# The Capinga Questions

## By

## Damian P.O'Connor

(Author's Note: This is a book about Apartheid South Africa. Authenticity demands that unpleasant racial and sexual terms are used throughout. In particular, the term 'kaffir' is highly offensive and banned in many parts of Southern Africa. It has similar connotations to the word 'nigger'. A Glossary of unfamiliar terms is provided at the end).

*

Between 1975 and 1990 the South African Defence Force fought a secret war on the Angolan border against the forces of Black Liberation supported by Cuba and the Soviets.

Black and White soldiers fought on both sides.

None of them won.

*

It's easy to ask questions. The hard part is listening to the answers. And the hardest part of all is asking the right questions and then listening to the hard answers.

*

Prologue

Capinga

1981

Freedom Topollo got out of her cot, pulled on her green fatigues and slotted her arms into her combat jacket, slipped her cold plastic flip-flops onto her toes and headed out of the smoky hut into the agreeable chill of the morning. Around her the camp was waking up to the familiar smells of wood smoke, ripe latrines and the dusty spice of the beaten earth and although the tannoy had not yet called out for everyone to arise and prepare for the morning parade, the sound of the squeaking water pump and the rattle of panniers was enough of an alarm clock to get most people out of bed. From over by the men's barracks she could hear the sound of throats being cleared and sneezing where a few traditional people were using snuff to clear their heads of the campfire fug. Up on the rickety, banana-palm shaded sentry tower, a man was yawning, stretching and scratching while his comrade appeared from beneath the waist high screen where he had been catching a strictly forbidden nap. Just below on the long ladder, a young man trudged up, pushed his AK47 over the side and flipped in to the guard post, reluctant to begin the tedious day.

People were slow today, thought Freedom, but it was the same every day here and it was her opinion that this camp was not run like a serious army camp. No, the *Forçes Armada Populares de Libertaçao de Angola*, the FAPLA army, in this camp did not seem to be very army-like at all. Not that she was any kind of military expert. This was something she freely

6

admitted and, to be quite honest, she had not enjoyed the little military training that she had undergone. She did not like the noise and jump of guns and had been happy to be assigned to kitchen duties where she felt much more at home but still, this was not like the camp at Oudtshoorn, South Africa, that she had worked in before leaving the country for the forces of liberation. In that camp where the white army trained, there was a lot more shooting and a lot more running and a lot more digging. Digging, digging, digging! All the time those white boys were digging! They were worse than porcupines for digging. Also cleaning. The white boys were made to clean their rooms time and time again even when there was no need for them to be cleaned. They were like hospitals. Everything was neat and clean and pristine. Clothes were ironed a lot too. She could not iron as good as those white boys and she and her mother had been doing it for boys like them for years and years.

A voice she recognised called out from the water troughs across the other side of the parade ground where the African National Congress boys were housed, for this was a shared camp for a lot of different liberation groups.

'Hey Freedom! You wanna toyi-toyi tonight?'

She looked up to see Jonny Mthetwa grinning at her with his piece in his hand. She looked away and ignored him. 'Remember the Struggle,' she muttered to herself, head down. 'All this will be worth it when we are free. Remember the Struggle.'

This was another thing that was not like the camp where the white army trained. The white boys marched about a lot and were kept busy always and they did not shout out at women going about their business – and if they did there would be a lot of other shouting going on from the white sergeants. All the soldiers here - FAPLA or the ANC, it did not matter -

7

seemed to have a lot of time on their hands and a lot of them seemed to be happy enough to eat and sleep and wait for the Struggle to call them. The eager ones ready to fight, always the new boys who had not had time to get used to the ways of the liberation armies, grew frustrated because so little happened and then they learned and slept and drank and loitered like the rest of them. The soldiers had political lectures and a lot of toyi-toying and sometimes they trained with their weapons but most of the time they sat around waiting for something to happen and talking about football. From time to time, a very few would be taken from the camp to be sent away to Russia to learn how to be officers and from time to time some very few would be allowed to take their guns and join in a raid but it was true that the FAPLA did not think much of her and her ANC comrades and the feeling was so mutual that fights often broke out about this. In truth, Freedom did not think very much of any of these soldiers and it made her sad and angry because the white soldiers from the white army were only very young men, only baby faced boys, and a lot of fine grown African men should have sent them packing all the way back to Holland or England by now. But this was just her opinion and her opinion was not often asked for. Perhaps that might change after Liberation too.

Flapping across the dust towards the kitchen, a big open, thatched *boma* with a deep fire-pit and some bottled gas canisters, she saw that big cauldrons of rice for breakfast were being prepared as usual and as soon as she got there she began opening the cans of fish that had come as a gift from the comrades in China. Fish and rice for breakfast, Mealie pap and sauce for dinner. Fish and rice for breakfast, Mealie pap and sauce for dinner. This had been the menu for the last week and the soldiers were grumbling about it; she could not blame them for she was grumbling about it too and it was at times like this that she really missed home. The food

8

here was not anywhere near as good as at home and not anywhere as near as good as she had been led to believe by the ANC comrades who had encouraged her to leave Oudtshoorn, take on her revolutionary name *Freedom* and come up to Angola. Opening up the fish cans made her think about the fish and chips she had grown up with, always a Friday night treat granted when her father had been paid, but this was part of the sacrifice that the Struggle demanded and she accepted it as just one more thing that had to be accepted.

'Breakfast is at eight today,' said Joyce, her supervisor, from under a large shapeless green bush hat. 'You must feed the white girl.'

'Again?' protested Freedom. 'I did not join the Struggle to become a Lady's Maid once more. Let the white girl join the line and get her own breakfast. And why does she have her own hut? Why can she not share the barracks with the rest of us?'

Joyce shrugged: 'I have been ordered to do this thing. Do you think I am consulted in advance?'

'What time is it?' said Freedom, deflating. 'I do not have a watch since my own one was stolen.'

'It is a quarter to eight.'

'I thought that was the time for the morning parade.'

'It was,' answered Joyce, pushing back her bush hat. 'But the tannoy is broken so the morning parade will be the same time as it always is and our good cooking will spoil while the men shout and cheer and wave their guns and the officers puff out their chests and shout out about the revolution in the same way they have been doing for years.'

9

Freedom tutted in resigned disgust, scooped up a pile of fish and rice into a red plastic bowl, tossed a spoon into it and turned to go to the hut where the white girl was kept. Outside the shade of the *boma*, the sun was up and the smell of food was drawing the boys out of their barracks to assemble on the parade ground in a big rough square with a clearing in the middle. Looking over, she saw the milling crowd of men, variously clad in green fatigues, combat jackets, bits of webbing and casually handling the selection of AK47s, RPD machine guns and RPG7 rocket launchers that they were never parted from and tutted once more. The white boys in the white army kept their weapons spick and span and locked away and only brought them out when they were to be used for marching or running or shooting practice; there was not much marching, running or shooting practice in this camp and she did not think the weapons were very spick and span at all. She tutted again and tried to find something good and uplifting to think about. Above, the sky was clear, still had something of the morning colour in it before the red dust rose up to mix with the humidity and encase them in the torpid day, so she chose this to think about and give her hope that there would soon be progress in the Struggle, that she would soon be marching home as part of a glorious conquering army to liberate her dear South Africa from the Boer, that she could see her family once more and perhaps go to the beach to swim. That was another thing that she missed, even though she had only ever done it once when her father and mother had been lucky to be granted a week's holiday together at the same time. With this wish, a wish that that she repeated to herself every morning even when the fulfilment of such a wish seemed a very long and distant prospect, she made a conscious effort to be happy and positive about the day.

The white girl was something of a sensation in the camp. Freedom knew there were white people involved the struggle but they did not often come to the camps and so when this one had arrived everyone was talking about her. Was she a spy or a prisoner? Was she a new recruit? Was she South African or perhaps a foreigner? Nobody seemed to know anything concrete, except that she belonged to the third group in the camp, the South West Africa People's Organisation, SWAPO, but no-one could tell why this should be so. Freedom sometimes thought that the people in this camp would not want to know if the truth were very simple because they preferred to speculate as wildly as possible and gossip endlessly because it passed the time more interestingly and made a change from talking about football. The thing that irked her about it all was that this white girl was getting the sort of special treatment that white people seemed to be very used to and which she, herself, had spent too many years of her life providing for them. And the fact that this white girl was kept in a hut which had a locked door on it was unusual; she did not know who held the key so could not tell if this white girl was being kept as a prisoner or if she was allowed her own privacy because she was white and being indulged in it. She would have liked to know, of course, but she did not expect to be told.

The hut wasn't far from the kitchen and it was possible to see the soldiers lining up on the parade ground from there and this drew Freedom's thoughts back to the ongoing comparison that she could not help making between this camp and the white army camp at Oudtshoorn. When she had been working in the stores there, she had always liked the way that the white boys always looked clean and pressed and eager and walked with their heads held high and marched with their chests proudly sticking out. The soldiers that she was looking at now did not look clean and pressed and eager. They did not stand up straight with their chests out and their arms straining down their sides. They did not march on to the parade ground. Instead they ambled, sometimes with their hands in their pockets, sometimes came late, as if they were coming to nothing so important as a football match. Even the ones who had been to train in Russia did not seem to march very well. Only a few seemed to think that this was a war camp at all.

She hopped across a trench that zig zagged across between the women and children's barracks and the schoolroom, turned by a banana palm and coming up to the white woman's hut, knocked sharply on the door.

'Room Service for you, Missy Princess,' said Freedom, trying to keep the snark out of her voice in the interests of being positive and hopeful for the day ahead.

The door opened and Freedom was met by a blonde girl in a pretty blue summer dress, the like of which she had once been used to wearing and longed to wear again.

'Thanks. Appreciate it,' said the white girl, taking the bowl. 'Fish and rice again?'

*Fish and rice*, thought Freedom looking at the girl. *Yes, it was Fish and rice. Fish and rice for breakfast, Mealie pap and sauce for dinner. Fish and rice for breakfast, Mealie pap and sauce for dinner. Just as it has been for weeks and probably will be for weeks more. Perhaps then we will get some tinned beef from Russia for a change.*

'Oh well,' said the white girl.

Was there the ghost of a smile there? Freedom did not think so. Rather she caught a trace of anxiety, nervousness, as though the white girl had a secret that she wanted to share but could not.

'Better than nothing, I suppose,' she said, moving the spoon in the bowl. 'Just.'

'What makes you so special?' spat Freedom, her positive resolution crumbling in the face of this ingratitude. *I should be used to this by now,* she thought, but the years of being subjected to the petty dismissals, the small daily humiliations and the routine indignities of being black in white South Africa had rubbed away at her carapace until it was such a raw and open wound that the unexpected presence of a white face was as bad as having salt unexpectedly rubbed into it. She snatched the bowl back out of the white girl's hands. 'Why are you even here? Why don't you go back to England or Holland or wherever it is you came from? We don't want you in Africa. You do not belong here.'

There came no answer, for at eight o'clock exactly, right out of a clear blue sky, four wide-winged frog-eyed aircraft flying side by side raced across the camp with a sound like ripping silk and a moment later Freedom caught the light flashing off a rain of hundreds of silver footballs scattering like ball bearings around a pinball table, which bounced once and then shattered the morning with a series of terrifying blasts that caught the men on the parade ground in a sudden maelstrom of shocking violence. Both Freedom and the white girl stood transfixed by horror as the camp buildings simply disintegrated under the terrible explosions and bodies were ripped apart and flung around in a spray of hot blood.

Time, the world, everything stood still, as Freedom realised that this appalling thing was what war really looked like and it did not look or sound like anything she had ever seen or heard before in a movie or even on the rifle ranges at Oudsthoorn. It was though she had been battered by an instantaneous gale and she felt her face become numb as though slapped, looked at her hands and saw they were spotted with blood and then stared in disbelief as the whole scene was suddenly engulfed in a thick mist of umber and brass through which splinters of wood and iron flew like black arrows. In that frozen instant of hot time, she saw with an intense clarity she had never experienced before that if she was to live then she must flee quickly and found that her body had already taken this decision without waiting for her conscious mind to galvanise it. It felt as though her limbs were wrenching themselves free of her control, her stomach convulsing in a terrible and fearful vibration and her arms pumping and trembling as she ran like a sprinter in a direction that her legs chose for her. She did not know if she ran a hundred metres or only two but she was instantaneously aware of her a trench ahead of her, gaping like a wound in the earth and she knew that she must jump into it as quickly as she could and cower down at the bottom of it if she was to escape the terrible rain of fury that was engulfing her; but to her astonishment she found that her legs had locked, frozen, so that she no longer commanded them.

And then, what seemed like an age later, sixteen shattering great explosions came down, one after the other – she counted them as though by counting she could gain a control of the monstrous forces of physics arrayed against her – and the air was filled with flying earth, blood, wood, timber, water, metal, matter and she felt her legs move as something hot seared into them. Looking down in a terrifying slow motion, she saw that a large bite had been taken out of her calf as though by a dog and then she knew that unless she got into that trench she would die on this day and she did not want to die on this day or any other.

14

The air roared once more and looking up through a tear in the veil of bloody mist and horror opened by the screech of a jet, she saw another line of aircraft droning through the sky like fat birds and she saw that from them fell figures in lines and then saw the terrible beauty of the opening of parachutes.

'Quickly,' said the white girl, leaping for the trench.

Freedom had ceased to be aware of the white girl at the moment the first screech of aircraft and she had been unaware that she had followed, or been followed, or run side by side with her to the shelter of this trench, and now her voice came into her ears like an unexpected guest that she did not know how to greet. Now she turned to look at the white girl and saw that she was afraid too, her round open mouth, ears covered, head down, hair flying, her terror a mirror image of her own.

'Quickly,' shrieked the white girl. 'Quickly.'

Freedom looked about, her eyes filled with smoke and dust and blood, her ears full of crackling violence, like screws and bolts flung hard at a cast iron roof, her nostrils full of the unfamiliar copper tang of burning blood and the roasting smell of flesh. Above her, the sky had disappeared in smoke but through it she sensed, rather than heard, the sound of a machine gun whirring and ripping like the sewing machine of a demon, the cannon shells flying down through the bed plate of iron dust to stab like needles and then explode in murderous fountains in parallel lines racing towards her as though she were about to go under the feed dog. And then, with no more than a single stab, the candle of her precious life was snuffed out by the strike of a cannon shell under her collar bone which took her head, right arm and shoulder clean off, boiled her blood and cauterised the wound.

15

*

01

Police Post 158

South West Africa/Namibia 1981

Friday

'No, they do not.'

'What?'

'Rivers do not always reach the sea.'

Sergeant Joshua 'Smithy' Smith of the South African Police sat up and passed the bottle of Redheart Rum to Sissingi, his Ovambo companion. They were perched on top of the water tank at Police Post 158, passing the time of day under a blue and red Cinzano beach umbrella that they had rigged up to protect them from the worst of the desert sun. It was the only human colour in that bleached landscape, incongruous and defiant under the hot, white glare of the sun, the hot white glare of the salt sand, and though it demanded a turquoise sea to give it real place and meaning, it had to be content with the endless, perfect, merciless blue of the desert sky.

'What do you mean?' he said.

Sissingi sat up too and drank from the bottle.

'I have never seen a river that has reached the sea,' said Sissingi. 'Whenever the rains bring it, the water is swallowed by the sand long before it reaches the ocean. Even the Okavango River disappears into the sand.'

'What about the Fish and Orange rivers?' said Smithy, taking the bottle back. 'They flow into the sea. The Fish River Canyon is one of the wonders of the world.'

'I will take your word for it,' answered Sissingi, lying back on the relatively cool metal of the tank. 'But I have never seen them.'

'Anyway,' said Smithy, petulantly. 'It's just a *fokken* saying. It's not meant to be taken literally.'

It was getting to the hottest part of the day and the rum was draining whatever interest he had in the discussion out of him. Around them the desert was flat, white, grey and white again. It would have been featureless but for the sparse, rank grass that stuck up like corn stubble after the harvest and Smithy was heartily sick of it.

'Oh,' replied Sissingi.

'*Oh*: is that all you can say?'

'What would you like me to say that I have not said many times before during this week, Sergeant Smith?' answered Sissingi, patiently, without opening his eyes. He was a tall man, with a broad, strong, intelligent brow above a strong nose and a face that tapered to a pointed chin and were it not for the wiry quality of the moustache, short beard and his dark skin, he might have been mistaken for a European. 'I understand that you are frustrated by your situation but it is your situation and you must just accept it. Perhaps something will change in the future and then you can go to the sea or to America or to another place. In the present time, it is hot and so you must just sleep.'

Smithy did not want to sleep, was too irritated to sleep, so he took up the binoculars beside him and scanned the horizon. There was nothing but salt sand and scrub reaching all the way to a distant purple hint of encircling hills; it was so flat and featureless that he swore he could see the curvature of the earth; the only thing of bare note was the straight scrape of the salt road that ran across the crater like a single string on a broken banjo. When they had driven down it two days ago they had not seen another soul in six solid hours of travel; at times they felt they were not moving but just marking time on some dreadful treadmill. Police Post 158 was so remote that the road down to it had earned the nickname of the Mouse Wheel Road.

'I can't sleep,' Smithy replied. 'I've slept enough.'

'Then go away and let me sleep.'

'*Fok*, Sissingi,' answered Smithy, gathering up the bottle. 'How long until we are relieved?'

'Four days,' replied Sissingi, without interest. 'One day less than yesterday. One day more than tomorrow.'

'I'm going to check the radio,' said Smithy, handing the bottle back on impulse and clanging down the rungs of the metal ladder. The water tower echoed emptily and dully, half empty, not half full, mockingly. 'That's if Scholtz hasn't broken it again.'

The radio was fixed in the back of the 9-ton, ugly armoured dog-faced dump truck *Casspir* parked by the side of the bare, four-square, white-plastered concrete pillbox that was home for one tedious week at a time. Swinging open the heavy rear door, he saw Scholtz, a pretty, stupid, blonde boy with a perfect complexion stretched out asleep on the floor of the vehicle with the handset clenched in his hand under his head.

'Scholtz, you *poes*,' he said, despairingly. The boy had kept the set on *transmit*, again, which meant that not only could no one contact them but no one could receive anything either because he was jamming up the frequency.

'Uh?' said Scholtz, waking, then starting up. 'I only closed my eyes for a second.'

'Get off the radio,' said Smithy. 'Go make some coffee.'

Scholtz sat up, bumping his blonde head on the seat, and then hitched up his khaki shorts and scrabbled out of the APC.

'And do your *fokken* shoe laces up, for *fok's* sake,' said Smithy, half-heartedly, before climbing in.

'You want a biscuit too?' asked Scholtz, almost apologetically. 'We've got brakeshoes. Sissingi ate all the Gypsy Creams though.'

The radio fizzed then returned to silence. Smithy shook his head and took up the handset.

'This is Whisky Golf. Radio check. Over.'

There was a hiss of static but nothing more.

'You're an educated man, Scholtz,' said Smithy, just as Scholtz was about to go. 'Rivers always reach the sea, right?'

19

'What?' answered Scholtz, a look of puzzlement spreading across his coffee blonde, blemish-free face.

'You passed Matric, didn't you?'

'Well, yes, Sergeant,' he replied, doubtfully.

'So you must have studied geography, *ja*? Rivers and all that shit?'

'Yes, Sergeant,' said Scholtz, frowning.

'So rivers always reach the sea, *ja*? Like the Nile, the Mississippi, the *fokken* Rhine and Amazon and all the rest of them?'

'Sergeant?' said Scholtz.

'If I got in a boat and sailed down a river would I reach the sea?'

'Well not the Nile, because the cataracts would upset your boat- and there is now the Aswan Dam to stop you too.'

Smithy grasped his mouth with his hand, let out a long sigh of frustration and then tried again.

'If I had a *fokken* Superboat made by *fokken* Superman and crewed by Jason and the *fokken* Argonauts would I, or would I not, reach the sea?'

'What's this about, Sarge?' asked Scholtz. 'You want some more Redheart, is it?'

'Just answer the *fokken* question,' persisted Smithy. 'Humour me.'

Scholtz sniffed and pulled at his nose. Since he had been standing in the full sun, a bead of sweat had gathered between his eyebrows and run down onto the bridge of his nose.

'Well, the rivers you mention *do* all empty into the sea,' he said. 'But the Volga, the Oxus and the Jaxartes in Russia don't.'

'Where do they go then?' asked Smithy.

'The Volga flows into the Caspian Sea and the others flow into the Aral Sea.'

'So, rivers always flow down to the sea then,' said Smithy, triumphantly. He called up to the water tower. 'Are you hearing this, Sissingi?'

'*Ja*, but *technically*, they are *inland* seas and so just big lakes really,' said Scholtz. 'They freshwater, not salty like the real sea.'

'Tell him about the Okavango,' called down Sissingi. 'He will only believe it if it comes from a white man.'

'*Ja*, that one flows into a swamp,' confirmed Scholtz. 'The wildlife is amazing there.'

Joshua closed his eyes in defeat. '*Fokken* communist rivers,' he said to himself. 'I might have known they would be fucked up.'

'Will I make some coffee now, hey?' said Scholtz, cheerfully, glad that he had passed a test.

Smithy nodded and as Scholtz stumped off, he returned to the radio set.

'Whisky Golf. Radio check. Over.'

The handset gave no answer and Smithy suddenly felt the silence crowd in on him. There was nothing out here in this endless desolation to make a noise; *nothing*. There were no birds to chirp or whirr the air with their wings; there was no wind to raise a rustle in the scrub, no rumble of traffic in the distance, not a bleat from a goat, not a bark from a jackal, the engine on the Casspir had long stopped *tink* ticking, Sissingi was dropping off to sleep and even the clumsy Scholtz could hardly make much noise with a spoon and a paper bag. It was as though the desert swallowed up sound as surely as it swallowed the rivers so that only the silent, shimmering heat remained; even their voices sounded tinny and empty in this vast emptiness.

He hated it. He hated it because it was in the silence that he heard the nagging, ticking voice of his conscience most clearly. Catching his reflection in the window, he looked hard at his brown hair, parted on the right nominally, his spade shaped face and the scar under his left eye and then rubbed his broken nose with his recently broken and only half-healed finger. He didn't like what he saw and dropped his eyes accordingly.

As a young Constable, Sergeant Joshua Smith had taken part in the murder of an anti-Apartheid activist and had been promoted and posted out to South West Africa as part of the cover up. Since then, he had called upon to investigate the battlefield murder of a white officer in a crack counter-insurgency unit up on the border, but his successful conclusion of the case had brought him more self-knowledge than joy; he did not agree with Apartheid, but his complicity had trapped him in the system. All he wanted now was to get out, go somewhere else and start again as someone else but he had no idea how this might be achieved without bringing down the ire of the Bureau of State Security on his head. They knew all about Sergeant Smith, the murder, and the fact that his mother was an anti-Apartheid campaigner – a situation so curious that he was under no illusions that they would look kindly on a request for a passport and an Exit Visa.

22

He knew that the right thing to do was to head north, get over the border into Angola and throw himself on the mercy of the ANC, but he could not convince himself that such a course would result in anything but disaster. As if to remind himself of his situation, he touched the bayonet on his belt; it had until recently belonged to Corporal Sanchez, a suspect in that last case, but it had come into his possession via a death threat from the ANC; they thought they knew about the murder of the activist too and had issued a Writ against him through their supporters; if he deserted and went over to them, they would surely shoot him. Sanchez's bayonet was like the sword of Damocles hanging over his head, held aloft only by the thin single strand of his dilemma.

'Whisky Golf. Radio check. Over.'

There was still nothing. Smithy checked the settings on the radio, then re-tuned it. There was a welcome crackle of static and the radio burst into life.

'Whisky Golf. Whisky Golf, Acknowledge, Over.'

'This is Whisky Golf. Over,' he said.

'About *fokken* time too,' said an exasperated voice. 'Remind me now who you have with you out there.'

'Sissingi and Konstabel Scholtz,' replied Smithy.

'*Fok.*' The voice belonged to Captain Botha, his immediate superior up in Windhoek HQ. Porcine, pasty and fat, he could never think of him without associating him with a butcher he had once known. 'Well OK, leave the kaffir in charge but tell Scholtz that he's in charge, but only *officially*.'

'Sissingi isn't a kaffir, Sir,' replied Smithy, doggedly, visualising the butcher's fingers wrapping around the handset like pallid sausages. 'He's Ovambo.'

'*Ja-nee*, Sergeant Smith,' replied Botha. 'The chopper will be with you in ten. Get your ballbag packed.'

'Chopper?' said Smithy, startled. 'Is this an early R&R?'

'Don't be a *poes*,' came the reply. Botha's voice was full of mocking sarcasm. 'There'll be no Intercourse and Intoxication for you for a good long while, Smithy my China! Not by the looks of this, there won't be. It seems you're wanted by the Big Boys again, Smithy! You are obviously their flavour of the month, Smithy, although I cannot for the *fokken* life of me think why. Parabats, indeed, Smithy! Parabats!'

'What?' said Smithy, his heart sinking. 'What do the Airborne want with me?'

'Oh, I bet they don't want anything to do with *you* at all, Smithy my China,' laughed Captain Botha. 'If you had seen the newspaper that I have here on my desk in front of me, you would know straight away that the Parabats would rather have a dose of the clap than deal with you just now, Smithy. So get your kit together like the good little detective you are and enjoy your flight.'

'No, wait,' said Smithy desperately. 'Captain – I'm sick. The Post needs to be defended. There are Terrs about – a big Typhoon unit is on its way, I swear!'

'Have a nice day, Sergeant Smith,' replied Captain Botha, laughing raucously. 'Out.'

Sergeant Smith put the handset back in its holder and put his head in his hands. Looking up through the hatch, he wished that he could escape up beyond the perfect, cloudless, bare, empty sky to some distant place where he could just do his punishment, get his private penance over with, be free of this prison and finally escape this Limbo life. All he wanted was a river that he could launch the boat of his life on and sail down it to the sea and a better horizon than this one.

'I think there's a chopper coming,' called out Scholtz, emerging from the white bunker, shirtless and carrying a tin mug. 'Maybe they will have some Gypsy Creams, hey?'

Smithy did not answer but continued to stare upwards into the sky, hoping that the chopper would turn into an angel to bear him away, but knowing full well that there was as much chance of that happening as it being a special delivery of chocolate biscuits.

'It seems that the rain is coming,' called Sissingi, standing and shading his eyes in the direction of the approaching sound. 'Perhaps a river will now come and take you to the sea.'

'Or straight into a *fokken* swamp, more like,' replied Smithy.

\*

The helicopter chattered and clattered across the flat brown slate of the desert below towards the unfamiliar sight of a collection of prefab buildings and squared off hangars. All around were lighter scrapes marking the thin fences of barren properties while the roads, straight as ever a surveyor could make them in the near-worthless scrub, turned at right angles on their way to nowhere. Seen from the air, Grootfontein airbase itself was not much more than a length of tarmac laid like the

25

silver-black skin of a cobra through the camel thorn and wattle but as the Puma banked, Sergeant Smith knew well that this was a sword pointed at the enemy over the border and one to which they had, as yet, no answer. As if on cue, two Mirage jets in sand and dark olive colours shot down the runway like silent salamanders, the roar of the engines masked by the sound of the rotors, and shot off into the air on some hunting mission to the north. Parked along the side of the runway were eight other Mirage jets, two or three old British Buccaneers and a more ancient Canberra with its frog-like cockpit, all kept in the air by sophisticated sanctions busting and farm boy ingenuity. Further on, Smithy saw the even more ancient Dakotas, troop carriers of Arnhem vintage, and then coming closer, saw the rows of Alouette helicopter gunships and the heavy-lift, three engine, bottle-nosed Super-Frelons all precisely lined up and attended by the mechanics as carefully as though they were thoroughbreds attended by grooms. Looking beyond them, he saw the huts that from this height resembled Monopoly houses and Smithy found himself wishing himself away once more. The Old Kent Road sounded lovely, he thought, just right for a stroll in the countryside surrounded by green hedges and apple trees, before going on to the bioscope in Leicester Square, followed by a *lekker koue een* in The Angel, Islington and home on the train to Vauxhall from Kings Cross. Before he could complete his fantasy with a high-born lady he had found in Piccadilly Underground though, the Puma veered away a little and headed towards a patch of black top away from the other hard stands, notable because of its proximity to a khaki walled bungalow shaded by bluegums. Smithy's mouth went dry.

Waiting by the landing pad was an impatient orderly in Air Force blues clutching a clipboard and as the Puma pulled up the nose and came down rear wheels first, the paper flapped and flickered violently in the down

26

draught, while the orderly squinted and shielded his eyes against the flying dust and whipped pebbles. Even before the decelerating rotors' whine had made hearing possible, he was there at the door waving to Sergeant Smith to disembark and follow him. Smithy did as he was bidden and as soon as he was clear of the rotors, he heard the whine pick up again and felt the enormous rush of air crushing down on his crouching back as the chopper hauled itself off the ground and into the air again. It was a moment before he could hear himself think, a moment when the silence came down for just a split second and made his heart quail once more, but it was a moment that could not resist the insistent beckoning of the orderly.

'In there,' said the orderly, without introduction or explanation, but indicating the bungalow with an outstretched arm. 'They waiting for you.'

'Who's 'they'?' asked Smithy.

'The Sniffy Tiffies,' replied the orderly, as though the thing was obvious. 'The *Snuffelhondes*.'

Smithy looked blank. There was something implacable about the way the orderly looked directly at him.

'*Detectives*,' explained the orderly. 'Isn't that why you here? It says so on my orders.'

'What else does it say?' asked Smithy, following him into the compound through a garden gate.

'In: One Detective Sergeant Joshua Smith.'

'That it? Does it not say anything about *Out: One Pissed Off Detective Sergeant Joshua Smith*.'

'You're a funny man, Mister Policeman,' said the orderly, without smiling. 'Have a *fokken* nice day.'

The door opened without being knocked upon and Smithy felt the orderly's hand on his back pushing him firmly through it.

'Keep going,' said the orderly, closing the door behind him. 'First on the right.'

Smithy did as he was told.

It took a little while for his eyes to adjust to the relative darkness of the bungalow, but when they did adapt, he saw that he was in a large, bare room, with stripped floorboards covered only by a postage stamp of a rug. In one corner was a grey filing cabinet and on the right hand wall were a row of Crittall windows, several missing panes of glass, the frames peeling beige paint, the fly screens rusted and holed while a tatty collection of net curtains tried to billow half-heartedly in the torpid air. The room smelled of stale tobacco and BO, which he found strange for a military compound where everything that didn't move was normally sanitised, disinfected, whitewashed and scrubbed. Before him, placed in the centre of the room was a blank trestle table with two unsquared chairs, one on each side and empty except for an ash tray. To his left, was another door, ajar, from which voices were coming.

'Sergeant Smith reporting for duty,' he called out. 'Anyone home?'

'I'll be with you just now,' replied a wheezy voice from the next room. 'Take a seat, hey?'

Smithy walked forward and scraped the chair back. The seat was polished, as though someone else had been recently sitting on it and as he sat down he thought he caught a faint whisper of perfume, a citrus smell that was so out of place but also so oddly familiar that it almost made him jump. It was only a fleeting sensation though and before he had time to ponder much on it, the door opened fully and preceded by a blast of cigarette smoke, a man shuffled into the room. He was tall, but stooped and round shouldered, somewhere in his sixties, with slicked back brylcreemed hair, shiny black and flecked with dandruff, which made a perfect match for his ancient suit. Underneath it, Smithy could make out a thin polyester shirt that might once have been white but was now closer to nicotine yellow and beneath that a string vest and as the man shuffled towards the table, he noted that he was wearing faded, red carpet slippers. Looking up into the yellowed face, he saw also that the man's eyes were a watery blue, but strangely alert, as if outraged, or expecting to be surprised at any moment. He was definitely not the ramrod steel and piano wire Parabat officer that he had been expecting but curiously enough, he had the impression that at some time, a long time ago admittedly, this man had been fit, hard and attractive, at least to someone.

'Do you keep up with the news, Detective Smith?' he wheezed, taking a seat and tossing a folded newspaper onto the table.

'Have the Springboks lost to England?' replied Smithy, making no attempt to keep the displeasure out of his voice.

The tall man ignored him, rooted in his pockets for cigarettes and a lighter, turning this way and that as though he had dropped them on the floor. Smithy did not move to help him. When he had found them, one in his right pocket, the other in his left, he lit up, adding a cloud of blue smoke to the one still hanging by the door and put the pack back in his pocket without even thinking that an offer of a smoke to Smithy might be required.

'My name is Pieters,' he said, and broke into a spasm of coughing. 'And if you believe that you'll believe anything.'

Smithy waited without replying.

'Chain smoker,' he apologised, coughing up a bubbling phlegm sodden ball into a hastily produced handkerchief. While his shoulders heaved, he tapped the newspaper and indicated Smithy should read.

'Which bit?' asked Smithy, sitting back in the chair and folding his arms.

'The headline, the lead story…' There was a further rattling cough. 'Don't be stupid….' He wheezed.

Smithy waited for a moment then, seeing as there was little else he could do, leaned forward and took the paper. It was a foreign broadsheet, the *London Times*, and as he unfolded it and laid it full length across the table a shiver ran all the way through him.


MASSACRE AT CAPINGA

APARTHEID DEATH SQUADS RAID REFUGEE CAMP

POISON GAS EMPLOYED

Dominating the page was a picture of a mass grave perhaps 7 metres wide, two metres deep and twenty metres long with a tangle of bodies, both male and female, two and three layers deep, at the bottom of it. The corpses lay in grotesque postures, parodies of life, limbs at strange angles, legs apart, arms flung wide, mouths open or shut as death had taken them. Even though the photograph was a grainy, smudged black and white of uncertain focus and clarity, the marks of violence were clear upon them; the ragged scatter marks of shrapnel ran up legs and torsos; black blood stains on soaked shirts; dust clogged hair; white bones shattered by high velocity bullets.

He looked up.

'Is it true?' he asked.

'No,' replied Pieters, breathing as though it was his last.

'So?'

'So, Sergeant Smith, we have a situation here that does not help us with our *Burgher sake*, hey? *Hearts and Minds*, hey? We are trying to win the hearts and minds of those whose hearts and minds are not completely and irrevocably closed to us and this…this accusation does not help us, you agree? Especially as it says that we are waging war on women and children.'

'Well, I suppose a grave full of bodies does look bad,' agreed Smithy, trying not to sound as facetious as he felt. 'It might upset people who did not know what we are doing to protect them from the Red Terror.'

'*Ja*, true,' said Pieters, shortly. 'And the Cape newspapers also have this story now and are demanding answers to their questions. If we do not do something about this then we will have an international media scandal, questions in Parliament from the Progressive Party and more and more problems with the UN. Something must be done.'

'Well, if the story isn't true, why don't you just say so?' asked Smithy. 'And even if it is really true, just tell a lie. You can always order some journalist to make a lot of rubbish up for you.'

Pieters placed his cigarette in the ashtray, took the newspaper back, shook it out and then laid it back on the table. He smoothed it flat with a liver-spotted hand and then examined the picture once more, widening his eyes to get a better look.

'Who are they and why are they in a mass grave?' he asked, more to himself than to Smithy. 'The international media have already decided that they are innocent victims of South African brutality.' He looked up. 'We want you to investigate this matter and report the truth of what really happened here,' he said.

'Who's *we*?'

'You know very well who we are, Sergeant Smith and, just so we understand each other, we know very well who you are and how that Writ got held up when it was attempted to be forwarded, hey?' Pieters wheezed a little more, rocking ever so slightly back and forward and then grimaced. 'Colic,' he said, forcing a smile. 'It can be a bit painful if I am not careful about what I eat.'

'And they've been feeding you nothing but Shrapnel Chicken and Spick and Spam, I bet,' said Smithy. 'So now you want me to feed you something more agreeable, hey? Why?'

'Why?' replied Pieters, lighting up another cigarette and breaking out into another fit of coughing.

Smithy picked the original cigarette, still burning, out of the ashtray and handed it to him.

'Oh,' he said, taking the cigarette into his other hand, sucking a last long drag out of it, then crushing it out in the ashtray from which it came. 'Why? Why? Because this investigation must be properly independent if it is to be believed, so it must be run by the police not the army, *ja*?'

'You think I will be believed?' answered Smithy, frowning. 'Why would I be believed? What makes you say that?'

'Think man,' appealed Pieters, narrowing his eyes. 'Your mother is anti-Apartheid, *ja*? *Ja*, we know this. And she is friendly with an English journalist by the name of Clive Merriman, *ja*? This we know too. And we know that you are soft on Kaffirs, *ja*? So you will be believed. People will think you are honest because you are not fully committed to Apartheid.'

'If you are considering involving my mother in this caper of yours, I would seriously advise you to reconsider,' said Smithy, with a smirk. 'If this wasn't a hare-brained scheme enough, I can guarantee you that she will fuck it up.'

'That's as may be for now,' conceded Pieters. 'But this matter is to be investigated and you have been chosen. You will have free rein to interview all those involved. This is not a matter for discussion…'

'Somehow, I thought not,' interjected Smithy.

'…and at the end of it, we will see what can be done about that Writ.'

'Shit,' said Smithy, looking up at the ceiling in something bordering despair. 'Look, you know I'm no good at being a detective – it's in the files just why I was promoted – so why don't you get someone who knows

33

what they are doing and send me back to the desert? What is it that you really want, man?'

'I want you to find the truth, that's all,' said Pieters, suddenly animated, leaning forward and wheezing flecks of spittle from a white line on his lower lip. 'I want you to find out who killed all these people, *ja*? Just the truth, the whole truth and nothing but the truth. Starting today. *Maak'n plan.*'

Smithy nodded in defeat.

'I'll make a plan, then, just now, hey?' he said, as the tall man raised himself to his feet. 'Hey, how about I get an office and maybe someone to help me with this *kak*?'

'The bungalow is yours,' said the tall man, his hand to his chest and his breath labouring. 'We'll see who's available for help. And I'll need an interim report in three days – Monday, after the weekend - and a full report by the following Friday. Any problems, wave *this*.'

He dropped a pass on the table. It was marked *Bureau of State Security*.

\*

Ten minutes later and Smithy was emptying his kitbag onto a cot in one of the bedrooms. There was no door to it, although the marks on the frame showed that it had once held hinges There were no curtains either and the windows were grimy with the desert sand, giving the light the quality of soiled and yellowed underwear. This was the better of the two sleeping options, especially as it had a lavatory that worked, stained like a smoker's teeth though it was, and did not smell of stale urine like the whole of the second room. At the back of the building was a kitchen, or something that once might have functioned as one; all the cabinets were broken, there were no pans or utensils, the gas bottle for the two ring stove was missing and there were mice droppings everywhere. The back door did not lock either and when he turned on the tap, the water gurgled like the Pieters' lungs then spat out a brown, brackish splatter the colour of chewing tobacco.

'Welcome to the *fokken* Ritz,' he said to himself.

He found a cloth and wiped down the surfaces so that they were clean enough to put his Esbit stove on, lit up one of the hexamine fuel tablets and then filled a dixie from his water bottle to make tea. When the water had boiled, he tipped it carefully into his tin mug and taking the newspaper went to stand at the back door. It was late, late afternoon and the sun was turning golden, lighting up the dun leaves of the bluegums, turning them to silver and raising up the cinnamon scents from the nutmeg coloured earth. He breathed in deeply, blew on his tea and then lifted his head up to feel the light on his face. Whatever crap the world threw at him, there was always the light of the veldt, he thought; it wasn't nearly enough compensation, but it did furnish him with some uncertain hope.

'Means, Motive, Opportunity,' he said to himself, looking at the newspaper picture. 'Agatha Christie, eat your *fokken* heart out.'

There was a sudden, enormous, rattling *Bang!* As though someone had just hit the corrugated iron roof of the bungalow with a sledgehammer and Smithy leaped, ducked and turned around simultaneously as he heard the tinkle of glass falling out of a window.

'What the…?' he cried out, looking for the smoke.

Up above, a Mirage jet streaked out across the veldt and hurtled into the argent distance.

'Make you jump, Sergeant?' said the orderly, appearing around the corner unconcerned. '*Ag*, man. It's just the Jet Jockeys showing off – going supersonic.'

'Is it now?' said Smithy, brushing tea off his shirt. 'And do they do this thing often?'

'You'll get used to it,' he replied, putting down a bag of tools and rummaging for a hammer. 'By the way, I'm attached to you. Never thought I'd become a Sniffie Tiffie's nark, I didn't, but I'm to be your clerk, gopher, rat-catcher and general *fokken* handyman.'

'What's your name,' said Smithy, eyeing up the young man. He was medium height, blonde, broad, general issue, straight from the farms and the rugby field, with a broken button nose and pursed lips; the only thing that marked him out as different was his unblinking, blue-eyed stare.

'Corporal Andrew Bridgeman,' he replied, taking out a hammer and putting three six-inch nails in his mouth. 'You want to go inside,' he mumbled. 'I got to nail this door up if we are going to be secure. The *jollers* use this place to smoke *dagga* in.'

'Sure,' said Smithy, going inside. 'What about the front door?'

Bridgeman held up a thick chain and a padlock. Smithy nodded with approval.

'Bridgeman,' he said, feeling his recently mended ribs. 'No one else comes in here but me and you, hey? No cleaners, no cooks, no tea-boys, no *jollers*, no nobody, get my drift?'

'As you wish,' replied Bridgeman. 'Top Secret, hey?'

'It's just that the last clerk I knew got blown to bits by a bomb planted by a cleaner.'

'Wasn't he paid on time?' replied Bridgeman, putting the door into the hole. 'The cleaner, I mean.'

Smithy's reply was cut off by the sound of hammering, so he went through the connecting door to the last room in the bungalow, which had been fitted out as a temporary office. There was a trestle table, a desk, a couple of chairs, a field telephone and on a filing cabinet, three or four box files; up above was a bare lightbulb with a couple of circling flies, while down below were bare floorboards in need of sanding. Sipping at his tea, he caught that sweet, sharp citrus scent once more and then dismissed it as the residue of *dagga* smoke.

The hammering stopped and a moment later Bridgeman appeared at the window. He stared for a moment and then put a finger to his temple like a school boy asking a question.

'I don't have to bunk here, do I?' he asked.

'No,' replied Smithy. 'Why do you ask?'

'No reason,' he replied. 'It's just that I was told to put two cots in here and I just thought the worst.'

'There are a lot worse places to sleep than this, Bridgeman,' said Smithy. It suddenly struck him as strange that a man as fit and healthy as Bridgeman wasn't up on the border in a combat role. 'How come you've got such a cushy job anyway?'

The orderly stared at him for a long moment, then tapped a glass eye with his finger nail.

'And you a detective,' he said, turning away. '*Jeez.*'

Smithy dropped his chin and slapped his forehead.

'No, Bridgeman, wait,' he said. I'm sorry. It's just that…,' he waved the newspaper. 'I've been told to work on this case and I haven't got the foggiest idea of how to begin.'

Bridgeman looked at the newspaper and then at Smithy.

'Why don't you start with the people who did it?' he asked. 'They're right here.'

Right on cue, the *bang* of a supersonic jet crashed down onto the building, making Smithy jump and spill his tea once more.

Smithy nodded wearily. 'I should have been a cook. Anything but a copper.'

It took Corporal Bridgeman no more than ten minutes to set up appointments with Colonel Templeton of the air force in an hour's time and Colonel Steiner of the Parabats for the following morning and by the time that Smithy had shook out his camo dress and put a bit of polish on his boots, he had also got the water – both hot and cold – running again so he could shave and shower before the meeting.

'You need anything else, Sergeant, or can I get over to the canteen, now?' asked Bridgeman, a mop and bucket in his hands. 'After the day I've had, I could use a Klippie and Coke, to be honest.'

'*Ja*, sure,' answered Smithy, tying up his boot lace. 'Where did you leave the padlock and chain?'

*

Smithy followed Bridgeman's neatly drawn, colour coded map, found the tiled bungalow flanked by feathery purple jacarandas and red flame trees and within fifteen minutes was being shown into Templeton's comfortable office. On the floor was a Persian rug and on one wall, next to a small bookshelf of novels, were hung portrait pictures of his wife and family beaming steadily out of the frames like windows onto a peaceful world, while against the other wall lay a rich red chesterfield sofa before a coffee table complete with copies of *Home and Garden* and more pictures of the family. Colonel Templeton was blessed with strawberry blonde hair and a yard-brush moustache to match, his face was open, intelligent, with a glint of humour in the eyes which was replaced by a hopeful yearning whenever he looked up into the sky, as though being earthbound weighed too heavily on his frame, turning his boots to lead and his brow to a frown. He was shorter and stockier than Smithy had expected for a fighter pilot, whom he had always imagined were all tall, slim, devastatingly handsome supermen and for a moment Smithy wished that he too could become a pilot. He envied what looked to him like a desirable detachment from the realities of war, envied the free floating individual who might drop bombs on the enemy but never see the results close up, envied the appearance of a war fought without complication or responsibility; you picked up your orders, went where you were told, did what you were told to do and the responsibility was entirely someone else's. There were no compromises to be accommodated, no dilemmas to be hung up on; just in, out and shake it all about and if it did get too much, there was always a well-paying civvie job at home or abroad waiting. If he had been a pilot, he told himself, his life would be a lot, lot simpler. That would also have been the case if he had been a cook; or a taxi driver; or a farmer; or anything else at all, he also told himself.

'Is this what they are calling us now?' said Templeton, when the courtesies and introductions were over. He held the newspaper up and read it while leaning back in his black leather, padded office chair. '*Death Squads.*' He put the paper flat on the desk and smiled out of the corner of his mouth. 'Well, I suppose that's one way of putting it.'

'Does this look like something that you are responsible for?' asked Smithy, tentatively.

Templeton studied the picture, making an attempt to count the bodies.

'Well, we didn't dig the grave or shovel the bodies into it,' he said, frowning. 'But if this is Capinga then it's probably our work.'

'Would you care to elaborate?' said Smithy.

'Sure,' replied Templeton, pulling a dossier out of his draw and tossing on the blotter. 'This is the operational order for the strike. Do you want to read it or shall I paraphrase it? It's pretty technical.'

'*Ja*, paraphrase would be great, Colonel,' said Smithy, taking the manila folder and flicking through it.

'As you wish,' said Templeton, putting his hands behind his head, leaning back, flipping his feet up onto the desk and beginning to recite as though he had it off pat. '0800hrs we go in with four Canberras line abreast, North-South axis, low level, 300 knots and drop a whole shitload of Alpha bombs on the Terrs as they're lining up for morning parade…'

'Alpha bombs?' interrupted Smithy.

'They're like bowling balls, weigh 10 kilos, designed to bounce on the ground to arm and then flip two metres up in the air to explode.'

'How many did you drop?'

'Twelve hundred between the four Canberras.'

'*Twelve hundred?*'

'No point doing the job by halves,' said Templeton. 'The airburst spreads the shrapnel over a pretty good area. One lethal splinter per square metre in a fifteen metre radius, if you're lucky.

'Jeez,' said Smithy, wincing as a vision of black, hot, iron rain burning and tearing through screaming flesh flashed up in his mind.

'0802 four Buccaneers come in and drop sixteen thousand pounders spread around the complex. Two tanks overturned, general Alarm and Despondency among the Terrs,' continued Templeton. '0804 four Mirage III begin strafing runs with 30mm cannon mopping up anything that's left, which isn't much, I can tell you – one shot hit the petrol tank and blew a jeep up a tree; never seen *that* before. Anyway, four minutes later, at 0808 *precisely*, all attack aircraft safely on their way back here while another Mirage comes up to act as close air support for the Parabats who are now dropping on the east side of the target. That's your lot. No poison gas necessary.'

'And you hit them when they were all standing to attention in parade?' said Smithy, looking at an aerial photograph of the parade ground. It was empty, but heavily cratered. There was still smoke rising from several of the buildings.

41

'What better time is there?'

'Were there any women and children on parade?'

Templeton thought for a moment. 'You mean: *was this a refugee camp*?'

Smithy gave a nod.

'Well,' said Templeton, sniffing. 'If you were to ask me to guarantee that there were no *piccaninis* on the base at all, I'd probably have to demur. That goes for women too. For one, SWAPO, the ANC and the Cubans all employ women in combat or support roles which makes them legitimate targets and for two, none of the little beauties can keep their knickers on for long in the presence of all that throbbing manhood; *ergo*, there will probably be a few kids around. Truth is, Sergeant, it's hard to tell tits from tots going at 300 knots from five hundred feet up with the imminent probability of anti-aircraft fire complicating your task.'

'But they're kids.'

Templeton's eyes flicked quickly towards the photographs of his own kids on the wall before coming back to stare straight into Smithy's.

'If they don't want their kids killed,' he said, looking straight into Smithy's eyes, and enunciating slowly and deliberately. 'Then they should not allow them onto military bases in a war zone. Unless, of course, you can invent some little gadget that allows an Alpha bomb to distinguish between a *piccanini* with a corn cob, a thirteen year old girl with a hand grenade or a fully grown Terr with an AK47.'

Smithy dropped his eyes and pursed his lips as he took the point, then looked at the aerial photo again.

'You sure it was a base not a refugee camp?' he said.

'Spread those photos out on the desk,' said Templeton, swinging his feet off the desk.

Smithy took out three or four reconnaissance photographs and did as he was told. Templeton took one and held it up.

'These zigzags are trenches,' he said, pointing.

'They could be air raid shelters,' challenged Smithy.

'True,' agreed Templeton, with a wry smile. 'If you are a journalist for the *London Times* they could be Buckingham palace. Except that the Queen does not keep ZPU-4 multi-barrel anti-aircraft guns on her roof.'

Smithy looked again. There were indeed gun emplacements visible, once his attention had been drawn to them.

'And I was not aware that the Royal Coach had been replaced by a Soviet armoured personnel carrier,' continued Templeton, pointing out a row of vehicles. 'Or that the English army fired their Royal Salutes with a Stalin Organ....'

'OK, OK, I get the picture,' said Smithy. 'So it's not a refugee camp.'

'Actually, it probably is in part,' said Templeman, sitting back. 'You know, the Terrs don't exactly stick to the Geneva Convention, hey? They don't take much care to separate the civvies from the *troupies*.'

Smithy ran a hand through his hair, chewed his lip, digesting the baldness and violent banality of Templeton's story. It rang true. It was too straightforward not to be true, he decided. He stood up to leave.

'Just one thing before you go though, Sergeant,' said Templeton, who had remained seated, watching Smithy from behind a smile.

'Huh?'

'That picture is inaccurate in one important respect.'

'Which is?

'We killed a lot more than the number in that grave,' said Templeton, with the glitter of a grim satisfaction in his eyes. 'I'd say about three times as many. And that doesn't include the ones that the Parabats *donnered*.'

*

02

Saturday

There were perfect miles of empty golden sand and the roaring waves were like white horses whipped up into a hissing frenzy by the keen onshore breeze. Marika, dark haired, dark eyed, walked along the Wilderness strand through the spindrift that came like a mist off the wave tops, and touched the hair away from her face as Joshua placed a soft hand on her shoulder. Looking far out to sea, she held her rope soled boat shoes in one hand while the other shaded her eyes from the aquamarine glare that lit up her skin like tawny gold. Together, they felt the soft grit of the sand gather under their toenails and revelling in being blown clean of all failings, all regrets, by the sharp blast of the salt spray, drank in the purest of clean air that came straight up from the pole. Pointing down to the inlet, Joshua smiled with delight as the steam billowed from the funnel of the Outeniqua Choo-Choo as it crossed the curved bridge, right there, above the sea and she laughed out loud with the pleasure granted by the beauty of a dolphin pod slicing, spinning, jumping and diving through the deep blue water of the great southern ocean. Later, they ate fish pulled from the sea that morning and picked apart the sage scented calamari with fingers tingling with lemon juice and deliciously smeared with mayonnaise. She left a kiss on the shared glass from which they drank the cool, grassy white wine and as a pink sunset turned the bleached wood of the beach bar to a stripped, pale blue, she touched him with a single finger that sent a bolt of electricity through his loins. The light painted the beach an intense, glowing gold and picked diamonds out of the turquoise surf to throw them glittering into the advancing darkness as he slipped his hand into hers, anticipating the release and the glorious abandon to come.

'Have you ever made love to a kaffir?' she asked, and he, overwhelmed by the need to preserve the integrity, the purity of the feelings that were flooding through him like the light from the last of the sun, answered honestly in the dangerous risk of the moment.

'I have,' he replied. 'She was called Ayize and she was my first.'

'Oh Joshua,' said Marika sadly. 'How I wish you had lied to me.'


\*


Smithy woke with a start, caught the sharp scent of lemons and for a moment wondered where he was.

'An erotic dream, hey?' said Corporal Bridgeman, placing a cup of tea by his bedside. 'You take sugar?'

'Two,' said Smithy, sitting up and jamming the heels of his hands into his eyes. 'No lemon.'

45

'I thought so,' said Bridgeman. 'There's dog biscuit porridge and Russians for breakfast. You want Mrs Balls'?'

'Uh?'

'*Ja*, OK, you need to wake up,' said Bridgeman, wiping his hands on a tea towel. 'You got a busy day today. I'll keep your food on the hot plate.'

'I thought it was broken,' said Smithy, sipping at the tea and feeling it warm through his body and lessen the tightness of his intestines.

'I brought another gas bottle and replaced one of the valves,' replied Bridgeman, moving over to open a window. 'It's a bit of a bush fix, but it'll do until I can get the proper *fundies* to look at it. Anyway, you got to meet with Colonel Steiner at 0800 hours sharp and it is better that you are not late.'

'He's a hard nut, is he?' said Smithy, pushing his sleeping bag down his legs and turning himself half out of the cot.

'Just about the hardest there is,' agreed Bridgeman. 'That man doesn't brush his teeth – he files them down with a rasp.'

*

If Colonel Templeton had attempted to create a home from home in his office and if this was a feature common to all the Commanding Officers on the base then it would not be too much to infer that Colonel Steiner had no home at all. The room was bare but for a trestle table that served as a desk, a single, simple hard chair, and a single filing cabinet rammed and squared into the corner like a sentry. There were no pictures, no pin boards, no aircon units, no nothing to soften the stripped bare functionality of the place; the only colour in the room was provided by the maps fixed up

46

behind the desk – none of which were marked in any way – and by a single telephone, which was pillar box red and connected to the wall by a long, twisted flex that was asking to be tripped over. The overwhelming impression of the room was that it was just about surplus to requirements and about to be abandoned like a useless piece of kit on a route march; that it was a soldier's room was obvious from the smell of polish and fresh paint and the packed rucksack waiting in readiness by the filing cabinet, but to Smithy's eye there was something extreme about it; it was more than just a soldier's room; he had seen soldier's rooms that were neat and tidy, also functional, but also somehow personal and home-like but this was entirely different in its nature; it was a Spartan's room.

Colonel Steiner was blonder than anyone he had ever seen before and in South Africa, where so many whites descended from pale, blond Dutch stock, that was saying something. He was a big, solid man in his late thirties, with a shock of platinum-blonde hair, his skin so white it was almost translucent - Smithy could hardly stop himself from thinking of macadamia nuts - his white teeth interrupted by one gleaming incisor made from Transvaal gold, and eyes so blue they could have been formed from ice. He stood with his shoulders back, confident, supremely fit, his weight balanced evenly on his boxer's feet and a mocking glitter of appraisal playing across his face.

'Sergeant Smith?' he said, in a flat voice, which Smithy decided carried a trace of a German accent laid across the pinched Rhodesian intonation. Later on, he imagined he could hear French there too; but this was not as strong as the contained resentment at being scrutinised evident in each clipped syllable. 'You've come to put us under the microscope, I believe.'

'Just a few questions about the Capinga operation, Sir.'

47

Steiner winced with irritation.

'We'd better get on with it then,' he said, through tight lips.

On the wall behind him were several large scale maps of southern Africa and it was to these that he now turned. Picking up a broken off car aerial from the desk, he extended it and began to point out the salient features of the geography.

'South West Africa,' he tapped on the map. 'Angola, Zambia and Rhodesia.'

'Zimbabwe now, isn't it?' said Smithy.

'Shut up. Don't interrupt,' replied Steiner, tersely. 'All hostile. The main terrorist bases are in Angola – as I presume you know – and the basic strategy is to keep them as far away from the border as possible. The base at Capinga is - was – a little further north than we usually strike, but the intelligence was good and we reckoned that they wouldn't reckon on us coming for them. Big HQ and supply dump.'

He paused, as though expecting a question. Smithy didn't oblige. Steiner pursed his lips and turned to a large, hand drawn map of the Capinga base and tapped it with his pointer.

'Yes, well' he continued. 'Shall I go through the air strike? I hear that you have already spoken to Colonel Templeton on this.'

'*Ja,* we can skip that bit,' said Smithy.

Steiner gave a tight smile and a shrug of indifference: 'Directly after the air strike, A, B, C and D Companies dropped onto their designated Landing Zones to the west and north of the base and proceeded to the attack. Initial resistance was sporadic and rapidly and effectively suppressed. Stop lines were quickly established north and south to prevent the escape of the officers and commissars that intelligence indicated were present. When B and C Companies pressed on into the centre of the camp, resistance hardened quite a bit, centred on several anti-aircraft guns firing horizontally.'

'Casualties?' said Smithy.

'Yes. I'll come to that,' answered Steiner. 'To overcome this difficulty, I led a platoon taken from A Company and assaulted the protecting trenches, cleared them and then destroyed the anti-aircraft guns and a recoilless rifle at close quarters. After that, resistance ceased to all intents and purposes, and the extraction began with the arrival of the helicopters.'

'It all went according to plan then?'

'Yes – well, as well as could be expected. We were delayed by the anti-aircraft guns which put us about two hours behind schedule.'

'And the poison gas?'

Steiner shook his head.

'The newspapers seem pretty certain.'

'Which kind?' said Steiner.

'What?' said Smithy.

'Which kind of gas do they accuse us of using on them?'

Smithy produced the newspaper and looked through the article.

'It doesn't say.'

Steiner smiled. 'Because we didn't use it. No soldier wants to use it, Sergeant Smith. It is too unreliable, too unstable in this climate and it means we have to fight wearing respirators – which we were not carrying.'

Smithy nodded. He had done his riot training with tear gas and knew just how impractical it was to do anything in thirty degrees heat while wearing a gas mask; the visor misted up whatever you did, the seals trapped your sweat and made your neck sting, your lungs were just busted and you ended up stumbling around blind in a rubber prison.

'Casualties, then,' he said.

'Twelve wounded, four killed,' replied Steiner. 'In return for around one thousand enemy dead and wounded; mostly dead – the air strike was more than effective.'

'The picture shows women in the grave,' said Smithy. 'Know anything about that?'

Steiner sucked at his teeth.

'There were civilians in the camp, certainly, and the Terrs employ both women and children in combat roles,' he said. 'So…it is possible that they were caught up in the crossfire.'

'You didn't try to avoid killing them?' said Smithy.

'Like I said, Sergeant,' said Steiner, looking him straight in the eye. 'The Terrs use women in combat.'

*

50

Back at the bungalow, Corporal Bridgeman was brewing morning coffee and as Smithy entered through the padlocked front door, the warm aroma of freshly ground beans and baked rusks greeted him.

'I'll be with you now, now,' called out Bridgeman. 'Would you like me to serve it up in your new office?'

'New office?' said Smithy, amazed. It smelled like real coffee too and not the bitter mix of instant and chicory that he was used to.

'*Ja*, sure,' said Bridgeman from the kitchen. 'I scrounged a few odds and ends from the quartermaster and the rest was just lying around crying out for someone to employ it.'

Smithy went through to the office. Gone was the trestle table, banished to a supporting role against the wall and in its place was a proper pedestal desk, complete with drawers and beside it a small cupboard. The stripped floorboards had been covered with a large rug and the light bulb had acquired both a shade and a mate below in the form of a green and brass banker's lamp. Pin boards covered two of the walls, while a large picture of an elephant had materialised on another. Smithy went up to the desk and saw a small ringbinder placed in the centre of the jotter, flipped it open and was surprised to see that it contained an alphabetised section, an address book, a map of the world complete with time zone calculator and a set of conversion tables for several sets of weights and measures.

'It's the latest thing,' said Bridgeman bringing a tray in and setting it down on a side table. 'It's called a Filofax and all the American Yuppies are using them. I got one for myself too.'

'What the fuck is a Yuppie and what is this thing for?' answered Smithy, mystified.

'A Yuppie is like a young, upwardly mobile professional person working in a bank or selling stocks and shares,' explained Bridgeman, pouring the coffee into a perfect white bone china cup. 'And the Filofax is a personal organiser; it's like a notebook but more modern and efficient.'

Smithy crinkled up one corner of his mouth as he looked at the folder and then smiled fully when he took the coffee and tasted it. Milk and two sugars; just as he liked it; real coffee too.

'You will make someone a fucking lovely wife, Bridgeman,' said Smithy, taking a rusk and dipping it. It was delicious. 'Better than Gypsy Creams, *boet*.'

'How did the meeting with Colonel Steiner go?' asked Bridgeman, pouring a cup for himself.

'As expected,' said Smithy, shrugging. 'He took me through the attack plan and a clinical job it was too. I believe him too when he says there was no poison gas or massacre of civilians; the air force went in and *donnered* the SWAPO base good and then the Parabats followed up in good order and twatted the rest of them. It doesn't help me but it all seems pretty straightforward.'

'*Ja*, you might want to get some original copies of that front page,' said Bridgeman, scratching his eye and indicating the newspaper. 'You already spilt tea on it and it will look like a rubbing rag soon. You want Engine mountings for lunch then? It is a bit better than the alternative.'

*Ja*, sure,' said Smithy. 'Just one thing though. Are you using some kind of air freshener or citrus cleaning product? I keep getting a whiff of what smells like a fancy perfume.'

Bridgeman sniffed at the air and looked around as though expecting to see the source of the fragrance.

'I can't smell anything,' he replied. 'But, you know, I've got a bit of a sinus problem. So is it Engine mountings or Spick and Spam?'

'Engine mountings,' replied Smithy, wondering just why Bridgeman seemed to have been born one step ahead of him.

'*Lekker*,' said Bridgeman. 'And there's an officer and a lot of files arriving to join you this afternoon – some big cheese *choti ghoti* from up on the border. I've to pick them from the helipad at 1400 hrs.'

*

'Smithy.'

He had watched her come in from the helipad, kitbag over her shoulder, beret tucked into an epaulette, honey-blonde hair tied up exposing her swan neck, military browns tailored to fit, and walking with her head down as though she was thinking hard. She only looked up when she reached the gate of the bungalow and as she did, he caught the flash of surprise and the flush of embarrassment.

'I thought you were going to call,' he said.

'I was,' she replied, hiding her blue eyes under lowered lids. 'It's just that...I didn't think that you would...really want me to. Given the situation....'

Trudi Mostert was the Lieutenant in the elite mixed race 23 Leopard Battalion who had been instrumental in solving his last case. She was also the only person to whom he had confessed his part in the murder of the anti-Apartheid activist. It made him nervous that he had trusted her; nervous that he had found it so easy to pour out the story under the influence of a starry night, a bottle of Klippie and a pretty face; nervous that he had gambled; nervous that he had given such a hostage to fortune in a world where fortune herself seemed to be held hostage to the future.

Smithy pursed his lips and looked at the bluegums. If she was a gamble, then she was also just about the only good thing to have come out that case; the way he had spent his days off since then had been determined by his proximity to a telephone. He hadn't actually stayed in and stared at one, admittedly, but he had confined his nights out to the mess bar, which was close by the switchboard.

'Never mind,' he said, holding up the newspaper. 'I am guessing you have been sent here to work on the Capinga business?'

'That's right,' she said. 'The orderly is bringing the files.'

As she passed him in the doorway, he caught her perfume; a soft musk, but also sweet and heavy.

'I'm glad you're here, Trudi,' he said, smiling.

'Me too,' she said, returning the smile and holding him in it for a moment. Smithy got that warm glow that he was hoping for and knew that the connection was still live even after all these months. Perhaps, perhaps, perhaps...something might come of it, second time around.

'Your bunk is in the room to the left,' he said, breaking the moment and embarrassed that he had let it go on so obviously. 'You can get Bridgeman to fit it with a lock - if you wish.'

'No need,' she said, flashing him a coy smile. 'I brought my own.'

'Why am I not surprised?' he said to himself, as she pushed open the door and went in.

*

'So you going to brief me on the situation, then?' said Mostert, settling down behind the desk in Smithy's chair.

'Pretty straight forward, it seems to me,' he replied, sitting down and pulling his Filofax towards him. 'The Air Force and Parabats *donnered* a Terr base up at a place called Capinga in Angola, the international media have declared it a massacre in which we used poison gas and the Brass want us to prove that we didn't and it's all bullshit.'

'Poison gas?'

'Like I say, it's bullshit,' said Smithy, pushing the newspaper towards her. 'I interviewed both the Air Force and the Parabat commanders and they are pretty definite that only the tried and trusted means were employed. If you ask me, it's just a load of SWAPO propaganda- my mother would love it.'

Mostert picked up the newspaper and quickly scanned it.

'Well, if it's an open and shut case,' she said, after a moment. 'Why did they drag you all the way from – where was it?'

'The end of Mouse Wheel Road,' answered Smithy. 'And they think that because I know Clive Merriman, I'll be able to persuade him that we are telling the truth, for once. And then, he will convince the international media.'

'Clive Merriman, the English journalist?' said Mostert, putting the paper down. 'The father of David Merriman?'

David Merriman had been the chief suspect in the murder case that they had last worked on together.

'That's him,' replied Smithy, looking down. 'You know BOSS killed David?'

'Yes, I guessed,' she said, wrinkling her nose. 'I saw the obituary. They even gave him a medal. This is going to be very tricky.'

'I suppose that's why they sent you along,' said Smithy. 'They needed someone with brains.'

'Or someone to keep an eye on you, Smithy,' she replied. 'You were going to let David Merriman go, weren't you?'

'I would have done too,' confessed Smithy, defiantly. 'But BOSS beat me to it.'

She held his gaze for a second or two and then leaned forward, her hands between her knees.

'I didn't tell anyone, Joshua,' she said, softly. 'Not about Merriman or …what happened back when you were just an ordinary Konstabel.'

Smithy took a deep breath, held it, rammed his own hands into his armpits and lent forward too, head down, nodding.

'I would be hanged,' he said, eventually. 'They have me by the balls.'

She leaned back in her chair and let the tension go.

'Well, let's not give them an excuse, hey? See if we can't steer some middle course through this?'

Smithy looked up sharply and nodded once again. He knew he was at her mercy but didn't mind. Being around her was worth the risk.

'Let me see the witness statements,' she said. 'And let's get some coffee.'

'Witness statements?' said Smithy. 'What witness statements?'

She shook her head in mock despair and rising from the desk, opened the door and called through it.

'Corporal Bridgeman? Can you make some coffee and then schlep over to the Air Force and the Parabats and get copies of the Capinga operational reports, please?'

'No problem, Ma'am,' he replied, appearing instantaneously from the kitchen. 'And what colour would you like the curtains for your room Ma'am? They have yellow or blue ones in the stores.'

*

Later that evening, after a dinner of clutch plate burgers, Smithy lounged about the office with a Klippie and Coke while Captain Mostert went through the operational reports that Bridgeman had provided before going off to his own meal.

'Well, like you said, it all seems pretty straightforward,' she said, stubbing a cigarette out. 'We'd do a few things different in 23 but by and large, it's all here.'

She spread out the pre- and post-op aerial reconnaissance photographs, maps, sketch maps, schematics, flight plans, fire plans, Battalion and Company orders, admin arrangements, re-fuelling schedules and all the other documents necessary to the efficient fighting of a secret war, flipping through page after page of heavily typed and treasury-tagged paper.

'You want another Klippie?' asked Smithy, trying to maintain his interest.

She shook her head. 'We're missing something.'

'Yeah. Drinking time.'

'No. Pass me the Parabat post-op report.'

Smithy selected the manila folder and slid it over. She opened it and began reading it again. Smithy poured himself another Klippie and went to look out of the window. The sky was purple and argent as the last of the light fled over the western horizon.

'In the great scheme of things,' said Smithy. 'What percentage of rivers reach the sea as opposed to disappearing into an inland sea or a swamp?'

'What?' replied Mostert, looking up sharply.

'Is just a question that's been bothering me.'

'I don't know,' she said, going back to the folder. 'Look in an Atlas.'

'I mean, most of them do, right? The Mississippi does and the Zambezi does and the Yang-tse does. Just because the Volga and the Okavango don't doesn't mean they are in the majority, does it?'

'Smithy,' said Mostert, drily. 'Take more ice with it.'

'I mean...'

There was a sound of drunken cursing from beyond the bungalow fence, followed by the unmistakeable sound of someone tripping over, breaking the gate and flailing hopelessly.

'It's Bridgeman,' said Smithy, going to the window then smiling out of the corner of his mouth, pleased to finally discover that his efficient orderly/cook/handyman/scrounger/fixer was, actually a human. 'Pissed up. I'll go see what state he's in.'

'Is he bunking here?'

'No,' said Smithy.

'Thank heaven for small mercies, hey?'

Smithy went outside and got to Bridgeman just as he hauled himself up onto all fours and, shaking like a dog, threw up into a bush.

'It's all *kak*,' said Bridgeman, between emptying himself and wiping his mouth. '*Fokken kak.*'

'You just worked that out, hey, Bridgeman?' said Smithy, stepping back quickly to avoid another acrid emetic spray. 'I bet you passed Matric and everything.'

'Everything,' he repeated, rolling over onto his back and panting. 'All *kak*. *Fokken kak. Fokken* Parabat *kak.*'

'You finished spewing now?' asked Smithy, preparing to pick him up.

Bridgeman nodded his head in the affirmative, then rolled over as a convulsion shook him and produced a spectacular projectile vomit.

'Why do pissed up people *always* say that?' said Smithy to himself. 'Why don't they just say that they have got more to get out?'

'*Fokken* Parabat *kak*,' repeated Bridgeman, this time with venom. '*Fokken* Capinga, *fokken* Steiner. All *kak.*'

59

'Alright, *bru*,' said Smithy, adopting the standard issue, universally accepted and employed fatherly tone necessary for dealing with drunks. 'Let's get you up and put you somewhere you can get your head down, hey? You can sleep in the kitchen where you can drink a lot of water and wait for that *babelaas* to wake you in the morning.'

'No. I mean it,' said Bridgeman, insistently. He tried to get up, but reeled over once more. 'Capinga was *kak*.'

'Yeah, you said,' said Smithy, catching him by the collar and wrenching him up into a kneeling position.

'That report is *kak*. That Steiner is a *blerrie leuenaar*. A bloody liar and a *fokken* bastard too.'

'What's that?' Mostert appeared in the doorway and switched the light on. 'What did he say?'

'He's drunk, Ma'am,' replied Smithy.

'And *bosbefok* too,' raved Bridgeman, climbing to his feet, his arms waving and tears starting from his one good eye. '*Ja*, completely and comprehensively fucked, hey? But it's still *kak*! You don't believe me? Ask Mickey Epstein, hey? Ask Mickey Epstein.'

'First thing in the morning,' said Smithy, propelling him towards the door. 'Now wipe away your tears and stop acting like a puff, hey?'

'Don't like what you see, Sergeant?' Bridgeman squirmed free and began tearing at his own face. 'Don't like anything that doesn't fit into your nice little macho world, hey? Well what does it say in your Bible? *If thine eye offend thee, pluck it out*.' He pulled out his glass eye and flung it wildly into the dark. '*Fok* you all!'

60

Smithy noted the trajectory as the eye caught in the flash of the outside light and sailed over the fence and then turning back to his sinking charge saw the tears streaming out of Bridgeman's remaining eye and the emptiness of the black pit next to it.

'Come on, Bridgeman,' he said, suddenly sympathetic. 'Let's get you into your bed.'

He looked at Mostert and gave a shrug. Drunk squaddies saying things they wouldn't normally say sober was part and parcel of military life.

'Bring him inside,' said Captain Mostert. 'You need a hand?'

'That would be most helpful, Ma'am,' replied Smithy, just as Bridgeman slumped into unconsciousness.

They found a blanket, improvised a pillow from a pack and put a bucket and a water bottle beside Bridgeman's head and then left him drooling and insensible in the recovery position on the cool tiles of the kitchen floor.

'Last Orders?' said Smithy, looking straight at Mostert with a hopeful sigh.

She poured a couple of Klippies and took ice from the fridge, threw them into the glasses and led the way back to the office.

'Stop looking at my bum,' said Mostert.

'*Ja*,' said Smithy. 'Sorry. It's been a long time these past couple of months. Light me up a *skyf*.'

'Do you believe him?' replied Mostert, flicking her hair back as she resumed her seat at the desk and tossing him a pack of cigarettes. 'About the report being a load of *kak*?'

'Not really,' said Smithy, looking up sharply. 'But I can see you do.'

'It's just that Mickey Epstein was listed as one of those killed at Capinga,' she said, sipping at her drink and waving away a whining mosquito. 'May be the details of what happened are not exactly the same as the ones in the report?'

'In *Chateau Libertas* vino veritas, you mean?' said Smithy, lighting up.

'The report just seems to me to be a bit *too* perfect,' she said. 'And just when did any battle ever go exactly according to plan?'

03

Sunday

'You did a lot of talking last night, *bru*,' said Smithy, squatting on his heels and handing over a coffee.

It was just after dawn and the cool air and soft light brought in fresh green smells from the bush to mingle with the warm smell of decent coffee. Bridgeman, wrapped in the blanket, covered in his own vomit and still sitting on the floor, snuffled, took a swig from the mug and nearly choked.

'*Ja*, I put a shot of Klippie in there,' said Smithy. 'Hair of the dog, hey? Now get it down you, Bridgeman, and then you can tell me all about Mickey Epstein and Capinga and Colonel Steiner and everything.'

Bridgeman shuddered and coughed again, keeping his eye down on the coffee, sipping, snuffling and shaking like a wet dog.

'And then you can stick this back in,' added Smithy, almost as an afterthought, holding out Bridgeman's glass eye.

Bridgeman reached out for it, but Smithy closed his hand on it before he could take it.

'How did you lose your eye – I mean your real one,' asked Smithy, looking professionally at the stretched skin of the empty eye socket. 'Bullet?'

'Shell splinter,' grunted Bridgeman, reaching for the eye again. Smithy handed it over. '*Fokken* Steiner's fault.'

'What happened?' said Smithy, putting another splash of brandy into the cup.

'I was aircrew on a chopper called in for a Casevac,' answered Bridgeman, blowing on the eye, polishing it and then slotting it back in. 'The enemy were close up and the LZ was coming under fire, so Steiner called in an artillery strike. Only he brought it in too close and I got this.'

'That's really tough,' replied Smithy.

'Yeah,' said Bridgeman. 'I got this and he wrote the report and got a medal.'

Smithy sipped at his own coffee while he digested this and then pulled out cigarettes, lit a couple and handed one to Bridgeman. Bridgeman took it and pulled deeply on it, then exhaled a great cloud of blue smoke.

'Better open a window,' said Bridgeman. 'The female officer won't like us smoking indoors. I should get cleaned up too.'

'*Ja*, in a little while,' said Smithy. 'And what was all that stuff about Mickey Epstein?'

Bridgeman gave a little start, then averted his eyes.

'I was just upset,' he said. 'Mickey is a friend of mine, that's all.'

63

'Mickey *was* a friend,' corrected Smithy. 'The post-Op report has him included in the KIA count.'

Bridgeman looked down into his cup and began to cry quietly.

'*Ag*, sorry man,' said Smithy, putting a hand out and taking away the mug. 'I should learn to be not so brutal.'

Bridgeman shook the hand away and quickly wiped the tears away with the heel of his free hand before taking another drag on the cigarette. He held the smoke deep in his lungs and then, pushing his head back, blew out the smoke in another volcanic gush.

'You people are here to investigate Steiner, right?' he said, a bright and direct light coming into his one blue eye. 'About the Capinga fuck-up?'

Smithy pursed his mouth and gave a nod of assurance.

'I know someone who was on it who can tell you a lot about what went wrong,' said Bridgeman. 'But you have to guarantee his anonymity. He won't talk otherwise. He wouldn't last five minutes in this place if it got out that he'd criticised the Colonel.'

'Well, why would he talk to you then?'

Bridgeman put his head on one side, appraised Smithy for a moment, and then blew out more smoke from the side of wryly smiling mouth.

'You want to speak to him or not?'

*

Bridgeman spirited 'Sergeant Bilko' out of the Field Hospital during Church parade and wheeled him over to the bungalow as though the pair of them were going for a Sunday morning stroll and by the time they arrived,

64

Mostert and Smithy had both gone back through the files to confirm that Mickey Epstein was indeed listed as dead and that their mystery witness was probably one of the eight wounded who had not been sent back to be treated in Pretoria. As they hauled the wheel chair backwards up the steps into the bungalow, Bilko said nothing but Smithy could see from the way he kept stealing glances at Bridgeman that he was uneasy about the situation, confining himself to the odd grunt of discomfort as the chair jarred against the woodwork and banged against the door frame. He was swathed in bandages that covered much of his face, his torso and his hands, while his left foot was encased in plaster but even under all that, Smithy could see that he was fit, muscular and in possession of at least one old wound, a star-shaped pucker just under the left collar bone. His hands were the most striking feature though; they were big, gnarled and without knuckles; without a doubt, the hands of a tough, street fighter.

'I hear you have something to tell me about the Capinga attack,' said Smithy, when they had manhandled the wheel chair through the too-small door into the office. He took up a pen and held it poised above the Filofax like a waiter about to take an order.

Bilko made a half-hearted attempt to salute Captain Mostert, gave up half-way through it and then looked over to Bridgeman and gave him a quizzical look. Bridgeman gave him a nod of permission without speaking.

'Too *fokken* right, I have,' said Bilko suddenly, his one visible eye watering. 'But this is Colonel Steiner we are talking about: so I'm not here, Bilko's not here, Bridgeman's not here and I don't know whether you are here or not. If you are, then that's up to you.'

'Yes, we get that,' said Captain Mostert, fiddling with a button on her blouse.

'Please, in your own time,' said Smithy. 'And Corporal Bridgeman – could you find a cold one for him?'

'It's ten o'clock in the morning,' warned Bridgeman.

'Are you his mother or something?' replied Smithy. 'This man looks like he deserves a *Castle*.'

Bridgeman gave a disapproving shrug. Smithy gave him a hard stare, a stare entirely defeated by the one returned by Bridgeman's glass eye.

'I don't need a beer,' said Bilko, his voice trembling. 'I need you to listen to what I've got to say because this was a complete fuck up from start to finish.'

'In your own time,' said Mostert, opening up the post-Op report and tapping a pen on the desk. Smithy noticed that the button on her blouse had popped open to reveal a glimpse of lace bra. He put down his Filofax and coughed meaningfully. Mostert ignored him.

'Nasty cough you've got there, Sergeant,' said Bridgeman. Would you like me to get you something for it?'

'Carry on please,' said Mostert, concentrating on the folder before her.

'It was the airstrike that was the problem,' said Bilko, holding up a bandaged hand. 'I mean it was *awesome*. I have never seen anything like it in my life. The shock waves looked like…like some *fokken* giant beating on a drum and the clouds of smoke were like…like thunderheads. There were secondary explosions going off everywhere. It was…'

'Yes, *awesome*,' said Mostert. 'Continue.'

'Well,' continued Bilko. 'The pilots carrying us Parabats were so fascinated by the spectacle that they over-shot the drop zone. *Ja*, it was only by a few seconds, but those few seconds were enough to put three quarters of the battalion down in the wrong places. My mob -B Company - landed in a field of tall mealies and we took much longer than expected to re-group and after that, we all headed off in the wrong direction for ten minutes before the Major realised what had happened and reversed our steps.'

'There is no mention of this in the report,' said Mostert, beckoning Bridgeman over. 'Show him, please.'

Bridgeman took the report, carried it the two paces over to Bilko's wheelchair and handed it to him. Bilko took it with one hand and held it up to read.

'*Ja*, this is all wrong,' he said, after a minute or two. 'It was why we didn't capture any SWAPO generals or FAPLA *fokken* commissars. The road out westwards was open for a full thirty minutes at least and by the time we'd got back astride it, they had bomb-shelled out.'

'OK,' said Mostert, waving a finger at Bridgeman. Bridgeman retrieved the folder, put it back on the desk and then resumed his position by the door. 'Go on, please.'

'Well, we headed towards the camp, coming under increasing fire from snipers concealed in what buildings were still standing and from groups of SWAPO fighters, more or less fleeing from the scene of the carnage on the parade ground,' continued Bilko, biting his thumb. 'Man, some of them were like zombies. They were staggering around in a state of shock with skin hanging off them like rags, some of them carrying limbs, all of them drenched in blood and covered in plaster dust. I never saw anything like it before and I've seen plenty of contact.'

'Were you involved in the attack on the anti-aircraft guns?' asked Smithy.

'Was I? Too *fokken* right I was,' spat Bilko, indicating his bandages. 'We'd just finished clearing some buildings and had lined up a couple of dozen captives when Steiner turns up and orders me and my platoon to follow him into some trenches. *Fok*! Those AA guns were spraying tracer around like free drinks in a burgled bar, so we didn't hang around and got straight into the section and platoon drills, hey? Putting plenty of fire down so that the corporals could crawl up and drop grenades right into them.'

'Was there any use of poison gas?' asked Mostert.

'Poison gas? Are you mad?' answered Bilko. 'Who wants to be running around in 35 degrees wearing a respirator? And anyway, we weren't carrying them. Where did you get that crazy notion from?'

'Carry on,' said Mostert, making a note.

'Well, we took out the guns,' continued Bilko. 'They fought well those Terrs. Tough nuts, they were.' He touched his bandages. '*Fokken* good shots, too.'

'And then?'

'Well, after that everything went to a can of rat shit,' said Bilko, sitting back and sighing. 'The word got out that there was a big Cuban armoured column bearing down on us and when the Brass started calling in the helicopters to extract us, the pilots came down in any old order and took off anyone who happened to be there at the time. I mean, there wasn't a rout or a big panic or anything, it's just that everyone was pumped up and forgot the proper order. It meant that we had to abandon a lot of the prisoners and the platoons and companies got mixed up, so when we got back to the rendezvous point – this was still inside Angola, right? – no-one quite managed to do a proper roll call. Some of the wounded had been casevaced straight away, some of the platoons were without their officers, some of the helicopters had gone back for others, and no-one knew exactly what was *fokken* up and what was *fokken* down.'

'Sounds like a standard issue SNAFU,' said Smithy.

'*Ja*, it was,' agreed Bilko. 'Except this was *different*. We left someone *behind*.'

'You left someone behind?' said Smithy, appalled. No-one was *ever* left behind, alive or dead. Not *ever*. 'Wait. Are you sure? How do you know? Steiner never said anything about anyone MIA.'

'He wouldn't, would he?' snarled Bilko. 'Rain on his *fokken* parade if it turned out he abandoned one of the boys, hey? I'm telling you, man: we left Mickey Epstein behind.'

'How do you know he wasn't killed?' persisted Smithy. 'You know; hit by a shell with not enough of him left to put in a chip bag.'

Bilko adjusted one of his bandages and made a conscious effort to control himself.

'Please,' said Mostert, beckoning Bridgeman over once more and handing him the folder. 'Can you explain why he is listed here as KIA?'

Bridgeman took the folder and passed it to Bilko. The button on Mostert's blouse was still undone and Smithy felt a little jealous flush come into his cheeks as he calculated the fine view of a soft bosom and deep cleavage that Bridgeman would be enjoying.

'*Ja*, this is wrong too,' said Bilko. 'It says Mickey was in my stick for the drop but he wasn't. He got shifted at the last minute to another one. There was a Recce officer and his Sergeant and Mickey and another guy got detailed to jump with them. They flew with us but jumped separately.'

'The report doesn't say anything about the Recces being involved,' said Smithy.

'Well,' said Bilko. 'They were.'

'Carry on with your account, please,' said Mostert, indicating Bridgeman to fetch the report once more.

'Well, we jumped into the mealie field with the Recces but a gust of wind caught Mickey's chute at the last minute and carried him onto the far bank of the river there. I tried to call to him but all hell was breaking loose and a couple of mortar rounds came down into the mealies and then we were up and off.'

'You told your officer?' asked Smithy.

'I did. Fat lot of good it did Mickey. He was stranded.'

'On the opposite side of a crocodile infested river,' said Smithy. 'I don't suppose he could've just lobbed a couple of grenades in to scare them off.'

'Fuck the crocs,' said Bilko. 'Mickey couldn't swim a river flowing that fast with all that kit on and it wasn't until we got back here that anyone noticed he was missing. Steiner sent a couple of choppers back to look for him but they were driven off by AA and so he declared him to be dead; just like that. Not *missing*; *fokken* dead. God knows where he is. If SWAPO have got him, well....'

'You think he was captured?' said Mostert, gently.

'Mickey was *ma bru*,' said Bilko, suddenly quiet. 'And Steiner left him behind to be captured and tortured.'

*

'What do you think?' said Smithy, standing by the window watching Bridgeman wheel Bilko back across the flat pan of the airfield towards the hospital.

'Well,' said Mostert, fastening the button on her blouse. 'I believe them. It rings true. Back in 23 Battalion, the guys say that just about the only thing you can guarantee about a paratroop drop is that it will go wrong. And I never believed that anyone would use poison gas willingly. It's just too unpredictable – one little change in the wind and it's coming right back at you.'

'Me too,' agreed Smithy, lighting cigarettes for them both. 'What about Mickey Epstein?'

'I believe them about him too,' said Mostert, taking the cigarette. 'It's obvious the pair of them were in love with him.'

'What?' said Smithy, squinting with disbelief. 'What? What? You think they were...?'

'Yes, of course,' said Mostert, smiling and taking the cigarette. 'Isn't it obvious? Bridgeman never once took even the smallest peep down my cleavage the whole time – the whole time your tongue was lolling out so far I thought you would get a carpet burn on it.'

Smithy thought back to the wry smile Bridgeman had given him that morning when he had asked about Bilko and screwed his face up in horrified revulsion.

'No,' he protested. 'Queers in the Parabats? I can't believe it. I mean, maybe the navy but....'

'Yes,' repeated Mostert, widening her eyes in mock horror. 'They *everywhere*, Joshua. Army, Air Force. Even in the Police.'

'Oh no, they are not,' replied Smithy, indignantly. 'There were no queers at Police College – or in Graaff Reinet, I can tell you!'

'What, you think they all English lords or drag queens?' she laughed, her eyes twinkling.

'*Ja*, well I can believe English lords being queer but – this is South Africa, for God's sake!' said Smithy, beginning to pace up and down the room. 'It wouldn't be allowed. It *isn't* allowed, dammit. The 1976 Sodomy Law specifically forbids it!'

'And we all know that the law is *scrupulously* observed in all its aspects throughout the whole of this wonderful republic,' she replied, enjoying his discomfort. 'You never been to the nudist beach at Seapoint?'

'What?' said Smithy. 'What do you mean? That's just for idiots and...well...weirdoes. Like Druids.'

'*Druids*,' said Mostert, sighing. 'Think about it, Sergeant Smith: you are a homosexual and you get your call up papers, yes? What you going to do? Join up with all your mates or tell them that you can't join up because of your particular tastes?'

Smithy took a moment to take this in.

'But we have communal showers! We have to live cheek by jowl in trenches and sleep in little bashas together!'

'What's the matter, Joshua?' said Mostert, laughing. 'Don't you feel comfortable in the company of men?'

'Yes! No! What do you mean by that?' said Smithy, knocking the end of his cigarette off by accident. 'You don't think...you can't possibly think I'm *one of them*, can you?'

'I don't know, do I?' she replied. 'I mean, you might just be faking. I don't know what you and the boys get up to together after a rugby match, all in the communal bath, do I?'

'Now that is well below the belt,' said Smithy, his voice dropping with disappointment. 'I mean, there is just no room for a limp-wristed mincer in the scrum. Rugby is a *man's man's* game.'

'I think you just proved my point, Joshua,' said Mostert, sniggering. 'I bet Bilko would be just the sort of person who'd like to get behind you in the scrum and reach between your legs to take a good firm hold of your shirt, hey?'

'No,' protested Smithy, flailing his arms about. 'It's unthinkable.'

'You don't mind Kaffirs,' she answered. 'Why should you mind homosexuals?'

'That's different,' Smithy gasped, still reeling from the thought of Bilko's hand between his legs.

'Why?'

'Because it just is!'

Mostert flashed him a big, wide smile.

'What a Neanderthal you are, Joshua.'

'*Ja*, well,' he said, calming down and stubbing out his cigarette in the ash tray. 'Jeez Louise! Queers, man! I should have guessed about Bridgeman when he started talking about curtains and baking his own rusks.'

'And you a detective, hey?'

Smithy lit up another cigarette.

'They call them *fags* in America,' needled Mostert. Smithy looked at the cigarette and stubbed it out.

'What we going to do about this Mickey Epstein?' he said.

Mostert smiled again, then shook her head as if to clear it.

'Well,' she said. 'This is something we need to check with Colonel Steiner. He'll be getting his lunch in the mess soon.'

'Hope it's curry,' answered Smithy, brightening up.

'Doesn't matter what it is,' she replied, tartly. 'It's the *Officer's Mess* and as you don't qualify, I'll just have to interview him alone.'

*

It was pleasantly warm in the sunshine and as she walked across the flat wide pan of the airfield guided by Bridgeman's colour-coded map, Mostert tried to get some order into her thoughts about Sergeant Joshua Smith. She liked him. That was certain; he was good looking in a raggedy teddy bear-ish sort of way and she admired the way that he bore the physical scars of his injuries so cheerfully. His optimism, she found childlike, and the curious way he blended a sharp, can-do, fix-it attitude with a jaw-dropping stupidity reminded her of some large dogs she had known. In other circumstances, she would have had no hesitation in accepting a date with him but right now she was not at all certain that this would be the right thing to do.

For a start, she was a woman virtually alone among men who were living warrior lives and she understood that even the slightest hint of availability given out would bring them down like wolves on the fold. Before they went out on operations, they were on edge, keyed up and sometimes, she could smell the raw energy of death in the air about them like ozone. When they came back, they resembled a storm about to break and their eyes flashed dangerously, hungrily, sometimes with contempt for those who had not shared the dangers, sometimes with indignation, as though she was intruding on some intensely private revelation. Their power was awesome, their physicality magnificent and the dirt and exhaustion they wore about them was an aphrodisiac she found hard to resist; it was a primeval instinct; but they were panthers too dangerous to dine with. One slip and she would be public property.

That these men had faced death, faced their enemy, closed with him and killed him was only one part of the equation because she knew from

75

experience that such things carried their own costs. Some – most - men accepted that they had killed and that what they had done was bad, yet they accepted that they had had no choice; it was kill or be killed. For the farmers and the hunters it was less of a trauma because they were used to seeing death at first hand and had acquired that extra skin, but there was no hard and fast rule for any of them. She had known city boys take to bush war like ducks to water but again, others were more troubled and prone to nightmares and Mostert had heard tales from back in Civvy Street of bleak, black depressions, irrational behaviour and the odd, unexplained death. She had also heard of reunions and parties and seen the quiet, dignified camaraderie of men who had shared this ultimate challenge, this ultimate experience, this ultimate vindication of their manhood and who knew they were now *different*. What was impossible to distinguish in advance was whether a man would survive or be destroyed by the war and though she felt able to make a decent guess that Sergeant Joshua Smith would probably be among those to come through with a lower personal cost, it just wasn't possible to be certain. She readjusted her beret, looked up at the sun and felt a little ashamed of herself for thinking this way, but she did not want to be married to someone who would not cope with the aftermath of war.

There was also the fact that Joshua was a murderer and though killing was what being in a war up on the border was all about, this was something different. Of course, she understood all the mitigating factors; he was young and stupid and impressionable and put upon by older men, men who were corrupt, thugs, and more stupid than ever Joshua would be, but whenever she tried to excuse him, the fact was that he had taken a shovel to a helpless man's throat and stomped on it so hard that the victim had been almost decapitated. There was no 'kill or be killed'; in those

76

circumstances, the more appropriate phrase would have been 'live and let live' but she feared that everyone in South Africa was long past that possibility and before long there would have to be a reckoning. And that weighed against Joshua Smith too; again, she could not feel proud of herself for thinking that she did not want to be hitched to a criminal, however remorseful. Joshua's crime would forever hang over him like the sword of Damocles.

And yet, she had liked him enough to slip her phone number under his door on the evening that he had confessed his crime to her. And yet, she had not summoned up the courage to return his calls. And here she was again, almost a year later, working alongside him, and glad in her heart that she was.

*

'Can I help you, Ma'am?'

Mostert looked up into a face that consisted mainly of broken nose.

'I'm looking for Colonel Steiner,' she replied, tapping the manila folder she had brought with her.

'And you would be?'

The man was big, even for a Parabat, with the look of a nightclub bouncer in a bad mood.

'*Captain* Mostert,' she replied. '23 Leopard Battalion.'

'*Ja*, and I'm the Queen of Sheba,' he replied. 'Since when did 23 start employing *bakvissies* like you?'

'Since just after the Parabats lowered the IQ tests to let a *dikbek domkop* like you in, Corporal,' Mostert replied, tapping the pips on her epaulette. 'Now, stand aside, please.'

The Corporal scrunched his face up into a broken toothed smile, looked down her cleavage, stood aside and saluted.

'*Lekke anties*,' he muttered. 'Absence makes the Ovambo girls look blonder.'

Mostert ignored him and walked through the doors into the Officers Mess, dropped her beret on the hall table and pushed on through the double doors to the bar, where she was greeted by an immediate silence from the group of men standing up against the counter.

'I'm looking for Colonel Steiner,' she said, her voice echoing under the corrugated iron ceiling.

'You won't find him in here,' replied a tall Lieutenant, after a moment's surprise. 'His office is through the other door. Shall I show you?'

'That won't be necessary,' she replied, recognising the pick-up tone immediately and backing out.

'Hello again, Ma'am,' said the broken-nosed Corporal looming up behind her and bestowing his best smirk on her.

'Colonel Steiner's office, please?'

'Off to your left,' he replied, extending an arm and bending slightly to bring his face a little closer to hers.

'Thank you, Corporal.'

'Anything I can do for you, *Ma'am*,' he grinned. 'Do not hesitate to ask, anytime, anywhere.'

'Get me a Martini from the bar then,' answered Mostert, taking the indicated corridor. 'And put it on someone else's bill.'

Steiner's office was at the end of the narrow corridor and all the way down towards the door she could feel the Corporal's eyes boring into her backside, so much so that the terse order to enter came as a welcome relief from the virtual groping he was giving her.

'Captain Mostert, welcome,' he said, rising from the chair behind the bare trestle table and extending a hand. 'I heard that you had taken control of the investigation from that young policeman. Excuse me, I am in the middle of lunch.'

Mostert looked at the plate of salad and the glass of water before him and took his hand.

'You are a vegetarian?' she asked, smiling. 'That must be a first in the Parabats, Sir. In 23 Battalion, they say you guys don't bother to wait until it's dead before starting.'

Steiner fixed her with his cold eyes for a moment, as if looking for something improper in her remark, and then gave a thin smile.

'Only in barracks,' he replied, indicating a second hard chair, folded, against the bare wall underneath a 'No Smoking' sign written in English and Afrikaans. 'In the field, it is my duty to eat whatever is put in front of me. How can I help you, Captain? I do not have much time that I can call my own and you are probably aware of my irritation at this needless investigation into our assault on Capinga.'

79

'Yes, Sir. I quite understand,' replied Mostert, taking the cue to get straight down to business. She flipped open the chair and then flipped open the folder. 'The investigation so far backs your story regarding the poison gas one hundred percent, so you are in the clear as far as we're concerned.'

'But?' said Steiner.

'But?'

'There is always a 'but',' said Steiner, putting his knife and fork together on the plate. 'No matter how well a soldier conducts his operations, there is always someone to cavil at the details. Sometimes it is politicians, sometimes the higher command, sometimes State Security and these things we must just endure. But I fail to see the need to pander to the international media – they will never take our side and will never be satisfied with our story. It has long been my belief that the only good journalist is a dead one.'

'You may be right about that, Colonel,' answered Mostert, with a dismissive flick of the eyebrows. 'But I have got to do the job anyway, Sir. Now, if I can just get a clear picture of how the four KIAs happened, we should be able to wrap things up finally and you can get on with your lunch.'

Steiner sat still, hardly moving a muscle, but Mostert could see that he was disturbed by the question.

'Is this for the families?' he asked.

'Something like that,' answered Mostert.

Without taking his eyes off her face, Steiner began to talk. His tone was even, factual, slow and careful, in an accent that she could not place.

'Private John Jacobs, C Company, killed while clearing a building; gunshot to the head. Nothing left of his face. Death was instantaneous. Private Piet Kruger, C Company, same manner of death, same place, but he lingered for ten minutes before what was left of his brain spilled out of the hole. Private Arnie Nelspruit, D Company, hit by 23mm AA fire. Both arms blown off, bled to death in the helicopter during Casevac. Private Michael Epstein, B Company, killed on landing, direct hit from 82mm mortar HE round. No substantial body parts remaining.'

Mostert felt the blood slowly drain from her face as Steiner related the cold facts, but it was the coldness rather than the facts that did the draining. She was used to war but not this icy relating of it.

'Any witnesses?'

'Plenty,' replied Steiner, sipping at the glass of water.

'And Epstein?'

'For Private Epstein too,' said Steiner. 'He was with a couple of Recces who had come along for the ride.'

'Recce officers?' said Mostert, feigning surprise. 'There's nothing in your report about the Recces.'

'Being from 23 Battalion,' replied Steiner, with a hint of exasperation. 'I am sure you are aware that the Recces count as Special Forces and prefer to keep their activities secret.'

There was a knock at the door and a moment later the Corporal entered carrying a tray with a Martini on it. Steiner saw the glass and betrayed the ghost of a frown.

'For the lady, Sir,' he explained. 'And the officers asked if you would be joining them for a drink, as it is your birthday, Sir. Forty, isn't it, Sir?'

'Thirty-eight,' said Steiner, bestowing his first small smile on her. 'Would you care to join me for a little celebration? I don't drink myself, but I'm sure there is a bottle of sherry suitable for a little lady in the Mess.'

On the way back to the bungalow, Mostert gave herself a small grim smile of self-congratulation and wondered about the vanity of men. For all their physical prowess, for all their bravery in the face of withering fire, for all their romantic ideals of service and of patriotism, whenever they were together in their masculine preserves a crassness came over them where women were concerned. It seemed that the lack of oestrogen in the atmosphere distorted their perceptions of women into little more than a series of oddly detached archetypes; they had sisters, aunties, mothers and wives, yet set apart from them in a world every bit as segregated as the one imposed by the Group Areas Act, they saw them only as the possibility of sex. These aesthetic, Spartan societies blunted the intelligence of men and herded them into a group-think that few of them would actually endorse in mixed company and would not do so in any kind of committed relationship. She thought of Joshua and realised what it was that she liked about him; he found group-think as onerous as she did and longed to be free of it, but he really had no idea about how to go about doing it. He needed her to show him.

Steiner, the callous, cold, controlling warlord was the opposite. He was just as entangled in the coils of this attitude but thought of it as a comforting scarf rather than a poisonous, constricting snake and so opened himself up to all the stupidities and weaknesses that went with it. His vanity was the one thing in his body, his personality, his habits that he had left to establish control over, yet it was the one thing he could not control and the merest presence of a women had led it to betray him. He had flirted with her, and thinking to give himself an edge had lied about his age and in doing so had given himself away; *falsus in unum, falsus in omnium.* Mickey Epstein had not been killed by a mortar round. Mickey Epstein had been left behind.

*

Smithy was holding a beer and scratching his balls as he looked out of the window across the flat airfield. He had just applied some Vaseline to his crotch against the jock-itch but it had simply added a stickiness to the level of his discomfort and he was now alternating between debating whether he ought to take a shower and thinking about whether airfields were chosen because they were flat or whether they were chosen and then flattened. In reality, he was thinking about these things because he did not want to think about Bridgeman and the whole issue of who was and who was not a homosexual but try as he might to think about bulldozers, hard hats and military engineering, his thoughts kept drifting back to it. Of course, he had heard all the jokes and insults and had seen Dick Emery, Frankie Howerd and any number of other screen queers, but he was doubtful if he had never actually come across a homosexual in the flesh, so to speak. Certainly, there was the chap with the long, well-manicured fingers and the lisp who occasionally came round for tea at his mother's house in Cape Town when he was a child and there was a teacher or two at school who had some peculiar mannerisms, but he could not connect them with the

83

concept of 'being a homosexual' nor imagine them doing 'it' – whatever 'it' was; the mechanics alone mystified him. Even in the old louche, liberal Cape Town District 6 where pretty much anything sexual, racial, artistic or political was tolerated, he could only think of the two, grey elderly old queens who shared a house on Arundel Street and always addressed each other as 'Mr Beyer' and 'Mr Crooks', who might possibly have been homosexual. In Krugerburg, the East Rand shithole that he had been taken to by his father after the separation, homosexuality was unknown, probably, he reflected now, because it would have carried with it a fatal risk; he had seen black men killed just for getting in the way there; God knew what would happen to a homosexual. Yet now, here, in the least expected of places, in the ultra-masculine world of the Paratrooper, here they were; Bilko, Bridgeman and Mickey Epstein and it did not seem right.

What, after all, was the point? There was no evolutionary point to homosexuality because it was hardly likely to result in the advancement, improvement or even procreation of the species. Surely there was something unnatural about it? Perhaps it was some sort of madness that could be cured with a quick bit of some psychology or maybe a pill or something? He gave an involuntary shudder. The thought of kissing a bloke was just beyond the pale. He finished his beer and went to get another.

Walking awkwardly back from the fridge to his position by the window, he saw Bridgeman approaching at a distance of about a hundred metres and concentrated on looking at him. He saw the normal, slightly rolling, gait of the farmer, the arms held slightly out on either side of the broad torso – probably more of a back than a forward when it came to rugby – and no hint of a dainty step, mincing gesture or swaying hip. Bridgeman's air force blues had the usual ironed-in regulation creases alongside the usual creases from normal wear while his boots had the requisite amount of polish on them and the expected amount of dust on them. There was nothing that his policeman's eyes could pick out as being out of the ordinary and he felt slightly let down that his powers of deduction were not up to lighting upon the detail that would give Bridgeman's homosexuality away. He wondered how Bridgeman himself knew he was a homosexual and wondered if he had a choice in the matter. Did a man just wake up one morning thinking of other men's arses? How come they didn't put on make-up or wear dresses? Scratching at his crotch again, he tried to remember when he had first become a heterosexual, but couldn't remember; was it eleven or twelve when he had kissed Flora McMicheals behind her mum's potting shed? Or was it when he had first started going out with Ayize? Probably somewhere in between, he thought; there wasn't a blinding flash, or anything. Really there was a very deep mystery here. Perhaps he should ask Bridgeman all about it?

Ayize. He had not thought about her for a long time. They had first met, aged 15 or so, in the Krugerburg Pick'n'Pay supermarket, which was just about the only public area in the town that was not officially segregated, and had then made a point of happening to be in there at the same time every few days. Not that they could say more than a few words to each other openly, not in a *dorp* as small as Krugerburg, but one day Ayize had dropped a rolled up note into his basket upon which was written her address. Her mother worked for Mrs. Parr and although they were supposed to be back in the Location by nightfall, Mrs. Parr had turned a blind eye to Mrs. Maquondo and her sweet daughter moving in to the servants' quarters on a more or less permanent basis. So it was that Joshua was able first to start talking with Ayize through a hole in the wall, then holding hands and then, when Mrs. Maquondo was busy in the house or away at the market, climbing over that wall to sit, shoulder to shoulder, arm in arm, backs against that same wall in the warm sunshine and dappled shade.

She was older than him by a year, with coffee coloured skin that made Joshua think she might be part-Indian. Her brown eyes were full of fun and a wide, shy smile above a narrow chin gave her an angular beauty that her straightened hair parted in the middle accentuated but the best thing about her was the easy way in which Joshua could relax with her. They had talked endlessly, about music and school and parents; anything but politics or apartheid because there seemed little point in doing so. They both knew that what they were doing would not be countenanced and that they would certainly be separated by their families if their secret became public. They both knew that this was a stupid and unjust world but being unaware of any other, they simply accepted that this was the way it would be until a storm or hurricane or tidal wave swept it away and brought something fairer along in its wake. Usually they talked about pop music, or school or dreamed up futures in faraway places like Cape Town or London or Australia without any real idea of how difficult it might be to realise those futures. Sometimes they dared each other to walk down the street together, but they knew that this was not possible and so instead would play a sort of follow-my-leader where they pretended not to know each other and yet never ventured more than five yards away from touching distance. They would look in the same shop windows, flashing messages in the blink of an eye in the reflections of the glass and on occasion, when they felt particularly daring, she would brush past him, the lightest touch of her shoulder sending a tingling shock wave through him.

The concealment, they acknowledged, was part of the fun and the frisson of danger added to the tension of sexuality building between them. Joshua wanted desperately to tell somebody about her but he knew that this would be fatal to the relationship and given that this was Krugerburg, possibly fatal in the literal sense for one or both of them. He had heard rumours about what happened to the black girls who had white boyfriends; and he knew exactly what happened to the white girls who were stupid enough to be found with black boyfriends. The school was awash with such talk and though he had friends, it meant that he could not trust any of them with this knowledge. It was also that he did not want the way he felt to be an object of mockery and he did not like the coarse way in which the black girls were referred to by the boys or the dismissive way they were dealt with by the girls. Ayize was not just a maid or servant in his mind, nor was she a rampant sexual beast open to any offer and ready to grant any favour in return for a ticky coin and a dagga cigarette. It had been better, he remembered, to endure the boiling frustrations of secrecy than to risk the loss of something so special, so fragile.

The sound of the gate squealing open brought Smithy back to the here and now and as Corporal Bridgeman came barrelling up the path to the front door, he decided that he would ask him to explain some of the more baffling points of homosexuality over a beer and went in to the kitchen to retrieve one for him.

'Thanks,' said Bridgeman, cracking the tin and slurping. 'I could really use one of these. I've got a mouth like Gandhi's flip-flop.'

'How's your friend, Bilko?'

'*Ja*, he's fine,' answered Bridgeman, sitting down. 'Thanks for listening to him, hey?'

Smithy shuffled his feet and took a gulp, giving him time to frame the question.

'About you and Mickey Epstein,' he began.

Bridgeman stopped drinking and fixed Smithy with his curious half-gaze.

'I mean,' said Smithy. 'I mean, were you…like…er…special kind of friends?'

Bridgeman did not respond. His glass eye did not blink.

'I mean,' stuttered Smithy. 'I'm as open-minded as the next bloke but…I mean. What's it…like?'

This was not the question he had intended to ask but it was the one that tripped off his tongue. Bridgeman said nothing.

'It's just that…well…it's to do with the case,' he explained.

Bridgeman was unconvinced and showed it by taking another swig from the tin without taking his one eye off Smithy.

'Like…er…how come…you don't like…er…breasts and that?' Smithy's voice trailed off weakly. 'Doesn't it…hurt…having your groceries delivered round the back?'

Bridgeman sighed, looked tired and resigned by turns, and then decided to put him out of his misery.

'Have you ever had sex with a woman, Sergeant Smith?' he asked.

'Of course! Yes! Loads of times!' replied Smithy.

'Well,' said Bridgeman, finishing his beer and getting out of the chair. 'I should just stick to that then.'

04

Monday

Pieters descended on them earlier than expected, just after dawn, shuffling up in his shiny black suit, rheumy eyes, an untipped cigarette dangling from his lip and looking like he had travelled all night. Mostert was still in the shower, Smithy still in his bunk and even the prepared-for-all-eventualities Bridgeman was caught unawares, breakfast not yet made.

'Tea, black, no sugar,' Pieters wheezed, his shoulders hunched, ready to start on a series of racking coughs. 'Tell the sleepy heads I want to hear their report in ten minutes. I see you have made some home improvements,' he said, going into the office. 'Very nice.'

'Black tea, no sugar,' repeated Bridgeman, backing out and shooting raised eyebrows at Mostert, who had appeared from the bathroom wrapped in a towel and a cloud of steam. 'Report in ten, it is, Sir – *Ma'am*, I mean.'

In considerably less than ten minutes, Smithy was up, dressed after a fashion (though unshaven), outside one cup of coffee cooled by cold water and proceeding through a second one while standing almost to attention in the office, gathering his wits and contemplating on the stark transition from Ayize's embrace to the vision of crumpled corruption now contemplating him. Mostert was cooler, having prioritised getting the report out from under her bed over brushing her hair properly and although she was in a far more presentable state than bleary-eyed Smithy, she would never have passed any decent sort of muster.

'Well,' said Pieters, screwing one eye up as the smoke from his cigarette irritated it. 'Give me the long and short of it – well, the short of it anyway; we don't want to be jawing on like some Groot Marico *stoep* gossip at ploughing time. *Ag* sit down – you look like a pair of tailors' dummies standing there like that.'

Mostert pulled her blouse into shape and sat down on the chair before the desk, placing the file on it. Smithy cast round, found a folding chair and drew it up.

'Sir, with respect, we can't find anything to substantiate the reports alluded to in the international media,' began Mostert. 'Preliminary interviews discount any use of poison gas at all and although the evidence seems to point to quite a few civilian casualties, these seem to have occurred in the confusion of battle. There is no suspicion of genuine and deliberate atrocities.'

She slid the report towards him, two meagre sheets of typewritten script held together with a red treasury tag. Pieters took it, shifted the empty tea cup, and scanned through it, his chest bubbling as though he were scuba diving. Mostert watched as he put his head down, resting it on the hand holding the cigarette and scanning down the side of the paper with two nicotine stained fingers of the other.

'*Ja*, Fly Boy Templeton knows his stuff,' he grunted, and coughed up a lump of phlegm into a hastily produced handkerchief that was already crunchy with snot. 'And Colonel Steiner?'

'A very efficient officer,' said Mostert, sitting almost to attention.

Pieters looked up, caught the lie in her voice, and then across at Smithy. Smithy shrugged and nodded in agreement. Pieters slowly dropped his eyes, took a drag off the cigarette, gave a choked off cough and went back to the report.

'Nothing else to report?' he said, keeping his eyes on the paper.

Mostert and Smithy flicked matching glances. They had argued about whether or not to bring Mickey Epstein up after Smithy had pointed out that Steiner's version of his death had the advantage of corroborating evidence and witnesses who would no doubt support it, while Bilko and Bridgeman's version had only hearsay and her female intuition to back it up. In the end, they had compromised; they would not mention it unless asked; but Smithy knew she would.

'No, Sir,' said Smithy.

'Just one thing,' said Mostert.

Pieters sat back in his chair, moving heavily, like some old battleship about to keel over and turn turtle.

'There is the possibility that one of our men was left behind,' she began, hesitantly. 'The evidence is confused but...'

'Left behind? Was he captured?' said Pieters, quickly.

'We have some Recce witnesses that say he was blown up by a mortar bomb,' said Smithy.

'And others that say Colonel Steiner sent back helicopters to look for him,' said Mostert, tightly.

'Recces?' said Pieters. 'This was a Parabat operation, I thought.'

'*Ja*, they just joined at the last moment,' said Smithy. 'You know what they are like. Always looking for action.'

'And they saw this man killed, you say?' Pieters dropped the stub of his cigarette into the ashtray and then rummaged in his pockets for another one.

'That's what Colonel Steiner told us,' said Mostert, dropping her eyelids.

'But you don't agree between you on this,' stated Pieters, lighting up and coughing heavily again. 'You don't think Colonel Steiner is telling the truth?'

Mostert looked down. Smithy looked up. Pieters waited for a long moment and then further until it was clear that no answer was forthcoming.

'*Ja*, OK,' he said, spluttering. 'I understand that you do not wish to accuse a senior and distinguished officer, so let us leave it.' He pulled his handkerchief out again, coughed into it, wiped a pendulous lower lip and went on. 'What concerns me primarily are the reports in the international media and what you have given me may well be true, but it will not be enough to convince these enemies of ours, so I am ordering you to continue with the investigation. What I need is something cast iron, something that a journalist would call a "killer fact", *ja*? Something that cannot be refuted, however hard they must try, *ja*? So look closer, hey? Look closer. I will telephone tonight for a further report.'

\*

'A "killer fact",' said Smithy, putting a hand up to shield his eyes against the down draught of the rotors as Pieters' chopper lifted off the helipad. 'I'd say Templeton's Alpha bomb airstrike was just about as big a "killer fact" as you are likely to get in a month of Sundays. Just how big does he want this "killer fact" to be? *Jeez*! The only way we could get the international media to accept that poison gas was not used is for the

92

SWAPO commander of that camp to go on the BBC and admit he had just made a bit of a slip of the tongue and he would like to apologise and set the record straight and say 'Really, assembled international media, in the interests of strict truth I would like to apologise to the South African Defence Forces for my mistake in accusing them of gassing up my terrorist camp.' And by tonight too. That is some *fokken* deadline.'

Mostert screwed her face up into a grimace to avoid the last whirls of flicked sand and then shaded her eyes to watch the helicopter move off into the electric blue sky.

'I mean, he *fokken* knows we don't have poison gas here. He's in the *fokken* BOSS, for Christ's sake,' said Smithy, enjoying a good rant. 'What does he want us to do? Go through the *fokken* warehouseman's log looking for a big box of canisters marked "Gas, Poison, Top Secret, Not To Be Used In Case Of Bad International Publicity"?'

The helicopter circled for a moment frowning like a boxfish unsure of its coral reef and then headed off purposefully southwards. Mostert watched it go, the grimace and the frown settling on her face as though it would be there forever.

'I don't understand either,' she said, finally. 'We missing something, Smithy. Something important.'

'You mean we should go back through the reports again?' he said. 'What good will that do? We've been through them ten times already.'

'He wasn't interested in Mickey Epstein,' she said, almost to herself. 'And if he was worried about the international media then a captured Mickey Epstein popping up at a press conference would be infinitely worse. We're not supposed to be in Angola at all, Smithy, and a captured Parabat would

93

be pretty strong proof that we were. I don't get it. There's something wrong.'

'You know, I thought that too,' said Smithy, who had not. 'So what is he interested in then?'

They turned to walk back to the bungalow where Bridgeman was making a proper breakfast for them but neither of them said anything more until after Smithy had polished off eggs and bacon and the best part of a pot of tea. Mostert hardly touched her toast, waved the ProNutro on and almost gagged at the Russians that Bridgeman laid before her.

'You pregnant or something?' said Smithy, eyeing the Russians, and feeling very greatly pacified since he had decided to disengage his brain until after it had been properly fed and watered.

'No,' replied Mostert, tartly. 'Well, not by you anyway. Listen, Joshua,' she waited until Bridgeman was out of the room. 'Listen Joshua, when I was a teenager...'

'A *bakvissie?*' said Smithy, taking two of the Russians onto his plate.

'Yes, now shut up: when I was a teenager, a friend and I...'

'Male or female?'

'Female, now shut up and listen: that's an order.'

'Ma'am,' said Smithy, saluting with the wrong hand. 'You should eat something. Make you less tetchy.'

Mostert gave him a glare.

'When I was a teenager, a friend of mine wanted to know if a boy she was sweet on would marry her – we were thirteen, OK? – and persuaded me to

94

go with her to see a *sangoma* to have her fortune told. So we went up to this village up beyond the farm in the Hottentots Holland to see this old lady who did the usual thing with casting bones and seeing visions and all that – it was pretty spooky –'

'Incense?'

'Incense too, Joshua. May I continue now?'

'Be my guest,' replied Smithy, taking the remaining two Russians from her plate.

'Well, in the end, she told my friend all sorts of things about her life and her family and her future so that we were convinced she really did have magical powers.'

'You do know it's a con, Captain?'

'Yes, I do now. But at the time we were both impressed,' continued Mostert. 'Later on, I found out how they do the trick. It's all about suggestion. They say a word or ask a question, but in reality they mean something the opposite of what they said and it works on your subconscious and you end up telling them the things that they want to know, even though you think you are telling them something different. Do you know what I mean?'

'No,' replied Smithy. 'I never believed in any of that bullshit.'

'It's like if someone says "don't worry", you know completely that you are going to worry, OK? Or if someone says, "don't think about getting shot" before going on an Op, you might as well put a bullet in your own foot because you are going to get shot because all you are thinking about is not getting shot rather than looking out for the enemy?'

'Well, OK,' replied Smithy, putting his fork down. 'I can see that logic.'

'Yes, but work it backward,' insisted Mostert. 'Pieters is not interested in Mickey Epstein, *ja*?'

'OK.'

'And he says to keep on with the poison gas stuff even though he knows it's bullshit, right?'

'OK.'

'And he says that we shouldn't accuse a "senior and distinguished officer" and so we must not suspect Steiner. So what or who is he interested in?'

'I don't know,' said Smithy.

'Steiner! Christ Smithy! Are you as thick as you pretend to be?' she said, pulling the teapot towards her. 'The power of suggestion, Joshua: he talked about Steiner didn't he? He hardly mentioned Templeton at all, so therefore he must want us to investigate Steiner!'

'Did he say that?' said Smithy, pushing the milk jug towards her. 'Because if he did, I must have missed it.'

'Yes! And Steiner was telling lies, wasn't he?' she replied. 'Not just about his age, but probably Mickey Epstein too. I think we should pull his file.'

Smithy shrugged and put more milk in his tea.

'Well, if you say so,' he said. 'This *domkop* hasn't got a better suggestion.'

\*

Getting hold of Steiner's personal file proved no challenge at all. Bridgeman knew all the other clerks on the base and armed with the carrot of a six-pack and the stick of Smithy's BOSS ID, he had two full copies of it, plus Steiner's BOSS file itself on the desk shortly before lunch. In the intervening time, Smithy had showered and changed and gone back through the operational reports, this time reading for discrepancies that might give a clue as to why Steiner was under unofficial investigation, but without success. Apart from the Mickey Epstein situation, they were as bald and as straightforward as the runway that the Mirage jets took off from through the morning. Mostert took the opportunity to do some personal admin, which meant washing her underwear, a chore that upon his return, an aggrieved Bridgeman, claimed for his own.

'If I told you how many pairs of smalls I have lost to randy soldiers from unguarded washing lines and laundries over the past months, it would bring shame down on the manhood of the republic,' she said, dismissing his protests. 'And I will tell you that the regulation issue looks and feels like it was designed by a blind Presbyterian bishop, so this thing, I'll do for myself. And don't look so hurt, Corporal Bridgeman. I'm not accusing you of anything.'

'And what use do you think I'd find for such things?' he muttered defensively in reply, retreating to the kitchen.

Once Bridgeman had been placated enough to produce coffee and some sandwiches, Smithy and Mostert began on the files.

'This is a bit on the thin side,' said Smithy, taking the Personnel File.

'Whereas this one is a bit on the thick side,' replied Mostert, taking the BOSS file in two hands. 'Start with his birthday. I want to know if he really is a lying bastard.'

'Leopold Ralph Steiner, born 3rd July1940…' began Smithy.

'See, I knew I was right,' said Mostert. 'He told me he was thirty-eight.'

'Congratulations,' answered Smithy. 'Joined 34th Parachute Brigade, 1974 and…that can't be right. He went straight into the Parabats, aged thirty-six, with the rank of Major and was promoted Colonel of 7th Parachute Battalion within the year.'

'Was he born in South Africa?' asked Mostert. 'Maybe he was in the British or Rhodesian army before.'

'Says he was born in Swakopmund, South West Africa,' said Smithy. 'So he's as good as South African. No National Service or Permanent Force record though.'

'Anything else?'

'Just the usual citations and medals; *Honoris Crux* Silver 1977 and Gold 1978. Fuck, he was hard. Climbed on a Cuban tank and disabled it by pouring a jerry can of petrol through the commander's hatch and threw a cigarette lighter in after it. The explosion blew his webbing off but he still made it back.'

'So nothing at all about previous service?'

Smithy pursed his lips and shook his head. 'Zippo – to coin a phrase. Even though he doesn't smoke.'

Mostert took a sandwich – crusts trimmed off, she noted - looked down, opened the BOSS file and began to read, nibbling delicately like a springbok on new grass until she came to the end of the triangle, and then took another. Smithy poured coffee.

'Well, well, well,' she said, when she had finished the second. 'The bastard's a Nazi. *Adolf* Leopold *von* Steiner was born 3rd July 1940 in Munich, Bavaria to Heidi and *Kapitan* Gunther von Steiner of the *Waffen* SS and was granted naturalisation papers in his current name in 1950 after arriving in Swakopmund by boat from Argentina with his parents. Daddy was wanted for War Crimes but kicked the bucket prematurely in 1965, at the sprightly age of 55; Mummy followed suit in 1975 after running a guesthouse popular with tourists. Is there anyone we won't let into this country? I mean...*Nazis?*'

'So? He can't help who his parents were,' said Smithy, topping up her cup. 'And there are plenty of people who think *we're* Nazis, if you hadn't noticed.'

'Well, I'm not one,' said Mostert, emphatically. 'The menfolk in my family fought *against* Germany in the war. What about yours?'

'My Dad drank for victory,' replied Smithy.

Mostert put her head down and began reading again.

'School but no university,' she said, turning over a page. 'Ran away to join the French Foreign Legion aged fifteen, succeeded on the second attempt. Served Algeria 1956-62 before drifting around the Middle East looking for trouble – attached to the Trucial and Omani Scouts, then to the Sultan of Oman's forces, service in the Dhofar war 1964...'

'What was that?' asked Smithy.

'Don't know,' replied Mostert, without looking up. 'Hello, here we go…1967-68 served in the Biafran War and then with the Rhodesian special forces from 1969 to 73 - did a couple of joint ops with our guys too - until he came over to us permanently in 74.'

'Any hint of an atrocity? Use of poison gas?'

'The Foreign Legion did a lot of torture in Algeria,' said Mostert. 'But I'm pretty sure there was no gas used.' She scanned through a series of loose sheets. 'Nothing mentioned here, at any rate.' She scanned through another series. 'No, nothing.'

'So he's a mercenary of sorts,' said Smithy. 'So what? There are plenty of them serving in the South African army. The whole continent of Africa is awash with mercenaries. What's different about him?'

Mostert looked up.

'Nothing,' she said, looking blank. 'Nothing is different about him.'

'Well, we'd better find something,' said Smithy, shuffling in his chair. 'Or Pieters is not going to be happy when he telephones us this evening.'

*

'There's nothing here, Joshua.'

Smithy looked up at the clock, cocked his head listening for the sound of a helicopter and then looked at the phone on the desk.

'There's nothing here,' he concurred.

Mostert gave a sigh of resignation, picked up the original newspaper, complete with the ring left by Smithy's coffee cup and with scant hope read through the article again and looked at the grainy photo once more.

'Corporal Bridgeman,' she called out. 'Can you get me another one of these?'

'Not that particular picture, Ma'am,' he replied, coming in with another pot of tea and some rusks. 'But I can call over to the photo-recon centre and get you some just like it. Do you want them blown up?'

Mostert nodded.

'That would be great,' she said, smiling and lifting the tea pot lid to sniff at the brew.

'Anything that helps find Mickey, I will do,' he said, wiping his hands. 'May I use the telephone? They will take an hour or so.'

'That's cutting it fine,' said Smithy.

'It'll have to do,' said Mostert. 'Now look again.'

'For what?'

'Anything,' said Mostert. 'There has got to be *something*.'

*

Smithy had given up, resigned himself to a bollocking and cracked a beer by the time that Bridgeman returned with half a dozen large sized photographs of the destroyed camp and two large magnifying glasses but Mostert insisted that he at least went through the motions of looking at the evidence.

'It's just a big pit full of dead bodies, Captain,' he protested. 'Can't we look at your holiday snaps instead? *Ja* – the ones with the bikinis.'

'Look at the other photographs too. Look for wounds on the bare skin,' she ordered. 'If they used mustard gas then there will be big blisters on exposed areas and the eyes of the corpses will be swollen up.'

'What if they used nerve gas?' said Smithy, reluctantly. 'That doesn't leave marks.'

Mostert shook her head. 'Just look, hey?'

He took up the magnifying glass gingerly, spun the handle between his fingers and then, sucking a deep breath and a glug of beer, began to look. At first he could make out nothing distinctive, save that the arms and limbs resembled the tangled roots of a felled tree, but then, only gradually, he began to pair up those limbs, match them to waists and torsos and then finally to heads. He picked out ears, individual fingers and toes, clenched fists but as most of the bodies had been tipped or thrown into the pit face down, there were few faces clearly to be seen. Instead, his mind began to play tricks on him, searching out patterns that might be faces in the same way that as a child he had seen faces hidden in the floral wallpaper of his parents' home after the lights had been switched out. The play of light and shade on the black and white photograph accentuated these imaginary shapes until it became difficult to accept the reality of so much death amid the strange kaleidoscope of butchered flesh. Switching one photograph for another, he picked out what might have been a woman's sleeping face and then the distinct shape of a crawling man heading for cover, frozen rigid, as he was caught by the blast of the flying splinter.

'Do you think these people had names?' he said.

Mostert looked up.

'Do you think SWAPO keep a proper register of who these people were, where they came from, who their families are?'

'What do you mean?'

'Do they have Personnel files? Pay books? That sort of thing,' said Smithy, softly. 'The things that make them exist. The things that make them people? Or will these bodies just disappear into the earth taking their whole lives with them?'

He looked at one corpse, crouching it seemed, head down with his hands protecting the back of his neck and tapped the picture with the glass.

'I mean, will these guys get a posthumous medal? Will their families be informed and given – what - a folded flag or a pension or something? Will their names be recorded and remembered?'

'They're Terrs, Smithy,' said Mostert, cautiously. 'Remember that these are the people who plant bombs in supermarkets and kill indiscriminately.'

Smithy continued staring at the hunched figure, strangely small even through the magnifying glass.

'This one isn't much more than a child,' he said, and felt a great balloon of grief inflate up in his chest. 'How did we come to this?'

He put the picture and the magnifying glass down and put the heels of his hands into his eyes.

'I don't know, Joshua,' she replied. 'But as long as we're in this swamp, we just have to keep paddling, hey? What else can we do?'

Smithy did not know how to reply. He did not know if there was an answer, or any point in looking for one. All he knew was that he was indeed in a swamp, and unlike Captain Mostert, no amount of paddling would ever take him to the edge of it and out into open water.

'Let's get pissed,' he said, suddenly. 'I am so sick of this bullshit.'

'Good idea,' said Mostert, dropping the photographs down on the table. 'I have no idea what is going on here but I can tell you that it has nothing whatever to do with Capinga and poison gas and until Pieters actually comes right out and tells us what he wants us to do, I'm with you. Corporal Bridgeman,' she called out. 'Two large Klippie and Cokes and have one yourself. And a big slice of lemon in mine.'

'Ma'am, it's only four-thirty and you are still expecting a phone call,' warned Bridgeman, appearing at the door. 'And we are out of lemons.'

'Bridgeman,' said Smithy, tersely. 'It's five o'clock somewhere. Don't be a puff. And we are not out of lemons. I can smell them.'

*

Well into his third Klippie and Coke, Smithy was feeling considerably braver when the phone rang just after five-thirty.

'*Ja*, Killer Fact, sir,' he said to a silent Pieters, while beaming sarcastically at Mostert, who was idling her way through the photographs, her feet up on the table and holding the magnifying glass in front of her like a lollipop. '*Ja*, the killer facts are in this order. One: there are no killer facts, sir, just the ordinary, regulation issue ones, sir. And two: this was a straightforward assault on the SWAPO facility at Capinga. The Air Force *donnered* them spectacularly and awesomely…'

104

'Smithy,' said Mostert.

'...in fact so *fokken* awesomely that they nearly ruined the whole Op because...'

'Smithy,' said Mostert, swinging her legs off the table suddenly.

'..the *fokken* para drop went astray- as I understand is *fokken* usual in these circumstances – and Mickey *fokken* Epstein got left behind or blown to smithereens depending on whether you want to believe a bunch of puffs or a Nazi...'

'Smithy! Shut up, for God's sake!' Mostert's eyes were wide with shock.

Smithy put his hand over the mouthpiece and gave her a quizzical look. She pushed one of the photographs towards him and pointed.

'What am I looking for?' he mouthed.

'Isn't it obvious,' she hissed, pointing with a trembling finger.

Smith looked again. Towards the top right of the grave, almost completely concealed by the twisted and headless torso of a man, was a body differently attired from the rest. The clothing was lighter, standing out against the more common dark grey and it looked more like a sun dress than the ragged cut of a set of Cuban issue fatigues. Nor did the skin tone of the face and one exposed arm fit in with the surrounding corpses even when the quality of the light and the distortions of black and white photography were taken into account. Mostert held the magnifying glass over it.

'It's a white woman,' said Smithy, taking the picture and uncovering the mouthpiece.

'*Ja*, bingo. Now find out who she is and what she's doing there,' said Pieters, hanging up.

'He wants us to find out who she is,' said Smithy, swaying slightly and feeling distinctly uneasy.

'I *know* who she is,' replied Mostert.

\*

05

Tuesday

Colonel Templeton had done his best to get them on the *Flossie* flight to Cape Town but even so, by the time they had picked up the vehicle from the car pool it was late afternoon before they got up the last necessary step of the escarpment and came into the shallow farmland of the valley below the Winterhoek. The fields, rich with wheat and barley in the summer, were empty and dun now, sprawled out like a desert camouflage jacket, but as they ran up in terraces towards the grey and powder blue mountains, they took on the deep green of vineyards and the dusty sage colour of the fynbos scrub. There they ran into the white blankets of cotton wool cloud lit within by a pearly light that gave them an unexpected solidity below and a swirling slow motion evanescence above as they rolled off one mountain range and ran up against the retaining wall of the next. Westwards, the beginnings of a warm, soft early evening glow spread ahead of the reaching shadows lifting glorious earth scents off the land into the clean, cool champagne of the air.

'Boy have I missed this clean air,' said Smithy, slowing down to admire a troop of deep chestnut bays galloping elegantly along the picket wire fence. 'When I'm in the desert all I can smell is metal and webbing and petrol and BO. This air scrubs out your lungs and makes you feel clean; *really* clean.'

'*Ja*, I know what you mean,' mumbled Mostert through a mouthful of hair grips. 'It's a great climate here; never too hot and never too cold and if there is a frost in the morning, it's always warm by lunchtime. And log fires in the evening. Perfect. Anna-Marie and I used to ride or play tennis every day we could when I knew her.'

'So you were pretty close?'

'Only for the one year – less really,' replied Mostert, tucking the last pin into the side of her head. 'We moved to a better farm outside Franschhoek and she got expelled so that was it. Plus she was a couple of years older than me. This is the place now.'

Smithy slowed the car down, felt it slide a little on the loose dirt and then turned in through the tall wrought-iron, white-painted gates and onto a good brick road shaded by oaks and willows, edged with whitewashed stones and flanked by cool, well-watered and manicured lawns tended by a couple of black men in blue overalls. Up ahead was a large Dutch gabled house decorated with extravagant rococo pineapples, rose chains and Greek urns worked into the gleaming white plaster. A Palladian triangular pediment stood over the double doors and only the thatch where there should have been tiles reminded him that he was in Africa not Holland. There was a swimming pool to the left and a next to it a tennis court built on top of a terraced bank planted with roses, oleander and bougainvillea, while to the right, shaded by a gold and glorious stand of more oaks and willows was a row of substantial cottages fronted by rose covered trellises and raised beds of agapanthus. Behind, the steep mountain reared up to a sky of clear, Prussian blue. When Smithy switched off, the hum of bees and the chirrup of crickets replaced the hum of the engine like peace settling down to rest amid the deep, full quiet of the farm, a quiet so unlike the silences of the desert that Smithy was more used to; there the silence was empty; here it spoke of solid, functional prosperity. Even the unusual mechanical clacking sound coming from behind one of the cottages could not upset the stillness for its rhythm was somehow reassuring, like the ticking of a clock in the dust motes of a library afternoon.

'Let me do the talking, first off,' said Mostert, as Smithy parked. 'They may not know she's dead.'

'Are you going to tell them?' he asked, getting out of the vehicle and breathing in deeply.

'No,' said Mostert, clunking the door shut. 'We have to be sure, first. We have to have *absolute* proof. Besides – her father was pretty traditional as I recall. He won't speak anything but Afrikaans and if your family did not get off the boat with Van Riebeck in 1652 then you are just a recent immigrant to be repatriated at the first available opportunity. To him, you are an English interloper in Afrikaaner paradise and so lower than a kaffir.'

'One of those, hey,' replied Smithy, with a shrug. 'Well let me just trample my muddy English kaffir policeman's boots into his *voorkammer* and see how he takes it. And he's not the only one with ancestry; there was a Smith on board the *Mayflower.*'

'*Ja,* and no doubt a whole deck full on the First Fleet to Australia.'

They walked up a flight of wide steps onto a pleasant terrace equipped with heavy wooden furniture and an oil drum *braai* complete with a full woodpile before knocking at the tall, dark double doors that towered over them.

'Fee Fi Fo Fum,' said Smithy, as the door swung back to reveal the narrow eyes of a small, golden skinned Khoisan woman, her face framed by a white deep brimmed bonnet and the loop of a long pinafore, who bobbed and curtsied nervously and gabbled quickly and unintelligibly in reply to their greeting, before firmly closing the door in their faces.

'She's missing the top four front teeth,' said Mostert.

'Too traditional for dentistry?' replied Smithy. 'Or too tight to pay the bills for his staff?'

A moment or two later, the door swung back and the woman emerged once more, this time armed with lace cushions and a table cloth, indicated the table by becks and nods, and proceeded to lay it. By the time Smith and Mostert had taken their seats, she had been back and forth three times, bringing glasses, a jug of lemonade and stone bottle of home-made *mampoer* brandy, rusks, napkins and more embroidered lace cushions, each time accompanied by frequent curtsies and a gabbled stream of high pitched words which might have been Afrikaans but might not. Neither Mostert nor Smithy could tell. The soft flap of her upper lip made enunciation impossible to understand for anyone not used to her.

'You know what that clacking sounds is?' said Mostert, thanking the woman, then cocking her head at the rattle and remembering. 'It's a handloom for making homespun cloth. They found it in one of the outhouses and were restoring it back then.'

'Ah well,' said Smithy, sniffing at the *mampoer*, sitting back on the bench and complacently adjusting a cushion. 'I suppose it's not all bad in the 18th Century.'

'It's a good job transport arrangements have improved though,' replied Mostert, nodding towards a dust cloud rising up from a dirt track westwards. 'Otherwise you wouldn't have time to finish that brandy. It'll take him at least an hour to cover that last mile.'

On the road, a team of eighteen white brahmin oxen were breasting a hill, swinging from side to side, tossing their heads, flicking their tails against the flies and lolling out thick, pink tongues as they smelt home pasture and refreshing water. On their humped necks, the polished yokes creaked as the lowing animals heaved against the traces and pulled the *disselboom* of the great canvas covered wagon making the harness jingle and the dangling leather buckets swing as the whip swirled and cracked high above them. Even at this distance, the light allowed them to make out the driver on the box. He was a large, corpulent man with a biblical beard dressed in nut brown cloth, tan *veldtschoen* and a wide brimmed hat and he flicked the long whip like a fly fisherman on a golden trout stream.

The crack of the whip cut through the air once more but Smithy's attention was drawn to the movements of the two gardeners down below, whose body language transmitted fear and dismay in equal measure. One of them was actually hopping from one foot to the other, like a schoolboy too afraid to ask for the lavatory; the other put down a pair of sheers and quickly taking up a broom, ostentatiously began to sweep the road. Looking left and right, he saw other figures until then unnoticed in the landscape, galvanised into action, scurrying about the farm; behind the cottages, the sound of the handloom went up a tone, as the speed of the shuttle increased like a keen runner on the last lap. He looked at the Khoisan woman who had come onto the terrace at the sound of the whip, saw the look of grey anxiety settle on her face and then exchanged a glance with Mostert.

'Let me do the talking,' she reiterated. 'You can't go bull at a gate with these *ous*.'

*

'Well now, *ja*, dear friends, we have prayed to God together and we have eaten of his wondrous bounty grown and killed on this farm and even though Sergeant Smith here has English blood in him, we are sitting on chairs and good furniture made to last a hundred years in the *voorkammer* built by my ancestors from the timber and stone cleared from this mountain when it was infested with Bushmen. This in a house lived in continuously, father to son, father to son, since the oldest of times, like civilised people. This is a good thing, hey? Now, you have come from different parts; tell me, how is the Kaffir problem that side?'

They had indeed prayed to God, hands clasped, pious faces plastered on, while the huge Mijnheer Cornelius van Zyl, master of all he surveyed read Leviticus from a tooled leather family Bible of ancient provenance, through an immense beard that grew down through mutton chops from a bearskin of black hair. They had also eaten of his wondrous bounty in the form of a plate of lamb chops piled so high it was almost impossible to come at the yellow mealie pap below, washed down with red wine so thick it was almost gravy, and in Smithy's case the wondrous bounty had been welcomed so greedily that he was now so dozy and greasy in equal parts that he almost missed the question.

'Oh, just the usual,' replied Mostert, kicking Smithy awake under the table.

111

'*Ja*, a *kaffir* is a *kaffir* anywhere and nothing can change that,' said van Zyl, in his booming patriarchal voice. 'They are really just a higher form of animal. Experience has taught me this. I think they are just above monkeys but not so far as to have true intelligence. I do not believe that they were given the opportunity to eat of the Forbidden Fruit and so gain knowledge of good and evil and have free will. This is something that I have come to know from experience and from my Bible study. The Kaffir lives and eats and drinks by instinct only.'

'Really?' said Smithy, raising one sarcastic eyebrow.

'You know, English,' he replied, pouring stiff tots of *mampoer*. 'I think they lucky really. They got no worries. They got a place to stay on this farm and plenty of mealies and they can sing and clap in their church and be very happy. Though it is not a proper church, you understand. It is more like a playground or like when you see the monkeys in a zoo having a tea party. It is imitation, not real religion, hey? *Kaffirs* don't have souls.'

'You pride yourself on being a Christian, then?' said Smithy, ignoring Mostert's warning stare.

'Of course,' replied van Zyl, sitting back with his glass. 'The Bible is the only place for real wisdom and it is a daily comfort and a comfort in difficult times too. Everything you need to know is in there. *Ja, ja*, I know many young people are turning away from religion right now, but this is only temporary. People will always turn back to the Lord. It is just to show different people different roads. It is his way of bringing them to the light eventually. All white people – even you English - know this in their heart of hearts. It is what gives us the strength to be good shepherds to our

112

flocks, to plough, plant and harvest in due season and to look after our animals and *Kaffirs* however difficult they can be.'

'That's very comforting,' said Smithy, taking a good pull at the *mampoer* and choking. 'Which do you think are more difficult to control: Kaffirs or animals?'

'*Ag* man, it depends on the animal. But the Kaffirs, you need to train them just the same as you train a dog or break a horse. You must use a mixture of pain and patting; give them a good *donnering* and then some mealies, turn by turn, and they will come around, though sometimes it takes longer with some than with others.' Van Zyl scratched his beard thoughtfully for a moment as though he was questioning himself. '*Ja-nee.* Especially when they are thieving. When they are thieving you must *donner* them so hard that they learn a good lesson or they will always be stealing. Wait! Haha. I know a joke, English. You will like this joke, I think. Take some more *mampoer* man. It will do you good.'

Mostert gave Smithy another warning shot under the table.

'Why does the sun never set on the British Empire?' wheezed van Zyl, already convulsed with coming laughter.

'I don't know,' said Smithy, who did. It was a joke so old it could have been in van Zyl's family Bible. It was also as out of date as Leviticus.

'Because God would never trust a *bladdy* Englishman in the dark!'

Van Zyl broke into a roaring belly laugh and reached over to place one of his bear paws on Smithy's shoulder, gripping it and shaking it so that the liquor almost spilled from his glass. Mostert shifted in her seat and decided that if she was ever going to get to the reason why they were at

113

van Zyl's table in the first place, she would have to break up this love-in before the pair of them were too drunk to make any sense at all.

'*Ja*, Mijnheer van Zyl,' she said, kicking Smithy once more and this time with enough force to make him sit up. 'Thank you for a good dinner but we must just ask you some questions regarding your daughter.'

'*Ja*, business,' said van Zyl, wiping his eyes and breathing heavily. 'Business, *ja*. What do you want to know about that hellcat of a daughter of mine? You know she was expelled from that school? If it was up to me I would not have bothered educating her at all. What does a good *boerefrau* need with anything more than the Bible and a head for casting accounts, hey? Why does she need her head filling full of rubbish, hey?'

He caught himself on the brink of a rant and pulled himself back. Taking up a tiny hand bell by his elbow, he tinkled it and when the Khoisan maid arrived from her station in the corner of the room, ordered coffee to be brought.

'Missy Mostert, what do you want to know? Is she in trouble?'

'Just what you can tell us,' said Mostert, ducking the question.

'I can tell you nothing. I have no contact with her. She is a Missing Person.'

'Anything will help,' she prompted. 'Something about her background or her personality?'

'Then that will be easy,' said van Zyl, heavily. 'She was a hell of a difficult child. Even as a baby she would not sleep and would stay up all night. Stubborn! She was more stubborn than any mule even as a small child. I will tell you a story, hey? One day, it was raining, really raining

114

heavily and I told her she must put on her coat so that she would keep warm and dry but would she? No, she would not. She stood in the yard of the farm and let the rain pour down on her and when I went to put her coat on her, she took it off – tore it off – and threw it away and just stood there in the pouring rain staring back at me in defiance. *Ja*, well she felt the back of my hand, of course – many times – but it did no good at all. She was always headstrong and her Aunt came up with the idea that she should go to boarding school run by the Catholic Nuns as they were good at installing discipline in headstrong girls and I agreed even though I do not like the Catholics very much. They are as bad as the Jews if you ask me. But then, I might not have bothered: she ran away from there too.'

'She ran away?' said Mostert. 'How did she get home?'

'Home?' said van Zyl. 'Oh, she did not come running home. She did not run *to* anywhere, as far as anyone could tell. Only *away*, but away from what, no-one could tell either. Once she was found in a railway yard in Cape Town, once in a farm in Stellenbosch and once half way to Port Elizabeth on a bus. Then she was expelled and stayed with us for only a little while before she ran for good.'

Van Zyl scratched his beard again, ran a hand through the huge mane of his hair and then got up and fetched a small framed photograph of his daughter. 'Here, you can keep this one,' he said, gruffly. Mostert took it and saw Anna-Marie just as she remembered her; an unremarkable, ordinary Afrikaaner girl, blonde, leggy, sporty with clear skin, a fine face waiting to flesh out from behind the shy smile.

'Did she ever give any explanation? To the teachers? Nuns? Someone in the family,' asked Mostert, her eyes still on the picture.

'Never a word. My wife, her mother, could never get through to her. It broke her heart.'

'Any suggestion of drugs?' asked Mostert.

Van Zyl flared: 'Drugs? Never! If a Kaffir so much as mentions *dagga* in my hearing, I will thrash the life out of him. My daughter was not on drugs, lady.'

'Boys?' ventured Smith, receiving a venomous look by way of answer.

'So, no boyfriend troubles, then,' said Mostert, pouring oil on water. 'That is comforting.'

'We fear God and honour the sanctity of marriage here,' said van Zyl. 'This is not Sodom and Gomorrah – or Cape Town.'

'Can you give me some dates?' asked Mostert.

'Born 1950, expelled 1965, disappeared 1966. Fifteen years ago. We made the police report, of course, but in all that time I have heard nothing.'

'And your wife?'

'God took her from me in 1968. Like I say, she died of a broken heart. Anna-Marie was our only child.'

\*

Van Zyl retired early, almost as soon as the meal was over and he had made arrangements with the Khoisan maid for Smithy and Mostert to stay over in (separate) cottages. Smithy extracted another bottle of red wine from her and took the stone jug full of *mampoer* with him too but when he asked for coke to go with it, the Khoisan maid wittered away unintelligibly

116

again and withdrew, from which Smithy gathered that if it wasn't available in the 18<sup>th</sup> Century, the article didn't exist on this farm.

'What is it with people like van Zyl, Trudi?' he said, sitting down next to her on a bench under scented roses and a spangle of stars. He handed her a glass of wine. 'Why do they think like this? Why do they have to spoil a good life in a beautiful place like this with all this rubbish about Kaffirs?'

'*Trudi* is it, now?' she said.

'Sorry, Ma'am,' replied Smithy, burping.

'I'm just chaffing you,' she smiled. 'Do you want an answer to your question or are you just talking?'

'Do you know the answer?' replied Smithy, putting his head back against the wall and looking up to admire the stars.

'They believe all this Old Testament stuff because the old Dutch settlers came here in the 17<sup>th</sup> Century and so missed the Enlightenment.'

'What's the Enlightenment?' said Smithy, enjoying the cool of the wall against the back of his head.

Mostert looked askance for a moment and then, taking a sip of wine, continued.

'It's when people started thinking scientifically and for themselves during the 18<sup>th</sup> Century and stopped accepting the Bible literally. The old Dutch settlers missed out on a whole intellectual movement and so they still think that when Noah came out of the Ark, God said it was OK for the children of Ham to be his slaves, literally. They think black people are descended from the children of Ham and that the Afrikaaners are the Children of Israel. Smithy, how did you pass Matric?'

'Truthfully?'

'Truthfully.'

'You don't want to know,' he said, standing up, scratching, his eyes beginning to glaze. 'I'm just going to see a man about a dog.'

'*Ja*, I should visit the little girls' room too,' said Mostert, putting her glass down on the floor and going towards her door. 'You are going to have a real *babelaas* in the morning, Smithy, hey?'

'You know he has a phone line in here,' said Smithy, indicating a line of telegraph poles that ran from the back of the farmhouse to the road. 'So much for all that 18th Century bullshit.'

He went inside the cottage, catching his shoulder on the doorframe and ricocheting into the room. There was a strong smell of paraffin from the Tilly lamp overlaid by the lavender that came off the bedclothes and the deep, comforting aroma from the beeswax polish that had brought a high sheen to the ancient wooden dresser and the newer yellow wood table. Over the fireplace was a forbidding portrait of two frowning, gothic ancestors, while on either side were old farm tools to match the black tripod and cast iron pot that stood in the hearth. It was a homely, warm room, certainly with something of the puritan about it but comfortable nevertheless. Still, Smithy didn't care for it; there was too much of the museum about it and the level of care, cleaning and attention required to keep it so could only be achieved by the constant labour of people who did not get paid enough – if they were paid at all - for their work. Going through towards the bathroom, he wobbled a little, put his hand out to steady himself and found himself holding a needlework sampler, slightly faded with age, but still a fine example of careful work. It showed two oaks in full leaf on either side of a house very like van Zyl's, an old galleon, two crossed muskets and an ox wagon very like the one that van Zyl had driven earlier, but it was the painstaking cross-stitch of the motto that took and held his attention.

*As ek omdraai, skiet my. As ek val, wreek my. As ek storm, volg my.*

'Can you believe this,' he said, outside once more, handing the sampler to Mostert after he had relieved himself. '"If I retreat, kill me. If I die, avenge me. If I advance, follow me." Do you know what that is?'

Mostert shrugged.

'It's the motto of the *Ossewabrandwag*.'

Mostert looked blank.

'It used to be what the South African Nazi party was called,' he said, pleased to know something that she didn't. 'I learned about it in History class. They used to go camping and pretending to be on the Great Trek fighting Matabeles and the English. They were all banged up during the war for sabotage, our late, great Prime Minister, Mr Vorster among them. So that's the connection with Steiner, then. Old man van Zyl and him were both Nazis. The girl rebelled and ran off to join the ANC and ended up dead because of it. Pieters will be happy, I suppose, but I was hoping to spin this little vacation out a bit longer.'

'Well done, Smithy. Bully for you, but I don't suppose that bit of miraculous supposition tops what I found on my pillow,' she said, lighting a cigarette and handing him a postcard. 'And if I was any sort of a detective, I'd say it was put there deliberately by the maid.'

Smithy crumpled his face up and took the postcard. On the front was a picture of the Britannia Hotel outside the Simonstown naval base. On the reverse, under a postmark giving the date as April 1968, was the address of the van Zyl farm written in a jerky but otherwise legible hand, but no message and no signature. It didn't need either. The message was clear enough. Someone had told van Zyl where Anna-Marie was.

*

06

Wednesday

They left shortly after dawn, fortified by a breakfast of fresh rolls, bacon and a steaming can of coffee provided by the Khoisan maid who had quite clearly been up long before them. She betrayed no hint as to the origin of the postcard, now nestling in Smithy's Filofax, but burbled and gestured to the effect that van Zyl had gone up the mountain for reasons unfathomable to them and would not be joining them for breakfast.

'Should we question her?' he had said, watching her go through bleary eyes.

'If we do, we won't be able to understand what she says,' Mostert had replied, lighting up a first cigarette. 'And if van Zyl sees us talking to her, she'll probably lose the rest of her teeth.'

Now, driving down the long valley as the sun lit up a silver and sapphire sky as it pushed the purple shadows westwards, Smithy settled to the morning's drive that would take them down through the glorious farmland of the Cape, the breadbasket of Africa, through the powder blue mountains, ringed and scaled like crocodile skin and then down off the escarpment, across flat Mitchell's Plain and then left side on to the peninsular and the naval base at Simonstown. He wound the window down to enjoy the morning air and sluice away his hangover and once again contrasted the delight of cool air and soft light with what he was used to up in the Namib. At one point, he slowed down to take in the view over a lake where the sky had suffused the whole landscape with the same cornflower blue so that it was only possible to say where the water stopped and the air started by looking at the crisp brown line of the dam wall; the second dam right by it reflected mountains floating indistinctly on a gossamer of cloud. A little later, he paused to count the folds of a hillside that looked for all the world like giant's toes and which then dropped sharply down from a steep cliff to a deep fissure; for all its homeliness, this was still wild enough to be leopard country. As if to underline this, a few miles on they halted to let a herdsman dressed in a leather *kaross* embroidered with intricate bead work in green, black, red and gold, lead a tinkling flock of goats out of a valley towards a mere and noted the spear alongside the shepherd's crook.

'Where does all the water come from?' he said, suddenly.

'What,' said Mostert, caught by surprise.

'Where does all the water come from if there are no rivers here?' he repeated, giving a friendly wave in reply to the herdsman's greeting. 'How can Cape Town exist if there are no rivers? I mean, Paris is on the Seine and London is on the Thames and New York is on the Hudson but in South Africa our cities don't have rivers; Jo'burg doesn't have a river and neither does Durban.'

'Durban does has a river – the Umgeni,' she answered after a moment.

121

'*Ja-nee*, but it's not a proper one,' said Smithy. 'It doesn't go anywhere. I mean, OK, there is the Sunday's river in Graaff Reinet but you can't put a ship on it and sail it down to the sea. And the Touws River is only ankle deep when it comes out in Wilderness. But even then, neither Cape Town nor Jo'burg has a river.'

'The rain,' said Mostert, as though answering an idiot. 'It rains. The farmers dig dams and store the water in them. What doesn't get stored, soaks into the rocks and the earth and then you sink a borehole, put in a wind pump and out it comes. You don't need rivers.'

'Well, where does Cape Town get water from then, Missy Clever Clogs? I've never seen a wind pump in Cape Town.' Smithy let the clutch out as the last clonking goat crossed the road and drove on. 'And like I say – no river.'

'From the Steenbras dam over Grabouw and the Berg river dam in Stellenbosch, if you really want to know,' replied Mostert, smugly. 'How long did you live in Cape Town without being aware of its basic geography? I take it you're not a farmer either.'

'*Bladdy boerefrau*,' retorted Smithy. 'It's a serious point. Rivers *don't* always reach the sea.'

Just outside Villiersdorp, Smithy pulled over once more, this time to relieve himself and admire the wide expanse of silver water stretching away northwards from the Threewaterkloof dam to the snowy caps of the mountains behind the Stellenbosch winelands. Just beyond a headland of pines, there were a couple of boats lazing by an outcrop of rock as the occupants fished for bass, drank beer and slept; Smithy envied them; nobody ever messed you around when you were fishing; it just wasn't done; but he hadn't cast a fly since he had been up here with his father years ago.

'Isn't Franschhoek near here?' he said, buttoning up and getting back into the car. 'We could go to your farm and you could introduce me to your folks.'

'*Ja*,' drawled Mostert, stubbing out the last of the cigarettes. 'Just after we pay a call on yours.'

'Be careful what you wish for,' said Smithy, winking. 'The Old Queen would love you, would she not?'

An hour later, Smithy pulled over once more, this time at the top of Sir Lowry's pass, a straight drop down off the escarpment to the great breath taking sweep of False Bay, to the green slopes of the blue-grey Helderberg and Table Mountain crouched long, low and sleek as the soft cloud swept back from it. Right down somewhere to the left, hidden now in the pink and silver haze, was Simonstown where they were headed.

'You know this country could be a paradise,' he said, quietly. 'Meat, wine, crops, sunshine, fishing, beaches, mountains; it's got it all.'

He looked again, but this time the surf line reminded him of the vapour trails of strike jets, the rugged folds of the blue-grey Helderberg erupting from the green vines of the winelands looked like a bomb strike and the great wall of Table Mountain brought to mind the clouds streaking back from the fuselage of one of the Mirage jets back at Grootfontein. Nearby the sound of clanking came to him again but this time there was no herdsman and his goats, just a chain gang clearing ditches by the road.

'*Fok,*' he said, turning back to the car.

The Britannia Hotel in Simonstown was an institution that Smithy had been on good terms with on several occasions. Now, standing in front of it once again, he marvelled at the Anglo-Dutch Victorian Gothic revival fantasy of ornate ironwork balconies, balustrades and arcades topped by two Dutch gables and one English and wondered what on earth was going through the mind of the man who designed it. The famous old pile had been built during the 1870s to cash in on the gold rush but those glory days had long passed it by and since the Purified National Party had taken over in 1948, it had gradually acquired a reputation, as much out of desire as necessity, to match the rust that besmirched the once pristine white of the paintwork. Being situated in the heart of a port that also doubled as a naval base, the owners had decided from the outset that any government-led moral crusade was likely to founder on the rocks of a sailor's need and so had never even bothered to pay so much as lip service to the law. It was liberty's own Gibraltar, a proud fortress tradition that had been kept up by successive owners faced with whole sieges of sanctimonious disapproval for more than a century and thoroughly approved of by anyone who wasn't permanently afflicted by a po-face and a narrow mind. By popular (though of necessity *muted*) acclaim, its rooms had done more for inter-racial harmony than the Swedish Council of Churches' Standing Committee on Anti-Apartheid Activities and had done more to damage the moral fabric of the nation's impressionable youth than the resolutely liberal lecturers of the University of Cape Town. True, there had been one or two half-hearted attempts to close the place down over the years, but each attempt had failed upon the arrival of cargo ships full of thirsty matelots of all nations, races, creeds (and none) who cared nothing for politics, but knew that the Britannia Hotel provided good beer, decent pies, hot baths and clean sheets

124

at a reasonable price charged in a variety of currencies and were not minded to let a few grass-combing coppers get in the way of a little friendly conversation between consenting adults. It was about as far from the ideal of Apartheid as it was possible to get without leaving the republic and loved the more so because of it. Smithy himself had come to know the place because he had been here once or twice too in defiance of the Morality and Separate Amenity Acts, with girls who shared a similar incomprehension for them; it was the only hotel that he had ever been in that didn't even bother with so much as a suspicious sniff when he wrote *Mr & Mrs Smith* in the register.

Looking at this piece of Henley now under a clean and clear day, all hint of grey washed out of the sky by a passing False Bay sun shower, he understood why Anna-Marie van Zyl might choose this as a place of refuge. There would be work, perhaps a room, few or any questions asked and papers routinely ignored; there might even be easily replaceable ones for a price and there was always the possibility of stowing away on a freighter heading somewhere better. Smithy looked at the gun emplacements, the asbestos roofs of the barrack buildings and the mole opposite the hotel and felt a kinship with this runaway girl. At that moment, with the salt tang of escape in his nostrils, he felt he needed to find out who this Anna-Marie van Zyl was and why and how she had ended up in a mass grave in Capinga, killed by her own countrymen.

'It's probably better if we don't let on that we are police or military,' said Smithy to Mostert, who was standing with her hands on her hips contemplating the hotel. This being the Cape and a long way from the border, they had decided to temporarily dispense with formalities and don their civvy gear. Mostert was neat in cheesecloth and jeans and looked like neat, just like any fashionable young woman of these parts. Smithy wore a bomber jacket and jeans and looked just like an off-duty copper would. 'We should just say that we are concerned family or something.'

Looking left and right, Smithy stepped out into the road and then quickly checked himself when he realised she was not following.

'Actually, Smithy,' she said, her eyes on her toes. 'It might be better if you go in there alone while I mooch about and see if there are some other clues around here.'

'Clues?' replied Smithy, puzzled. 'What clues?'

'Well, you know, I could go into the base, ask around in the Officer's Mess. That sort of thing.'

There was a slight flush rising at her throat.

'Do you know people here?' he asked. 'Family or something?'

'Smithy,' she replied, beginning to blush. 'It's just better if you go in without me, OK?'

'What? Do they know you in there?' said Smithy, joking.

Mostert blushed bright red. Smithy's jaw dropped two long moments after the penny. She dropped her eyes and folded her arms across her chest.

'None of your business,' she said, before he could ask. 'So you go in and I'll go somewhere else for a while.'

Smithy watched her as she walked off quickly, enjoying the sway of her hips only half as much as the way she tossed her hair from side to side and jammed her arms straight down by her sides.

'Well,' he said, breathing out and scrubbing his nails through his hair. 'There's hope yet.'

*

Inside the heavy mahogany wood reception area, the manager greeted Smithy with what might have been a flicker of recognition from out of a face that had been badly disfigured by a petrol fire. The putty-like skin was melted across the brow and cheeks, leaving only a few red bristles where the beard and eyebrows had grown back, while a heavy skin graft across the man's jaws had done little to mask the terrible pain of burning and replace the bare lips. His nostrils were mere pin holes, his ears no more than rebuilt flaps of skin while his tongue flickered, lizard like within his puckered mouth.

'Can I help you, Sir?' he said, mumbling a little, but with surprisingly clear diction and a recognisably British accent. 'The name's Markham, Charles Markham. Don't be put off by my appearance, please. I'm afraid it can be rather disconcerting at first but underneath it, I'm just an ordinary chap.'

Smithy was not dismayed or put out by the injuries; he had seen enough of them in his line of work and knew that the best way to treat those who had to carry the burden of disfigurement was just as they requested.

'I'm trying to get in touch with someone I knew years ago and well, this was the last place I came across her, so to speak,' said Smithy. 'It's *delicate.*'

'Are you with the Police, Sir?' said the manager, in a tone of innocence.

'No,' lied Smithy. 'It's a sort of, well…have you worked here long?'

'Twenty years, Sir,' said the manager, in the same tone. 'Man and boy, so to speak. And I should say that we like to maintain a certain discretion where our guests are concerned, Sir; a courtesy we extend to *all* our clients.'

'*Ja,*' said Smithy, with a hint of a wink. 'That's what we were relying on back then.'

The manager made no comment, his face settling into a professional opacity enhanced to fortress depth by the scarring. Smithy pulled out the photo that van Zyl had provided.

'Look familiar?'

The manager gave a little start: 'Who are you?'

'Like I said, she's an old girl friend of mine.'

The manager raised one patched eyebrow: 'She must be a very old girlfriend then. May I ask what led you to the Britannia Hotel?'

'Well, actually, it's *business* related,' replied Smithy.

'And what business are you in, may I ask? If it's not too impolite.'

'Cars mainly,' replied Smithy, plucking a profession out of the air. 'Mechanics. That sort of thing.'

'Really? How very interesting, Sir. I've been having more than a little car trouble lately. I do believe the cylinder head gasket has gone and where to get a new one - what with sanctions and so on – is proving rather more complicated than I had anticipated.'

'If you let me have the make and model, I'll see what I can do,' said Smithy. 'Now, about this girl.'

128

'Are you a relative?' asked the manager, with a wry smile.

'Like I said, old girlfriend and business related.'

'And you have a name for this girl?'

'Now that would be telling,' said Smithy. 'You got to give me something before we bandy a woman's name about in a place as *liberal* as the Britannia Hotel, hey?'

The manager looked Smithy square in the face for a long moment and then coming to a decision, ran a hand over the braise marks on his cheeks.

'If it's business, I should think you are probably pursuing a debt,' he said. 'In which case, if you do catch up with her you'd earn my undying gratitude by letting me know her whereabouts. She owes the Britannia Hotel a substantial sum of money – and myself a new face.'

*

She had arrived on the doorstep of the Britannia Hotel sometime in the autumn of 1968, another waif led there by strays, looking for shelter and a job and clearly in need of both. Back then her Christian name was still Anna-Marie but she had jettisoned the van Zyl and had fished up Lovell from somewhere to replace it. Markham had taken her in, just as he had taken in girls like her many times before, started her off in the kitchen where she could eat to her heart's content and given her a bunk in the shared dorm that he kept for such eventualities and which was always home to the flotsam he was so fond of. He called them *Les Marginelles*, the people who live on the margins of society; the buskers, the artists, casual labour, transient poets, the unsettled, the displaced, the undecided, the hopeless dreamers, the genteel refugees. Most of them were white – or so near to that apartheid classification as to pass for whites in the eyes of the law – who were alienated from the society that claimed to stand up for their colour and doubly alienated by their rejection of officially sanctioned 'respectability'; they wore paisley prints, kept their hair long, rejected materialism, nationalism, capitalism, racism; talked of liberation, mysticism, socialism, going to India and thought there was more meaning in rock music than in the Bible. In unguarded moments, he envied them for their freedom but he had become too convinced of the truth of the balance sheet to give up his chains and join them. He had learned early on that freedom was not free and that what bestowed choice was not the open road to a far horizon but a full wallet and a healthy bank balance. The people he gave space to had yet to stumble on this inescapable truth and he saw his role as providing such space and in return for his troubles he got a steady flow of youth, effervescent life, stories from afar and the fresh lime of hope to sting into retreat his ever-present tendency to cynicism.

Yes, his hospitality had been abused and Anna-Marie Lovell *nee* van Zyl was not the first to empty the till and disappear into the windy night, but he took a hard-headed approach to these incidents, writing them off as a business expense to set against what he saved on the lower wages he paid; most of the time, he was actually up on the deal. Often, they drifted back, shame-faced and apologetic, were forgiven, worked off what they owed and then went on their wandering ways a little the wiser, knowing that there weren't many berths as soft as the one that Markham provided. In other times, they would have found a refuge in District 6, the louche, multi-racial piece of Cape Town over by the fort but since the demolitions had begun that refuge was no longer open to them and the new township over Table Mountain on the Cape Flats had been more strictly segregated. The truth was that he expected transgressions from his charges; he

130

regarded them as children; some of them were not much more than children; some of them would always remain children.

There were those, however, who were *not* children; the chaos and unwelcome attention from the law that drug addicts and petty dealers brought, he would not abide. He hated drugs and made it clear from the beginning that the merest hint of *dagga* - or the worse things that came ashore from the ships in the harbour - about anyone he extended a helping hand to would terminate both accommodation and employment immediately, no exceptions. He regarded addiction as a rejection of life and a self-inflicted wound; the drug made those it mastered prey and predator and he had a business to run. Not only that, but Markham needed the police to turn a blind eye to the blind eye that he turned to the draft dodgers who took a room and never came out of it until the night a ship came in. There was a steely nervousness about them that he learned to spot as they became more frequent; they carried the mark of the soldier not the hippy in their bearing, and the conflicts between desertion and loyalty, patriotism and idealism, bravery and cowardice, warred across their brows however hard they tried to conceal it under a brusque normality.

Markham was an hotelier and dealt with people, secrets and lies every day of his life; there wasn't much he couldn't tell from the way a man, a couple, a woman alone came into a hotel like his and asked for a room. Anna-Marie he had marked down as a runaway the moment she came through the doors. She was carrying a black vinyl Adidas bag that was way too large for a weekend but not big enough for a life and was dressed in a denim jacket that needed a wash, sandals against the beach tar, chipped red toe-nail paint, a cheesecloth shirt above a blue floral skirt and a grubby silk scarf wound around her neck like a torque. She was also anxious and hesitant, smoking as she came up the boardwalk, before flicking the cigarette away, taking a deep breath and putting on a professional cheerfulness as she came into the lobby. Markham had seen someone that looked like her only a day or so before and decided before she asked that he was going to let her take up the spare bunk because she would be company for Liesl, a teary mixed-race girl claiming to be Greek from up in the Transvaal, who was just finding her feet as the hotel's newest chambermaid after what he suspected was an illegal abortion. They would be good for each other, he thought, and he was right.

Anna-Marie worked hard, kept her nose clean and was such a hit from the outset with the customers that he promoted her to the bar almost straightaway. She teased the old salts like a favourite grand-daughter, flirted with the crown-and-anchor sailors, feigned the ignorance of innocence at blue jokes and fended off the young men who fancied themselves the first to pull a barmaid. She lit cigarettes, poured pints, learned drinks, listened to the same stories from the same mouths at the same time every day, asked for help with lifting the crates and rewarded the assistance with a smile, pretended to understand cricket, golf and rugby, and always kept up that same professional cheerfulness, to which she now added the vivacious dizziness that she had shown on the day she arrived. She was the perfect hostess and her popularity rang up the tills as much as it lit up the bar on a grey Tuesday. Before a month was out, Markham was trusting her with the cash and allowing her to sign off on the deliveries, two areas which were the traditional preserves of the pilferer and in which he was sometimes guilty of placing small honesty traps. She never took the bait or gave an indication that she knew it was bait. Markham quickly grew to like her.

At forty, and on the wrong side of a separation that had prompted him to seek out a new life in South Africa, he knew that he was far too old for her and had no desire whatsoever to be on the receiving end of the jibe that there was no fool like an old fool. He was suspicious of women in general, generally preferred the bar to the bedroom and stuck to the wisdom that had been drummed into him during his National Service that generals did not bed privates if they expected to maintain respect and good order; he had worked in too many places where that rule had been observed more in the breach than the observance, with disastrous results in each case; it was hard enough to get good staff. He liked Anna-Marie, hoped she would stay for as long as it suited her and would wish her well and count himself glad to have known her when she moved on – as he always knew she would.

Looking back, of course, he should have seen it coming. With hindsight, it was the row she had with Liesl that marked the beginning of the end. They had been for the best part of a year the same couple of happy young girls enjoying their freedom and the jingle of money in their pockets, breaking hearts up at the Brass Bell, swimming off the beach at Muizenberg, sitting on the rocks to watch the whales come in and gracing the yachts in and out of the marina. What the immediate cause of the break up was, Markham did not know and did not ask. He expected them to patch it up in the normal course of events but the breach was serious and would not be sealed. Liesl packed up and headed off, an event which made him review just what might have been the cause and which led him to keep a sharper, paternal eye on just who exactly Anna-Marie was seeing, which in turn led him to notice the young black man who had taken to sitting on the wall across the road by the marina who seemed to be wearing clothes which, though ordinary enough, seemed rather too good for a man who didn't seem to have a job. He was not a drug dealer, Markham decided; those same clothes were wrong for that profession and he was neither approaching or being approached by anyone who might be described as a customer. He certainly had time on his hands and though he sloped off from time to time when it got hot, he seemed to have found a couple of favourite spots where he could swing a leg in relative comfort or fold the newspaper that he read rather ostentatiously from cover to cover. Markham wondered if he was a suitor but then decided that rather than having the lover's air of ardent impatience, he looked like someone who was being paid to watch something without making it obvious that he was actually watching. What was more, Biggs (as he christened him) seemed to be about the only person in Simonstown who was unaware that the colour bar at the Britannia Hotel was of the distinctly grey variety; as long as a man was discrete, sat in the back bar where a passing police car wouldn't be obliged to take notice and was prepared to pretend to be a foreign sailor unaware of the regulations if asked, then Markham would take his money and give him a beer; yet this fellow appeared prosperous enough to be able to afford the prices but no matter how hot it was, he never developed a thirst. This, Markham concluded tentatively after a day or two of discrete observation, meant that he was a either a copper's nark sent to report on who or what was going on at the Britannia Hotel - not the first, nor would he be the last – or he was casing the joint for a robbery. There was still something different about Biggs that intrigued him though and Markham was both proud enough of his professional judgement and curious enough about what he wanted with Anna-Marie to follow her up to the railway station by the Brass Bell one afternoon, when the young man wasn't in his customary place on the marina wall.

Markham stood at one end of the platform while Anna-Marie went down to the Blacks Only end and stood side by side with Biggs, though not talking.

A few minutes later, a black woman with fine features and her hair done up in a ponytail came along and stood behind her and he distinctly saw the glint of keys surreptitiously handed over. Anna-Marie took them without looking backwards and within a day or two was the proud owner of a ten year old black VW Beetle.

From then on, her behaviour became more erratic. Though she maintained a cheerful visage, Markham knew that something had changed and her increasingly frequent and implausible requests for time off confirmed him in his belief that she had got mixed up in something that was beyond her capacity to handle. At first, it was just a few hours here and there and a quick check of the odometer showed that she was going no further than Cape Town or perhaps Hermanus, but the trips gradually got longer and her return sometimes coincided with the arrival of a young man evading the draft or a coffee-coloured person claiming to be Portuguese and wanting a room at the back for a couple of nights. When she came back from a three day break with the car covered in red dust and went straight to her room to sleep for twelve hours straight, all his suspicions were confirmed; that was Botswana dust; she was running people for the ANC.

It was in the days following the acquittal and re-arrest of Winnie Mandela in 1970 that things came to a head. There were serious riots at the university and in the Black Locations on Mitchells Plain and the police were in a state of high excitement; he was warned by the BOSS that the Britannia Hotel was *known* and that they had their eyes on it. This he dismissed as bluster but it did decide for him that he could not just let Anna-Marie drive that car straight onto the ferry to Robben Island without warning her of her likely fate. That same day, after she had missed a shift without giving notice, he had tried to warn her about the dangers of her involvement with the ANC, explaining gently that it was not because he did not sympathise with the cause but because he just thought she was out of her depth. Not surprisingly, she had disagreed; indeed she had *vehemently* disagreed and had used some language towards him that he did not think she was capable of. In fact, her response quite frightened him; he had not seen this side of her before and the black glow in her eyes had taken him aback. And then, that night, she emptied the till and the safe, got into that Beetle and disappeared. He never saw her again.

That was not quite the end of the story though. A couple of days later, a note came through the letterbox informing him that 'the parties involved in the recent financial misunderstanding were keen to make restitution' and that if he was to find himself in the parking lot behind the Caltex on the edge of Mitchell's Plain that evening, 'these poor words would be made good.'

\*

'Well,' said Markham. 'Like a fool I went. There was a gang there and they smashed the windows of my car and put a Molotov cocktail in and made me into the beauty I am today.'

'That's pretty tough,' replied Smithy, putting the bottle of beer down. They had moved from the lobby to the back snug and were now sitting uncomfortably on hard, bare chairs at a basic wooden table. On the wall was a poster from the Ali vs Liston fight, showing a snarling Ali standing over the prostrate Sonny Liston and looking like he was going to hit him again. 'You think the ANC used Anna-Marie to rob you then set you up?'

Markham smiled and though his nose twitched it did not wrinkled as might have been expected.

'I do not,' he said. 'In fact, I know they didn't because they sent an apology later on. The Molotov cocktail was just coincidence. I was white, they were black and they happened to be there just before the ANC people turned up.'

'Just bad luck then? Being in the wrong place at the wrong time.'

Markham smiled again: 'She told the ANC that I had reported her to the police, then she disappeared with the cash *and* the car. She ripped both of us off. Don't look so surprised, *detective*.'

'You rumbled me straight away?'

Markham nodded: 'You have *Policeman* written all over you. But a reluctant one, I think. Judging by the company you kept when you stayed here.'

Smithy felt a pang of guilty embarrassment followed by a surge of relief that Mostert wasn't here with him. This in turn was followed by an intense desire to ask Markham about her, which his conscience demanded he quickly force down.

'And you're giving me this information because you want your revenge?'

Markham's hand went to his throat and produced a small silver crucifix on a chain.

'I let God into my life and have found it in my heart to forgive her,' he said, with a sigh. 'But, in that moment of her decision, I think that she was possessed by a demon. I am sure that I saw its coal black eyes staring out of her head at me and I think that she must be found and made to make restitution or she can never find her own salvation. This is something that goes for all of us. If we do not reconcile ourselves to brotherhood with our black friends then – well – mine will not be the only face that will look like this in the future.  So she must return the money she stole from me and the car that she stole from the ANC.  That would be God's way.'

'Would you still have the number plate for the VW?'

'I remember every detail of those days,' replied Markham, touching his lip. 'I am reminded of them every day, but I am afraid that the licence plate of that car was changed rather more than once.'

'Would you have a contact address for this Liesl girl then?'

'I have the address that I sent the balance of her wages to,' he replied.  'But that was many years ago.'

Smithy gave a little shrug:  'Maybe it'll lead to something.  You never know,' he said, hopelessly.  'Tell me, did her family ever coming looking for her?  The police?'

'No,' replied Markham.  'But we get the odd call asking us to look out for missing persons from time to time.'

'Which you ignore,' said Smithy.

'The people who come here for shelter are lost more than they are missing.'

Smithy nodded and finished his beer.  'But sometimes, you let their parents know.  Just so they don't worry.  A postcard, posted discretely?'

Markham allowed a small smile out.

'But nobody came for her?'

Markham shook his head.

'You know you're a decent bloke, Mr Markham?'

'I do my best,' he replied.

*

'A demon?' said Mostert. 'And he runs *that* Hotel and calls himself a Christian?'

'He spoke highly of you,' replied Smithy, winking horribly and starting the car. 'Besides, there are some very funny sorts of Christians. You've heard of the Swedenborgians? No? They're into Free Love and all that hippy shit. And as for the Osmonds, well, *Mormons don't drink.*'

They drove northwards with False Bay glinting in the sunshine. In among the kelp beds, Smithy caught the occasional glimpse of the whales that were returning to the bay with the onset of the Antarctic winter while further across, he could see the mountains of the escarpment lying blue against the deeper blue of the sky. He smiled a little at his memories of previous drives up this road from the Britannia Hotel when he was full and happy and sated with love and it seemed like the world was as full of possibilities as the continent of Africa was big. Driving past Cecil Rhodes' cottage at Muizenberg, he had often been seized by the desire to do the whole Cape to Cairo route and had seriously considered jacking in his job, buying a car and heading off into the unknown. That had been before he had been forced to take part in the murder of Onyele Namyana, the ANC activist who his colleagues in the Graaff Reinet police force had beaten into such a pulp that the only way to avoid a charge of attempted murder was to murder him properly and hide his body out in the Karoo desert. He had no dreams now, beyond survival.

'Joshua,' said Mostert, breaking into his thoughts. 'Don't you think that this case is a little fishy? I mean, *why* are we trying to track down this woman? And *why* have we been given the job? If this is a regular BOSS thing, *why* don't they have regular BOSS officers investigating? And *why* all the bull about poison gas? Why didn't Pieters come straight out and tell us to find out what happened to Anna-Marie van Zyl?'

'No idea,' replied Smithy. 'If it's a BOSS thing it will be wheels within wheels. That is a given. Who cares anyway? Enjoy the sunshine.'

'What do you think she was doing up at Capinga?' said Mostert. 'Do you have a theory? I mean, back there you said that she had rebelled against her father being a Nazi and had gone off to join SWAPO or the ANC and I agreed with you.'

Smithy shrugged: 'She might also have been a BOSS spy and that is why Pieters is interested. To be honest, I'm just enjoying being here in civilisation and I'm going to string this out as long as I can. That's why we are going to follow this Liesl lead.'

'We have a deadline,' said Mostert, primly reminding him of his duty. 'She was a spy, hey? Working for BOSS?' She mulled the idea over for a moment. 'No: I don't buy it.'

'She wasn't a tourist, that is one thing that is for sure,' said Smithy, changing gear and revving the engine.

'These hippy chicks are always rebelling,' said Mostert, working through the possibilities. 'They call it *radical chic* in America. They do it for the fashion. I'm going with the theory that she had gone over, left the country and joined SWAPO or the ANC.'

'*Spy or Traitor*, is it?' said Smithy, grinding the gears. 'Let's flip a coin, hey? Heads I win, Tails you lose. Ten Bucks on it?'

'Pieters thinks this thing is a little bit more important than a coin flip,' said Mostert.

'Big deal,' replied Smithy. 'What will they do if I'm wrong? Post me somewhere worse than Police Post 158? The way I feel right now, I don't think there is such a place. And if you want fishy – look over there.'

About fifty metres from the shore the huge black bulk of a whale suddenly erupted from the sparkling blue surface of the sea, rose up ponderously like some huge airship and then, defeated by its weight and bulk, rolled and fell back into the sea with a great boom and splash like a fat drunk at a pool party.

'*Ja*. Amazing,' said Mostert, shifting in her seat and craning her neck to see if the whale would breach once more. 'You know there is someone who might help us – might give us a short cut.'

'I am not going near my mother,' replied Smithy.

'No, no,' said Mostert. 'I mean that journalist Clive Merriman.'

Smithy's stomach flipped.

'We are not going near Clive Merriman. We sent his son down for murder, remember? Only he didn't get sent down, did he? BOSS murdered him in cold blood and cooked up a story about him dying in combat as a true South African hero.'

Smithy drove in silence for a while. Unbeknownst to Mostert, he had got the suspect David Merriman to confess by torturing him and that

141

uncomfortable memory, plus the fact that he had been with David when BOSS killed him, told him in no uncertain terms that he dare not risk an interview with the grieving father. Clive Merriman was known to hold committed anti-apartheid views and was probably aware of the Writ that had been issued against Sergeant Smith for the murder of Onyele Namyana; he knew that he and David had been in the same place at the same time (though not the context) and would be bound to ask for more details; one little fib and his journalists' nose would be sniffing at him like a bloodhound in a butchers' shop; his wife, Sheila, was also friendly with Smithy's mother; it would be like sticking his head into the lion's mouth.

'So all we've got to go on is a number plate and an ancient forwarding address?'

'It'll have to do,' replied Smithy.

There was another splash in the bay like a shell exploding but further off and Mostert only just caught a glimpse of a whale's mermaid tail sliding smoothly down into the water.

'OK,' she said. 'But if nothing turns up today, I'm going to pull rank.'

'Pull whatever you like,' replied Smithy. 'I'm not talking to him.'

'I'll talk to him myself then,' replied Mostert. 'You can wait in the car.'

'Fine,' said Smithy. 'But we're going up to Montagu first and as that means another four hours in this shit heap on wheels, I'll be grateful if you don't mention my *bladdy* mother or Clive *bladdy* Merriman for the rest of the *bladdy* way.'

*

142

Montagu was one of those places that tourist guides always called 'hidden gems' because it was so difficult to find. Up until the late 19<sup>th</sup> Century, it *was* difficult to find because anyone wanting to go there would have to make quite a long detour around the mountain barrier that separated the Karoo desert from the green of the Cape. Then some enterprising road builder had blown an omnibus sized tunnel through it and woken up the inhabitants of that dusty *dorp*, who no doubt cursed at the march of progress and went back to doing what they were doing before, which mainly consisted of sitting on the *stoep* and complaining about the lack of rain and how the country was going to the dogs. Sure, it was pretty, but so were all these little Karoo towns scratched out of the desert. There was something Andalucian about the place, if only they had known it; all the soil had been washed off the top of the pink, barren mountains to form the fertile valleys below and what nature had started irrigation had developed into ideal areas for fruit growing. KWV had been producing (bad) wine there for decades which meant the town had grown fat and rich enough to afford a school, a couple of fine whitewashed churches and some classy, bay fronted villas with lots of frilly cast-iron work to add to the solid Dutch farmhouses that had taken root there in the 1860s. The distinctive thing about the place was not so much the corrugated green and zinc oxide red iron roofing and certainly not the ugly utilitarian apartment blocks imposed on the place by an architect who would never have to live in the place or look at them, but the bold colours that some of the people had painted their houses. These ranged from the flat roofed Swedish blue house with bright white quoins that gave it the look of a wild west bank done up to look like a fancy iced cake all the way through to the pink Dutch gabled thatched villa, complete with Georgian sash windows, that looked like it had been drawn on a bit of paper in Sunday school and then handed to the builder with a terse instruction to get it built. Even where walls were white and roofs plain silver, they exploded with cerise, apricot, orange and white bougainvillea while the gardens kept neat by native labour were deep with luxuriant foliage, oleander, hibiscus and every sort of exotic.

The surrounding mountains were beginning to take on the first glow of the late afternoon as they followed the line of grey-green aloes that right now had put out stamens as tall as telegraph poles and then turned onto a deserted Long Street. Smithy wound the window down in anticipation of asking for directions to the local police station and caught the warm and clean breath of a breeze which carried the healthy sound of children laughing and shouting somewhere off to the left.

'Is it a fete today?' he asked, slowing down to call up to an open window and the head and shoulders of a young housewife.

'Soap box derby,' she replied. 'Go left side and up the hill.'

'Excellent,' said Smithy, with a grin. 'I used to love that as a kid.'

'Great,' replied Mostert. 'But we have a job to do.'

'And you think there will be a single person in the police station, right now? Come on.'

The police had closed off a couple of streets for the event and placed a row of hay bales at the bottom of the hill to stop the competitors hurtling into oblivion. It seemed that the whole town had turned out for the event because the sidewalks were lined with people, there was bunting fluttering cheerfully among the shade trees, a couple of braais going and plenty of soda pop fizzing down kids throats. Smithy bought a couple of hot dogs from a teenage entrepreneur, sloshed some tomato sauce onto them and handed Mostert one.

'I never *ever* won a prize for this,' he said. 'But it was not for the want of trying.'

From up the hill came the sound of a starter's pistol and a minute or so later, a collection of ramshackle carts came hurtling down the hill towards them. There were big carts, small carts, ones with three wheels, fat tyres, thin tyres, some with arrowed fronts to cut down on the drag and some with no consideration for wind resistance at all. Some had stabilisers, one had been painted like a chequered flag, another looked like it might actually have two storeys because it had been built with a turret like a tank. What they had in common was a lot of cheering, a lot of hopeful pulling on steering ropes, very little skill and a reckless disregard for safety plastered all over the wide eyes of the drivers.

'That one is never going to make it,' said Smithy, smiling and pointing out an especially rickety example of the soap box cart builders' art. 'His backside will be on the road before he reaches the bottom.' Right on cue, the cart swerved to one side, hit the kerb and disintegrated in a spectacular display of flying bicycle wheels, cardboard and old rope. The child, who wasn't above eight was caught by the arm and yanked back like a swinging monkey just before he went nose first into a tree.

'I bet someone put glue in his oil can,' laughed Smithy. 'Or loosened the wheel nut. That's what I used to do.'

'You cheated at this?' said Mostert, as another small boy in a badly built death trap hurtled by.

145

'Of course,' replied Smithy. 'It's the same as raiding wood from someone else's Bonfire Night pile. Part of the game. Where were you brought up?'

'In civilisation,' replied Mostert. 'Let's find a cop who can tell us where our witness can be found.'

'Back into uniforms it is, then,' said Smithy, reluctantly. 'They'll never take our words for it otherwise.'

*

## Last Wednesday: Capinga

The mortar round blew Mickey Epstein backwards and off his feet and for a moment he was merely disorientated but it was the second explosion that did for him. When he woke up from that one, it was nearly dark, the camp on the far side of the river was still burning and there was a pall of smoke and dust hanging above the shredded trees. He could hear the faint sounds of voices but they were indistinct and he could make nothing of them above the sound of the wind in the river bank reeds. What he could hear absolutely nothing of was the one sound he really wanted to hear; the *chop chop* of helicopter rotor blades.

He knew that he wasn't dead but wasn't sure if he was injured or not and, keeping a remarkable calm, he went through the drill of wiggling his toes – no broken bones down there or spinal injury; wriggling his fingers – arms OK; patting his torso and groin with his hands – no cracked ribs, but he had pissed himself; and finally his face – pretty as ever. After that, he rolled over and reached for his weapon; right to hand. On to one knee; check pouches – grenades OK, magazines OK, water bottle, full – *should have brought two*. Assured that he was reasonably in one piece and with his kit intact, he put his head up, looked around, made a plan.

146

He was missing presumed dead; if the guys were coming back for him, they would have been here by now; by morning SWAPO would have anti-aircraft guns re-mounted or fresh ones on the way, so he could forget about uplift. He had no radio either so basically, he was on his own, which meant a long walk in a southerly direction, five days minimum at a reasonable speed; he had water for one, perhaps two and rations ditto, or perhaps three at a stretch. He didn't have a map, but he had paid attention at the briefing and so he knew that there was a rough road that went in a South Easterly direction which cut a river before turning south for the border. So no problem there. All he had to do was avoid SWAPO patrols, the Cubans, FAPLA checkpoints, friendly fire from UNITA and whatever assorted bandits were lurking about in this blasted bit of the world, plus wild animals. Problematic, he thought, but definitely do-able. He set himself a goal; first would be to reach the treeline without being seen and then use the night and the cover to put a few good kilometres between him and the camp. He stood up, pulled his pack and webbing into a more comfortable position and keeping low, made a quick survey of the dead ground available, and then moved off into it.

That first goal was an important one for he was more than reasonably confident that if he could put distance between himself and the camp, the chances of being caught diminished with every step because the search radius would proportionately increase. Mickey had been good at maths at school and began to make the calculations as a way to keep his brain active and push back the moment when he would need to stop and sleep; this was already the seventeenth hour since he climbed out of his pit this morning and he wasn't sure if he wasn't slightly concussed, so this was important. At five kilometres from the camp and assuming that any pursuit would discount the possibility of him heading in a North Westerly direction, then the area to be searched would add up to roughly 59sq km; ten kilometres would become 236sq km; fifteen would be 530sq km; and if he could rack up his target of 50km for the first twenty four hours then at the end of it, the pursuit would have the glorious task of looking for Mickey the Parabat Needle in a haystack just short of 600,000 square kilometres big; *ja*, good luck with that. He reached the treeline and the night swallowed him.

Or rather, the mosquitoes swallowed him. Within moments of entering the forest, he was engulfed in a cloud of mosquitoes whose dentist drill whine blotted out all other sound entirely and immediately his ears, face and neck were assailed with attackers so dense that when he wiped his hands across his exposed skin, he found them smeared with his own blood. His immediate instinct was to keep walking in the hope that he could leave behind whatever pond, stream or stretch of marsh was home to them but within half an hour he was forced to abandon this particular sub-plan. It was so dark under the canopy that he could barely see his hands in front of his face and he had to factor in the possibility that his next trip over a low hanging vine could cost him a broken ankle or the next time he hit a branch, one of the iron hard, two inch long thorns might pop an eyeball. He found a tree with a bole wide enough that he could nestle into and sat down. In an instant the mosquitoes settled thickly on him, which he tried to count as being in his favour as the whine, the itching and the constant irritation would prevent him drifting off into a deep sleep but no amount of self-delusion could work under such torment. He pulled out his sleeping bag, climbed into it and prepared for a long night under siege from the vast array and variety of winged, crawling, biting, stinging insect life that only Africa could provide in such profusion.

The maggot bag provided a little protection but not much; it was too hot to spend more than twenty minutes encased in it and Mickey was forced to strip it back from his head and shoulders and take gasping, panting breaths of the relatively fresher air outside before his sweating body went mad. The night seemed endless and when the mosquitoes departed with the first rays of the sun, Mickey knew that his face had puffed up, his eyelids were almost closed and his hands and arms were one long white weal of mosquito venom which shrieked at him to scratch. This urge he resisted, instead holding them up like stiff branches to cool a little in the precious early morning air. After that luxury, he allowed himself a second indulgence; one biscuit and a single, large mouthful of water to wash it down. Then it was *up, up and away*, he sang to himself, *for a beautiful, a beautiful kay-eh?*

By midday it was hot and whatever breeze had come with the morning had died with it but Mickey had made the decision to keep moving because travelling by night was too slow and too dangerous. Above, the sky had had all colour seared out of it by the sun while the rocks over which he was working vibrated with the baking heat. This was mirage heat, he told himself. This was heat that made the ground disappear in sheets of white light, heated up clothing so much that the wearer was tempted to accept a devil's bargain and abandon it, and added weight upon weight to every last shred of equipment until the bearer of that weight felt his heart hammer, his knees crack and his arms go numb. He was drooping and his lips were cracked and his chin was on his chest. He put his hand inside his shirt and found that it was still wet from sweat, still soaked, which meant that he was not dehydrated, however much his dry mouth and thick tongue complained; Mickey had it in his head to go another thousand steps before he gave the day a compromise. Then, and only then, would he take the water bottle in his shaking hands and taste one warm mouthful.

By late afternoon, Mickey was feeling a sense of grim achievement; he was still here, still free, still alive and if the prospect of another night with the mosquitoes was unappealing, he could think of ways in which a FAPLA or SWAPO jailor could make it even less so. He had been pushing along down an animal track – elephant probably – and so fresh that he could afford to pay a little less attention to his own tracks given the wreckage of stripped branches and broken trees that were the calling card of *Loxodonta Africanus* and had made good time, he reckoned. He had counted his steps and at every thousand had tied a small knot in a piece of string that he carried for this express purpose; there were thirty nine knots which he reckoned would bring him close to his target of 50k in his first twenty four hours. He intended to celebrate that fact with the tin of Beans in Tomato Sauce from his ratpack.

By the end of the second day, Mickey was beginning to get concerned at the water situation and he knew his tactical awareness was beginning to suffer because of it. It was still hot, felt hotter, but he was encouraged by the fact that there was more shade to be had than yesterday but still, he knew he needed water, much more water and if he didn't get it soon then he would have to find it or die. His feet were on fire now, the result of having been bitten along both insteps somehow, sometime, in the sleepless night and his weapon was now sometimes slung through his webbing straps rather than in his hands because it too was becoming too hot to comfortably hold. He put his hand inside his shirt. The skin there was cool and clammy; a bad sign; he had stopped bleeding from the scratches, cuts and bites that screamed through his body; another bad sign; he was

150

beginning to dehydrate and he had a ringing in his ears that was quite distinct from the screeching cicadas. He did not want to resort to drinking his own urine even though he had saved the lemonade powder to mix with it in the hope that it would be rendered a little more palatable. He pulled out the string of knots, tied an extra one and wondered if the tally was correct; had he already counted this last thousand steps or had he not? He looked up and for a moment found the fact of a tree incomprehensible; another symptom, he noted. He needed water. Tonight he would eat the Viennas, more for the moisture than the sustenance, and then he would go through his kit and see if anything, anything at all, could be jettisoned.

Day three would be crucial, Mickey decided. If he made it through this one, he would make it and if he didn't he wouldn't and with that stark logic, he decided that he would eat whatever he could from the ration pack, drink the two mouthfuls of water left in his bottle and then prepare to collect his own piss in it. There was a river somewhere up ahead and he should hit it today; if he did, he would survive and if he didn't, he wouldn't. That was it. No point moaning. It was time to just get on with it. He ate. He drank. He began to walk. He had been brought up among Zulus in Ballito and so he started to hum the repetitive wheeze of a Zulu squeezebox walking song; these songs drove white people mad because they misunderstood what the melodies were for. Mickey knew though; it was his secret weapon; the walking songs were repetitive because they were supposed to induce a sort of hypnosis, so a person didn't notice the miles; it was why Zulus could cover so much ground so quickly; this would help him make it; And he had not abandoned his kit. So he *was* going to make it.

And then, to his intense dismay, he heard the sound of shots. Someone was looking in the right haystack for him.

*

They found Liesl Aristedes a little way out of town past the warm springs on a desert road marked by rows of tall cactus and low scrub everywhere where the irrigation didn't reach. Where it did reach were good meadows of bright grass, orderly orchard rows of apricot, apple and plum trees and willow in the valley bottoms amid which were situated sold, square farmhouses shaded by poplars and oaks. Scattered here and there on the scrub side of the road were small homesteads of broken glass, neglected whitewash and mangy, barking dogs while at the further end of one of the fruit farms was a substantial block of sturdy construction, barred and meshed windows, bolted doors and what looked like a large loading bay.

'She's running the bottle store,' said Smithy. '*Jeez.* She must be a real tough nut.'

Crunching to a halt, they got out of the car and entered the cavernous entrance only to find, once their eyes had adjusted, that it was not a loading bay but just a large bare, concrete and breeze block room around which ran a high counter, fortified with more bars and thick wire mesh. In two or three places, the run of the bars was interrupted by a swing bin arrangement whereby money might be deposited, the bin swung in to the person behind the counter who would take the money and replace it with a bottle of beer. Behind the counter against the back wall were crates and crates of beer, stacked up almost to the rafters, alternating with shelves of cheap white rum and even cheaper brandy, loaves of bread, packets of candles, boxes of matches, cartons of cheap cigarettes, large 25kg paper sacks of maize, sugar and rice, tins of tomato, fish, cheap pots and pans, a

152

bolt of printed cotton cloth, charcoal, firewood in thick plastic bags and a glass container for keeping pepper steak pies warm. There was also a framed portrait of the president peering out from under his heavy lidded spectacles and smiling the thick lipped smile that reminded Smithy of that English funny man, Eric Morecambe, but the whole place was still dominated by the towering crates of beer. Looking up, he saw hanging from the ceiling a large, hand painted sign which declared with a definitive confidence that Smithy couldn't share: NO GUNS ALLOWED. NO KNIVES. NO WEAPONS OF ANY KIND. NO CREDIT. NO TABS. NO OWN FOOD. NO TOILETS.

'Not really your sort of place, hey, Trudi?' said Smithy, grinning. 'This is a real black man's pub. A hardware store, corner shop and general haberdashery rolled into one. I doubt they serve cocktails here. I doubt they serve *women* here.'

'Like I said, Smithy,' she replied. 'I was brought up in civilisation.'

'Can I help you?' said a voice out of the gloom.

'Liesl Aristedes?' asked Mostert.

Liesl's appearance was nothing less than striking. Her face was a light olive colour dominated by small but fleshy lips, a likewise fleshy nose, rather heavy jowls and dark, kohl rimmed eyes. It was a face which marked her out as someone who had worked harder that she should have had to in an ideal world and which was now beginning to collapse into a double chin long before it needed to. It was an alert face though, not passive at all and Mostert associated the quickness of the eyes and their ability to penetrate the gloom with those of the soldiers she knew up on the border. She was wearing a jacket which was dark and really too thick to be comfortable in this heat and as Mostert's eyes adjusted to the darkness, she saw that it was ripped in a couple of places, repaired in a couple of others and covered up something lacy underneath. Combined with the scarlet fingernails at the end of strong hands, the effect would have been almost entirely gothic if it had not been for the coils and coils of turquoise hair that rambled and tumbled about her head and shoulders like the snakes of Medusa. It was also evident that she carried herself with a slight stoop, as though wincing under a falling blow.

'Police.' It was a statement not a question. Stalking warily along behind the counter, Liesl eyed up the uniforms and then said in a mocking American accent: 'One blue, one brown. From out of town.' She paused and then abandoned the joke. 'Whatever rape, killing or robbery you are pursuing, you will find no information here. No-one knows anything here. Ever. Not anything at all.' She gave a little snort that made the turquoise snakes on her head shift. 'The Kaffirs can barely remember their own names an hour after they come in here.'

'Is there somewhere where we can talk?' asked Mostert.

'You're standing in it,' replied Liesl, picking up a bag of chips from the floor and tossing it onto a shelf. There was a framed photograph there, of a boy sitting on a chequered soap box cart holding a shiny silver cup. 'Talk away.'

'It's about an old acquaintance of yours,' said Smithy and then, taking in the picture. 'Your boy did well in the race today. Shame you missed it.'

Liesl looked at the picture, nodded and said: 'Delivery. Do I need to tell you what would happen to a beer delivery if I wasn't here and just left it to the staff to handle? Who's the old acquaintance?'

Mostert came forward to the counter and held the photograph up to the bars.

'Anna-Marie Lovell,' said Liesl, without emotion. 'Though I wouldn't swear that was her real name. Mixed up girl. What's this all about?'

'You worked with her in Simonstown a few years ago,' said Smithy.

'About ten – twelve - years ago, I'd say,' replied Liesl. 'What do you want to know?'

'What can you tell us about her?' said Smithy.

Liesl looked at Mostert for a clue, shrugged and then bent down to heft a crate of beer up waist high from the floor and smack it down onto a pile by the wall. 'You ask the questions and I'll answer them if I know what the answer is.'

'Can you tell us what she was like, what sort of a girl she was and what she was doing at the Britannia Hotel?' said Smithy.

Liesl bent down for another crate which she then swung up with expert ease and crashed down onto another pile.

'She was OK. Normal. Well, normal for the Britannia,' she said. 'I guess you know about the Britannia or you wouldn't be here. Is this a political thing?'

'Missing person,' said Smithy.

'*Missing person*,' replied Liesl. '*Ja*. Well; we worked; we went out together and crashed parties; we drank a hell of a lot, mostly for free. Smoked some *dagga* too.'

'How did your employer feel about this?'

155

'Who Markham?' said Liesl, surprised at hearing the name. 'Is he still working there?'

'You know what happened to him? The...*accident*?'

Liesl picked up another crate: 'Markham was alright. I read about him in the papers. I guessed it was something that Anna-Marie got him mixed up in but I don't know anything certain because it happened after I left. He had a soft spot for her. It wasn't good for him to have a soft spot for her. She was not someone to let an opportunity go by to milk a person who could be milked. And she was milking him already.'

'Was she involved in anything political?' asked Mostert.

Liesl gave a little pout as she weighed the question up in her mind and then nodded quickly.

'Like lots of white people there,' said Liesl. 'They thought that if they sucked up to the blacks they might get spared when the ANC took over. I think she ran errands for them.'

'Can you be more specific?'

She shook her head: 'I wanted nothing to do with it. She was playing at being a revolutionary agitator as well as milking Markham.'

'We heard that you fell out with Anna-Marie over something serious,' said Mostert. 'Was it to do with her political involvement with the ANC or something else?'

Liesl nodded again as though this was something obvious. 'I'm National Party. Always have been. She was radical. Black majority rule. Like I told you, she was sucking up to the blacks. I told her that when the blacks take over they will just do what they do everywhere they take over – they will kill any whites who aren't quick enough to get on the plane out and then they'll do the same to the Coloureds. I'm National Party because there isn't an alternative to black communism. She didn't agree. We argued. I left. That's it.'

'Because of politics?' said Smithy. 'You sure?'

'It's pretty important these days, hey?' replied Liesl.

'What were you doing down in the Cape?' asked Mostert.

'Trying to get reclassified,' replied Liesl, as though the question was redundant. 'Try to get reclassified from Coloured to White in the Transvaal and they think you are about to start a rebellion. Down here in the Cape, it's a lot more easier. I got a Japanese guy to help.'

Mostert looked puzzled and gave a little uncomprehending shake of her head. Liesl replied with a tired smile.

'Japanese are classified as 'White' so I got the guy to say he was my grandfather,' she said. 'One white grandparent and you're on your way. We got around the paperwork by telling the authorities that the birth certificate originals had been nuked in Hiroshima and just submitted a lot of Japanese letters in their place.'

'And that worked?' asked Smithy.

'What would you do if a lot of Japanese stuff landed on your desk?' said Liesl. 'Check it through thoroughly? Get it translated? Write to the Japanese Embassy? Make your life very complicated? Or just take the bribe and stamp the papers? *Ja*, you understand now. You going to arrest me for this, hey?'

Mostert shook her head again. 'Let's get back to Anna-Marie,' she said. 'You fell out over *politics*, right? And then you left and came up here? Did you see her again?'

'A couple of years later, yes,' admitted Liesl, heaving up another crate of beer. 'She called by and stayed a little while. Not long. Then she left again.'

'You got a date for that?' asked Smithy. 'Roughly?'

'27th November 1971 was the day I last saw her.'

'Wow,' said Smithy. 'That's pretty impressive. How do you remember so precisely?'

'Because it was the day I got arrested and reclassified back to being Coloured,' replied Liesl. 'All because the stupid bitch couldn't keep her knickers on and her mouth shut.'

'Uh?' said Smithy.

'She was one of those girls who like women,' said Liesl, as though explaining to an idiot. 'She tuned me a couple of times back at the Britannia but I wasn't into her and she wouldn't take no for an answer. In the end, I got tired of her coming on to me every time she got drunk. It was one of the reasons I left. Then she followed me up here, got *really* drunk when I turned her down again and then went around the town telling everyone that we were lovers. In a small town like this, the police take notice of these things so the inevitable happened. Her father, a big old Boer, came down with a van and a couple of police from out of town and arrested us. They put me in the Cape Town *tronk* where I was reclassified and her, I never saw again. And now I'm *here*, stuck out in nowheresville saving up to get robbed by the Kaffirs when they take over and no way out. The worst of it was that it was all bullshit. It was all show. She didn't really like women at all.'

'How could you know this?' asked Mostert.

'Because I *do* like women,' said Liesl. 'And when I kissed her back once, her flesh crawled. You can tell.'

*

'Lesbians?' said Smithy, wide –eyed and on the verge of exasperation. 'I thought that was just sexy girl-on-girl stuff that they made up for porn mags! I never knew they were for real. Anyway, she can't be – she's got a kid.'

'You lie,' replied Mostert, sniggering. 'You going to tell me you thought she was really, really Greek. Like from Lesbos in Greece.'

'There's a place called Lesbos? Is that why they are called Lesbians? Because all the people there are queers?' Smithy, got into the car and started up. 'I need to apply for a refund on my school fees because I never learned any of this stuff in Sex Ed. I mean, how come she has a kid?'

'You had Sex Education now?' answered Mostert, sliding into the passenger seat and rolling down the window to let out the hot air. 'I'm amazed. Truly, I am.'

'*Ja*, well, not much,' said Smithy, pulling out. 'They gave us a lesson on reproduction in fruit flies in the morning and then Father Norman spent the whole afternoon telling us why sex before marriage would get us damned and the Sin of Onan would make us blind or round-shouldered. He never mentioned anything about the actual mechanics and I doubt he knew what

159

a Lesbian was any more than I did. *Ja,* I had a proper Catholic education. *Jeez,* man. I learned what I learned mostly in the back of the bioscope and it seems I'm still filling in the gaps. And *turquoise hair, man.* I have a *lot* to learn.'

They drove down the pink desert road for a while in silence watching the mountains undulate under the deepening sapphire of the late afternoon and listening to the rough hum of the tyres on the tarmac. There was a big sky here and though the mid-day light of the hot, yellow sun tended to bleed the colours out of the mountains, turning them pumice-grey and gauze, the westering sun now picked out every pock mark, striation, ledge and rock slide in sharp shades of salmon pink, mauve, red fire, sharkskin and tanned flesh. Even as the silver darkness came down ahead of the Prussian blue, Smithy found it comforting to know that they were still there, patient, hulking, watching like the shoulders of benevolent giants. There was something pleasing about this space, this isolation and the loneliness of this road through the desert that made it a different desert to the one back at Police Post 158, for unlike the flat dead of the salt desert back there, here the mountain sides were full of snaking, sinuous movement and full of wildlife, even in the stillness. Hawks could be seen hanging high in the last emptiness of the day, bats were beginning to rustle in the fruit trees, there were baboons on some of the higher kloofs and from time to time, Smithy would steer around the boulder sized tortoises that swam ponderously across the road towards the oncoming shade of the dusty olive trees.

'I mean, how?' said Smithy suddenly, flicking on the headlights

'How what?' answered Mostert.

160

'I mean, if you are a Lesbian how do you get to meet other Lesbians?' he said, uncertainly. 'I mean, it isn't as though you can just walk up to a girl at the bar and start tuning them, hey? People would notice. And if they don't have *turquoise* hair, how do you know they got the same tastes as you in the first place? It's not like they wear a badge, is it?'

'Start with the hockey club, I'd say,' answered Mostert. 'Or maybe the *Wine Barrel* in Cape Town'

'I've been in the *Wine Barrel*,' exclaimed Smithy. 'I tuned a few girls in there.'

'Any luck?' asked Mostert.

'They weren't biting,' said Smithy.

'Now you know why,' scoffed Mostert.

'Nobody tuned you then?'

'Never,' replied Mostert, firmly. 'I've heard about them, but I never met one who was open about it before today.'

'So, you're just like me,' said Smithy, triumphantly. 'You a lesbian virgin too.'

Mostert gave him a hard stare.

'*Ja*, OK, sorry, hey? I didn't mean anything by it.'

They drove on for a moment.

'Don't even think it for a minute,' said Mostert.

'It never crossed my mind Ma'am,' replied Smithy, secretly relieved. 'You want a cold one?'

The evening was coming in quickly now and Smithy was glad to get under the street lights of the town. It wasn't that he wasn't used to driving at night, but he wasn't familiar with the road and the last thing he wanted to do was to hit some buck or stray cow and have it come in through the windscreen into his lap, especially as the thought of Mostert getting it on with another girl had given him an extra gear stick, a fact that he was particularly concerned to conceal. There was a pub on the street, just before the church, which had been recommended for food, beer and rooms and Smithy steered towards it, pulled up and switched off the engine.

'You picked up that old man van Zyl lied about when he last saw Anna-Marie?' said Smithy. 'He said he last saw her in 1966. Liesl the Lesbian says he was there when she was arrested in 1971.'

'And why would Anna-Marie pretend to be a Lesbian?' asked Mostert.

\*

07

Thursday

'What next?' said Smithy, tucking into bacon and boerewors over the gingham table cloth.

'Well, we should corroborate the arrest with the local police, I guess,' answered Mostert, sprinkling muesli on her yoghurt. 'Check out the old man van Zyl was actually there and see what happened. There may be an address or something.'

162

'It's been nine years,' cautioned Smithy. 'And these little dorps aren't big on paperwork.'

'*Ja*,' said Mostert. 'Liesl Aristedes might want to forget being arrested for immorality but that pretty much guarantees that she won't be. These little dorps have long memories.'

That, thought Smithy, was undeniably and uncomfortably true.

*

'*Ag,* man.  Shame,' said the Sergeant.  'No forwarding address given. Actually though, we did do the arrest but it was on the word from the higher-ups.  Normally we turn a blind eye to things like this.  It's just trouble, man.'

'Higher-ups?' said Mostert. 'Like Cape Town?'

'Pretoria as I remember,' replied the Sergeant.  He was a standard issue sort of man, perfect for police chief of a town like Montagu; belly, greying temples, pistol, complacent, pragmatic and thoroughly convinced of the value of a quiet life.  'Phone call.  Down comes a detective with the girl's father.  We pick the two girls up as instructed and they take them away.'

'But Liesl came back,' said Mostert.

'*Ja*, that was tragic,' he said, rumpling up his nose.  'Losing her classification like that.  But she does a good job out at that bottle store.  It's a good business, that way.  She makes more money than I do and she has a good bank balance, especially as she hates the Kaffirs.  I mean, *really* hates them.  Even when they are her customers.  Actually, that is probably because they *are* her customers.  It is not really a place for ladies, man, but at least it keeps them out of the town at the weekends.'

'This isn't a 'Whites Only' area?' asked Smithy.

'*Ja*, it is but the only supermarket is here and so we have to let the Kaffirs in,' replied the Sergeant. 'And if they were allowed to buy booze here, we'd never get them out. That bottle store is a public amenity man. I think it is more of an important public amenity than the library. It keeps the peace, hey.'

'And you never saw Anna-Marie van Zyl again?' asked Mostert.

The Sergeant shook his head.

'Or her father?'

He shook his head again.

'Anything you can tell us about the officers who arrested her?' asked Mostert.

'They came from Pretoria,' replied the Sergeant. 'Or that's what they said, so I believed them. They were pretty heavy, hey? They weren't too keen to answer too many questions.'

'You think they were BOSS?' asked Mostert.

The Sergeant held his hands apart and shrugged. 'If they were, they would not tell *me*.'

Mostert pulled out the BOSS ID that Pieters had provided for her.

'Shit, man,' said the Sergeant, taken aback. 'Sorry, hey? I thought you were just detectives. But I don't know anything. Really. Except what I told you. Here, look at the file.'

164

Smithy took the file and ran through the forms. There were two of them, with carbons, filled out in thick pencil by thick hands. One of them noted the arrest, the other the handover of two prisoners. Everything was as the Sergeant had said. It was just a routine arrest which had then been taken out of his hands. There was one detail there that interested him.

'Is the registration of Anna-Marie van Zyl's car?' asked Smithy.

The Sergeant looked at the number and nodded. 'They took it with them.'

'Thanks,' said Smithy. 'Thanks for your help.'

'*Ja – nee*,' said the Sergeant, swallowing. 'Look, I don't know what this is about but I'm just a dorp Sergeant, hey?'

'Don't worry,' said Mostert, tucking away the ID. 'But you don't need to mention that we came here either, hey?'

'Whatever you say, Ma'am,' said the Sergeant.

They stepped out into the bright morning. It was already warm and it promised to be hotter.

'It's a Vredenburg registration,' said Smithy. 'CFG. Pretty new back then, I'd guess. I would have thought it would be more on the Cape Town side. It's not her old man's car either because that would be CCM. How could she afford a new car?'

'CFG is also Saldanha Bay,' said Mostert, thoughtfully. 'There's a Recce base there at Langebaan.'

'There were Recces on the Capinga drop,' said Smithy. 'The ones who turned up at the last minute.' He paused to light up a cigarette. He offered

165

Mostert one but she refused. 'I guess we should find out who that number plate belonged to. Maybe they still own it.'

'In you go then,' said Mostert, indicating the police station. 'Go back and ask the nice Sergeant if you can use his phone.'

It didn't take long. The car was back with its original owner, a nun at a Catholic boarding school in Saldanha Bay.

\*

It was more than a couple of hours drive up to Saldanha Bay and Smithy, lulled into contemplation by the hypnosis of a steady fifty limit, went back to thinking of those years growing up in Krugerburg. Something about the soapbox carts, the plain old dorp copper, and the bougainvillea of Montagu had given him a fleeting homesickness which wasn't really homesickness at all because no-one could be homesick for an East rand shithole like Krugerburg, but he didn't have the words to describe just exactly what it was. It was like a feeling of reluctant parting, but, again, he had never been reluctant to part with Krugerburg and had spent a good portion of those teenage years just waiting for the moment when he could finally part with the place. His great wish was to shake that dust from his heels and head for the hills, pausing only briefly and momentarily to piss on the boundary stone. What had sparked this? Of course, it was the bougainvillea because the orange, white and cerise paper tissue flowers that spilled over the white Montagu garden walls mirrored almost exactly the flowers that crowded along the top of Mrs Parr's wall back in Krugerburg.

'Can you smell citrus?' he said, suddenly overpowered by the scent of lemons and oranges. 'Is it your perfume?'

166

'Uh?' said Mostert, waking up from her own reverie. 'Citrus? No. I'm not wearing any. I left it at Grootfontein.'

'Wind the window down,' he said. 'Maybe there's a farm nearby.'

'I can't smell anything,' she said, sniffing.

'Wind the window down,' repeated Smithy. 'You must be able to smell it.'

'No,' she said, opening the window half way. 'Nothing.'

'Well that's odd,' he said, sniffing again. 'For a moment there, I could definitely smell lemons and oranges.'

This was slightly disturbing because it was the second or third time he had smelled citrus this week. He had smelled it during the first interview with wheezy old Pieters and then again in the office that Bridgeman had fixed up and then again when Bridgeman was bitching about them starting on the Klippies early.

'Besides, I don't wear citrus perfume,' she said. 'I like the heavier, musky kinds. Citrus is a bit teenager, don't you think? Musky is more sophisticated.'

'That isn't your perfume?' said Smithy, puzzled.

'Not me,' she replied. 'I don't wear it when I'm in uniform anyway. And certainly not up on the border. It makes the boys go *chop* and they're bad enough at the best of times.'

'It's probably your shampoo then,' said Smithy. 'Mind if I smell your hair?'

167

'Joshua,' said Mostert leaning away. 'Are you tuning me again? Because if this is a routine you use, you should get a better one.'

'No, really,' protested Smithy. 'I'm just eliminating the possibilities.'

'*Ja*, you have done that already.'

They drove on in silence while Smithy thought about the citrus. He had definitely smelled it, he decided. Of that, he was positive, but the mystery of where it came from remained. He wondered if Bridgeman was secretly wearing perfume to make himself more attractive to the Parabats but although he enjoyed the thought of a load of hard men sqweeming like *bakvissies* while trying on the *Charlie* and the *Rive Gauche*, he couldn't really entertain it seriously; especially if they were busy sharing lipsticks and eye shadow at the same time; they'd be scratching each other's eyes out in no time at all. And then Bridgeman had ruled out cleaning products, Mostert had ruled out perfume and Pieters would have to be hosed down with carbolic twice daily for a week if he was to smell of anything but stale tobacco and BO, so just where did the scent come from?

'Maybe it is psychosomatic,' said Mostert, suddenly. 'Maybe it is in your mind. And it is playing tricks on you.'

'I use my nose to smell, Mostert,' replied Smithy. 'And I am not in need of a trick cyclist.'

'No, seriously,' said Mostert. 'I read an article about people smelling things that weren't there for no apparent reason.'

'*Ja*, go into any pub around closing time and you'll get that.'

'It's a symptom of schizophrenia,' she continued.

'Like I said,' repeated Smithy. 'I do not need a trick cyclist. Especially not like the ones in *Cosmo*.'

'It could be your brain telling you something,' said Mostert. 'Do you hear voices in your head?'

Smithy was about to say something very rude but caught himself just in time. She was smiling at him sideways.

'I definitely smelled citrus,' said Smithy. 'And even if I am going mad – and who is not likely to do this in these times, hey? – I am not going anywhere near a shrink.'

The road ahead bent around to the left and cut through a long stretch of bare, brown earth beyond which were two hazy outcrops of striated rock that seemed to have been slotted into the flat landscape at a 45° angle giving Smithy the impression that he was looking at two separate pictures stuck together in a collage. One of them was clear and in sharp focus and dominated the foreground while the second was much more indistinct, the edges blurred and smudged, the lines vague and the horizon uncertain.

'What were you thinking of when you thought you smelled citrus?' asked Mostert.

'The first time, I was wondering what Pieters wanted with me,' replied Smithy, with a sigh. 'When he showed me that picture of Capinga in the newspaper.'

'And the next time?'

'About ten or fifteen minutes later. I was with Bridgeman, wondering what the hell I was supposed to make of this job.'

'And after that?'

'Just after I'd interviewed Steiner,' replied Smithy. 'I asked Bridgeman if he was using citrus bleach or something like that. It was in the office. The day he gave me that Filofax.'

'Is there a connection, do you think?' she said. 'Anything in common?'

'Are you shrinking my head now, Mostert?'

'You said you could smell lemons when Bridgeman tried to stop us getting into the Klippies just before I spotted Anna-Marie in the photograph,' said Mostert, frowning. 'Do you remember that?'

Smithy nodded.

'So?'

'So, that's three times you smelled citrus when looking at the pictures of Capinga,' said Mostert. 'It's a connection.'

'No,' replied Smithy, waving his arm around the landscape. 'It isn't. No Capinga here, is there? No piles of bodies strewn in a heap. No stray arms and legs.'

'OK,' said Mostert, slowly. 'Were the pictures around when you asked Bridgeman about the lemon bleach?'

'We were in the office,' offered Smithy.

'So that's four,' said Mostert. 'The odds are shortening, Smithy.'

'Coincidence.'

'And after you had interviewed Steiner,' asked Mostert, with a light of amused triumph growing in her eyes. 'You were where, exactly?'

'In the office,' conceded Smithy.

'Where the pictures were,' said Mostert, wagging a finger at him. 'Five out of ...how many? You are definitely having some kind of psychotic episode, Joshua. You definitely need a shrink. Go on then, tell me what you were thinking about when you smelled lemons just now, hey?'

*

St Xavier's was one of those late Victorian boarding schools that dotted the country towns across white South Africa. It was built in a curious mix of Cape Dutch and Colonial Gothic, complete with quoins, a small white clock tower topped with a fox and hounds weather vane and a steeply pitched roof pierced by mullion-windowed garrets. Wrapped around it were fine lawns sloping down to a soft mere full of wildfowl and shaded by willows so that the only thing to mar the impression that a substantial piece of Newmarket had been dropped down in the arid semi-desert of the Northern Cape were the sandy tracks that ran through them. That, of course, and the ubiquitous mimosa and acacia and the sound of the Atlantic surf hissing in the bay.

The building was proud and painted well, exuding an air of defiance at the withdrawal of government funding that had resulted from the Church's refusal to submit to the Christian National Education curriculum. It was also half empty for that same reason and although the bell still tolled for classes, there was never the numbers for the usual chattering magpie cacophony of a schoolyard yet the school sailed on, its yellow wood floors polished into a varnished gleam, its chapel humming with prayer and a wheezy harmonium and its kitchens steamy and clashing above the shouts and occasional singing of the cooks. It was a school with a brave face for

171

difficult times and the nuns and lay staff who chivvied and clucked after the girls did so with hope in their hearts and one eye to the north.

'Is this the school that you went to,' asked Smithy, dusty from a long drive punctuated by two punctures and a long wait at a garage to get a 1000k fix on them. 'It's *lekker.*'

'No, Smithy,' replied Mostert. 'This is the school that Anna-Marie got expelled *to* and the last one she attended until they waved her off too.'

They had phoned ahead and were expected and were now ushered into the Headmistress's study by a burly nun with a disapproving air. The room was close and comfortable, the contrast between the strong, warm outside light and the darkness within achieved with the use of awnings and dark furniture that seemed to have an air of old Spain about it. What light was not diffused by the awnings was sucked in by the heavy bookshelves and imprisoned in the impenetrable tomes of theology, philosophy and political economy that lined them while the air was full of dust motes which swirled like phosphorescence whenever anyone made the slightest move, conjuring up images of space, the universe and eternity. Smithy caught the faint smell of incense and under it, the more prosaic scent of cigarette smoke, something from which he drew a temporal comfort.

'May I offer you a sherry?' said Sister Margaret. She was English – by which Smithy understood she was proper English, having clearly been born, brought up, educated and then stamped with the indelible stamp of a Headmistress in England before being shipped out here. Her accent was like the posh, upper class ones he had heard coming out of the mouths of aristocrats and dukes and bowler hatted chaps in films at the bioscope; the ones that usually provoked a volley of catcalls from the Afrikaaners in the audience, but he found it rather pleasant. It was clear, plain and devoid of

172

artfulness or coyness; perhaps it had something of the stables about it and he had the strong impression that this nun would probably call a spade a bloody spade when she needed to. Tall, austere, fifties probably, with an aquiline nose and sharp nostrils, there was something masculine about her, though her figure under her light grey robes was slight and spare and he wondered if she had gone out of her way to suppress any suggestion of femininity in order to accentuate something rather more angularly intellectual in her make-up. 'It isn't too early, is it? Really, I have never been quite able to reconcile myself to the absurd rules requiring a reasonable person to wait for six o'clock. It isn't Lent either.' The clock that ticked away under the crucifix on the wall indicated that it had just gone four. He took an instant liking to her.

She poured three schooners without waiting for an answer and handed them over on a small, finely engraved silver tray. Smithy sniffed and tasted. It was pale and better than the usual brown cooking stuff, that was for sure.

'Bottoms up,' said Sister Margaret. 'And no heel taps.'

Smithy caught the glance from Mostert telling him that he shouldn't knock it back in one go and limited himself to a delicate sip of the bone dry, sticky liquid. Sister Margaret took a sip too, put the glass on the blotter and then sat back behind her desk, folding her fingers together.

'Perhaps you might like to take off your firearms?' she said. 'Although a girls' school is fraught with many dangers, ambush and massacre are not among them.'

Mostert and Smithy unclipped the holsters from their belts, laid them on table under the window and tossed their caps down beside them.

'Anna-Marie van Zyl,' said Mostert. 'This is a Missing Person enquiry and we'd like to get your take on her, if we can.'

'Indeed. I was not aware. How long has she been missing?' asked Sister Margaret.

'Nine years, give or take,' answered Mostert.

Sister Margaret looked up sharply. 'If she wanted to be found, she would certainly have made her feelings known about the matter by now. Have you considered that she might have fled the country and is now comfortably settled abroad?'

'We're trying to establish these things,' replied Mostert, as the photograph of the mass grave at Capinga leaped into her mind. 'Hopefully you could give us some pointers as to her character which might in turn gives us a clue as to what might have happened to her.'

Sister Margaret thought for a few moments in silence, her gaze fixed on the wall high behind them.

'Well, I betray no confidences, I suppose,' she said. 'And after such a long time has passed, it can do no harm to help.' She sipped the sherry again and then looked into the middle distance, as though gathering her thoughts at the lectern before embarking on a sermon. 'Who knows? It might even do some good. Bring some *closure* in the modern parlance. I do so hate the way this American psychology seems to be invading our lives. I always thought Freud to be a complete charlatan, to be honest. But I suppose that is by the by. Anna-Marie van Zyl is the subject for today and since your telephone call this morning, I confess that I have thought of no-one else.'

'Please,' said Mostert. 'Anything you can give us will be a help, I'm sure.'

'In a long career in three continents and any number of schools,' she began. 'There are only a very few pieces of wisdom that I am tolerably certain of. Of these, the most important is that despite impressions to the contrary and despite the nonsense spouted by psychologists and other sundry educational reformers, *children love rules*. They are happiest when they have clear boundaries, clearly explained to them and the consequences of crossing them clearly explained. They respect *certainty* and *predictability*. They crave *stability*. They are happy with *authority* as long as that authority is clear, fair, constant and consistent.'

Smithy began to switch off in disappointment. He had heard variations on this theme many times before and it usually presaged a caning.

'This is something that goes for all children without exception,' she continued, the certainty in her voice, iron hard. 'Those children who are brought up without these disciplines *will* be unhappy. They will challenge, fail and sink into frustrated unhappiness until they are brought to realise that it is the rules that create the framework to be free. For some people, this fact will occur naturally to them; others will be taught it; others still will discover this truth for themselves after long tribulation; some will never discover it and will spend their lives railing against God or the world, blaming anyone and anything for their condition when in reality, it is they who are responsible. These are the people who refuse to accept the staves and bars of the score and so cannot make music; they refuse to accept the reality of line and shade and so cannot paint; they reject all grammar and so cannot express themselves; they damn Pythagoras and so cannot discover the science that God ordered the world with. They lack the courage to submit and understand. They lack the courage to face

175

reality. They lack the courage to be free. Anna-Marie van Zyl was such a creature.'

'Any chance you could be a bit more specific?' said Smithy. 'Some dates or...'

'Sergeant Smith,' said Mostert, icily. 'Let her speak.'

'Thank you,' said Sister Margaret, without rancour and a small smile. 'I do have a tendency to preach, Sergeant Smith. You will forgive me, I'm sure. It is an occupational hazard. Would you prefer something other than sherry? I'm not an habitual beer drinker but I'm sure something might be found somewhere in the kitchens.' She picked up a small silver bell. 'Shall I call?'

'He's fine with sherry,' said Mostert. 'Please, continue.'

'It is a long story.'

'We have time,' said Mostert.

'Very well, then. I shall begin at the beginning,' she said. It was clear on her face from the outset that she had spent the day preparing this exposition and her ordered mind had been composing it, refining it and polishing it like an essay. 'Once or twice in a lifetime one comes across a person whose life has been burdened with a curse - or perhaps 'secret' might be a better word. It matters not. This is not a trivial curse; not a secret of birth or bastardy. Not the sort of secret that you would prefer to forget out of shame for your own foolishness; the time when you were cheated so comprehensively that you still flush with anger at your stupidity and even more so at how you saw all the warning signs – now revealed in glorious technicolour hindsight – and still walked right into the trap. At least this sort of secret teaches a little wisdom, gives you a heightened caution, makes you cock a sharper eye over a pig in a poke, so to speak. No, this was the sort of secret, or curse, that taught no wisdom and allowed for no backward glance at a naivety that could be grown out of. It was much, much more terrible than that. I'm talking about Anna-Marie's mother here, who I became something of a confessor to – not sacramental, mind! *Not* sacramental. But someone to whom she came for solace and guidance which I could not refuse. Her name was Annabel Goodwin-Chalmers before she married Cornelius van Zyl and she hailed from Oxfordshire in England, not far from where I come from too.

'Her secret was not of a crime committed either, Sergeant Smith, if that is what you are hoping for. It never appeared on a record or on a character reference. It was not marked on her driving licence; it did not stop her at the border or from working in sensitive positions in the armed forces or the police; it never held her hostage to a newspaper reporter for she had committed no crime in the accepted sense but only, perhaps, in the one way that did matter; against herself and, if it is not too large a charge, against the life that God gives itself.

'There never seems to have been a time when she was without the burden of this curse but, of course, there must have been one; she was not born with this particular Original Sin. Exactly where and when she acquired it though is known only to her for certain; but somewhere along the way she accepted Eve's Apple and took a bite from it and was from thenceforth expelled from Eden. The sullen regret and bitter glance that often broke out from her was, we might imagine, similar to Adam's regret, Adam's glance, when looking back at the flaming sword of the Angel set at the gates of Eden to guard against his return.'

'Ma'am,' said Smithy. 'I'm not really religious so could you make it a little easier for me?'

'Certainly, I beg your pardon,' she said. 'Do you know what the Curse of God is?'

Smithy did not.

'In punishment for eating the Apple of Knowledge, God condemned Adam to suffer in toil for his daily bread,' she said. 'And Anna-Marie's mother was filled with sheer bloody resentfulness that God had similarly cursed her with the necessity to work. From the beginning, she always gave the impression that she was due a royal pardon, or a partial exemption at least, from work in recognition of the special weight of her particular personality.'

'That's it?' said Smithy. 'She was cheesed off at having to get a job? That was her secret curse?'

'Please, Sergeant Smith, bear with me. It is important for your understanding,' said Sister Margaret.

'On you go,' said Smithy.

'The conviction that she should not be required to work for a living did not, I think, come from her background,' she continued. 'Her parents were reasonably well off, Officer class when that still counted for something, with a comfortable, well-appointed rustic house on an Oxfordshire village green and her father's frequent service abroad entitled her to a place at a decent boarding school; not Eton or Winchester, Sergeant Smith, but still good enough to give her an attractive bearing, the formal social graces and outward self-reliance then thought essential to a well-rounded education,

178

and a confident determination when it came to horses, tennis or croquet. On first acquaintance, the impression she gave was every bit the country-bred public school girl, at home in a clubhouse in Henley or a cocktail party in St. James, destined for a good marriage to a familiar family connection; that would be a young man with a commission in a good county regiment and later on a place as something in the City. She would happily fill the role as wife and mother up at the big house – providing 'an heir and a spare' in the vulgate – and spend her days hosting coffee mornings or handing out prizes as wife of the Chairman of Governors and, quite possibly, acting as chief supporter to a husband with a safe seat on the back benches eventually. And yet she would achieve none of these things.

'People in this country like to dismiss we English as terrible snobs –,' Smithy caught himself before he said anything. ' – but the world of inherited wealth and privilege has been dying for some time now. When Annabel came of age, the men she would have married were all at war. Those who came back came back to a country broken and impoverished by that war. Their investments were in worn out companies whose best men were dead and whose customers were grubbing around the ruins of bombed out cities. Whatever business was left had been snapped up by the Americans and whoever was still standing and still had wealth was soon felled by the socialist government. The Old Boy Network was collapsing, deference was dying, an old school tie was not the automatic door opener it once was; social mobility, Sergeant Smith, was beginning to mean *down* as well as *up*. There were many fewer big houses to look forward to. Many fewer eligible bachelors on the lookout for a debutante – and she was no longer nineteen. So she did what so many other girls did after the war; she

179

took ship for the colonies in search of a husband who would help her evade the curse and keep her in the style to which she was accustomed.

'And all she could find was Cornelius van Zyl?' asked Mostert. 'Was he really the best that she could do?'

'Cornelius van Zyl is a brute of a man where the blacks are concerned but he is not wholly unredeemable,' said Sister Margaret. 'He offered her a life of servants and horses, tennis parties, a swimming pool on a farm that would make a Duchess with deer park in Devonshire envious. In return for which, she would provide him with an heir, of course. Oh, he was slightly rougher around the edges than the men she was used to in England and the church was Calvin rather than Catholic but the compact was tolerably the same. And she took it. It was not Cornelius' fault that she reneged on it. The spare never arrived; Anna-Marie was it; he had no male heir, so he was bilked.'

'He beats the staff,' said Mostert. 'Did he beat her?'

'Not more than is normal,' answered Sister Margaret. 'By which I mean rarely and always with remorse.'

'Bastard.'

Sister Margaret gave a tight smile and went on: 'The child, Anna-Marie, was born within a year or two and the inevitable happened. Annabel had little time for the joys and duties of motherhood; they seemed to her too much like hard work. She handed the baby to other hands as soon as she decently could – *before*, some people thought – and tried to go back to the world of cocktail parties and tennis but it was not possible to do this because those young people who she loved to play tennis and drink cocktails with were busy with their own young families and no longer had so much time for her. So she went further afield, to Cape Town and Johannesburg, but these places weren't London or Paris or New York and although the country life suited her well, she began to miss the sophistication of the Old World. The child, she washed her hands of almost entirely, leaving her to Cornelius and the servants and by the time it was brought home to her that the neglect of the child that her curse demanded was at the root of Anna-Marie's behaviour, it was too late to do anything about it. The child's essential nature had been formed by the very formlessness of the world she had been left alone in.'

'Stubborn and defiant,' said Mostert.

'Unloved and unwanted,' nodded Sister Margaret. 'And she came to us aged fifteen. Which was about ten years too late.'

'Anna-Marie: what was she like here?'

'She was a natural sportswoman. Tall, fit, blonde, clean limbed, without anything that might be called fat, she possessed a body of classical beauty topped by a head of leonine elegance. She moved with her mother's grace, was strong, skilled, confident and attacked physical challenges with absolute relish; she would watch the soldiers from the base when they were out on endurance runs and she would go out and match them. From her father, she had the Captain's air and a physical presence that belied her slightness but she played in no teams; she would sail single-handedly, or row; she would run or play tennis; but never would she contemplate hockey or lacrosse unless forced to by the games mistress; and then she would take up a position in goal where she could lean on the posts and ignore what was going on in front of her.

'In the schoolroom, she performed no better. Though far from unintelligent, something held her back from even a basic diligence; she could learn with enthusiasm when the mood took her; history and astronomy fascinated her to begin with; the stories written in the past and in the stars appealed to the romantic in her, but she would not submit to any sort of discipline when it came to the formal aspects of study. For her, the constellation of Orion was far more than a dreary classification of hydrogen and orbits, and her interest was in its mythical rather than mathematical aspects; the thought of looking deep, deep into those sparkling lights of the past appealed to her but she showed scant interest in radio telescopes, infra-red spectrums and the rest of it; she was a stargazer not an astronomer; History was a pageant, nothing more. In Literature class, the only author that he had any time for was Thomas Hardy and only then because she was fascinated by Bathsheba in *Far from the Madding Crowd* .'

'Who?' said Smithy, receiving a withering look from Mostert in return.

'The heroine of the story is a woman by the name of Bathsheba, who is pursued in love by three quite different men but cannot make up her mind which one to choose,' explained Sister Margaret.

'Oh,' said Smithy.

'Her English teacher saw hope in this and encouraged her to read, but she would not do so seriously,' she continued. 'She claimed that there was nothing worthwhile in books and that real life was happening while she was wasting her time in a classroom. Of course, the reality was that like many immature people she was good at asking questions but rather poor at listening to the answers. When it became obvious that she would never matriculate, her mother came to me and begged me to intervene. So, to my regret, I did. I challenged her to choose a book at random from my shelves and to prove that it was worthless by reading it and then explaining how meaningless it was. It is an old trick of mine but I confess this time it backfired spectacularly. She chose *A Brief Guide to Existentialism* and it turned her into a monster.'

'What's *Existentialism*?' asked Smithy.

'That is a very short question with several very long answers,' said Sister Margaret, drily.

'Just the basics then,' answered Smithy.

'It is a philosophy that divorces an act from context, motive, tradition, morality, law or religion and absolves the person committing the act from responsibility for it.'

'Can you make that a bit easier for me?' said Smithy, frowning.

'The philosophy means that you may do as you please in life.'

'Sounds alright to me.'

'It is a superficially attractive philosophy to those of weak mind,' said Sister Margaret. 'For they take it to mean that they may do as they please and absolve themselves of the consequences. They develop a superciliousness to those of us who have not abdicated responsibility for ourselves and our actions and come to regard us as little more than blind slaves. They use it as a justification for any and all actions that a reasonable person might regard as wrong.'

'Such as?' said Mostert.

'Often the actions are of a sexual nature, which a Catholic might call sinful,' said Sister Margaret. Smithy half expected her to blush, being a nun, but her demeanour remained austerely academic. 'But they avail of the same justification for acts of barbarous violence.'

'Terrorism,' said Smithy, coming to an understanding. 'You turned her into a Terrorist.'

'If she has become one, then it was I that set her on that road, certainly,' admitted Sister Margaret. 'But I should say that the chaos that would result from a universal adoption of Existentialism as a philosophy was already present in Anna-Marie; the formless rebellion, the pointless resistance to team sports; the rejection of disciplined study and the destination-less journeys that she undertook as a runaway all pointed to this.'

'But she didn't just run out and start planting bombs,' said Mostert. 'What happened?'

'There was a creeping habit of introspection to begin with, of self-absorption rather than self-awareness, growing stronger in her in the remaining time she spent here. She began to smoke marijuana occasionally, like many teenagers in search of some spiritual awakening that they cannot find in the church, but though she would indulge this drug from time to time in the following years, it did not take a hold of her.'

'The *following years*?' said Smithy. 'You saw her after you expelled her?'

Sister Margaret nodded but would not be interrupted: 'Neither was it a gateway to other, worse things; she could not be tempted by cocaine or heroin or any other of the myriad temptations of these times, mainly because she learned very early on that they could not relieve her of her

184

burdens. She was also aware of the costs and dangers that brought drugs to the market and wanted no part of them; once, while out on an expedition to an African village to buy marijuana she caught sight of some white boys on a similar expedition except that they were being offered *moonlight* which she discovered was an eight year old child being prostituted for pennies. She sought *tranquillity* in smoking marijuana, she once told me, and she could not achieve it with that thought in her mind. I took hope from that. As a Catholic, I believe that the Divine Spark is always present in a person and that through the actions of God's grace even the greatest sinner can be brought back from the lip of the pit. I believed that she possessed a fundamental decency and there, in that revulsion, was proof if it was wanted.'

'You still expelled her?'

'She was caught *in flagrante delicto* in the dormitory with a younger girl. There were also drugs present and the proffered explanation was inadequate. I could not break our own rule without opening the floodgates,' answered Sister Margaret. 'The Headmistress had to come before the Nun in this case but I used what influence I had to get her into Varsity. Her parents were grateful for this, at least, and paid her fees even though her chosen Major was philosophy.'

Smithy looked across at Mostert and she nodded in understanding. Van Zyl had denied all knowledge of Anna-Marie after she was expelled from school. Another confirmation that he was lying.

'In did little good though,' she continued. From the beginning her malaise was total. She attended few, if any, lectures or tutorials and certainly nowhere near the bare minimum needed to see her through the formality of First Year exams. That she survived into the second year was due to a

185

judicious change to a less demanding course, but even so, her reluctance to commit to academic study remained; she professed an interest in Ecology, but again, her interest was expressed in terms of an attachment to animals rather than the economics, geology, meteorology and chemistry of the subject, and that interest quickly dissipated. She also burned through her allowance and ran up an overdraft to add to the credit she had run up at the Greek shop, so that she was existing on funds that were restricted to say the least; her daily meal was usually restricted to mealies and whatever she might scrounge from others. And, of course, what I would loan her from time to time when she made the journey up here for that purpose. She slept late, rarely emerged before midday; ate; returned to her room until the late afternoon when she would re-emerge, eat once more and then visit the shop to buy cheap wine, which she would drink while reading into the early hours. This, of course, was not an outrageously unusual lifestyle for a student; what made it remarkable was its relentless nature and the fact that she utterly resented it and utterly resented the need to learn from her experience and make changes. In this, she was very much like her mother in her refusal to compromise with the facts of her existence.

'Where money was concerned, instant gratification was her unvarying rule, a rule that she never subsequently broke. She could not hold on to it. Over the years, her landlords learned and demanded and got payment in advance; whether she would turn up for an outing with friends, I soon discovered, depended on which route she took from her house; if her chosen route went past a record shop, she would invariably go in, buy music and arrive broke or not at all. She would indulge in pointless extravagances like going to expensive restaurants and then sending back the food. Whenever she started a job, she would always buy the best of whatever she wanted at that moment, hang the cost and put it on tick. Of course, she was soon penniless and varsity had had enough of her, so in 1968, she was sent down from there too.

'For her mother, it was the last straw. Or rather, Annabel took it as the excuse she needed to bring the disappointments of her life to an end. While she was flitting between Cape Town dinner parties and Johannesburg cocktail parties, Cornelius had slipped back into the traditional Boer way of life and, of course, every time she heard a tale of the Swinging Sixties in London, she resented that she had missed it. She felt that both age and geography had conspired against her to cheat her of the life she had always imagined would be hers. In her last years, she had tried to shake free of her curse and of her regrets. She tried to make up for her neglect of Anna-Marie, but of course it was too late. Anna-Marie's upbringing alone made her unrecognisable from the girls that Annabel had known back in wartime England; she was South African, not English, in all but parentage and her erratic, uncontrollable behaviour was mysterious, unfathomable, to her. So one day, she went out for a last ride, retired to her room and took an overdose of barbiturates.

'Anna-Marie did not go to the funeral,' she said, after a pause. 'As one might expect, she had no feeling for her mother. I suppose they might have overcome this given time and patience but…they did not have the chance.'

'But you still saw Anna-Marie,' said Mostert, quietly.

'She would borrow the car from time to time, but that was not the real reason she came back,' said Sister Margaret, sitting back in her chair. 'She came back to challenge me. She came back to throw my religion, politics, apartheid, abortion, the state of the world in my face as though it was all my fault. She questioned, but wanted no answers and each time I did answer a question, she came back with another. Sometimes she would slam *The Communist Manifesto* or some other banned work on my desk and challenge me to refute it but even such a simple task as that she would not suffer to be completed. She was not rational. She was very angry but unable to express that anger because she had rejected all the disciplines that would allow her to articulate it. Rage had overcome her.'

'Were you aware that she was arrested in 1971 while in possession of your car?' asked Mostert.

'I was,' answered Sister Margaret. 'Cornelius and a policeman brought the car back and Cornelius pleaded with me to find a convent for her. Of course, I told him that the days of packing off difficult women to be confined in convents were long over. He then asked if she should be sent to an asylum.'

'Should she have been?' asked Mostert.

'I am not a psychologist,' answered Sister Margaret. 'And I distrust the discipline but I thought that perhaps she might benefit from such a course of therapy and suggested a physician in Cape Town. In past times we might have called for an Exorcist, so deep was her disturbance...'

'You think she was possessed?' said Smithy.

'There is Evil in the world, Sergeant Smith,' said Sister Margaret. 'It is capable of taking physical form and inflicting terrible suffering. Horns and Tails *do* exist, even in these modern times, but fortunately they are rare and in this case, I think *not*. Anna-Marie was a creation of her circumstances and of her education undoubtedly, but she was also a creation of her *self*. She *chose* her paths, even though they began in less than ideal circumstances. And unlike the Existentialist philosophers, I hold that she is responsible for those choices.'

'When did you last hear of her?' asked Mostert.

'Cornelius took her away, I do not know where, though I think she might have been sent abroad. There was an enquiry made about the dates of her attendance here at the school that came from a London address a few years ago – 1975, I think – and one from the police the following year but nothing more. They were not unusual enquiries and they were of the type that do come to us from time to time from potential employers.'

'That's it?' said Mostert. 'Sure? Any detail can be a help.'

Sister Margaret looked sideways out towards the window. Out over the Atlantic the sun was beginning to set and the gold of evening was rising up from the land.

'She was not a demon,' said Sister Margaret, quietly. 'But I do think she was a remarkably dangerous young woman.'

'And you never saw her again?'

'Only once,' said Sister Margaret. 'I caught a glimpse of her going into the military base over the water at Langebaan in 1976. I called to her but she did not hear. I presumed that perhaps a course of psychological therapy had worked and that she had finally settled down and got a job in something defence-related. Hence the police enquiry of the preceding year. I understand that the military can often find jobs for highly dangerous young women.'

'That's about right,' said Smithy, under his breath.

189

'And you're sure it was her?' said Mostert, ignoring him.

'Her appearance had changed somewhat,' replied Sister Margaret. 'She had put on some weight and her hair was much shorter, but it was certainly her.'

'You didn't attempt to make contact with her again?' said Mostert.

'I did not,' said Sister Margaret. 'To be quite honest, I am more than a little afraid of her. She is the only pupil I have ever taught that I really can say that about.'

\*

'So she's ANC one minute and on an army base the next,' said Smithy, lighting up and handing Mostert a Lucky Strike. They were driving back into Vredenburg where they had booked rooms for the night and Smithy, wrenching on the handbrake as he waited for a military convoy to pass before hanging a right, took the opportunity to sum up the state of play. 'She's a lesbian and she's not a lesbian. She smokes *dagga* but hates drugs. She hates school enough to keep getting booted out of it but keeps going back to debate with the Headmistress who booted her. She's brainy enough to go to varsity but not clever enough to pass the exams. She's richer than a Joburg goldbug but runs up tick at the Greek shop. Her father wants to do right by her but denies any knowledge of her.'

'And the BOSS wants her investigated to find out why her corpse is mouldering in a mass grave,' added Mostert, blowing out smoke into the evening air. 'But they don't want to do it themselves. You forgot that bit.'

'So what do you reckon?' said Smithy. 'You still think our little rebel is just a bit misguided and went off to seek meaning for her life working for the Liberation in a SWAPO camp in Angola?'

'It's still a possibility,' answered Mostert.

'A remote one,' said Smithy. 'Hippy chicks don't usually join the army and especially they do not join the Recces. I'm telling you; she's a BOSS spy. And I am willing to double up on the coin flip on the strength of that fact alone: twenty bucks?'

'Twenty bucks it is. All that Existentialism nonsense is just the sort of thing to make a disturbed girl like that become disturbed enough to go completely nuts and run off to SWAPO or the ANC,' said Mostert. 'Sister Margaret should have spanked that rubbish out of her seeing as she was the one who put it into her.'

'And now we must go and get our heads shrunk by some bullshit trick cyclist in Cape Town,' sighed Smithy.

'Who will no doubt claim it is all a matter of *client confidentiality*,' said Mostert, wearily. 'And tell us precisely nothing.'

'Look on the bright side. We still going to get a free weekend in Cape Town,' said Smithy. 'If you don't fancy that, you could take me home and introduce me to your Mom.'

'Right after you introduce me to yours,' replied Mostert, drily.

The stream of Samil trucks rumbled on and on, each at a regulation distance from the vehicle in front, each one with a couple of brown uniformed conscripts peering over the tailboard in identical attitudes of resigned boredom.

191

'Did you do your basic here?' asked Smithy, without real interest.

'Heidelberg,' replied Mostert. 'There weren't that many of us so they just tacked us on to the Gymnasium there.'

Smithy looked left and saw the end of the convoy in sight and slid down in his seat to rest his head on the back of it while it went by.

'Fish and chips?' he asked. 'And then a couple of cold ones?'

'Sounds good to me,' replied Mostert, airily. 'Do you know a good place in Vredenburg?'

'Me? No,' said Smithy, as the last truck rumbled by. 'Maybe there'll be *Spur* there. We could get a steak, if you like.'

'Sure,' said Mostert, indicating the road. 'You can go now.'

'Let's give them a minute to get ahead so we don't have to eat their dust all the way. Finish up the cigarettes,' said Smithy. 'Or maybe we could get in the back seat and while away the time that way.'

Mostert flicked her eyebrows up. 'I heard one psychologist say that men think about sex every eleven minutes,' she said. 'You could ask about this tomorrow, hey? Get yourself checked out while we are questioning him?'

The light was nearly gone now and Smithy was about to pull out when he registered a set of headlights on an approaching car quickly flick on and off, followed by a movement of the windscreen wipers and then finally the illumination of the interior light.

'Let's let the Hire car go by,' said Smithy, letting off the handbrake and balancing the clutch.

'Fuck, Smithy, get down!' hissed Mostert, as the car hurtled by and the clean, white shock of Colonel Steiner stood out pearl and yellow in the quick moment before the interior light was extinguished.

'What the fuck is he doing down here?' said Smithy. 'Please, please tell me that it is just a coincidence.'

'Somehow, I doubt it,' said Mostert, rising up. 'He'll be off to that Recce base. Follow him!'

'I think we can just safely assume that that is where he is going,' replied Smithy. 'Unless you want him to know he's being followed and on a road as bare as this, we can make another safe assumption that he would notice us following him.'

'Get after him, Smithy,' she said, removing her beret and shaking loose her hair. 'This is South Africa. All the roads are bare. We need to be sure. And take that stupid police cap off or he's bound to notice.'

They followed at a distance. Steiner was going to the Recce base. And Smithy could smell citrus.

*

Sunday Last

It was not so much the pursuit that screwed things up for Mickey as the fact that he had to change direction to lose it. The shots that had alerted him to the fact that SWAPO, FAPLA and probably the Cubans were coming for him were not dangerous or even very close and he doubted whether they were aimed at all; possibly some *oke* just clearing his weapon or letting off a negligent discharge; but they could not be ignored and so Mickey quickly began to weigh up his options. He had already been going for three days and making good progress but clearly something or someone had alerted the enemy to his presence – if indeed it was him they were looking for. It was possible he had been spotted from the air, more likely that he had been spotted by some villager or other; perhaps his spoor had been found and read. He didn't know but he had to do something to take account of this unwelcome new development.

There were a number of schools of thought on how to evade a pursuit. The first held that the correct thing to do was put on a course of 180° and proceed with all speed to the home objective. It had the advantage of being simple but also the disadvantage of being obvious and a pursuer would seek to leapfrog the hunted and so trap him between the hammer and the anvil; this was very near the principle of establishing a stop line dropped in the rear of the enemy and then sweeping up towards it that the Parabats used in attack. The second option was to go to ground, lay up somewhere well-hidden and camouflaged and hope the enemy got tired of looking for you. Mickey thought this was a good tactic for night but didn't like the fact that it handed the initiative to the enemy the rest of the time. He was inclined to be pro-active in matters of life and death so he decided on a third method. This was to head in an unexpected direction with frequent changes of course designed to convince the enemy that you had evaded them and that they could now give up and go home. If you were heading south, then take a north easterly course, then a westerly one and then a south easterly one, effectively making a great loop that hopefully would take you behind the enemy while he wandered off in pursuit of something that wasn't there; the safest place to be, in effect, was behind the enemy.

The down side of this was that it could add days to the journey. Worse; it meant more nights being preyed on by insects.

\*

## 08

### Friday

'*Fokken client confidentiality?*' roared Smithy. 'You giving me *fokken client confidentiality* when you just handed over the *fokken* files to the first person who wanders in here with a badge and bad manners, hey?'

Dr Maybank was not long qualified and certainly not qualified to deal with Smithy in one of his professional rages. He was just into his mid-twenties and sported a beard and long, unruly black hair like Cat Stevens on a bad day, which for him, this was. Right now, he was on tip toes against the rear wall of his consulting room while Smithy hand one hand at his throat and the other poised to deliver a very hard, hard right.

'For God's sake, Smithy,' said Mostert. 'Put him down. He's just a baby.'

'Just a *baby? Just a baby?* Captain Mostert, he is the same age as me,' answered Smithy, squeezing the throat a little more.

'*Ja*, well, you must have had a hard life, hey?' she answered, in her best tone of professional boredom. 'Now put him down.'

Smith let go and Dr Maybank dropped onto his feet and massaged his throat.

'Sit on you chair,' ordered Mostert. 'You say he was a tall, blonde soldier type. Did he leave his name?'

'No,' said Maybank, pulling himself into his wheeled office chair.

'It's *No Ma'am* to you,' said Smithy, slapping him round the back of the head like he was a naughty schoolboy. 'Can't you see she is an officer? I presume you did do your National Service? Please do not tell me that you are one of these hairy draft-dodging mompies?'

'No, Ma'am,' repeated Maybank, massaging his throat. His face was flushed and puffy and the marks of Smithy's fingers were still visible on his neck while his left eye was beginning to swell up into a fine silver medal. 'But he was definitely Parabat or Recce or something like that.'

'It's Steiner,' mouthed Smithy. 'Steiner has nicked the *fokken* files.'

Mostert nodded.

'Right, so now you will tell us what was in Anna-Marie van Zyl's file,' said Mostert. 'And I'll need details. And don't say *client confidentiality* again; it upsets Sergeant Smith here.'

Smithy slapped him once more for good measure.

'Look, I just assisted,' said Maybank, ducking his head in anticipation of another blow. 'It was one of Dr Scheepers' clients but he thought it would be good experience for me. It was a pretty rare case…and, well…I just assisted, OK?'

'So what did you *assist* Dr Scheepers to do to Anna-Marie van Zyl?' said Mostert.

'Look, Scheepers is one of these old time guys, OK?' began Maybank. 'National Party, Dutch Reformed Church; he's really into this crazy racial stuff and gives up a lot of his time to the Youth Preparedness camps. He goes out camping with the youth and tells them all sorts of things about Communist Terrorists and shows them pictures of dead bodies in the hope that they will toughen up for the army. He does a bit of preaching too. He is right up there with PW Botha.'

196

'Is he in the *Broederbond*?' asked Mostert.

'I don't know,' replied Maybank. 'But he's hardly going to let on to an English speaker like me if he is. I'd say he was pretty thick with the apartheid crowd though.'

'If he hates the English so much, what's he doing employing you?' said Smithy, pushing the back of his head forward.

'He thinks I can be educated,' answered Maybank. 'I'm another one of his pet projects.'

'OK,' said Mostert, giving Smithy a nod. Smithy hit Maybank round the head again. Mostert sent her eyebrows up. Smithy grimaced an apology in return.

'OK Dr Maybank,' said Mostert. 'From the beginning please.'

Maybank shook his head, stretched out his arms in front of him so that they stuck out of the sleeves of his white coat like sticks and began to explain.

Dr Scheepers had not been the first port of call for Anna-Marie but her case had been referred to him by Sister Margaret's preferred physician because he had been called up to do psychological evaluations for the new intake of conscripts. This suited Cornelius van Zyl because Scheepers was an Afrikaaner of the right sort for what he wanted done to his daughter and Scheepers had always wanted to work on a case that would prove that the American Psychiatric Association was wrong to try to declassify Homosexuality as a mental disorder. He was convinced that with the right combination of aversion therapy and hormone treatment, a person might be cured of the disease and re-enter society as a full person, free of perverted desire and ready to play a full and normal role in society.

'Tell us about this 'Aversion therapy',' said Mostert, offering a cigarette.

'I don't smoke,' replied Maybank.

Anna-Marie was subjected to twice daily sessions of Aversion therapy over a period of ten days at the clinic. They consisted of connecting her upper arm to electrodes and then handing her images of naked women to look at. While she was asked to describe how she felt about the pictures, she would be given a series of electric shocks which increased in intensity until she was experiencing real discomfort. At that point the shocks would cease and the pictures would be replaced with images of handsome young men and she would be encouraged to talk in a positive way about them. The procedure would be repeated several times in the hour long session at the end of which she would be given a cocktail of drugs which would induce a mild euphoria even as the hormone tablets worked to 'correct' her hormonal balance and turn her back into a 'real' woman.

'How much electricity was involved?' asked Mostert.

'Not much,' replied Maybank. 'It's just enough to twist the muscle in your arm. The pain never gets above someone giving you a mule bite like they did in school. It's nowhere near what you guys use…'

'You know, I might put that to the test,' said Smithy, administering another slap. 'Where's the kettle flex?'

'Later, Smithy,' said Mostert, frowning. 'Did the therapy work?'

'Did the therapy work?' replied Maybank, smiling incredulously. 'Of course, it didn't! Being a Lesbian isn't a disease! Are you people completely *bevok*? I can wire you up right now, if you like, and cure you of that – (given time and enough current).'

'Don't be cheeky,' said Smithy, handing out another slap.

'Anna-Marie *did not respond to treatment*,' said Maybank, adopting a tone of officialise. 'Scheepers was really disappointed.'

'And the hormones?'

'Yes, well, they did have an effect,' admitted Maybank. 'They made her even more bad tempered than she was when she came in. She didn't want the treatment in the first place and…well…we did have the consent forms signed…but…'

'Her father signed them for her,' said Mostert.

'I think so,' replied Maybank. 'Anyway, she had to be physically restrained before, during and after the therapy.'

'She screamed the place down?'

'The opposite,' said Maybank. 'She was in hysterics the whole time. Scheepers thought this was a resistance response to the treatment. I think she just thought the whole thing was so ridiculous that all she could do was laugh. And curse. She cursed a lot. I can't say I blame her. She also kept asking me to get her more Valium. After ten days of this, even Scheepers' patience was busted and he ended the treatment. She was sent up to Pretoria to the Military Hospital there for a while.'

'For more of the same?'

'I guess so because she came back here a year or so later and Scheepers went through the whole rigmarole again,' said Maybank. 'With exactly the same success as before. That's when he gave up.'

'Her father took her away?' asked Mostert.

199

'No,' said Maybank. 'It was the guy who came yesterday and took away the files. He turned up and Scheepers handed her over and she went back to the military hospital at Pretoria. Then Scheepers told me to keep quiet as it was all Top Secret.'

'That's twenty bucks you owe me,' mouthed Smithy, triumphantly. 'I told you she was a spy.'

*

Luanda, Angola

1975

Steiner was cool. Steiner understood. From the minute he had come into the ward in that stupid, stupid hospital he had seen and understood and she in turn had seen and understood him. She remembered every detail of that sharp, white outline; the tense bearing that was simultaneously relaxed; the poise and the cold eyes that saw through things, right to the heart of things, right to the heart of complicated things and perceived in an instant the truth, the *real* truth, not the bullshit that she had been served up all her life. The way he knew she had not taken the Valium had come as no surprise to her; all either of them had to do was to look around to perceive that in a ward full of zombies they were the only sane, clear, clean ones. Even the staff in this place were doped up; and Steiner knew that she was making a little money by selling her pills back to the dispensary staff, who sold them on to the *moffies* and addicts in Ward 22, who needed them to stay out of the war.

'It is the *act*,' he had said, without introduction. 'It is the purity, the cleanliness of the *act* that counts. Nothing else. To *act* is to live life honestly, fully and naturally. Disregard anything but the *act*.'

200

And then, he had taken off the handcuffs and told her to follow and she had done so, on the instant, without pausing to collect her meagre possessions, without bothering with a bag, without regret, without doubt and desirous of nothing but to *act*.

He had driven her in silence through the night, northwards and westwards she thought but, really, she had hardly cared. There was something in his demeanour that was so absolutely commanding, so overwhelmingly masculine that she hardly dared speak and when she thought that she might, she realised that she did not want to. The silence was all encompassing and neither the turn of the engine, nor the passing of other vehicles or the sound of her own breathing could break it. Sometime in the night they had arrived at a compound and he had dismounted from the vehicle to open a wire gate in a chain link fence and then they had passed through and into an island distinct from the rest of the veldt, the country and her life to date. He had shown her to a bungalow, handed over the keys and motioned her towards the door. She turned the lock and then threw the keys into the bush and her education had begun.

First, it was physical. An instructor took her through gymnastic exercises, pull ups, push ups, sit ups, star jumps, parallel bars, rings and weights and would then accompany her on long endurance runs.

'You must prepare your body for the *act*,' Steiner had said and though he had said it evenly, without command, she took it as one and accepted the discipline for now there was a point to it. 'Your body is not clean. It must be purified so that the *act* might be venerated.' In the months that followed she found her strength again, found that the years of dissipation could be repealed, regained her athleticism and pushed it further until she was fitter and stronger, more confident in her prowess than she had ever

201

been. The pain of exercise she accepted, waited for it to come and go so that the pleasure of tingling, fully formed, tight limbs might assert itself when the sweat had been sluiced off.

Later, it was philosophical but Steiner conducted it in a way that was beyond the meagre powers of the pettifogging varsity hypocrites, for whom the subject was no more than a meal ticket and an excuse to seduce their students. Outside, under the vast, vast ocean of the Milky Way, Steiner taught her to read, not skim; to think, not repeat; to wonder at the universe, not rage at it; to brush away the fogs and mist and see the sharpness and clarity.

'To see the *essence* of ourselves is to see the commission of the *act*,' he told her and she realised that she had been blind to all true things up until that moment and that there was a euphoria in that liberating knowledge greater than anything she had ever received from a chemical. Later, as he picked out for her the constellations that she dimly remembered had once interested her, he went further and declared that there was no *good* or *evil* in the world, beyond that which a person might decide for themselves to be *good* or *evil* for these concepts were constructed by society and it was absurd that society might dictate to the autonomous individual. 'You must always be true to your own truth,' he had said, and it seemed to her that he had handed her a telescope to make the stars leap into focus.

'And I am Zarathustra,' she replied. 'This is the point of this education. To become *übermensch.*'

'Partly,' said Steiner. 'The overcoming of the limitations of the self and of the body are only preliminary to the commission of the *act*. The *act is all.*'

Next came weapons training.

'For why?' she had asked.

'For the discipline of mind and body,' he had said. 'For the sharpening of reflex. For the understanding of what differentiates the small *act* from the greater, the ultimate *act.*'

'Am I being trained to kill?' she had asked.

'You are not,' he had reassured her. 'You are being trained to *act* and to understand that the *act* is justification for itself.'

Pistol, rifle, assault rifle, grenade, machine gun, RPG; then mine, plastic explosive, fuse, timer.

She lost track of time but it did not matter because she tuned her body to the simpler, older rhythm of night and day, and the coming of weather and although she was aware of other people on the compound, she rarely caught more than a glimpse of them but found that she did not need company other than her own, Steiner's and the brief and meagre interactions of her instructors. Steiner was away, often for quite long periods, but she felt his presence around her with each passing day. For a while, she went away to a place which she thought might be the Lowveldt on the Mozambique border where she learned to live and move and hunt in the bush and there was another week or so in what she thought might be the Caprivi Strip for the same purpose. A year, give or take, went by she thought, but such things as time had little meaning to her now that she had learned to live according to Steiner's existentialism. She needed no-one but Steiner and she felt sure that she was close to arriving at the moment where she had overcome this last desire and achieved the state of *übermensch*; after that she would truly be free.

It came the day she shot the springbok, gutted it, skinned it, cooked it over coals and ate its toasted heart and it was a day that was precious in her memory. The tingle in her finger as she controlled her breathing, took in the wind strength and direction, put the sight on the creature's head and then *willed* the bullet away on its perfect trajectory was as nothing to the blood rush of adrenalin as the triumph of her conquest coursed through her being.

After that things moved at a different pace. She was briefed, very quickly, on a mission and within a day or so was in a car heading for the Zimbabwe border. Once over it, she had boarded the plane for Amsterdam on a false passport, caught the train to Hoek van Holland and then the ferry for Harwich and from thence the train to London. In a pub in Camden Town she had gathered up the package that a man she never saw left on the seat for her, taken the tube to an address in Kings Cross where she checked into a hotel that wasn't interested in names or whether the room was for a day, a night, a week or an hour. There she unwrapped the package, made sure the fuse was appropriate, checked the timer and then as soon as the neon had replaced the daylight, set out for a third address across the city in Fulham. It was a third floor flat in an Edwardian block and she entered the building with the key provided, skirted past a bicycle under the arch of the hall way and went quickly, ordinarily up the stairs. Outside 311, she took out the package from the Tesco bag, switched the timer – one minute would be plenty – placed it against the door and went down the stairs in exactly the ordinary way that she had come up them. By the time the bomb tore off the door and sent a sheet of flame through the flat within, she was already two streets away on a bus heading for Fulham Broadway. By the time, the Fire Brigade arrived she had picked up the suitcase handed to her by another man she never saw and was on her way to catch the evening flight to Cape Town on another false passport. The next morning, Steiner picked her up from D.F. Malan, debriefed her and sent her on to the base at Langebaan. She had been away from South Africa for less than a week and yet had burnt out SWAPO's London intelligence cell, killing one operative and leaving two others with life changing burns, which BOSS rated a major success. For her, she remembered, it had been the vindication of her philosophical training. The last vestiges of those petty nonsenses of restraint - good, evil, morality, religion, law, tradition - she had slewed off like a snake shedding a skin. She had passed the final test. She was free.

After that, Steiner had said there were no more tests, no more orders, no more missions for she was *übermensch* and need only choose the *acts* that she chose to commit herself. If she wished to accept his suggestions and help, then he would be willing to help her *act* and when she indicated that she would be prepared to consider such help and suggestions, he sent her to walk among the enemy.

'It will be like dining with panthers. The Portuguese will leave Angola and there will be revolution and civil war. I will need eyes and ears there,' he had said and she had nodded and returned to London. There she claimed asylum, enrolled at the university to study Portuguese and became involved in the student anti-apartheid movement. There were meetings and demos and chanting outside the South African Embassy in Trafalgar Square and trips to Lunar House to have her visa extended, more meetings, more demos, more chanting, a period which she had been warned would go on for much longer than she might imagine before an opportunity to move further up the chain would present itself. In the end, it was the opportunity of a study trip and student exchange to Cuba that provided it; these were common ways for the Soviets, Cubans, SWAPO and the ANC to recruit gullible students to their cause. When the next university vacation came around, she was granted a visa for Angola and, most fortuitously, landed herself a placement teaching English at Sonangol, the newly nationalised state oil company of the newly independent People's Republic of Angola, as part of her gradual induction to the SWAPO underground. It was a position that so suited her, she told Mr. Mason of the British Embassy who came to visit her, that she intended to stay in Luanda for the foreseeable future, even though the outbreak of civil war made it an increasingly dangerous place.

Steiner was pleased with her she knew, and yet that mattered less to her than the fact that she was able to slip so completely into the skin of another personality while retaining her own *essence*. It was indeed like dining with panthers and she fed off the tension and savoured the heightened sense of reality that a diet of adrenalin gave her until she came to believe that Steiner's description of her task was wrong in one important respect; she was not dining *with* panthers, but *among* them, for she herself had become a panther, perhaps the greatest of them and the sense of power that she drew from that thought was intoxicating. As she grew into the role, so she attracted more attention to herself; she ceased being an English teacher and became an aide, an assistant, to a series of men, always black, who saw a white woman serving them as the ultimate status symbol; she realised that she was something of a curiosity among both the Angolans and the SWAPO people, but played to its strengths; she was not the only white South African in exile and playing a part in the struggle, she explained, and they could expect more as time went on. She expected to be seen as an ornament at both the company events and those chicken and rice dinners that SWAPO organised and accepted the role willingly for the doors that it opened – and those doors often contained filing cabinets which she duplicated and sent back in the direction of Steiner. It was she who sent the first detailed information on the Cuban forces entering Angola to ensure the Communist government won the civil war. It was she who alerted Steiner to the possibility that one of the factions involved in the fighting would be prepared to accept asylum in South Africa; from them would be born the formidable 23 Leopard Battalion.

And now, she was here, armed with nothing more than a torch and a battered old sedan on a beach by the oil refinery in Luanda Bay waiting for extraction before the South African Defence Force began its advance on the city during Operation Savannah. It was with regret that she was leaving because she felt that she could have taken the *act* much much further, perhaps even to the point where she might hunt a president or at least a senior minister but she had allowed Steiner to persuade her that with the army closing on the city, she would be vulnerable to the formless violence that always went with the fall of an African city and such trivialities were beneath the notice of the *übermensch*. Besides, he wanted to debrief her in person; there was only so much that a document could reveal. It was her insights that he sought and these were best shared at length and in person. It was time to come in and a submarine would be waiting for her. It was the submarine that persuaded her; childish though the impulse was, this would be an experience that would be new.

*

'Friday night in Cape Town,' said Smithy, stretching gloriously as they entered the bar. '*Lekker*. How about the *Wine Barrel*?'

'You know I hate it when you hit people when you are interrogating them,' replied Mostert, irritably. 'You always get more by co-operation.'

'True,' replied Smithy. 'But it's not so quick. And we got a lot quick, hey? We know now that Anna-Marie was definitely mixed up with Steiner. She was spying on SWAPO for him, *ja*? And she got wasted in the air strike when she went up to Capinga on some sneaky beaky, which wasn't in his plan I bet. So now his nuts are in the mangle for the fuck up, he's trying to clear up his spoor now that she is dead. So it's case closed. Mystery solved. Pieters gets the answer to why a white girl is in a mass grave and we can go down into Cape Town and get really wasted with a clear conscience knowing what a good job we have done and make our report on Monday morning and collect our medals for good work and meritorious conduct on Tuesday. And don't forget the twenty bucks, you now owe me.'

'It's a theory,' said Mostert.

'It's more than a theory,' said Smithy. 'It's a fine excuse for a weekend and a viable story which nothing now is likely to disrupt.'

'And I still don't like it when you hit people.'

'That trick cyclist really tuned me. Really, Trudi, I'm *gatvol* of his kind. You just know he's going to be on the plane somewhere *lekker* with his qualifications packed up in a suitcase the minute things get really tough with the blacks here.'

'Isn't that what you want to do?'

'*Ja*, of course,' replied Smithy, with a grimace. 'But with my particular qualifications I can't see either Her Majesty's Bobbies or the ANC welcoming me with open arms.'

'Sorry, Smithy,' she replied, softening a little. 'For a moment I just forgot.'

'Lucky you.'

'Get some drinks in, Smithy, and I'll call in,' she said, going towards the public phone booth in the corner. 'Then we'll maybe go down to Muizenburg or someplace.'

'The Britannia Hotel?' said Smithy, hopefully.

'No,' replied Mostert. 'And drive carefully, hey? This isn't the border. There are other cars on the road. You nearly hit most of them - mainly when you were looking for the gears.'

'Maybe we should call in *after* the weekend?' said Smithy. 'Just in case you reconsider?'

Mostert ignored him and going under the Perspex bubble of the canopy began to dial.

'Two double Klippies and coke,' said Smithy, to the barman. 'Do you do pies here?'

'Sausage rolls, Mutton curry or pepper steak?' answered the barman. 'Wait while I get some ice, hey?'

While the barman rattled around the storeroom, Smithy pondered happily on his rapidly advancing education in the mysteries of sexual attraction. The news that homosexuality was not a disease had brought him a great deal of comfort because he had been considering the possibility that as he spent a lot of time in the company of men he might actually be at risk of catching it. This was not something that he wanted to happen and he had hoped that the psychological evaluation that all conscripts went through would have weeded out those who might infect him if, indeed, homosexuality was a disease. He was pretty sure that this process had worked in the police because he had never come across any *moffies* in blue but he could not say that with complete confidence about the army brown jobs, especially now that he knew about Mickey Epstein and the Parabat *moffies*. He didn't even want to consider the navy because he thought that it might even be compulsory there or at least rife in epidemic proportions. So now that the Doctor had assured him that homosexuality was not catching, he felt much happier and an awful lot more secure.

He also drew comfort from the fact that Aversion therapy did not work because, so he reasoned, if you could make a Lesbian like men by giving her some electric shocks and letting her see some dirty pictures, then it stood to reason that you could do the same in reverse to a healthy heterosexual, red-blooded male like himself. The thought of swapping an appreciation of *lekker anties* in a skimpy bikini for a pair of hairy bollocks swinging free from a sweaty jockstrap filled him with horror. He could feel the blood draining from his face and swore that from then on he would never electrocute anyone again, just in case.

'Smithy,' called Mostert, two minutes later, while the ice was still rattling around the bucket. 'Mickey Epstein's turned up!'

'What?'

'He came out of the bush two days ago! We've got to get up to Grootfontein right now.'

'You lie,' swore Smithy, banging his hand down on the counter. '*Fok.*'

*

If salt were required to rub into Smithy's disappointment, then the vision of eighteen partially drunk soldiers full of grins and gins tumbling off the tailboard of the afternoon *Flossie* at D.F.Malan airport just about covered it.

'I told you we should call in after the weekend,' said Smithy. 'I just *fokken* knew this would happen.'

'I'm sorry, Smithy,' said Mostert, tucking her beret under her epaulette. 'I sympathise, I really do but it can't be helped. Duty calls, hey?'

'*Fok* duty,' said Smithy, despondently, taking one last look at blue mountains and the green vineyards of the Cape as he rolled towards the plane. 'Absolutely, you can *fok* it.'

As conversation was not possible in the back of a C-130, Smithy meditated on bad luck all the way up to Grootfontein but to no real avail. How was it that everyone seemed to have better luck than him? How was it that Mostert could sit there in a bucket seat reading *Cosmopolitan* and a sixteen week old copy of the *New Musical Express* as relaxed as if she was in her own beach house on the dunes at Wilderness? How was it, that that *fokken poes* of a trick cyclist could defer his military service by going to varsity and then when the *poes* did have to turn up and put a *fokken* uniform on, could land himself a *lekker soet* job doing psychological evaluations at the Cape Town naval station? How was it that Mickey Epstein, being left for dead in the bush behind the lines and hundreds of kilometres from nowhere could come breezing through the enemy's defences and so come home safely just at the *fokken* moment when he had a whole weekend to work on Trudi?

*Ja*, he knew the answer; it was because they were all sitting in boats on their personal rivers, heading out through whatever swamps and rapids they might encounter and so on until they came to the sea and were picked up in a luxury cruise liner to a future life of beaches and cocktails and umbrellas and villas and smart cars. They had been given paddles too, by virtue of their superior education, family money or, in Mickey Epstein's case, because he was a tough, little fucker who could make it through the shredder of Parabat training and so wear the wings that would get him a job in security consultancy anywhere in the world, any time. He thought about Scholtz, *kaking* in the same place every day out at Police Post 158 and fucking up his radio drill, but still in possession of an Irish passport that would allow him to jump into a boat paddled by his own personal *fokken* leprechaun and sail right out of the desert and into a future of Guinness and randy mad redheads. And Scholtz also knew which *fokken* rivers actually did reach the sea so wouldn't get lost in the delta.

Reaching into his pocket, he pulled out a Crunchie bar, tore off the wrapper and bit into it. It was soft; somewhere, somehow, water had got into it. He spat out the yellow glob of cinder and chocolate into the sick bag and tossed it ruefully across the cabin.

It was just so *unfair*! Yes, he had murdered an activist; there was no getting away from that, but so had lots of coppers; but how come the ANC had chosen to pursue him particularly with charges and writs and that sort of thing? How come it was only him that they sent bayonets to? OK, OK, so it was a war and they were going after who they could get; he understood; but it seemed doubly harsh that rather than protection, he could expect only blackmail from his own side because he had also been implicated in the murder of David Merriman, who he had at that the time, been trying to save from a death sentence. OK, OK; it was a fuck up and most of that fuck up was due to his own stupidity, but he was only stupid because he was young and did not have the family connections or varsity education that might have found him a cushy number for his National Service, like counting shithouses in a Durban military warehouse. Instead, he had joined the police and because of doing that he had murdered Onyele Namyana, the ANC activist and here he was *not* sitting in a boat on a river that would reach the sea, but up Shit Creek without a paddle in a barbed wire canoe, surrounded by crocs on a stream that just disappeared into the dry desert –with a Crunchie bar that wasn't crunchy.

This last thought cheered him up a little. At least now he could think about Onyele Namyana without immediately throwing up; now he just associated the name with a soggy chocolate bar, so that was a plus. On the other hand, God was still laughing at him because having relieved him of that burden, he had immediately sent a plague of citrus down on him; and it was a plague because he simply refused to admit the validity of Mostert's theory that there was a subconscious connection between the smell of oranges and lemons and that mass grave at Capinga. How could there be? He knew what dead bodies smelled of and citrus wasn't it. He had also got the whiff when they had spotted Steiner after sherry with the Mother Superior and although Steiner was obviously connected to the mass grave having personally despatched a few of its occupants, there was no possible connection between him and his first girlfriend, Ayize, who he had just happened to be thinking of when they drove out of Montagu.

'*Jy is en boer,*' his father had always said to him. '*Maak 'n' plan.*' It was good advice, he reflected, even if it came from a man who was never more than two drinks away from an empty bottle, a man of twelve trades and thirteen accidents who spent his life looking for sausages in the dog house. It was advice for those who could rely on no-one but themselves and had nothing to help them but what was immediately to hand. It was the sort of advice that he needed.

He shifted in the bucket seat and stretched out his legs. If there was no river for him, he thought, no river that would lead to the sea, no road that would lead him to Rome, then he would just have to be like Noah. He would have to construct an ark and hope to weather the coming flood that way; and until then he would stock his ark with options, two by two, starting with his pay, which he promised himself he would start to save and not just piss away every time he got leave; and then his record, which he would try to make exemplary so that one day it might add up to forgiveness, redemption, pardon or at least a little *fokken* slack; which meant he would have to start taking this bullshit case seriously.

Well, perhaps at some stage he would. In the meantime, and in the absence of even the teeniest bit of a green light at the robot from Mostert, he would shut his eyes, get some kip and perhaps dream of Ayize.

*

The black man had burst out of Mrs. Parr's millinery store half way down the arcade on Constitution Street, breaking open the heavy sawdust silence of the *stoep* with his cursing and flailing his arms trying to wrench free from her grasp. She was shrieking as she lost her footing and the man almost tripped over her, dragging her along the wooden boards, trying to high step out of her entangling limbs. His eyes were wide, terrified, as though he had been pounced on by a lion while stealing meat from its cage and his only thought was to get away from the stick-like creature, to flee, cart-wheeling his arms as though he would swim through the pedestrians

214

tumbling into and out of his path. He had a red shirt on, a round necked soccer shirt, cheap faded jeans and he had the lean look of frustration and desperation about him; and regret that he had given in to this stupidity.

Joshua was just sixteen then and he was carrying the pistol that his father kept in the house for dealing with uppity Kaffirs and robbers that never came. It was heavy, but he was used to its weight and kick from the times he had shot cans with it down by the waste ground. On the boards was Om Van Heerden, his mouth forming a perfect circle only marginally smaller than the perfect circles of his outraged eyes as the black man elbowed him out of the way and next to him, just a little way in front were Koos and Charles, two big-bellied boers in empire-builder shorts and long socks, and it was they whom the man collided with when he managed to shake Mrs Parr off. Joshua did not hesitate. He dropped into an approved crouching stance, held the pistol firmly in two hands, pulled back the hammer and, as soon as he was sure he had the man in his sights and that Om van Heerden, Koos, Charles and Mrs Parr would not be hit, he squeezed the trigger in the way he had been taught in school cadet training. The bang was expected. The shock wave that put a momentary target roundel on the man's shirt was not; nor was the back flip that the man executed as his torso was blasted back and his feet thrown up in front of him; nor was the heavy, blunt sound of the body hitting the wooden decking and the heavy full silence that descended for full ten seconds afterwards.

'*Het Boet!*' shouted Om Van Heerden. 'Did you see that? The *laatie* nailed that Kaffir good!'

As Joshua straightened up, hands reached out to congratulate him, to pat him on the back, to tell him what a hell of a fellow he was for such a *laatie*

215

and how he was sure to get a mention in the newspaper for helping to end the kaffir's crime spree.

'*Ja*, that should get you a guaranteed place in Police College after your Matric,' cried Koos, wheezing and chuckling. 'They probably will forego you training now you have learned everything you need.'

'Young man,' said Mrs Parr, restoring her dignity, gingerly stepping over the corpse and composing her creased distress into a pinched nose and a sniff. 'Thank you very much for helping a defenceless woman in the course of her legitimate commerce. I know people complain about the youth these days, but I can see now that they are all wrong.'

Joshua realised that he had done something big, something for which neither cadet training nor Youth Preparedness class had actually prepared him for. He had imagined in the split second before he fired that pulling the trigger of the pistol that lay heavy now and silent in his hands would make him a man in the eyes of the community, a person to be reckoned with and respected in the world of Krugerburg which, though a small town, was still a big place to him then. Instead, he felt strangely dirty, as though the town had soiled him and as he put the pistol back in his waistband, he felt the overwhelming urge to scrub his hands in caustic soda until the skin peeled off them.

'Will he die?' he asked.

'Never mind about that *laatie*,' said Koos. 'The Kaffir doctors will fix him up just fine.'

*

216

It was only a day or so after he had shot the thief that Mrs Parr invited Joshua around to her house to say thank you for his brave actions. In truth, he was planning to go there anyway but it was to see Ayize rather than the owner of the house, for he was experiencing a heaviness, a sort of numbness and a feeling of detachment, and although he was not sure he wanted to talk about what he had done, he knew he did not want to boast, or be lionised for it. Instead, he just wanted to sit down by her, side by side, shoulder to shoulder and feel her skin on his and look at the ankle bracelet that he had bought for her from CNA with his pocket money.

'What you want to go hang round that old crone for?' said his father, reaching for another beer and slouching down on the battered sofa. 'You hoping she's got a daughter or a grand-daughter who will get her tits out for you now that you have shot a kaffir?'

Joshua flushed red and dropped the cup from his shaking hands down into the sink where it shattered.

'Clumsy as a Kaffir too,' added his father, scratching.

'You know you are a pig, dad, don't you?'

'What? Where's your respect?'

'I sent it back with Mother that last time she came for a visit,' answered Joshua, trembling and heading for the screen door. He pushed through and let it slam before calling back. 'Get a job, you pig. And take a bath – you smell like a *fokken bergie*.'

A bottle flew across the kitchen and smashed on the yellow wood floor, but Joshua had crossed the yard by then and was hurdling the gate into the street.

Mrs Parr lived alone in a bay fronted Edwardian villa that she had inherited from her parents, who had built it themselves, sometime after the Boer war. It was quite unusual in Krugerburg because it was built from a shade of red brick that had weathered to a dark rust colour and wasn't available now. All the new buildings that had gone up recently had a different shade of brick, mottled usually, or had been rendered with concrete. Built high on a bank, solid and dependable, the house looked like it had stood for a century already and would stand for a century more, looking down its dignified nose at those who passed beneath the windows of its eyes. Mrs Parr felt the weight of the old house acutely and because of this kept its lace doily dignity and dark wood floors spruced, polished, spick, span and double waxed at all times, in case by neglect she might offer disrespect to her parents' sacrifices. As if to add a sacerdotal depth to this respect, she had fixed a sign on the wicket gate to the rose garden that directed *Salesmen to please call at the side gate.* So forbidding was this aura of dependable fortress respectability that no one ever went in through the front door and although Mrs Parr sometimes left by that route, she always received on the rear *stoep* under the *broekie lace* ironwork by the perfect lawn, close by the kitchen. Joshua noted the instruction and duly abided by the custom, coming through the pink cosmos and blue agapanthus, and ducking under the willow.

He wasn't quite sure why he had accepted Mrs. Parr's invitation, except that sometimes he felt a bitter sweet hole where his mother should have been and though he chose not to admit it to himself, he felt abandoned for it sometimes. Mrs Parr would substitute for a little while, he imagined, even though she was really much closer to his grandmother's age and in some respects resembled something from the last century, rather than this one. It was also the case that he enjoyed trailing his coat a little and thought that it might be exciting to see how Ayize reacted to his appearance in the Madam's house. Brushing aside the thought that this might not be a good idea after all, he decided that he would very much like to see Ayize and that in fact Mrs Parr's invitation provided really all the excuse he needed. Nor would he have to go employ his usual means of alerting her to his presence – an obvious whistle and an even more obvious pebble over the wall – because the invitation also did away with the need for the subterfuge.

Closing the gate carefully, he looked down the garden towards the servant's quarters but he knew in an instant that they were deserted because there was no washing out on the line and there was *always* washing out on the line down there. He looked at the *stoep*, saw Mrs Parr busy about something in the kitchen and slipped quickly down the path while she wasn't looking. The banana palms and bamboo hid him once he was past the first few yards but his sense of dismay grew when he saw there was no light on in the house and a padlock on the closed door proclaimed that there was no one at home. This was not usual; the door was almost always left open and the interior visible from the garden. He had been over the wall and behind it often enough to note the pattern of life in Mrs Parr's garden. He felt the tremor of discovery run through him.

Mrs. Parr caught sight of him from the kitchen window and came bustling out, wiping at her hands with a tea towel before he could grasp what the empty house portended. She had her white hair piled up and permed like those ladies in the black and white movies and was wearing a sort of baggy blue plaid skirt which went down to her ankles. An embroidered blouse, clasped at the throat with a regency brooch and black pumps rounded off her rather Victorian attire, while a strong sharp nose and small spectacles gave her something of a bird-like appearance.

'Ah there you are, young Joshua,' she beamed. 'Come on in and have some tea. We are making pâté today and I am sure you would just like to help now, would you not? Besides I must give you a present that I have made for you.'

'*Ja*, sure thing Mrs Parr, but I can't stay so long, you know,' he replied, hesitantly, desperate to know what the closed door meant.

'Of course, of course,' she said, shooing him into the kitchen. 'I am sure I am keeping you from a very suitable young lady, but I am also sure that she will not mind me borrowing you for a while. Come now. Will you have tea? Take a seat now at the table and I will see what cakes we have in the pantry.'

The long kitchen was open to the *stoep* and above an ancient blackened stove hung several copper pans like clouds in a mackerel sky while on a worktop to the side metal trays like silver linings lay side by side, waiting to be filled. Joshua sat down at one end of the yellow wood table that seemed to stretch the whole length of the room while Mrs Parr hummed a little tune then reappeared with a cake stand, some fly covers and a series of pink and yellow fancies.

'Eat, *ja*,' she fluttered, producing primrose china and silver cake slices. 'They were fresh baked yesterday and are full of goodness. Help yourself now while I bring you a little present.'

Joshua looked at the cakes arrayed over three levels of nickel-silver and then chose a Bakewell Tart with a luscious glazed cherry in the middle. He went to pick it up with his fingers but then remembered his manners and reached for the cake slice, which he held like a bricklayer's trowel and began the delicate operation of shovelling the tart on to his plate. It had stuck a little with the heat and as he slid the blade across the silver he felt the base begin to disintegrate under the pressure. He tried again from a different angle as Mrs Parr reappeared with a small, black, woolly object which she placed in front of him before drawing water hot from the kettle into a teapot and spooning in several teaspoons full of black leaf tea.

'It is just a little something to keep you warm when the frost comes,' she said, going over to the pantry again. 'We make them at the church for the poor black children in the townships.'

'Thank you, Mrs Parr,' he said. His fingers were weak, he noticed, and he could not hold them to his will and so put the cake slice down with a clatter. It was easier to pick up the woollen object, which turned out to be a knitted balaclava, so hideously uncool that he dreaded the thought of having to try it on. At the same time though, the softness of the wool reminded him of the ones his mother used to knit for him all that time ago whenever they ventured out of the mild winter of Cape Town and into the frosty interior. He dropped it back on to the table.

'Do you need help, Joshua?' she said, looking around.

'I'm fine, Mrs Parr really,' he replied, trying again with the cake slice held in his left hand.

This time, he was even more awkward. Aware that he had probably broken the Bakewell Tart, he decided to pick out a sturdier looking piece of heavily iced lemon sponge cake, but once again the generosity of Mrs Parr's measures of sugar defeated him as the rich base melted in the summer heat. His left hand was now shaking worse than his right had

221

done and for a reason he feared to understand, tears were welling in his eyes. He dashed them away.

'Are you needing a hand with the cakes, Joshua?' she asked, over her shoulder.

'*Ja*, it's not a train smash or anything, but I think I must have a trapped nerve somewhere. Is Mrs Maquondo working today?'

She came over to the table and sat two seats down on his right side, so the light was on her, scattering filaments of shadow across the creased leather of her face.

'She has gone back to the Location since…since….Let me serve up this Bakewell Tart for you,' she said, expertly whipping the cake onto a fresh plate and leaning over to place it before him. 'Would you like to pour the tea?'

Joshua was sitting on both hands now and feared greatly to take up the pot in case he spilled it. He was also aware that there was a flutter in his bottom lip that he couldn't explain but wanted to, desperately.

'I'll pour,' she said, taking up the pot. 'You know when the boys came back from the war – the last war, that is – it took some of them a long time to get over what they had seen and experienced in Egypt and in Italy. It was a terrible shock, you know, but they mastered themselves and went on with their lives.'

She poured tea into the china and added milk and two lumps of cane sugar without asking.

'You were in the war?' said Joshua, his eyes trying to find a view of the garden.

222

'Oh, I have been in three wars,' replied Mrs Parr, with mock indignation. 'I was born the year the war with the English came and I was fifteen when the first war with the Germans came. My son was killed in the second war. And there was also the Zulu rebellion in Natal, but I was only a little girl then and knew nothing of it.'

'I'm sorry Mrs Parr. I did not know. I am sorry for asking.'

'There's no need to be sorry, young man. It is finished with now and I am at peace with God for taking James from me so young.'

'Was he in the army or the air force?' asked Joshua. There did not seem to be any sign of Mrs Maquondo or Ayize about the house.

'He was in the army and commanded a tank,' she replied, primly. 'He was always interested in tanks, from when he was just a little boy. I think it must have been because I was pregnant with him when I saw the tanks going to Johannesburg in 1922.'

She smiled again and though the creases doubled some of the years fell away.

'There was a parade?'

'No, it was a big rebellion. The mine owners wanted to sack all the miners and employ cheaper blacks so the Communists in the Trades Unions declared a White Worker's Republic which had to be put down with troops and soldiers. *Workers of the World Unite and Fight for a White South Africa,* they called out. That's when I saw the tanks driving up on their way to Johannesburg.'

'Did they succeed?' asked Joshua, feeling his hands become confident enough to pick up the Bakewell Tart. He had recognised Mrs Maquondo's housecoat draping from a hook in the pantry.

'Oh, I'm not sure now. I was too busy with my family and children to take much note of politics. We had to move around a lot for my husband's work then. He was an engineer so we had to go to some out of the way places. Some places, my boy would not go to school and would go barefoot in the dust like a little *piccannini* with the other Kaffirs. These were happy days, but of course they had to come to an end and we must just send him away to school. *Ja*, we were happy though, until the war killed him.'

'Is it Mrs Maquondo's day off today?' asked Joshua. His hand began to tremble again and he put the cake down on his plate after a single bite.

'Come now,' said Mrs. Parr, getting up and going to the pantry as if she hadn't heard the question. 'You sit there and take your ease while I get on with making this pâté or it will never get made.'

She indicated the cakes and then went into the pantry once more, returning with a bread tin lined with bacon and a white enamel dish covered by a bloody cloth. Bringing a chopping board and a sharp knife from the worktop, she slipped out the liver from under the cloth and began to skin it and then cut out the fat white artery and veins that ran through it. Joshua had the Bakewell Tart half way to his mouth when she slid the knife in, deftly slicing at the chocolate brown, glutinous mass that wobbled like a gutted toad with each sharp incision. He put the cake down.

'Are you a little squeamish?' she mocked, gently. 'You are not country bred, this thing is obvious. Usually I have the maid do this, but Mrs

224

Maquondo cannot be here today and I like to cook from time to time. It reminds me of the days before I could afford to have staff. It is important to be grateful for what you have, you know. And you must recognise that it is not achieved without struggle. This goes, even if you are not country bred, too.'

Joshua picked up the cake again, but the sight of globules of blood oozing from the unctuous liver brought on another quake in his hands and he only managed to avoid dropping the cake by cramming far too much of it into his mouth. There the sweetness made his palate sweat and he felt as though the crumbling mash would ball up and choke him if he did not swallow soon. It was as though someone had crammed a bottle stopper into him and his palsied hands reached for his tea cup, urgent for moisture to wash the cloying, crunching sugar icing down.

'Will Mrs Maquondo be back later – to help with the washing up?' Joshua was conscious that his interest was becoming obvious, but Mrs. Parr continued to cut and slice until she had a pile of eviscerated connective tissue and veins in one jelly fish like mound and a row of carefully filleted meat tranches on the other. The meat was a deep red-brown colour mottled with a green khaki tinge.

'This is a recipe that my mother showed me how to make, just like they make it in France,' she said. 'They call it *pâté de compagnie* there; it means 'country pâté', but I am sure you know this language from school.'

'We just do English and Afrikaans,' said Joshua slurping and swallowing and desperate to know what had happened to Mrs Maquondo and, more importantly, Ayize.

Mrs Parr began to chop the liver more finely now, drawing the blade confidently through the flesh so that the tranches became rough squares and then, tiny slugs and worms.

'Now for the pork and brandy,' she announced, as though letting Joshua in on a secret. 'You must use quite fatty pork for this part because although there is a lot of fat in the bacon, it is not enough to really cook the liver.'

From the pantry she brought another muslin covered enamel dish and tipped the pale pink contents onto the board in a small diced avalanche. She picked out some small piece of gristle that she was not happy with and dropped it onto the pile of discarded liver parts, then broke the mass up and began to add it to the chopped material on the board. Each time she mixed the two kinds of flesh, she sprinkled a little brandy on to it, as though it were a blessing and then, when she considered it seasoned enough she pronounced herself satisfied.

'Now we must just fry this quickly and for a moment and then it can go into the tin. It is important to cook pork properly and thoroughly you know.' She retrieved a wide frying pan from over the stove and scooped up the mixture into it. 'This is why the Jews don't eat pork,' she opined. 'It is because they did not cook it properly once in the Bible and they became very sick. Please, take another cake.'

Joshua was finding it harder and harder to control the outbursts of shaking that were now spreading beyond his hands to his knees as the realisation that Mrs Parr was concealing something grew. Had someone told Mrs Parr about him and Ayize and Mrs Parr had dismissed them from her service back to the Location? He drew himself together, knotting his shoulders, clutching his hands, driving his knees inwards and bracing his legs against the chair legs. With a supreme effort, he unbound one hand and reached out for the cake slice, but got no further than touching it before he had to draw it back.

Mrs Parr moved over to the stove and lit the gas with a pop and a hiss, then turned it down a little before allowing the heat to build up and sear the meat. He could see the brandy flame, red and blue as she allowed the gas to light its aromas and then gave a start when she splashed in a generous helping from the bottle. The alcohol flared up in a conflagration that hung in the air like a spirit of fire before consuming itself and disappearing, leaving the heady aroma of brandy above the meatier base of the liver and the saltiness of the pork.

'Did I make you jump, Joshua?' she asked.

He nodded tersely.

'*Ja*, Joshua, you must not let the incident of the other day affect you, you know?  It is natural to be a little shocked but you must not let it show.' She stirred the spitting pan, rattling it against the ring. 'You must contain yourself and not be like those hippies who are always letting it all hang out. There, now we are ready.'

Joshua nodded again, blankly.

'Joshua, are you not well?' she asked, and then frowning, took the pan off the stove. Some small part of the meat had overcooked, had jumped from the pan and onto the ring and had sent up a spiral of burnt offering that filled Joshua's nostrils with a revolting acridity. 'Joshua? Joshua? Can you hear me?'

'Where is Mrs Maquondo?' he said quietly, his stomach like lead.

'She has gone, Joshua,' replied Mrs. Parr, quietly. 'She and her daughter left this morning for Johannesburg. They went without handing in notice, Joshua. It was her son that you shot, Joshua. He was a bad hat, Joshua and you should not feel bad about what you did. I never allowed him to set foot here.'

'Her son?' said Joshua, his insides lurching violently. 'Ayize's *brother*?'

Mrs Parr pursed her mouth and nodded simply and with understanding.

'Johannesburg?' said Joshua. It might have been the moon.

At that moment a huge sense of distance and detachment intruded on him and with a start, he understood that this sense would not be enough on its own if he was to survive his life in Krugerburg. In that moment, he realised that he must grow an extra skin, perhaps several extra layers of skin, if he was to cope with the realities of a life splintered by the divorce of his parents, then cracked open by the death he had just meted out to the black man who he sometimes thought of as a brother-in-law, and now destroyed by the disappearance of Ayize. For a moment, he felt sick and then he began to hear Mrs Parr as though she were speaking down a tube from a distance.

The next thing he knew he was lying on the cool floor with the faces of Mrs Parr and Doctor Levy floating above him. He could barely hear them speaking but even so, he was surprised to find that he was the object of their conversation. They were calling to him and then he felt Dr Levy's reflex hammer tapping at his knees and elbows, followed by the cold ring of a stethoscope pressed against his chest, and then the soft wool of the balaclava being placed under his head.

'We must take him to his father,' said Dr Levy.

Dr Levy was a Russian Jew; his skin was olive, his hair and eyes intensely dark, his brow heavy and he operated with a slight hunch to his shoulders and Joshua knew that his father did not approve of him. Mrs Parr's kindly concerned face, he recognised as belonging to the sort of house where there would always be a jar of freshly baked, home-made rusks on a tray in the kitchen and which smelled faintly of lavender and rosemary, but he had forgotten for the moment just who she was exactly. He was dimly aware of his condition, but really only conscious of a sharp cramp in his shoulders and dryness in his mouth and the damp sound of the voices above him.

When next he was aware, the perspective had shifted and he seemed to be hanging in the air, his toes barely touching the ground, his sight blurred, but his hearing strangely sharper.

'No, I don't believe him to be epileptic and he is not mad,' Dr Levy was explaining in his Russian accented English. 'He is just having reaction to the shock of shooting Kaffir. He must just be put to bed and given rest and he will be right as rain in day or two.'

Joshua was surprised to see his father but not surprised to see that he was swaying backwards and forwards a little, drunk as he usually was by this time, but he could not be sure because he himself seemed to be swaying too. Mrs Parr had her hand on his arm and he could smell her lavender perfume quite clearly now.

'So just let us enter into house and we will make sure he is laid down and steady.'

Joshua watched disinterestedly as his father stood aside, scratching at his string vest, and waved them on into the room. He recognised the threadbare rug balled up against the fireplace, the familiar crate of beer bottles by a broken down and stained armchair and wondered why the radio was still on. Against one wall was a two seat sofa, just by a patch of exposed lath and plaster which Joshua could not ever remember seeing before.

'His room is through there.' His father was pointing one moment and then snarling the next. 'What? What is it Mrs Parr? You don't like the way I live, hey?'

'It is none of my business,' she replied, haughtily. Joshua liked the tone and felt a ghost of a smile creep around the corners of his mouth. 'But if you wish I will send my new maid around to help you with Joshua if you please. She will begin work tomorrow and she can help clean up too.'

'You think I want a dirty Kaffir in my house?'

'As I say,' replied Mrs Parr, handing Joshua along. 'It is none of my business.'

'*Ja*, Mr Smith, she does not mean any harm.' A blurred Dr Levy was pushing his spectacles back on his long nose as Joshua took a faltering step forward. 'And it would help this boy if he was given some soup or broth at regular intervals. He might not feel like eating but little bit nursing would not hurt him.'

'You think I'm a Kaffir nursemaid now?'

'*Ja*, Mr Smith, why don't you just take seat and we'll handle this OK? We don't need any aggravation and this boy needs some peace and rest, is all.'

Joshua looked at the faces gathered round him and wondered who they were arguing about.

'*Poes,*' spat Joshua's father. 'He has only killed a *fokken* Kaffir.'

'*Ja*, well it is big thing for *jong*, hey?' answered Dr Levy. He was nodding to Mrs Parr and Joshua felt himself being guided forward. 'He may need little bit time to get over.'

'And I am not used to hearing such language from gentlemen, Mr Smith,' said Mrs Parr. '*Drunk* or sober.'

'Then why do you come here then? Sticking your long nose in to other people's business, are you? And who will pay the Jew-boy Doctor, hey? That's what I'd like to know.'

'There is no fee,' answered Dr Levy, tiredly. 'Come, Mrs Parr. Sooner we are done, sooner we can go.'

Joshua still could not fully understand what was going on but the mention of the killing called to something in him.

'You are correct as ever, Doctor Levy. Let us see Joshua to bed and then take our leave,' said Mrs Parr.

'Just dump him on the sofa there,' Joshua heard his father say. 'What? Is he royalty now? I know you just want to have a good snoop around here. What a *poes* to turn to jelly because he kills a *fokken* Kaffir!'

Joshua again became aware suddenly that they were talking about him.

'We are all God's children, Mr Smith,' said Dr Levy, lowering Joshua to the sofa. 'My, you are well built young man. Good for rugby.'

Mrs Parr fluttered a little and brushed Joshua's dark hair back off his brow. The soft leather of her hand reminded him of Ayize and his memory came back to him, called into sharp focus as if he had been looking through the lense of a camera.

'Are you sure you will be alright here, Joshua? If you like I can make a bed up for you in my house.'

'Stop fussing, woman,' Joshua heard his father say. 'Leave him be and stop treating him like a *fokken* milksop. Jesus, you'll be wanting him to be a choir boy next.'

'Dad,' said Joshua, as if from a long, patient wait. 'Shut up.'

'Shut up, is it now?'

The feeling in his arms and legs was coming back now and he could feel a curious tingling of pins and needles in his elbows. He saw his father lurch but couldn't decide whether it which one of them was actually moving. Dr Levy stepped forward and laid a long restraining arm across Mr Smith's chest.

'Come back now and keep calm,' he said. 'Give him some air. You must take no notice because he is shocked.'

'Shut up, is it?'

Joshua saw his father flinging away Dr Levy's arm.

'Shut up,' he repeated, more firmly.

'Rest quietly, now, Joshua,' said Mrs Parr, her voice reedy and nervous. 'Do as the Doctor says and remember you are in shock.'

Joshua saw his father take an unsteady step forward, looming over him, his fists at the ready. Doctor Levy intervened once more but was pushed back a second time.

232

'Please Mr Smith,' said Mrs Parr, growing agitated. 'This is not right. Take your seat again, please.'

And then it happened. The thought of Ayize disappearing forever sent a though a jolt of electricity firing through every single cell in Joshua's body, whipping through every single muscle and blowing out the fuses in his brain. The thought that the only thing that made life in Kurgerburg worth living was gone was the straw that broke the camel's back. The casual cruelty, the bone-headed stupidity, the contempt for anything different or out of the ordinary, the crushing dullness of an ugly, small-minded small town that revelled in its ugly small-minded cruelty and dullness was just more than he could take anymore. He lived among people who thought kicking an old man to death on a Sunday morning was not out of the ordinary; he lived among people who thought that shooting a young, black man with his whole life ahead of him was nothing to get worked up about, was indeed, something to get used to, something necessary, something no more serious than killing a chicken for the table; he lived among people who thought that the simple, pure love-making that had lit up his soul and Ayize's was something disgusting, something on a par with bestiality. He was not going to live with them any longer.

In less than an instant he shot out of the sofa and head butted his father with every last ounce of rage, strength and being that he possessed. There was a flash of blood as Mr. Smith's nose exploded and a bellow of bull elephant rage as he went over backwards, hitting the floor like a dropped coal sack. Joshua answered instantaneously with a screaming, desperate, animal desire to kill him and leaping upon him, locked his hands into his father's throat so hard that the nails began to gouge at the skin. He clenched harder, furiously, so that the blood vessels across his father's

233

cheeks, nose and brows began to shatter into black pin points as he tried to squeeze the life out of each pore. Though he was dimly aware that a horrified Dr Levy was wading slowly towards him, he did not feel his father's arm drive up under his chin forcing his head back but concentrated all his might into holding that grip on the throat beneath his hands. Not even when Dr Levy took hold of his shoulders did his grip slacken but rather he tightened it as if he would wrench the windpipe out.

'Get help,' he heard Dr Levy shout. 'Go for neighbours! Quick! Quick! Look lively now!'

Joshua felt his father writhe beneath him but the strength of his madness equal to the strength of Krugerburg's banal, murderous stupidity and a sense of triumph began to flood through him as he heard the desperate drumming of his father's heels behind him. He squeezed harder at the fat neck, the greasy stubble and the beer stained breath, defying Doctor Levy's attempts to prise apart his fingers and howling like a dog at the moon in a stasis of spuming, cataleptic anger.

The cleansing terror of the moment was only broken when Bokkie Adams and his two sons burst in through the door and flung themselves on Joshua, tearing him off and driving him back bodily onto the sofa. He was panting, raging, spitting like a cat, yet the weight of Bokkie's sons was too much for him and they pinned him down, then thumped him so hard, twice, that he gave up the struggle as useless. He saw his father dragged to his chair by the corner, his throat being massaged all the while by Dr Levy as Mrs. Parr held her hands to her mouth, her face a prison pallor.

'What the *fok* is this?' cried Bokkie Adams, panting heavily and staring around at the scene. 'How can a son do this to a father?'

Mrs. Parr went over to Joshua and waved the two restraining boys away with a handkerchief.

'You should ask how a father can do this to a son,' said Mrs Parr, leaning over and mopping at the black eye that they had given Joshua.

'You should ask deeper questions than that,' thought Joshua, quiet now and filled with a strange peace. 'You should ask much deeper questions than that. Like why does everything smell of citrus here?'

*

Mostert looked up from her magazine and then checked her watch and frowned. It was too noisy for conversation, so she got up from her seat, and manoeuvred herself round to look out of the window.

'Smithy!' she shouted, against the hiss of the air and the roar of the engines. 'Look down! That isn't Grootfontein!'

Smithy started awake and did as he was told, took one look at the bush below and went forward to the intercom.

'*Ja*, we're diverting to a bush strip beyond the Cut Line,' crackled the voice of the despatcher. 'They putting in an Admin Box for an Op and they want you there. You must be very important with the Higher Ups to get this special treatment.'

'*Fok,*' said Smithy. '*Fok, fok, fokken fok.*'

*

09

Angola 1976

235

Steiner had sent Anna-Marie back in after Operation Savannah, the South African attempt to install an Angolan government more favourable to itself, was called off just as the armoured columns were ready to strike. She went through the same channels as before; back to university in London ostensibly to finish her degree and then out to Luanda as part of the struggle. Not surprisingly, she was met there with a certain scepticism but her cover story was good; she had been a scared kid in a chaotic situation; she had received death threats from BOSS and had panicked; the gaps in her timeline she filled in with backpacker tales of India and Thailand. As neither the Angolan government nor SWAPO had the skill or resources to properly check her story, she was put on a sort of probation and sent to work at the Karl Marx Reception Centre near Lubango where her job was to help assess the authenticity of South African, American and European activists volunteering for the struggle in order to screen out potential spies. She was also aware that she was being screened herself.

The camp was divided into two parts, she quickly became aware. The part where she was stationed was made up of a compound of secured accommodation, offices, interview rooms, a small guardhouse and a communal kitchen and it ticked over slowly, without drama and without undue pressure mainly because the number of comrades dealt with was usually very small; one or two a week was normal, although from time to time there would be a sudden rush which usually coincided with a big security operation down on the border. Most of those who presented themselves were deserters from the UNITA rebels and they were usually after just one thing; promotion. Anna-Marie took statement after statement from these men (and the occasional woman), filed them and, at a convenient moment, duplicated them and sent them off to a dead letter box in Luanda to be forwarded to Steiner. From time to time, however, there would be a white South African, hoping to join up with the ANC and then she would be required to test their stories by asking the sort of questions that only local, and therefore genuine, knowledge would be able to answer. It was true that she never knew if any of these people were genuine refugees or just people sent in to test her integrity, but she put this all to the back of her mind and adopted the position of someone who just wanted to serve the struggle in whatever way she could. Steiner took the product of this work and used it to inform BOSS of the names of virtually every single dissident real or suspect across a swathe of Africa, plus a good number of SWAPO intelligence operators.

It took her longer to penetrate the second part of the camp. Much more heavily guarded, much more comprehensively wired-in, it was clear that whatever went on in there was intended to happen away from prying eyes and, as she found out, for very good reasons. Much of it was underground, camouflaged by the flimsy buildings constructed above them that were never intended to be occupied and although she saw very few people in there, she was able to count the number of buckets of rice or sadza that went in each day brim-full and came out empty, which told her that a considerable number of people – well into the hundreds at times – were in there. She also noted that the guards locked up at three in the afternoon and that the women employed on construction duty or gardening came from within the camp, never left it, and were not visible after three o'clock, which told her that they were prisoners too. Sometimes there was a terrible smell of roasting flesh even though no meat ever seemed to go through those gates and though few sounds ever came out of those underground rooms, she noted the occasional report of a bullet. There were also times when a man might be driven out of that detention centre in a car that contained two uniformed men and a shovel; most times only the uniforms and the shovel came back. This knowledge she passed on in the normal way to Steiner, from where it found itself via intermediaries in the hands of those journalists and clergymen who had not yet fully convinced themselves of the simple equation that *black* was *good* and *white* was *bad*. It was never enough to strip away the blinkers completely but it did prompt a few reporters to make a token effort to investigate the truth of the reports that SWAPO was maintaining a fully equipped centre for the torture of people deemed insufficiently credible or ardent in their support for the Revolution. Taken together with the product from her routine work though, Steiner counted it as gold dust.

*

Angola.

Monday Last.

The bridge was guarded. At the near end of the box girder construction was a guard post. There were two armed men. AK47s. Not alert but they would see him when he tried to cross the sandy floodplain that stretched out a hundred metres and more from the turgid brown water. He would have to wait for darkness. It had been a week since he had left Capinga and the food and water that he had lifted from that badly parked vehicle while its occupants slept off the booze and dagga were now exhausted. FAPLA and SWAPO, he had become convinced, must be mightily pissed off at what had been done at Capinga to have kept up the pursuit for so long. He would have to drink the piss again.

Around the middle of the afternoon, Mickey became aware of the sound of a vehicle on the road below. So far, he had not seen so much as a donkey cart on the road and summoning up his curiosity, he prepared to observe it;

type, speed, number of passengers, direction, load, general condition, general comments; the checklist; the discipline; do the job. It was not travelling fast, indeed it seemed uncertain and as the truck – Ural-375, 4.5 ton, 6x6, Russian, stinking, bad petrol and clouds of black exhaust fumes – passed him, Mickey saw the expression on the driver's face really quite clearly and realised in an instant that the *joller* was lost. He watched the truck all the way to the bridge where it was halted, some arms were waved and fingers pointed, whereupon the driver executed a three point turn taking five to do it and came back towards him, grinding gears and pumping out the thick oily smoke. It was at that point that Mickey realised that the smart thing to do was to hijack it and use it to get across the bridge and then drive very quickly home.

He had chosen a vantage point to watch the bridge on a small rocky hill at a bend in the road and reckoned now that if he was quick enough he could get down the rear side and on to the road before the wheezing truck rounded the bend. There it would just be a stick up job and after that he would not walk but ride. The guards at the bridge, he decided, would be no obstacle that a grenade wouldn't overcome and it would be ten rand to a ticky coin that the driver would have something to drink in the cab; it might even be water. Once over the bridge, he would be back over the Cut Line and safe by morning, given even odds.

He snatched himself up and hobbled quickly down the hill, his pack over one arm and using his rifle as a crutch to allay the red hot fire in his boots and reached the road just as the truck chugged and ground into sight, twenty five metres away. It was not doing more than 10kph and making hard work of that, so Mickey had plenty of time to make sure he had a bullet up the spout and to plan his shot. Positioning himself in a ditch on the passenger side of the vehicle, he waited for it to draw level, swung himself up onto the running board by means of the mirror and then thrust the barrel through the window.

'Stop the *fokken* truck!' he croaked. 'And get out!'

The terrified driver did as he was told on the instant, but Mickey still shot him in the head once he was out.

'Sorry, hey?' he said. 'But it's a war and you started it.'

He turned the vehicle around, took out his two grenades, straightened the pins which he had previously bent over to prevent them accidentally slipping out and placed them in his lap. The rifle, he laid by him on passenger seat. Had the guards heard the shot? Probably, thought Mickey, but if they did, they would probably think the driver was coming back to report it. It was a gamble, but it would have to do. He touched the brakes, wiggled the gear stick and then, with shaking hands, poured the entire contents of a litre bottle of warm Coca-Cola down his throat without spilling so much as a precious drop of it. Only then did he began the long, slow trundle towards the bridge.

He was filthy, burned brown by long months in the sun, the windscreen was dirty and he pulled the sun visor down but even with these precautions, it was clear that the two soldiers on the bridge were uneasy. There could be no doubt that they had heard the shot because they were gesticulating at the truck to hurry up and pick them up.

'*Fokken* cowards,' said Mickey. 'One *fokken* shot and they want to bombshell. Looks like I won't need the grenades at all.'

Fifty yards from the bridge and the two guards started to run towards the truck, hopping up and down in anticipation while shooting terrified glances beyond it.

'How do they expect to beat us with material like this?' he said to himself, steering with one hand and reaching for his weapon with the other. 'Kaffirs, man.'

Sticking the barrel out of the window, he flipped to automatic and fired a burst. He knew he would never hit anything but it was enough to send the two guards flying off into the bush and by the time he arrived on the bridge, Mickey was confident enough to stop, put on the handbrake, go into the guard post and lay claim to a full yellow jerry can full of water.

'Just what the doctor ordered,' he said, pouring the cool liquid into him and over him, before regaining the cab and clattering on over the bridge.

Drinking steadily and almost continuously, the rest of that day became a surreal experience for Mickey. It was as though the water made him drunk. With each gulp, he felt his body respond; at first, the water seemed to disappear in his mouth before he even had time to swallow and anything that spilled onto his skin was instantly absorbed, as though the pores themselves were drinking. His eyesight suddenly became sharper and he became more alert, more alive, able to calculate again, a realisation that he tested by measuring the distance travelled by estimating speed over time as given by speedometer and a cheap alarm clock wired into the dash board by some early rising SWAPO star. As he chugged down the road and across a series of unguarded box girder bridges that spanned vast floodplains, he noted the complete absence of any life whatsoever in the landscape. There wasn't so much as a bird in the sky and though he leaned out of the window when crossing the bridges, there was no sign of hippo or crocodile and no sign of the villagers who habitually used the river to wash clothes in. Though there was maize in the fields, it had not been cultivated and had run wild, right into the abandoned villages whose plaster walls had cracked like eggs, making the graffiti scrawled across them look oddly disjointed. At intervals, on high points there were villas, remnants of the Portuguese occupation and their gaping empty windows menaced the landscape below and made Mickey scan them twice for the possibility of snipers. The villas were dead though, like everything else in this much fought over landscape. Within an hour or so, he was sweating again and the white salt that he had previously brushed off his clothes, he now found himself licking at like an animal. And within him grew a feeling that he was going to make it. He was going to make it. He was going to beat the odds. He was going to become a living legend in Parabat messes across the country because he was Mickey Epstein; Mickey Epstein who once was lost and now is found; Mickey Epstein who flew in on a Dak and drove out in a *kak* old Ural; Mickey Epstein who was MIA and is now Back In Town.

And then a hundred klicks from the Cut Line, just as he came through an empty town that seemed to consist of only two roads, one from the river to an overgrown airfield, the other past a burned out post office and governor's residence to another maize plantation run wild, the bloody old truck coughed, spluttered, slipped its clutch one last time and juddered to the most pathetic of rolling halts.

'Probably just out of fuel,' said Mickey to himself. 'Let's see if there's a jerry can in the back.'

Going round to the tailboard, he undid the fastenings that held a corner of the canvas closed and climbed in. The normal smells of stale sweat, oil, diesel met him but as his eyes grew used to the darkness, he was surprised to find that the load consisted almost entirely of filing cabinets. This didn't bother him unduly and certainly it did not bother him as much as his disappointment at not finding a jerry can full of fuel, but once he realised that he would be back to walking once more, he thought that it wouldn't do any harm to take a look inside a couple of the cabinets in the hope that, like any other office in the known world, one of the drawers would contain a bottle of something drinkable.

He retrieved a screwdriver from the toolkit under the vehicle and jemmied open a couple of the drawers, hitting jackpot on the third attempt. It was just cheap brandy, but it was better than nothing and in his heightened state of euphoric awareness, the effect of even a small sip reminded him that he was still stuck well out in the bush with an unclear fix on his exact position with the strong possibility that his movements had been reported by the two heroes on that first bridge. He screwed the top of the bottle closed and, just out of curiosity, took out one of the files to look at.

'My giddy *fokken* Aunt,' he said, quietly, as a cold flush of fear and realisation ran all the way down his back. All those troops that he had been dodging these past days weren't looking for *him*. They were looking for *this*.

*

Bloemfontein

1978

It was while driving home from Pick 'n' Pay on one of her home runs that Anna-Marie was seized with an overwhelming sense of panic. All of a sudden, she found her knuckles tighten on the steering wheel, a balloon of horror welling up in her chest and a sudden notion that swerving off the road and sending the car over the pavement and into a ditch was the correct thing to do at this particular moment in time. Coming towards her out of the black clouds gathering at the end of the slick wet road was a truck from the builder's merchant heavily laden with sand and gravel, a fact that probably saved her because in another instant she understood the possible ramifications that such a wild and irrational act as deliberately driving off the road and into an accident would bring.

For a start, there would be questions; why had she done it? Was she drunk? Did she need glasses? Did she swerve to avoid an animal? Was there something psychological wrong with her? Was she cracking under the strain of being undercover? There would be endless questions and those questions would go on and on and on from doctors, psychologists, Uncle Tom Cobley and all and they would never ever stop until she gave them the answers that were apparently required. These she would have to fabricate because she did not want to admit the real reason for that panic and this was a problem because Anna-Marie did not like telling lies because they had a tendency to stick to one like burrs. Once you told a lie, you could not get rid of it without ditching your whole life and starting off again somewhere else, which of course, she had tried to do many times in her old life but which she now could no longer contemplate; a lie could compromise the bigger lie of her cover and the best way to maintain a safe and deep cover was to stick to it as though it was indeed the truth. Lies just complicated things.

There was a lay-by just ahead and taking care to indicate safely, she pulled into it, put the handbrake on and wound down the window of the ten year old Ford. Just beyond the verge lay a field of sunflowers, the flat leaves green and the heavy heads nodding in the breeze; in a few weeks' time, they would be a raging, van Gogh yellow under a fine blue sky, but just now they were more like bits of cabbage under a grey, damp, dish cloth of a sky. The air was fresh though and Anna-Marie drew in three or four big breaths through her nose, enjoying the clean smell and feeling a calming effect on her racing pulse as she gradually and systematically brought herself back down to earth. Glancing in the rear view mirror, she saw the truck thunder off in a spray of wet road and thought back to all the trucks she had hitched lifts in during those turbulent days of school age rebellion; she had seen a lot of places in a short time that she would otherwise have had no reason at all to go to. Now, she did not go to many places; just the same dismal camps in the dismal Angolan bush, interspersed with the odd weekend in crumbling Luanda and the annual home run, which she was supposed to be spending visiting her exiled relatives in London. She didn't drive too often in Angola either and wondered if she was so out of practice that she ought to pack it in altogether but she also knew that that was a ridiculous idea. The only question that needed answering on this subject was whether the Ford would pack up before she had driven the miles that she wanted to drive.

She took in several more breaths, consciously willing herself calmer and refusing to give in to the symptoms of the Great Scare of Before Christmas. Before she had even begun to do this though, she knew that this was not similar in nature to the attack that had briefly hospitalised her then, but was something quite different. In her opinion, *that* attack had been a result of eating something less than wholesome but food poisoning, malaria and the other routine diseases of an insanitary condition had been ruled out; the most distressing part of the attack was how difficult she had found it to rid herself of the vision she had endured of a pair of shears cutting through her sinews and dropping her like a marionette. She had been outside, walking across the camp at Lubango on a grey day in the rainy season when the attack had occurred. She had just stopped dead as a great weariness came over her, felt her shoulders drop and the next thing she knew she was breathing in from an oxygen mask on a jogging stretcher headed for the camp infirmary.

She had not wanted to go to the infirmary but, with a thrill of horror at the memory, at that moment a feeling of complete resignation had overcome her; she didn't really care what happened to her. Indeed, she had quite liked the idea that she was being whisked off somewhere without having to make any decisions about where, what, how and why she was being whisked off. It felt good to be relieved of such duties and responsibilities; she felt better, more peaceful and strangely ecstatic, and she minded not at all being parked on an iron bed and left alone for some hours. When the doctor finally came and poked at her, she was a little disappointed that he could find nothing wrong with her because that bed suddenly felt comfortable in the same way as the one in the Pretoria Military Hospital Psychiatric Ward that she had spent so long in had felt comfortable. When he came again the next day, she felt much the same, the only concerning moment being the one where he speculated about prescribing some anti-depressants – but they were expensive and hard to come by; Anna-Marie assured him that she was fine really, and there was nothing to worry about. He gave her two days bed rest as the best he could do.

So no, this attack was not the same as the Great Scare of Before Christmas, but something very different and she was glad that she was alone, now that it had happened, because she would not have to go to hospital again and answer a lot of questions from doctors, especially as these would be South

African doctors who were probably more competent and, more to the point, would tell Steiner.

Was it *fear of getting caught*? She had asked herself that question and had admitted to herself that there was something in it. She now knew in detail what went on in that secluded part of the camp and the dread of being incarcerated in there grew on her like ivy.

She let go of the steering wheel and stretched her fingers; though she did her exercises and jogged as a normal young woman might, she missed the real challenge of physical training and the bad diet of the camps made her feel weak and bloated. Her eye sight was no longer so sharp either and sometimes she needed glasses to read; once, she had borrowed a pair of varifocals, but they had first made her stumble about like a drunkard and had then produced a remarkable illusion of disembodiment. For one terrifying moment, she could not see the rest of her body when she looked down and for a moment, had endured the sensation of just being a head floating in the air; a marionette.

What was similar to the feeling of panic, that she was now successfully mastering with her self-prescribed deep breathing exercises, was the shot of unwelcome adrenalin that she had felt when, last year, three youths had attempted to hustle her outside a bar in Luanda. She was just crossing the street when she had felt a sharp push in the back and looking up sharply, she had seen the second youth to her left and then the third to her right. All of them wore dangerous and surly looks but she had taken them to be no more than seventeen or so and, being confident in her unarmed combat skills, she had simply barged the one on the right out of the way and that was the end of that. It was full daylight and already a security guard from the bar was moving them on. The adrenalin had been sudden and decisive but was decidedly more of the *flight* rather than *fight* variety and this in itself was cause for worry; her first and overwhelming instinct had been to run. Somewhere along the way, it seemed, she had allowed cowardice to creep up on her.

She steadied herself and then, satisfied that she had mastered this attack, Anna-Marie released the hand brake and being careful to indicate even though the road was empty, continued her journey home from the shops. A little further on, she turned once more, this time, feeling a little more relaxed, without indicating, into her own cul-de-sac and drove carefully onto her own driveway and then with a shuddering realisation that she was home, began to shake uncontrollably. The trembling was profound and two great sobs escaped from her lips as she struggled to master himself and fight down the terrible fear that seized her once more. *This is just stupid*, she told herself. Ahead of her was the red garage door. Behind her on the back seat was the shopping. Above her were the feathery leaves and purple of the shading jacarandas. All she had to do was get out of the car, open the rear door, remove the shopping and take it into the house, yet there was before her a barrier so great that she could hardly bring herself to think about it. From out of the sky, a single hail stone dropped through the jacaranda tree in the drive way, hit the car, and then bounced off like a little polystyrene pebble.

*

Angola.

Monday Last

As Mickey Epstein made an attempt to push the truck, he cursed his own conscientiousness. He could, he told himself, just ignore it all and head off

248

for the Cut Line with his jerry can full of water and a more than reasonable prospect of making it to safety before the inevitable hornets' nest came down on him. The bridge guards would report the attack; they might even find the body of the driver and when SWAPO or FAPLA or whoever these files and filing cabinets belonged to put two and two together they would come up with an answer that would undo all his calculations as to radius, distance and kilometres squared. The handbrake was off and the truck had come to rest on a raised part of the road, just by a donga, so all he had to do was to get it rolling, push it down off the camber and gravity would take the old rust bucket down the gradient into the bush below. After that, all he would need to do would be to camouflage it and then hope upon hope that it would be enough to keep it concealed long enough for him to make it back and raise the alarm.

He was weak though. The water had given him a bit of new life but he needed food, was feeling sick from the bites – malaria? – and had taken to sucking his shirt to get the salt out of it and back into him. He had eaten the driver's lunch – tinned fish courtesy of the People's Republic of China – but it wasn't enough and he reckoned that his body fat was coming to the end of its reserves. And he reckoned he still had two days hard march ahead of him.

The truck was a dead weight and he wondered if it might have slipped into gear when it had broken down. He had checked the tank – bone dry – looked under the bonnet to see if anything might be done there but without petrol he knew it was hopeless. Climbing back into the cab, he decided to have one last try at starting her up; the clutch was shot, he knew, but the gear stick moved freely, so he discounted it being stuck in gear; sometimes there was a bit of petrol left in the engine and even if it was just fumes, all he needed was for the blasted thing to start rolling. He pressed the starter; nothing but the last coughing gasps of an exhausted battery. Next, he thought about lightening the load, but then dismissed the idea; the load was the vital bit and he was too weak to be shifting steel cabinets full of the weight of paper about. There had to be a solution, he told himself; hadn't Archimedes moved the world with a lever? This was just one *fokken kak* Russian truck.

If he couldn't push the truck, he reasoned, he would need to get some other force on to it. He couldn't pull it, that was also for sure, and he could not make it fly either so the only force left to him that was freely available, to hand and in abundance was gravity. He slipped out of the cab, went to one of the side panniers and opened it. There was a jack there.

'That is a *fokken* miracle,' he said, out loud. 'The only *fokken* pannier in Africa that the Kaffirs haven't emptied. They must have no traffic stops in Angola.'

Placing the jack under the rear right wheel axle, he attached the handle and quickly pumped it up. It was a flat headed device, he was pleased – ecstatic – to note as his plan would not work with the type of jack that held up the axle in any sort of groove. The wheel came off the ground slowly – ever so slowly – but it came up. When it was as high as it would presently go, he went back into the pannier, hauled out a length of oily hemp rope and tied it around the jack.

'Here goes,' he said, taking the strain on the rope. 'Now move it, you *bladdy goffel*.'

He yanked at the rope, tugging at it with all his strength, shocking the jack as hard as he could. It moved. A little. He yanked again. It moved. A little.

'Third time for luck,' he said. 'Come on *choti ghoti*. Be a beauty, hey?'

The jack stayed put; the truck stayed put; the downward pressure of the weight of the truck was simply too much for him to overcome. He might as well have run a rope round the back leg of an elephant.

Mickey nodded.

'Shovel and pick, then' he said, glad that he had not abandoned his kit.

Mickey retrieved his entrenching tool from his kit and began to pick at the earth around the left front wheel. This, he realised, was a task that needed to be completed with some care and so he filled himself up with water in the hope that it would help him to stay sharp for the moment when, with the right rear wheel high on the jack and the left front wheel undermined, the whole shooting match might be persuaded to tip up and roll down into the donga below. The dirt was dry and came up easily, crumbling under each quick peck to reveal the sandy soil below and Mickey was careful to ensure that he dug from the lip of the road inwards towards the wheel rather than the other way so that he always had his eyes on the green bulk of the stranded monster. When he was satisfied that a few last shovelfuls would do the job, he paused and then decided to make sure of things by undermining the rear left wheel too and the middle one for good luck. It was not a long job; a couple of cubic metres to shift or so and when that was done, he returned to the front wheel. Encouraged by what he took to be a slight list to port, he rested one hand on the front bumper and then began to pick away at the earth supporting the tyre. The moment was close now, he thought, and to make doubly sure, he went back to the jack and screwed another couple of turns; the truck groaned. Another turn. Another turn; another groan. He went back to the front, pecked a little more earth out and was gratified to see small fissures beginning to crack open in the crumbling dirt.

Would it go? He stood back and then went to the other side of the cab to give it a shove. The vehicle didn't budge, but he sensed that there was a definite change in the stubbornness of the *bladdy* thing. Before, he was convinced, the heap of Russian *kak* had refused point blank to move; now, it was *afraid* to move and Mickey took heart from that as he tried to rock the suspension. Again, the truck didn't move much but now Mickey was convinced that he had got the measure of it and it was time for the *coup de grace*. Kneeling down once more, he very carefully dug out a couple of handfuls of dirt from under the left front wheel, then scooped out the hole further until it was a horizontal hands length deep, before reaching for a grenade, pulling the pin and popping it in.

There was a dull report and a spurt of earth came out of the hole, like bubbles from a straw. And then the ground finally gave way, slowly at first and then quicker as it slid. The truck went with it, front left side first and then full broadside, under the impetus of its own weight, until it flipped, rolled and plunged down into the donga with a sound like a bag of tools being thrown through an oil drum tunnel, coming to rest upside down, its wheels spinning slowly, as though dying of exhaustion.

'That'll keep the recovery Tiffies busy,' said Mickey, smiling to himself as he surveyed the area. There was no sound that he could make out beyond the inevitable cicadas, which he took as a very good sign indeed. 'Right then. Now to cover it up.'

This was a much easier task as the donga was already riot with vegetation. The bamboo felled easily and many of the thorn bushes were already partly rotten for being submerged during the rainy season, so a couple of kicks and a blow from a panga were enough. After that, he got a bit more subtle and remembering how the gardeners at home would lay a hedge, he cut only half way through three or four more acacias, bent them over and hoped that they would grow up quick; *ja* it would take a while but long term, it was a nice touch.

Looking up, he saw that they day was nearly over and that night was advancing at the trot. He picked up his pack and weapon, made a mental note of prominent local landmarks so that he would be sure of finding the vehicle again, and then set himself the target of two thousand steps before offering himself up to the night and the mosquitoes once more.

*

Winterhoek

1963

The hail stone was followed quickly by the ticky-tack of more and the cold wind lifted her skirt as Anna-Marie took shelter under the canopy of the pie shop by the Caltex. It was 1963 and Johnny Kongo's *Tulips for 'Toinette* was sliding out of the tinny speaker, making the thin girl grimace and put a cigarette in her mouth. There was a tap on the window and a finger directed her to the *No Smoking* sign; she gave a tart grin in return, put the matches away, but kept the cigarette in her mouth and looked up at the darkening sky. The hail did not come often but everyone knew the warning signs and made sure they were quickly under cover for when it did come. Across the street some of the black people were scuttling into the

253

cover of the shops, some struggling with umbrellas, others holding folded newspapers over heads hunched down into their shoulders. On the forecourt, the car drivers switched off, climbed out and stood with hands on hips or struggled into rain jackets against the sudden cold. It wasn't possible to walk in the hail and dangerous to drive so, really, there was nothing to do but wait it out.

'Hi Anna-Marie,' said the little blonde boy, barefoot, in shorts and white school shirt. 'Do you like this kitten, hey?'

She looked down at the mongrel cat and then at the boy. Like her, he was a regular truant, but unlike her, he didn't seem to understand that what he was doing was wrong. They met sometimes, here, or in the Super Eight café where there was a pinball table and an owner who didn't care whether they went to school or not.

'Sure,' she said, hardly interested. 'Cool.'

'Would you like me to give it to you as a present?' His voice was sing-song high, innocent of design but full of curiosity. 'Do you think it might make you happy?'

She shook her head. 'You keep it. This is a big storm coming, hey? Keep under the canopy here until it was gone.'

The ticky-tack of the hail suddenly increased in tempo and strength, as though the sky had shifted up a gear and white pebbles began to bounce down into gutters already swollen with the sudden and intense rain. The cat, which was no kitten but a full grown Tom, squirmed in the boy's full arms and became agitated as the storm began to ratchet up from pebbles to golf balls. The first of the windows in the shop across the street shattered as the golf balls swelled up into rocks and then a whole volley of these cannon balls flung themselves against the storefronts, punching through the windows and shattering the glass in a sudden frenzy of violence. The canopy over the petrol station clattered and banged as though rocks were being pitched onto it, while the street was suddenly covered in lime green feathers of jacaranda as the hail stripped the trees that lined it. Somewhere, a burglar alarm had been set off and its klaxon insistence added irritation to the anger of the storm.

'*Jeez*,' said Anna-Marie. 'That has to be a record for broken windows in one storm, hey?'

'Cool,' said the little boy, trying to sound grown up.

Anna-Marie frowned: 'You don't need to grow up so fast,' she said, weary beyond her thirteen years. 'Be a kid for as long as you can.'

'Sure, Anna-Marie,' piped the little boy. 'Do you like Coke or Pepsi best? Which do you think is the best?'

At that moment the wriggling cat squirmed free, bound out of the little boy's arms and ran swiftly out into the street.

'Hey, come back,' cried the little boy following.

'Don't go into the hail!' cried Anna-Marie, tossing her unlit cigarette aside and chasing. 'Stay under the canopy.'

'I will just grab this cat,' he answered. 'It will be all fine.'

As he stepped into the road, a hail stone the size of a fist hit him on the temple, killing him instantly. The cat did not look back.

'He just went,' said Anna-Marie, later. 'One second only, he was in that storm. One second only. We really do not have any control over things,

255

do we? One tiny decision and we can be dead. How can anyone live so? Why even bother to try?'

*

Angola

Tuesday Last

The morning air was clear and fresh and Mickey held up his swollen hands and arms to the breeze like a votary offering up a prayer. A baboon barked somewhere off to the right setting off a wild screeching of birds while up above the mewling of a hunting bird hanging high in the sun dripped the honey of hope into the morning; that bird would be able to see the Cut Line from up there, perhaps even farther towards Rundu and the bases of 41 Mech or 23 Leopard battalion; there might even be patrols in the area; he resolved to remind himself to look out for their spoor; it would keep his mind alive in the coming heat and force him to use his gritty eyes, now swollen and almost closed by the bites. His eight day old beard had given some protection to his face in the night but not enough to ward off the creatures with stings so deep and so hard they would go through three layers of clothing and although he knew that he had to maintain a positive mental attitude if he was to make this last hundred klicks, his hunger gnawed at it constantly, devouring it bite by bite, even as the insects had done. The buzzard mewled again and Mickey forced his cracked and swollen face into a rictus grin; at least it wasn't a vulture, he thought.

The bush here was thick and so close that the moisture that evaporated from the *vleis* and marshes remained trapped under the dense canopy. In some places, the green looked like a solid wall and though it would have made his life so much easier to travel on the road, this was just not something he could risk in daylight. Actually, he was surprised that there had been no following patrol already, given what was on that truck and though he was prepared to guess that the bridge guards had not yet reported in – or perhaps reported in a report that did not bear any resemblance to the ignominious truth – he was not willing to bet his life on it and that was what was at stake. He washed his arms in water from the jerry can in the pursuit of momentary relief from the irritation and then gritted his teeth against the day.

He found a path, a tunnel that meandered a little but held to a general course south and with the jerry can in one hand, his rifle in the other and the pack on his back he put his head down, entered a very private misery and ploughed on through the steaming heat. Throughout the long day he was plagued in turns by mopane flies that got into his eyes, nostrils, mouth and ears and then by butterflies that came to drink on his bloody sores and then by the sharp burn of a bite from the tsetse flies. The game trails he was following conspired against him too by disappearing into flat green walls forcing him to retrace his steps and thus add to his journey rather than subtract from it. From time to time he was overwhelmed with the sensation that he was being watched and although he tried to dismiss it, he knew that he probably was being observed but whether by man or beast he could not tell; probably beast; something had made these game trails. Later in the day he heard the snuffle of a rhino feeding but the bush was so dense that though the animal might have been a yard away, he caught not a glimpse. It was only a little while after this that he stumbled out of the bush and into a patch of stinging nettles, a final insult that in its sheer cruelty left him close to tears.

Each kilometre that day was a tortuous, pain filled marathon which Mickey grimly embraced because he had no choice but to do so and made worse by the need to do everything slowly because in his numbed state anything done quickly usually ended in a trip or a fall and when he went down he did not always know if he would be able to rise. The jerry can was something that he began to curse for its weight and sheer unwieldiness and then for the temptation it offered; he could throw it away and trust to his water bottle for luck; but that would be stupid and very possibly death. His rifle, he did not curse, though it seemed to catch in every bush, for it was now a valuable crutch; each little bit of weight it bore was one little bit less that weighed down on his weeping feet; he used the antiseptic ointment from his First Aid kit that day, but he thought that he should, perhaps, have used it earlier. The painkillers he would not take for they took off the edge and Mickey needed all the edge that pain could give him. At one point he gave in to necessity of doing something about his swollen, bleeding bites and reluctantly, hurriedly, stripped off in a clearing where there was a pool of water cascading over rocks. There he rubbed himself with wet sand and mud, as the Ovambos did, which gave some relief and then, dressed once more, took more of the mud and coated his exposed skin with it, as protection against both the sun and the flies. For a season, it worked, but the night was not far ahead.

*

Karl Marx Reception Centre, Lubango, Angola

1980

*Thomas Mashaba*, wrote Anna-Marie, readying her report for Steiner. *Native of Durban educated in Bulgaria certainly and Moscow probably. Genuine, intelligent, honest and sceptical of Marxist-Leninist theory. He commented to me in private that if he was offered the choice between a plane ticket to New York or Moscow, he would take the New York option every day of the week. Although guarded, as everyone is here, he thinks that multi-racial democracy is the only way forward for South Africa because without the educated white population fully committed to progress then the economy will collapse. Is also privately critical about the corruption in the camps with certain comrades enjoying privileges beyond what is justifiable by increased levels of responsibility. When a white South African comrade came to give a speech – you know his name – on the subject of 'Armed and Dangerous, We Will Overcome', Mashaba listened to the talk and commented; 'That fellow has rarely been armed and never has he been dangerous'. He is a talented man and widely liked and respected. He is not feared though. He expresses a desire to fight, as all the comrades here do, but while there are plenty of comrades who want to avoid anything that might entail some real personal danger, I believe he is genuine in this wish but I doubt whether he would pass basic training. Sometimes I have thought that he might be turned to serve our ends but I would dismiss this possibility now. He might be useful as a contact in the future, if ever some sort of negotiations like those undertaken with the Rhodesians were happening. He seems to be more reasonable than most. More research on his background might reveal something useful. AMvZ.*

The report went to the dead letter box. Three months later, Thomas Mashaba was killed in Luanda by a single gunshot to the head just as he left for the British Embassy on his way to apply for a study visa. When she heard the news, the glass she was holding cracked in her hand.

'He was my friend,' she said, as the bar owner cleaned up the mess.

'He was a good comrade, this is true,' said her companion. 'And so soon after Uncle MJ too. Truly we are under an attack of very bad luck, sister.'

*

*Peter Moloti*, she wrote. *Returned from operations in South Africa. Based in Johannesburg area, his adopted terrorist name is Uncle MJ. Clever, light on his feet and ruthless, he claims to have been responsible for several attacks on police stations including landmine operations. Accepts that civilian casualties are inevitable in landmine operations but justifies it as being a necessary cost of the struggle. He is an absolute bastard, I reckon, and is more of the gangster than the committed ideologue. The girls in the camp are wary of him for good reason, I think. His way of avoiding arrest while maintaining an aggressive team in constant contact is to break his cell of eight to ten men down into four or five different sections who never meet up except to carry out an operation. He accepts no contact of whatever sort from local organisations, refuses all messages or offers of support even from friendly bodies and takes what he needs, when he needs it by straightforward robbery. Those he suspects of informing the police, he kills on the spot. In this way, he hopes to choke off sources of information available to us while ensuring that his supplies of food, money etc are protected. He makes a big noise of wanting to go back to South Africa at the earliest opportunity and I think that the authorities here would like nothing better. For a start, his active nature puts them to shame and second, I believe some of the other ANC comrades here would like to see him meet a bullet, the better to protect their own ambitions.*

*Steiner. There are people watching me. I know they do this routinely but I have the impression that this is being stepped up. I am meeting too many people who are a bit too obvious in wanting to befriend me. I feel that I am close to being compromised. I cannot be sure but extraction at short notice may be needed in the near future. AMvZ.*

\*

Angola

Wednesday Last

Another tortured night. Another tortured empty day and Mickey knew he was coming to the end. He believed that he might now be actually be walking in circles as only one eye was open, his left leg was dragging and he was trembling constantly. This was it. This was the Day of Reckoning, the *Dies Irae*, the Last Judgement. He held onto that thought because at school he had played the trumpet in the orchestra and the music master had got them to play Verdi's *Dies Irae* because he thought that boys liked all the drama, *sturm, drang* and explosions in it. Actually, Mickey had liked that music almost as much as those Zulu walking songs and so now, to keep himself sharp and keep himself going, he tried to imagine the trumpet part he had played and when he had remembered it and got it clear, several hours had gone past and he was still moving, so he went back to remembering all the other pieces of music that he had played and when he had remembered about half of them it was mid-afternoon and he was still moving and judging by the sun he was moving south which meant he was going in the right direction so he went back to playing Verdi over and over in the hope that by the time he had played it to death he would still be alive and somewhere near the Cut Line.

And then in the last hour before sunset, Mickey heard it. It was unmistakeable. It was the sound of angels and gathering up the last of his strength and will power out of the bush he came at a last run, staggering more than jogging, out into the open, waving one arm wildly above his head while his rifle slid off his shoulder and the jerry can thumped against his legs. It was coming towards him, quite low, like a vast dragonfly, the whine of its rotors echoing the mosquito whine that had so tormented him and as soon as he saw it dart off quickly to one side preparatory to circling, he knew he had been spotted. His knees buckled under him and the weight of his pack keeled him over, but he did not care because he, Mickey Epstein, euphoric and victorious, was back from the dead and bearing gifts beyond riches to boot.

And as the chopper crew piled him into the spare seat he thanked God and the music master and promised himself that as soon as he got back to Grootfontein, he would drink two of the coldest beers that the biggest deep freeze in the whole of South West Africa could provide, then shortly after that give Corporal Andrew Bridgeman the rogering of his life and after that, he would take his boots and webbing off.

*

10

Saturday

Ahead and below the double line of petrol tin fires stood out in the darkness as well as any set of landing lights in the otherwise stygian landscape and the aircraft banked around to line up for its final approach. Dropping like a stone out of the sky, it hit the end of the runway with a sickening lurch sending clouds of dark earth up into the total darkness, feathered its rotors with a maddening rush and slid more than rolled down the runway, extinguishing the fires as it came on until the only light was the single bulb of the small torch of the controller at the end of the runway.

'Welcome to Angola,' said the despatcher, indicating the lowering tailgate. 'Have a nice day.'

Smithy tightened up his belt, checked his pistol and tried not to think about his rotten luck any more. He was back on the border, over it indeed, and out here the only law that mattered was the law of survival and that law demanded guns, no compromise and keen senses; there was no room for anything else. Mostert was not armed but she too was grim as she shouldered her holdall and followed him off the tailgate. The aircraft did not stop and as it turned in a tight, ponderous circle, Smithy saw the petrol tin fires light up again and then, only minutes later go out again as the aircraft roared down the strip and disappeared into the vastness of the African sky.

'Follow me, Ma'am, Sergeant,' said a voice out of a camouflaged face. 'The Major is going to give you a briefing and then you should get some shut eye, hey? Tomorrow – today actually - is going to be a bitch.'

The darkness of the bush was disorientating but strangely comforting as they followed their escort for in among the cinnamon and spice of the earth and the soft green smell of water, there were the harder smells of metal, oil, rubber, fuel and rations that told them that 41 Mech were here in force. 41 Mech: Smithy and Mostert had been up with this elite unit last year to investigate a series of murders and they both knew just what a tough nut unit it was. Being in the middle of it made them feel safe, for if a person was not safe when surrounded by this much muscle, this many armoured vehicles, this many automatic rifles and enough testosterone to repopulate a famine stricken country, then that person could not feel safe anywhere.

Mostert tried to affect a sort of disdain for 41 Mech, she being from their rivals over at 23 Leopard, but it was only the sort of concocted disdain that the Springboks felt for the All Blacks. She knew what they were capable of. Smithy, being a mere copper, was looked down on by anyone in a brown uniform, but he didn't care at all; he had been in combat with this mob and could afford to shrug off any jibe, especially as it was most likely that the normal rotation of National Service meant that there had probably been a 90% turn over in personnel since last he was with them.

A tent flap was lifted momentarily and the smell of damp canvas and warm coffee was added to the ambience as they found themselves propelled into a busy command post. Along one long wall was a row of trestle tables, topped with radio sets of different types and backed by boards full of figures that told of ammunition, fuel, food, water supply states; vehicle readiness states; artillery, helicopter, aircraft on-demand states; medivac stand-by; and maps, lots of maps, covered with shiny plastic and marked up with tactical symbols, grid references, arrows, question marks and all the arcana of remote battle. From hand to hand, folders, papers and chits were passed, checked, ticked off as armed clerks corrected numbers on the boards while trance-like signallers scribbled down Morse messages translated in real time. Here and there, an officer or NCO barked terse jargon rich demands into handsets and then froze in impatience while the replies came through.

'How much do you know?' asked Major van der Merwe. He was too busy for introductions; too busy for anything superfluous. Smithy put his copper's eye over him and noted that he was thinner, more drawn, stripped down and steelier than last year. Then, he had thought him too sensitive for the job he had been given but there was no evidence that such a quality remained now. The yardbrush moustache was still there and his uniform was still creased and starched but the troubled conscience of the rightness of the cause of this war and the suspicion of indecision seemed to have disappeared. He had seen something to change his mind, guessed Smithy. It wasn't unusual; a liberal disposition was often tempered into hardness on contact with the heat of reality and there was no sharper place to experience that heat than up on the border where illusions were burned away faster than a struck match in a blast furnace.

'Mickey Epstein has come out of the bush after being posted Missing Presumed Dead at Capinga,' replied Mostert, looking around the command post. 'That's it.'

Van der Merwe nodded. 'On his way back he came across a truck full of SWAPO intelligence files. He buried them in a ravine and we're going to retrieve them – which is what all this drama is about. SWAPO and FAPLA know this too and have got similar intents.'

'How many files?' asked Mostert.

'All of them, by the sound of things,' replied van der Merwe.

'All of them?' said Mostert, wide-eyed.

'A truck load at any rate,' said van der Merwe. 'Whoever loaded them up must have got a tip-off about the raid and had them away before the airstrike went in. The driver got lost though – *ja*, hard to believe, I know, but that's Epstein's tale. And that's your problem, not mine and I'm not interested in anything else beyond the *kak* I've to deal with in the here and now. My problem is that SWAPO and FAPLA are coming with tanks and my Ratels aren't equipped to deal with tanks. Your job is to take responsibility for the files once we've seen them off and the Tiffies recover the vehicle. So, Captain Mostert, you will go with the Tiffies – they're just next door. We're going in at first light. Sergeant Smith, you will go with Charlie squad.'

'What's that?' said Smithy, his heart sinking.

'Ratel 90.'

'Where's Mickey Epstein now?' asked Mostert, as Smithy's eyes went up to the ceiling.

'In our medical centre,' answered van der Merwe. 'Under guard. Someone from BOSS told us to keep him away from everyone until you speak to him.'

'Has Colonel Steiner been to see him?' said Mostert.

'No. BOSS were insistent. I turned him away. Epstein is under guard,' said van der Merwe. 'Which is why you're going in the Ratel 90, Sergeant Smith. I'm short-handed again, thanks to you.'

'Well thank you very much, Mickey *bladdy* Epstein,' muttered Smithy. 'Your timing is impeccable. Why could you have not waited until after the weekend to be a hero?'

Smithy felt a tug at his sleeve and turned to face a ginger-haired man, large, bearded with wild hair and a fair skin that had been roasted cricket ball red by the sun.

'That's Corporal Naude,' said van der Merwe, turning away. 'He's your commander. Do as you're told.'

Corporal Naude stood there, almost stupidly, a quizzical smile on his face, waiting for the protest that would naturally come from a sergeant's three

266

stripes and ready to bat it away. Smithy, however, knew that any sort of protest was pointless and anyway, three inexperienced stripes were not as much use in the survival stakes as two experienced ones. It did bother him a little that Corporal Naude was a year or two younger than him, a fact that rankled more than it logically should, but this too was just something else he would have to swallow. There was some comfort to be drawn from the sheer size of the man though; he was at least a head and a half taller than him and barn door wide.

'Shouldn't I stay with Captain Mostert?' said Smithy, hopefully.

'Do as you're damn well told, Sergeant,' replied van der Merwe.

'We'll talk later,' said Mostert. 'When we've got the files. *Ja* and,' she dropped her eyes and brushing past him, touched his hand lightly, almost imperceptibly. 'Keep your head down, hey?'

'No fear,' answered Smithy, as he watched her go, pleased by that tiniest of lapses.

'What a wonderful little lady,' said Corporal Naude, politely. 'How marvellous it is to have the pleasure of female company from time to time.'

*

Karl Marx Reception Centre, Lubango, Angola

1981

*Steiner. There is talk about Capinga camp. Something is up. I don't know exactly what it is but there are rumours that high ranking officers are being quietly moved out of it in anticipation of something big. The Capinga camp commander was here a few days ago and three new villas are being constructed. An order for office equipment has also been placed. Are you planning to raid it? AMvZ.*

*

Saturday

'Got a weapon for me?' asked Smithy, patting his pistol holster. 'I mean, one a little bigger than this?'

'None bigger here than a Ratel 90,' grinned Naude, leading him out of the tent. 'And we're bombed up to the gunnels too.'

'And where on earth does that accent come from?' asked Smithy.

'From the fine County of Suffolk in God's own country, which is England.' The burr and ring was as thick as a rich loam after ploughing. 'By way of the Royal Tank Regiment.'

'You're a mercenary?' asked Smithy.

'Soldier of Fortune is the term I prefer,' replied Naude, kindly. 'Though I am, in fact Afrikaaner on my father's side, as the name might betray.'

The darkness swallowed them and it took Smithy a moment or so before he was able to distinguish the solid shapes of men and armour from the penumbra of the night. The starlight helped a little as he dandled alongside Naude's giant figure, made larger for being identifiable mainly by silhouette. He wondered just how it was possible for such a large man to fit into the commander's hatch of a Ratel but then he remembered how smaller, slimmer-waisted men complained of bruised hips after being bounced around the turret ring when bundu bashing over rough terrain. Perhaps Naude was just jammed in, hammered like a peg into a hole?

268

'This is ours,' said Naude, knocking on the rear door. 'Let's just see who's at home, shall we?'

The door opened to reveal two faces distorted by the eerie red glow of the cabin lights. Both of them were bearded and pale skinned, their eyes made black by the light and there was an unwelcome intensity in their gaze.

'Jif is our driver,' said Naude, indicating the man on the left. 'He isn't a bad one either, when he is sober.' Jif nodded but offered no greeting. Smithy thought he had the look of a car thief about him; slippery-eyed, with a SlimJim never far away. 'And Grobbler is the gunner.' Again a nod, but no greeting. Grobbler was blonde and unblemished and just the sort to steal your girlfriend away at a pool party. 'And aren't we are all just one big happy family? Yes, we are. Are we topped off with diesel?'

Jif nodded. 'She's full. Who's he?'

'Sergeant Smith will be replacing Arnie for this operation,' announced Naude. 'So let's make him welcome, shall we?'

'What's his job?' grunted Jif.

'He can manage the rear Browning in need, but mainly it will be his job to clear away the empties,' said Naude. 'If that's agreeable?'

'*Clear away the empties*?' said Smithy. 'What does that mean?'

'Just what it sounds like,' replied Naude, good humouredly. 'When we start to hose down the enemy's ardour with our several weapons, it will be your job to stop the empty cartridges from getting in the way of the turret ring mechanism and jamming it up. All you have to do is scoop them up wherever they may fall and dispose of them in a suitable manner, *viz* out of a convenient hatch, of which there are plenty.'

269

'*Viz*,' said Smithy, his neck back and his eyebrows arched.

'*Viz*,' confirmed Naude. 'Tickety-boo.'

'*Tickety-boo*?' repeated Smith.

'Tickety-boo,' confirmed Naude. 'Now, it being as near to 0300 as makes no different, I suggest we make our preparations. I'm sorry, I can't offer you a tank suit, but I'm sure you'll feel just as comfortable in your own gear. Jif: final checks, please. Grobbler: you too please. I shall see to the cam nets while Sergeant Smith makes coffee for us all.'

'Are you sure we shouldn't be having Earl Grey and scones,' remarked Smithy, drily.

'Coffee will be just fine, thank you, Sergeant Smith,' said Naude, refusing the bait. 'And porridge too, if you can manage it.'

'He's a sad disappointment to his parents,' said Grobbler, pushing past. 'Got thrown out of school for complaining about the kiddy-fiddling vicar.'

'He's alright,' added Jif, tapping a finger at his temples. '*Bosbevok*, but *lekker*.'

'An observation that I welcome, even though you are not qualified to make it,' said Naude, climbing on top of the vehicle. 'And it was a priest of the Roman Catholic Church not a Vicar of the C of E, to be precise. And I take my coffee NATO standard which, for the uninitiated, means milk and two sugars.'

Smithy shrugged his shoulders, gave a wry smile and got busy with the Esbit stove while Grobbler checked the 90mm rounds in the racks and then opened up the boxes of link for the machine gun.

'Five ball, one tracer,' he said, in Smithy's direction. 'Four hundred round belts – you know how to connect up link?'

'This isn't my first time in a Ratel,' he replied.

'That isn't what I asked,' said Grobbler. 'Do you know how to do it or not? This isn't a *fokken* braai we're going to, so answer one way or the other. We're depending on you today, copper.'

'I know how to do it,' said Smithy, firmly.

'Show me then,' replied Grobbler. 'Because it will also be your job to connect them up when we call for replenishment.'

Smithy took the belts proffered and snapped the two long crocodiles together. They were heavier than he remembered from training college and, he admitted to himself, he was glad to refresh himself.

'Hand them up to me,' ordered Grobbler, climbing into the turret. 'Put them into my hand just *so*, hey? Naude likes them to be handed him just *so*. It makes a difference in contact, *ja?*'

Smithy felt the seriousness of the business and did as he was told; he knew that these small details were war winners in the confusion of battle.

'*Lekker*,' said Grobbler. 'Now you watch him good when he is firing and have another belt ready always.' There were boxes stacked in rows all around the crew compartment. 'You won't be on the intercom, so he'll just shout for it and you tug his trouser leg and then put the belt into his hands as I have showed you. You understand this now? Good. Now make the coffee – hot and strong, hey?'

271

Smithy made the coffee hot and strong and then boiled water and powdered milk for porridge. Up above, Naude rolled up the camo nets, patiently unsnagging the lines as they caught on hatches, branches and kit fittings until they were neatly stowed, all the while humming a tune that Smithy found vaguely familiar but couldn't quite place.

'*Men of Harlech*,' whispered Grobbler, taking a cup. 'You seen that movie with Michael Caine and Buthelezi in it about Rorke's Drift? It's his favourite. Sees it in the bioscope any opportunity. He's saving up to buy a video player so he can have his very own copy and watch it every night.'

'It is a fine example of the cinematographer's art,' said Naude, who had overheard. 'My father took me to see it in the Odeon in Bury St. Edmunds when I was a boy. Unfortunately, I did not draw the lesson from it that he intended to impart and got a beating for it.'

'*Ja*, what was that then?' asked Smithy, proffering a cup.

'I came away from the cinema rather admiring the Zulu warriors,' said Naude, with a smile and reaching down for it. 'Mind you, I also wanted to be Welsh for a little while afterwards –I'm not sure which was more disapproved of. Still, it made me want to join the army from quite a young age. And here I am.'

'I thought you were in the British Army?' said Smithy, pouring out a third cup and handing it to Jif, who had arrived, spanner in hand.

'I was,' answered Naude, pleasantly. 'But all I could look forward to was the North German plain. I rather wanted to see a real battle. Always wanted to shout '*Fix bay-o-nets*' just like Michael Caine does in the film.'

'*Bosbevok*,' mouthed Jif.

'And have you done that?' said Smithy, concealing a smirk.

'Oh, once or twice,' answered Naude, tying up a loose end on one of the net fastenings. 'Once or twice.'

'And is your father proud of you now that you are in the South African Defence Force?' pushed Smithy.

'Oh, I wouldn't know about that. I haven't seen him for years,' replied Naude, rolling the netting into the spare tyre on the roof. 'He ran off with a pig farmer's wife from Bungay when I was ten. Some people do like to live interesting lives, it seems. The man in the Chinese chippy in that same town used to say that to rude customers, you know? He would say: *may you live in interesting times*. He meant it as a curse.'

'Any porridge ready?' asked Grobbler, handing Smithy his empty cup and then, suddenly, stiffening. '*Fok!*'

'What?' replied Smithy looking around, his heart leaping into his mouth.

'Wessels has got bacon again,' said Grobbler. 'How does he do it? Where does he get it from?'

Smithy deflated, his heart hammering.

'Some *fokken* cook, you are,' said Grobbler, sniffing at the wonderful piggy-salt smell and then screwing up his face. 'Wessels' crew gets bacon sandwiches and we get porridge.'

*

*Steiner. I'm to be sent up country to the camp at Capinga. Nothing has been said but I'm to go up very soon. If you are planning an operation against it, I don't want to be there when it gets hit. The people here know something is going to happen, I'm sure. AMvZ.*

\*

Smithy watched as Naude went through his routine. He knew that the longer a soldier was in contact with the enemy, the more precise, the more logical, the cooler they became and yet paradoxically, they also became more superstitious. They had seen so many inexplicable effects of the physics of violence that they came to believe that there was no order, scientific or otherwise, and no predictability either in battle and that as there was no science or predictability at work, adherence to a lucky charm or ritual might just provide the hair's breadth difference that kept a man on this side of the great chasm. Jif had a Holy Medal blessed by Mother Theresa hung around his neck; Grobbler had a bullet with his service number engraved on it, which he kept in a matchbox in his breast pocket. Naude had seen plenty of action, Smithy was sure, and he had convinced himself that left sock first, then right sock second, then right boot on, then left boot on was the sort of tattoo that a war god might respect. A great calmness was on the man too as he prepared for the day and though he remained cheerful, there was within that mild manner concealed a deeper seriousness.

\*

*Mason. Steiner has gone quiet. What do you want me to do? AMvZ.*

\*

'*Oh Lord thou knowest how busy I must be about this day,*' said Naude, quietly, with great sincerity and depth of feeling. '*If I should forget thee, do not thou forget me.*'

274

'Amen,' said Grobbler and Jif, shaking hands.

'Smithy coughed, embarrassed by this display of humility, as only a man without religion could be.

'It was Cromwell's prayer,' said Naude, gently. 'It is a soldier's prayer from the lips of a God-fearing man from my part of the world. There is none better.'

*Amen*, Smithy wanted to say, but even in the sepulchral red light of the Ratel crew compartment, he could not bring himself to mouth the word. Praying would not help him. Praying would do him no good. And the irony of Naude being here when, being the proud owner of a British passport, he did not have to be struck him with full force. Here was another one paddling a boat down a river that led to the sea; someone else with a command over their own destiny that was denied to him; and here he was again, just Joshua *bladdy* Smith clinging to a *bladdy* life raft on the edge of a *bladdy* whirlpool. He would need something a lot more potent than prayers to turn his swamp, his inland sea, into a broad, fair, mile-wide river that would take him home to the gulls, the beach and the free horizons of the open sea.

\*

*Steiner. I'm going tomorrow. It's Capinga, definitely. I need to know if and when you are going to raid it so I don't end up getting hit. AMvZ.*

\*

'This is our job,' said Naude, simply and plainly. 'On the left is a tear drop shaped hill which will be occupied to protect our flank. Ahead of us is a belt of thick bush which extends all the way to the right. Beyond that on the right is open country leading down to a broad, what you fellows call a *vlei* – full of crocs and hippos, I shouldn't wonder – so we needn't worry about anything coming from that direction. In the centre is the road. So this is our mission: we are to move into that bush, keeping to the left hand side of the road and use it as cover to shoot out across the open ground at anything that comes towards us. I repeat: Mission: left hand side of the road, shoot out at anything that comes towards us. Expect infantry and BTR-60 armoured personnel carriers.' He paused before his next statement, as though overcoming a great reluctance to utter it; as though naming would call. 'We are expecting tanks. Our main armament will kill a T-55 but probably not with one shot so, Jif, we will need to jockey back and forth, in and out of that bush as quick as you may, but always on my word and just as we have practised. And don't ride the clutch.'

Jif nodded.

'Grobbler, you will need to be accurate and quick on that gun. Aim at the join between the turret and the chassis if you can. I will give you time for two shots before moving. I hope to find a flank or rear position, but you know that isn't always possible. I will also try to get in as close as possible. Pick your target and use the co-ax to make sure you're on target if you need to. Listen to me for directions. I will mark the target with tracer if it's needed.'

'*Ja*, boss,' said Grobbler, swallowing. '*Ja.*'

'Now then, we are Charlie Bravo,' continued Naude, calmly but seriously. 'On our left will be Charlie Alpha and on our right will be Charlie Tango, each moving in their lanes fifty to thirty metres from us. Charlie Tango has the 20mm and the infantry squad. We have mortars in support and there is word that the air force might pay us a visit. Happy?'

276

'Cuban MiGs?' asked Jif.

'The Major thinks we're a little further out than they care to venture.'

Jif and Grobbler both nodded, hands in pockets, eyes down.

'The job is to hold the line while the Tiffies recover this special truck,' said Naude. 'Engines start at 0415. After that, strict discipline on the net please. No casual chatter. Follow the drills. Any more questions?'

'How long?' asked Smithy, his voice croaking out of a dry mouth.

'And how long is a piece of string?' replied Naude, drawing out the question. 'The Major says that the Parabats made a right proper job of dropping that truck down a donga so I should think that we might be here for a while. Never mind.' His voice became reassuring. 'We must just do our jobs and hope for the best. Now, I think there might just be time for another coffee, eh, Sergeant Smith?'

\*

At 0415, the radio squawked and in an instant eight 12-litre, twin turbo diesel engines came alive, roaring out black jets of exhaust fumes like some dangerous black dog growling into life. The whine of hydraulics added to the grumbling roars of the Ratels as all silence was abandoned and shouted orders competed with the clanging of metal doors and the metallic rattle of rounds being ratcheted into machine guns. Smithy heard Naude give the order to Jif to let the clutch out and swing in behind the leader for the advance to contact. He opened up the hatch above his own head and without waiting for instruction, put a belt into his Browning and got himself into a position where he could see both forward and back.

It was still dark in a way that only Africa can be dark but as he looked up into the great swatch of stars above him, he could see that away to the East there was already a hint of the silver to come. Ahead, westwards, it was still ink but as the vehicle pulled this way and that way, sliding up and down through the loose sand and following the tiny red tail light of Charlie Tango, and then with a thump up onto the road, Smithy's eyes grew accustomed to the night and he was able to pick out the grey scar of the road and imagine the green of the mimosa trees that lined it. They were away and it was exhilarating to be in an armoured vehicle, with a machine gun in his hand, off into danger where all thoughts of right or wrong, all consideration of ethics, all hesitancy, all doubt, every guilty past could be forgotten in the urgency of the moment. For now, survival was everything; moffies, poofs, lesbians, spies, mad Parabat bastards coming back from the dead, *Ossewabrandwag* Nazis, Communists, mothers, drunken fathers, dead activists, BOSS, the *Bruderbond*, Apartheid...*everything*... and *all* of them could be forgotten. All he had to do, above all other considerations, was to come out at the end of this day with a skin reasonably intact and it would be a victory. All he had to do was keep his boat on the river afloat.

The cool air of the morning was beautiful and while Naude, sitting high up in the turret a good couple of metres above Jif's driving position, guided the Ratel along the road, Smithy peered out into the bush absurdly hoping to catch a movement of buck; they ought to be moving at this hour, he thought, and if the deep rumble of engines, the whirr of rubber on sand and the whine of hydraulics couldn't start them, then nothing would. Of course, the forest disguised the sound and dispersed it; that was the reason for the engine start drill for if FAPLA or SWAPO would know that 41 Mech were out there and on the way, they would not be able to distinguish

278

the number of vehicles or even the particular direction. And, he realised, what buck there was had been eaten, land mined or scared off by now.

They were travelling in a single column, line ahead now as the sun began to crack open the horizon behind them, firing up the sky in livid streaks of orange, red, bloody purple and brass all to the high pitch of turbochargers driving the run-flat tyres through the yielding sand. Smithy looked forward from time to time to see that Jif was following in the wheel tracks of the vehicles in front, now becoming deep furrows, and thanked the Lord he didn't believe in for the fact that they hadn't been mined. Naude stood hugely in the commander's hatch, waist and upper body high out, his helmet giving his head a strange alien-like silhouette, one that hardly moved with the yawing of the vehicle, he being jammed in there tighter than a Russian doll second in the stack. Grobbler's hatch was open too, but his head barely protruded – just enough to allow him to smoke a cigarette without filling the turret with smoke.

As the light came up, Smithy was able to see more and more than just the odd silhouette and red tail light and as the forms of the Ratels became more defined in the growing dawn, he thought once more of boats and battleships. The last time he had gone out with 41 Mech this comparison had struck him head on; the Ratels were 41 Mech's battleships, their lifeboats and their landing craft but now he pushed the comparison further. He had once had a book as a boy, all about Jackie Fisher and the Royal Navy of the First World War, and he remembered how he had read about Admiral Fisher scrapping all the old sloops, cutters, frigates and what-have-you of Nelson's navy to make a lean, tough, armoured force that was all war and no sentiment. There would only be four classes of ships, Fisher had declared; fast Destroyers, lean, quick dogs of war, ready to tail the enemy and then come out of the smoke and fog to torpedo them; Cruisers, fast, long range with medium guns to chase down the German fleets in China and Africa and protect the lifeblood of trade; Dreadnoughts, massive, thick armoured, all big gun ships with no other duty than to stand in the line of battle and slug it out with the heavyweights; and somewhere in between, the fast cats, the Battlecruisers, just tough enough to stand with the Dreadnoughts, fast enough to run with the Cruisers.

The Ratels were quick, but not quick enough to be destroyers, he considered. They had long range – 100k sometimes, before they needed refuelling – but not long enough to really be called Cruisers. In terms of protection they were nowhere near being Dreadnoughts; the designers had given them enough armour to stop a big 14.5 mm Soviet cannon, but only on the front – the sides and rear would only stop small arms and shrapnel. It certainly would not stop the 100mm gun of a T-55. They had clout in terms of firepower though; a 90mm gun that would fire HE, anti-tank HEAT and a big shotgun round full of ball bearings for anti-personnel; a co-axial .50 Browning alongside the 90mm operated at the flick of a switch by Grobbler and a 7.62mm MAG machine gun in Naude's capable hands. These would shred bone, muscle, people and boil blood; bricks turned to sand when hit and breeze blocks offered no more resistance than a stretched piece of paper did to a sharp pencil. And there was another Browning at the back, which Smithy operated; so the Ratel packed a punch. So perhaps he might think of them as half-Battlecruisers; it was a comforting thought. Until he realised that this half-Battlecruiser was going up against T.55s which qualified as Dreadnoughts.

Just after the great fire of the African sun shot up over the horizon, the line of Ratels fanned out into line abreast and Smithy lost sight of all but the two vehicles left and right of him as the bush took them and swallowed them as surely as if they had headed into the grey waves on an arctic convoy. The radio hissed from time to time as nervous commanders checked they were not alone and still keeping station; most were now in a bubble fifty metres or so in radius and would probably not see anything beyond the edges of that bubble until they left the bush. Smithy peered right and left and caught the outline of Charlie Tango to the right, easily recognised because the infantry were riding atop the Ratel with hatches open and weapons out. On the left, Charlie Alpha was a little harder to spot, but then he caught the plume of black exhaust as it shouldered its way over a fallen tree.

'Slow advance,' said Naude, dropping down into the turret as the vehicle braked to a walking speed. Smithy could hear him speaking into the intercom but could not hear the replies from Grobbler or Jif, but a sixth sense seemed to fill in the gaps for him. 'Enemy two clicks front. Eyes peeled.' Only his head and chest were now discernible and Smithy took this as notice to do the same. Looking right he saw the infantry de-bussing from Charlie Tango and going forward, crouched, hesitant, moving one foot at a time, putting security, concealment and caution before speed until they too had been swallowed by the bush. Checking his watch, he was surprised to see that an hour had gone by in the flash of a few moments; this was a good sign, he knew, because it meant his brain was speeding up, becoming more alert, honing up his senses.

'Halt,' said Naude, his voice quiet and even. They had finally found their way through the bush and were now ten or fifteen yards from the front edge of it. Beyond there was an open stretch of gently undulating ground, divided laterally by bands of good green grass alternating with drifts of sawn pinewood coloured sand, perhaps six or eight hundred metres across to another band of bush. His copper's eye told him that the tree-line contained something suspicious; his soldier's eye told him that there was a lot of dead ground between here and there and the impression of it being open was deceptive. Looking rear and then to his front, he noted that the infantry had gone to ground at the near edge of the bush and then, as he raised his eye to the far tree-line, he saw the movement of dark figures.

'Infantry at One o'clock,' said Naude, quietly. 'Browning on my command. The left file.'

The figures formed themselves into the scrawny forms of SWAPO guerrillas, wrapped up in baggy olive green fatigues held together with a motley collection of webbing. Even at this distance, Smithy could see that there were more tennis shoes and bare feet than boots and that this particular outfit had been the grateful recipients of a donation of red football socks. One or two carried their weapons on their shoulders, one hand clasping the barrel, the other holding a joint. He counted thirty, in three lines ahead, striding across the open ground a hundred metres apart and giving the impression that they were almost without a care in the world; almost, there were one or two who carried their AK-47s at the ready, banana magazines clipped on with a second taped widdershins to it for ease of a swift change; and he noted another carrying a light machine gun who had a pair of binos to his eyes and was scanning the bush in which 41 Mech was concealed. To no avail; Smithy watched as he rubbed his eyes between sweeps; the sun was directly behind 41 Mech and blinded him each time he attempted to scope them.

'Fire,' said Naude, and opened up with his MAG. Grobbler fired the Browning too as all along the tree-line, 41Mech opened up, filling the morning with cordite and smoke, the crackle of small arms and the *chunk-chunk-chunk* of the machine guns. Charlie Tango's 20mm also came into play and Smithy watched as the ball, tracer and exploding shells ripped up the ground all around the advancing troops, catching one man in a yellow T-shirt and cartwheeling him over for yards and yards and yards. 'Check fire,' said Naude. 'Reverse left twenty metres.' The Ratel suddenly shot back, jerking Smithy off the gun and into the crew compartment. Naude saw him but did not see him; the look on his red face was one of complete concentration. 'Halt. Forward. Straight thirty metres.' The machine obeyed, flinging Smithy backwards once more, but now Naude was looking forward and did not see his hopeless flailing.

Ten minutes and Smithy felt the breeze and caught the scent of water and decaying vegetation amidst the diesel fumes and the bad egg smell of cordite. There were people who got off on that heady smell and the gunners of the artillery would put the freshly ejected shell cases into their jackets to warm them up on a cold morning. The price was the stinking out of the latrines next day because the cordite fumes went straight through you and not even curried eggs could match it for sickly sweet intensity. Here in the bush, he noticed its intensity and drew comfort from it. That much ordnance would surely discourage the enemy and though he could not find it in himself to muster much personal hatred for them, he was happy that they were on the receiving end of it and he was not.

There was a crackle of automatic fire from the far side of the clearing. It was speculative, thought Smithy; just some guy giving himself a bit of courage because the chances of hitting anything at eight hundred metres with a Russian RPD machine gun were pretty low at the best of times, but he ducked instinctively anyway and was concerned to see a twig snap and a few leaves come fluttering down from high above him as one of those bullets zipped through the bush.

'Close hatches,' said Naude, and then repeated it for Smithy's benefit. Smithy did as he was told and pulled the overhead door down over him. It was stifling hot inside and he could see very little out of the gun ports that lined the bulkhead and as the Ratel began to manoeuvre, the beginnings of a nausea began to come upon him. When Naude ordered a halt, all he could think of was opening the doors to gulp at the relatively fresh air outside. A few minutes later and the sound of whistling dispelled all desire to open anything. It was only faint at first but then it gained pace and intensity until it was replaced by the *crump-crump-crump* of artillery rounds landing no more than a hundred metres ahead of them.

'Ours or theirs?' asked Smithy, but got no reply. Naude though seemed satisfied and shoving up his cupola into the open position, quickly thrust his head out, looked around and then ordered the Ratel forward once more. A little air came in with the movement and Smithy decided it was enough to justify him staying put for a little while longer.

'Man your gun, Sergeant,' said Naude.

Smithy did as he was told, opening the hatch and carrying out his own survey. Whoever had fired had done a good job of shredding the forest foliage and the front of the tree-line had been stripped clean. To his inexperienced eye, it looked like good shooting; the down-side to this was that it was SWAPO doing the shooting. The radio splattered once more and then they were off, this time moving forward from the tree-line and out into the open. Right and left, the other Ratels of the Battle Group were also on the move, running fast across the open ground, weaving as they

284

drove forward to pick out the best line until they reached the bush opposite and plunged into it.

'Range closed,' reported Naude, and then to Grobbler. 'This close we'll be on equal terms. I'm loading HEAT. Eyes peeled. You too, Jif.' And then to Smithy. 'Keep low but watch our Six.'

Automatic fire started to crackle again, some staccato, others lengthy, sustained but Smithy could see no-one and nothing beyond the confetti drift of stripped leaves and brittle twigs. The enemy, it seemed to him, were inexperienced, firing way too high and sustained fire like that from light machine guns would heat up barrels so fast they would melt and bend. This was a worrying factor because he could not believe that SWAPO would send a bunch of *moffie loskops* to retrieve the entirety of their intelligence files. If it was him, he thought, he'd be sending the crack troops, top of the class and tooled up with everything except the kitchen sink and coming in from… behind. He checked the Browning again as his admiration for Naude's anticipation went up a notch.

And then the bush in front exploded in a shattering torrent of ferocious bullets flying *zeep-zeep* through the ether, interspersed with the *thud* of mortars spitting out shells high, high into the air. Rounds pinged off the Ratel, making even Naude duck, but then the vehicle was suddenly and quickly reversing, left-hand down, while Grobbler sprayed whatever was in the bush to his front with the co-ax Browning, blowing off branches and sending tracer flying in all directions. Charlie Tango was doing the same, except his 20mm cannon was acting like a buzz-saw, levelling trees and sending them flying like skittles.

'Halt. Forward. Straight,' said Naude, heading straight back into the bush. 'Keep the co-ax firing, Grobbler. I'm unloading HEAT and loading HE. Halt. Target. Base of large tree. Watch my tracer.'

Smithy watched as Naude sent a long burst into the wide base of a big ficus whose bushy leaves reached right down to the ground. The hot white streaks of the tracer marked out the target as though he had put a laser on to it and it took no more than three tracer rounds to hit the spot before Grobbler shouted 'Ready! On!'

'Fire' said Naude. There was a dull thud, a metallic ring, a two metre wide flash from the muzzle of the 90mm and then Smithy felt a slap across his face like he had been hit with a wet towel. A moment later, there came another *boom* and the ficus tree, forty feet high, lifted up a little and then, like a pissed old lady in a hooped crinoline, keeled over and crashed to the forest floor as Naude raked it with his MAG.

'New Target,' said Naude. 'Watch my tracer.'

Smithy waited for it but then when no tracer happened and the realisation that no tracer was happening was because Naude was out of ammunition, he leaped forward, banging his head on the bulkhead, and handed up the long belt. Naude took it without comment, cracked it into the breach and slapped down the top cover. 'New Target. Watch my tracer.'

There was another burst of machine tool, another bang and the 90mm cartridge case was ejected onto the base of the turret. Smithy picked it up, filled it up with the handfuls of .5 and 7.62 cases that lay around the base of the turret and then tossed it, not without difficulty, out of the rear hatch.

So it went on for the next hour. The Ratels went forward, fired, reversed, sought out a new target and went forward. The 20mm cannons shredded everything; the High Explosive burst eardrums, kidneys, livers and blew arms and legs away from their owners while the constant spray of MAG and Brownings ploughed up the bush more thoroughly than the most destructive herd of panicked elephants could hope to. But each time the Ratels went forward, they went forward a little further and each time they reversed, jockeying around in their own lane, they reversed a little less and it seemed to Smithy that the few SWAPO soldiers he saw were all going one way and that way was not towards him. About this, he felt good, but he could not shake the feeling that in going forward he was less the lion tamer pushing the beast back with a chair and a whip but rather a tasty bit of meat being sucked down into a gullet; at some time there would be teeth to this SWAPO mob, he thought.

'New Target. Two o'clock' said Naude. 'Loading HEAT.'

Smithy watched as the turret wound round. From where he was in the crew compartment, he could see Grobbler frantically winding the hand wheels to get the gun on just that little bit quicker. Putting his head out of the hatch, he followed its line until he could see some fifty metres away the long, ponderous cockroach shape of a BTR-60 creeping forward. Atop it, a man wearing the ribbed cap of a soviet tanker's headgear was cocking the massive cannon ready to let fly while alongside it two olive green troopers pointed their Kalashnikovs forward, their heads turned slightly away as if they were afraid of what would happen when they pulled the trigger.

'On. Ready,' called Grobbler, his voice oddly muffled.

'Fire,' said Naude, and before the backwash of the blast could slap him again, Smithy saw the BTR turned into something for which the word 'explosion' was simply inadequate. There was a split second flash and then the armoured vehicle was nothing but roiling black smoke. The men he had seen, flesh and bone a moment earlier, were now gone. There was no trace of them. Nothing. 'New Target. One o'clock,' said Naude, mechanically. 'BTR. Loading HEAT.'

'On. Ready,' called Grobbler, once more.

'Fire,' said Naude, the same flat calm in his voice, and Smithy saw a second green vehicle disappear in a flash and a mass of thick oily smoke. 'Reverse. Thirty metres. Left–hand down.'

Smithy could not quite believe that he had seen what he had seen until one of the 90mm cartridge cases clanged out of the turret and began rolling to and fro across the crew compartment floor, like a discarded milk bottle. He picked it up. It was warm and stank of cordite.

'Browning, Sergeant Smith,' called Naude, as the vehicle went into a bouncing reverse. Smithy did as he was told, just as a shower of spent machine gun cartridges clattered down out of the turret like coins out of a one-armed bandit.

By now the noise was terrific and it seemed like there was nothing in the air but the rattle of machine guns, the deeper *chunk* of cannon fire and the deep *boom* of 90mms going off. Around him, the grass was now on fire and latching on to the trees and so adding the crackle of flame and thick white smoke of a bush fire to the growl and revving of powerful engines. Naude was waist high out of the turret, looking this way and that for more targets, locating friends and distinguishing them from enemies, his red face lightened by his white teeth and a mouth that seemed alternately pursed and chewing in a jaw that was set so hard that even the beard could not conceal it. Smithy wondered why he didn't make more use of the turret periscopes but then, looking around at the disintegrating bush, the smoke from burning vegetation to which was added the oily smoke of burning vehicles, he realised that anyone who fought closed up would be fighting blind. Naude was trusting to speed and movement and heavy use of the machine guns to make his opponents close up and fight blind.

There was a *pock*, followed by two more and then *pock, pock, pock* and Smithy saw Naude duck down. A moment later there was a dull explosion close by and the sound of someone slinging a handful of bolts at the side of the Ratel, which Smithy took a moment to recognise as the sound of accurate rifle fire and incoming mortars. He ducked down, only to hear Naude calling forcefully through the crew compartment for him to get his head up and start shooting the Browning. This seemed like suicide, but when Naude stuck his hand down and gave him an insistent wave with one thumb, Smithy took a deep breath like a swimmer going for the diving board and then sprung up and began to fire in the direction of the *pock pock* sound. He could see no target but if the man out there was anything like he was then just the sound of the gun would put him off his aim long enough for the Ratel, now going forward into the two o'clock channel, to disappear into the smoking bush. He eased off the gun, looked down into the crew compartment to see Naude's hand waiting for another belt and went to provide it.

In this moment, Smithy realised that he really had no control over what was happening to him. He had no idea whether they were winning the battle or not. He did not know whether the precious truck had been recovered – the truck! He had entirely forgotten about it – and nor did he know whether Mostert was alive or dead. His entire universe was now confined to this Ratel and the area around him, an area that would take no more than ten or twelve seconds for him to run across and considerably less for a shell to traverse. Life and death were not his to decide; he might be dead by the time he had finished taking his next breath; he might at this exact moment be in the sights of a SWAPO gunner; in the great scheme of things he counted for nothing, he realised, and all his worries about rivers reaching the sea meant absolutely nothing to anyone, including himself; his future was as irrelevant in this moment as his past and everything he had done, everything he wanted, owned, lusted for, hated meant nothing at all. He was utterly powerless to decide even the smallest of matters for a machine gun bullet was an unanswerable argument and a mortar round the ultimate judgement. The only thing that he could do was to do the things that came to hand; replace the machine gun belts, throw out the empties, stand up on the Browning when he was not doing either of those things and do them faster and better than he had done them so far. He would concentrate only on the things within his control, trusting to Naude and Jif and Grobbler to do the same and so, perhaps, come out of this maelstrom alive.

The Ratel lurched forward and Smithy found himself looking at open ground. Away to the right was the road and on it a line of military trucks were drawn up looking like frowns under stiff Cuban kepis.

'Target. Three o'clock. Soft-skinned vehicles. Loading HE,' said Naude.

*Soft-skinned*, thought Smithy, as he brought the Browning to bear. *Soft-skinned; like women*, he thought and then pulled the trigger. The tracer flew away like hot bees as he hit the cab of the lead vehicle and then watched as three or four Ratels opened up on the line, obliterating it within seconds. Incredibly, there were troops in some of the trucks still and he caught a glimpse of burning bodies staggering away from the smoke, the exploding petrol tanks and the fizz of automatic weapons zipping into the inferno. *Soft-skinned; like people*; he fired the Browning again, two long bursts into the canvas cover of a truck and saw the bullets hit like punches until one of his tracers hit the fuel tank and lit the whole thing up. A wave of sympathy began to engulf him at the thought of the families that he had just deprived of a son, a brother or a father but then pushed that wave right back down into his boots and out through the soles; *you chose to be here, brother*, he hissed. *I didn't.*

He came back to the harsh reality of the here and now and became suddenly aware of an upsurge in the excited chatter across the radio net. Jif was shoving the Ratel back hard and Naude was facing backwards directing so Smithy swung around and readied the Browning with a fresh belt. Glancing left and right, looking for the rest of 41 Mech, he realised that the whole line was reversing at speed, giving up all the gains that they had taken, until they were back at their start point; tear drop shaped hill on the left, *vlei* on the right, road up the middle, bush line all around, tree line, now burning and stripped, right ahead.

'New Target,' said Naude. 'Grobbler. This is it. Jif. Right-hand down hard back twenty metres on my word.' There was a pause, as though Naude was gathering himself. 'New Target. Tank at ten. Loading HEAT.'

Smithy followed the barrel as Grobbler spun the wheels and there, just where Naude had spotted it, was the T-55. It was low to the ground, front sprocket raised, a pan-handle turret with the gun elevated to an optimistic angle, while hanging off the back, like a bustle on a crinoline, was an oil drum of reserve fuel. Above the noise of the Ratel, he made out the dreadful squeal of metal sliding over metal and wondered how the thing did not simply grind itself to pieces for want of lubrication. Although he

291

felt his heart rate go up, his mind stayed strangely unimpressed; this was his first tank and it was smaller than he had imagined; that fuel tank was just asking to be shot up; he was no more afraid of it than he was of a dalek. There was a *bang* as Charlie Alpha took a shot at it and a moment later a great spume of earth fountained up in front of the tank.

'Jif. Forward ten metres. Grobbler. The seam between the turret and the chassis.' Naude was head and shoulders out of the hatch, quickly scanning left and right. 'Ten metres more. Grobbler? Ten metres more.'

Smithy put his head up as Naude stalked the tank. It was still moving forward but he noticed that the hatches were all firmly closed. Charlie Alpha sprayed it with tracer to keep it so as Naude looked for a flanking shot.

The earth shook and a long stab of flame erupted from the 100mm tank gun and less than a second later there came a terrible *clang*, a ringing like a cracked bell and the loud whine of a ricochet. Smithy saw something dark fly up out of the trees going at an incredible speed. It was only a spot in the sky and it was gone in a moment but he could guess what it was. A moment later, the sound was repeated, much louder, much, much louder and something long, black and solid screeched down the side of the Ratel with the sound of brakes going into a car crash. The metal of the side door glowed a cherry pink which faded slowly to leave a black, smoking gouge mark.

'Ten metres forward,' said Naude. 'Grobbler. Fuck. Take the shot.'

Grobbler fired and the Ratel immediately shot backwards.

'New Target,' said Naude. 'Tank twelve o'clock. Loading HEAT.'

Smithy did not care whether Grobbler had hit his mark or not. The round that had nearly ended his life had come from the tank in front of them, the tank that Naude had not seen, and he was only concerned with that. It was head up straight on the tree line and Smithy saw its gun fire once more but the shot went short, ploughing a long furrow through the sand in front of them before burying itself too deep to do harm.

'Fire,' said Naude.

Grobbler hit the tank first time and Smithy could see a piece of track go flying off like a snapped elastic. The T-55 ran off the rest of the track, slewed around a little and came to a stop.

'Repeat.'

Grobbler had fifteen seconds before the gunner in that T.55 got a third bite at them, but he was good and put a shot on the turret in ten.

'Repeat.'

The T-55 fired but the shot went wild, strong evidence that all was not well inside that tank. Grobbler hit it a third time and the tank barrel drooped like a drunk's penis.

'Repeat,' said Naude.

The fourth shot went in and blew off the turret as though it was nothing heavier than a frying pan.

'Reverse thirty metres.'

There was a rattle of shrapnel against the side of the vehicle but Smithy was sure, almost instinctively sure, that it would not touch him and made no attempt to duck. Only the *pock pock* sound was to be worried about

293

because he was now convinced that if he heard the sound of an explosion, it had missed him.

'Target Nine o'clock. Follow my tracer.' Naude let off a long burst at the T-55 that he had first selected and then shoved a black tipped HEAT round into the breech. 'Fire when ready.'

The Ratel lurched back on its suspension as Grobbler fired. Smithy saw a tiny white flash as the round struck home, just below the turret on the left side. The top hatch flew open almost immediately and the commander jumped straight out and began to run. Closely following his exit, a billow of flame and thick smoke boiled out of the hatch; no-one else made it; HEAT rounds were designed to fire a stream of molten copper through tank armour.

Smithy saw the commander run. He was no danger any more. He was no threat, but Smithy swung the Browning round and decided to kill him. There was no reason for this, but there were also no consequences for him and with a squeeze he sent a horde of bullets after the fleeing man, caught him with the second squeeze and watched as three or four huge splatters disintegrated the tanker's head in a spray of red mist, chinks of skull and a splurge of grey and tallow brain. There were advantages to this Existentialism bullshit, he thought, grimly.

'SITREP,' called Naude, grinning happily. 'The truck is out. Home time soon. Tickety-boo.' Smith watched him as he carefully took off his helmet, hauled himself half out of the turret and then threw up copiously and noisily down the side of the Ratel.

*

*Mason. Nothing from Steiner. I'm being posted to Capinga. What do you want me to do? AMvZ.*

*AMvZ. Prepare for Extraction. Mason.*

\*

Though the T-55 attack had failed, there were still plenty of SWAPO operatives determined to bite a piece out of the 41 Mech apple and it was still necessary for Naude and Grobbler to fire off belt after belt as the Ratels began to withdraw. RPGs were now the weapon of choice for the enemy but as each rocket was fired, the position of the firer was given away by the back blast and the cloud of white smoke produced; and as the firer had to kneel or stand to fire, he became a target for the Brownings the moment he pulled the trigger; and knowing this was a great disincentive to take too long about aiming and firing so the rockets flew in all directions but rarely in the ones that mattered.

'Floor it, Jif,' called Naude, as a succession of mortar rounds exploded around the vehicle. 'Back a hundred.'

Jif stamped on the pedal, driving the eighteen ton monster back hard through the bush, completely blind, relying for direction entirely on Naude; there hadn't been a wing mirror on 41 Mech's Ratels since the second week of the Bush war. And then, Smithy watched in slow motion as a mortar round came right down and exploded on the roof of the Ratel. His head was only half out of the crew compartment but he saw the distinctive slim teardrop, almost dolphin-like shape of the bomb, its fin stretching out behind it, come down and strike. He saw the red flash and then felt rather than heard the bang before being flung back into the crew compartment as he was enveloped in a thick, black cloud. Ahead, he saw Naude's legs

295

buckle under him as he dropped down into the turret like a sack of potatoes, before he too disappeared into the smoke.

He was not dead. This was a strange certainty, but one that Smithy was convinced of because if there was an after-life, he was sure it would not be like this. Though he could imagine feeling a deep calm similar to this one, he could not conceive of heaven consisting of a jolting vehicle, a puking Naude, the horrified look with which Grobbler turned to look at him, briefly, before shoving his own head out of the turret hatch and shouting something into the intercom or the rapidly clearing smoke and the distinctive wet dog smell of burning rubber. Also, he could not imagine being festooned with a 400 round belt that had dropped like a boa constrictor into his lap. He touched his face. It was not wet. He could feel his fingers and his feet inside his boots. His breathing did not hurt, so his ribs were not broken. He was alive. So was Naude.

Gathering himself he hauled himself up out of the hatch. His Browning was gone, the pintle just twisted metal and turning to look forward he saw the spare tyre alight and shredded. That was what had saved both him and Naude; the round had landed bullseye in the centre of the spare directing the blast upwards. A split second either way and one of them would be dead; probably all of them would be dead because if the round had exploded in either the crew compartment or the turret, the splinters would have whizzed around inside the containing shell of the vehicle and they would have been minced in a blizzard of shrapnel. His eyes came up to meet Naude's as he emerged from the turret hatch.

'Tickety-boo?' mouthed Naude, grinning horribly.

'Tickety-boo,' replied Smithy, grinning back, overwhelmed by a surge of exhilaration so strong that he was half crying and half laughing.

'Halt,' said Naude, regaining command. 'Check for damage.'

The Ratel came to a juddering halt in a stand of trees stripped bare and broken. Naude leaped like a cat out of the turret and went around the vehicle while Smithy stared blankly at the scene around him. Two or three other Ratels pulled up close to them, figures piling out, more or less intact as they went about their checks. There were some bandages evident but mainly there was sweat, grime, cigarettes and determination.

'Two close shaves,' called out Naude. Grobbler was head and shoulders out of the turret with the co-ax trained forward while Jif got out to look at his vehicle. 'Look at these big black streaks. 100mm, I shouldn't wonder, but not hitting us at quite the right angle. Lots of shrapnel.'

Smithy hung over the edge of the hatch and saw the smallpox rash where steel splinters and small arms had scarred the Ratel. He had no recollection of being hit so many times and though he remembered the first near miss from the T-55, he could not recall the second at all.

'Five of six tyres shot out,' said Jif, ruefully.

'And no spare either,' said Naude.

'Radiator's popped too.'

'Hmm,' said Naude. 'The Tiffies won't be pleased. Will it get us home, I wonder?'

'Recoil gas is fucked,' shouted Grobbler.

'Well, I daresay we'll manage,' answered Naude. 'An extra shove on the breech is all that's needed.'

There was a shout from Charlie Tango: 'Naude! We gotta get forward! Van der Merwe's ordered a Fire Plan. Your radio is down?'

Naude looked rather surprised at this question, but then saw that the mortar strike had stripped away more than just the spare tyre. There wasn't an aerial in sight.

'Oh dearie me,' he said. 'We'll just stick by you then, if that's all right?'

'Eat my dust, Naude,' came the mocking reply. 'Tickety-boo, you *poes*.'

Mounting up, Naude took the Ratel forward but angled back a little to Charlie Tango's left. Fifty metres closer into the enemy, the two vehicles came to a halt and Charlie Tango indicated the target. It was not difficult to spot, being the front edge of the position that they had originally occupied, except that now it was no longer pristine bush but an apocalypse of flattened trees, white smoke and flaming grass backed by the deeper black towers of ugly burned out armour. The commander of Charlie Tango waved in the direction of the target and then held up his hand, as though about to start a race. When he dropped it, everyone opened up with whatever they had. Brownings, MAGs, 20mm cannon went crazy, flicking out mechanised hornets in a continuous stream of directed violence into the enemy position while above them flew a ripple of mortar rounds that *clumped* down every five seconds for a full two minutes. Naude chose this moment to alternate between HE and the ball-bearing round, firing a pattern that swung through an arc of 90° across his front, while keeping up a steady fusillade from his 7.62. The noise was industrial, terrific, like some massive, monstrous machine stamping out metal blanks on the devil's anvil and for the first time that day, Smithy put his fingers in his ears and opened his mouth to prevent his teeth from rattling out. And it went on for twenty minutes until Charlie Tango stopped firing and Naude followed suit. The Ratel was almost knee deep in empty cartridges and Smithy wondered just how much all this brass would be worth to a scrap metal dealer; probably enough to retire on, he thought. There was no sign of the enemy.

'Break contact!' called Charlie Tango. 'We're pulling out!'

'Job done,' said Naude. 'Well done, one and all. I wonder if the beer is cold?'

'Thank you, Mickey *bladdy* Epstein,' said Smithy. 'I hope you are pleased with yourself.'

\*

*AMvZ. Go to Capinga and await further orders. Steiner.*

\*

11

Sunday

Every time a mortar round sent her diving for a foxhole, Mostert was tempted to curse Mickey Epstein for the fine job he had done in sending the truck down the ravine. Straight sided and steep, the head-scratching recovery Tiffies had almost had to abseil down to it before they could begin the job of shifting the tangled mass of thorn bushes and get a line on it. After that was accomplished they discovered that the cab had managed to wedge itself tight in amongst a bottleneck of rocks at an angle of just shy of 45° through which a muddy puddle of a stream flowed. When they realised that the truck was soft skinned and that therefore the weight of the vehicle was resting on the precious filing cabinets they really did curse because it was no longer a case of just hacking the cab free with crows and picks then winching the *bladdy* thing up and out. If they did that, the canvas would come off, the cabinets would spill out, crack open and that gold mine of paper would flutter away in the breeze or spill out into the muddy water. Mostert made herself *very* popular went she pointed this out and even more so when she absolutely insisted that the cabinets came up un-opened and undamaged. The tiffie sergeant responded in great detail and at no small length what complex and time-consuming engineering processes her strictures laid on an already burdened crew but he might as well have tried to persuade her out of her knickers.

'Tough job, hey?' was her final remark on the subject. 'Best not waste any more time then.'

The tiffie sergeant booted an oil can long and high and if there had been uprights he would surely have split them, but Mostert simply ignored him, let him have his tiffie tizzy and then pointed with raised eyebrows and a curt nod at the truck.

They cracked it in the end though. After several failed attempts to uncork the cab from the bottleneck, the cutting gear was sent down and with the deployment of a combination of angle grinders, hacksaws, files and rasps, the Ural-375 was persuaded to detach itself from its cab, which remained where it was, and flip itself over by means of several lines attached by several extremely frustrated Tiffies. Only then could the detached portion be winched up – a process delayed by two or three stonkings from a 120mm mortar, of which one resulted in Mostert receiving what was considered to be her just deserts in the form a small, hot splinter in the upper rear of her right shoulder blade. While this minor wound was treated (to the sound of wolf whistles, inevitably), the flatbed was inspected to determine if it was towable and on discovering that it was, hitched up to the recovery truck and Major van der Merwe informed that the Tiffies had sorted the Parabat fuck-up – *again*, as *usual* – and that he could now break off the action and let everyone get back to real soldiering in the bar of the Oshadangwa canteen.

Mostert, none the worse for the bit of shrapnel, unfazed by the catcalls but really cross at having a scarce bra fatally wounded in the strap, took charge of the filing cabinets, had them loaded aboard the C-130 sent specially for them and re-united with a grimy but grinning Smithy once more, flew down to the airstrip at Oshadangwa where they collected Mickey Epstein over the protests of the medics and went back to the bungalow at Grootfontein.

*

Corporal Bridgeman had been busy while they had been away. The aircon had been fixed, a decent kitchen along with a fair display of pans and utensils had been liberated, cleaned, scoured, polished and set up proudly under good lights and mended windows. There were curtains in each room, clean blinds for the office, some improved bits of carpet and the walls throughout had been freshly painted, transforming them from nicotine yellow to a functional but clean air force issue magnolia. Best of all were the bedrooms, which Bridgeman had transformed from dosshouse chic to boarding house comfortable – or as close as the issue horse blankets would allow at least; sheets and pillow cases had been laundered and starched and the stained mattresses replaced with something that he could look at without wincing. And in anticipation of doing his bit to nurse Mickey Epstein back to health, he had raided the medical stores to fill up a raided fridge with antiseptics, alcohol wipes, painkillers, cold compresses,

301

bandages, unguents and ice packs. He had even got a selection of gun and hunting mags for him to read while he convalesced.

It was because of all these efforts that he regarded Pieters with an air of frustration; the yellow cigarette smoke was twirling up to the ceiling, the ashtray was already spilling over, his collar looked like the tread of bakkie and he was just about to put out one of the two cigarettes he was smoking by dropping into a cup of his freshly ground and brewed coffee. That, and the fact that Mickey Epstein had been sequestered in his room with strictly no visitors, nursemaids, well-wishers, comrade-in-arms allowed on Pieters' orders and those orders included him. He snatched the cup just before the cigarette could go into it and handed him a clean ashtray.

'You interview him, Sergeant Smith,' wheezed Pieters, his watery eyes almost starting out of his head at Bridgeman. 'Leave the files to Captain Mostert. You'll have just a couple of days before Pretoria will want them. Now I must go to the helipad or I shall not get home in time for church.'

Bridgeman headed for the kitchen, his fingers clicking with impatience. Smithy shrugged and did as he was told. Mostert sent him off with a single raised eyebrow that said *I thought* he *was Pretoria.*

*

'Well, Mickey *ma bru*,' said Smithy, pulling up a chair by the bed. 'Some R&R trip you've had then. Bet you just can't wait to get out of bed, get back on the horse and back into the shit.'

The medics had done a good job. Mickey's face looked like it had only gone three rounds with Muhammed Ali and the swelling around his lips had gone down enough to let him drink his *Lion* through a straw. It was still too early to make out the real features that lay under all the swelling but somewhere down there was the sort of round Slavic face that was a perfect match for the stocky physique and cubic chest now wrapped up in bandages, lightly covered by the sheet and through which spots of blood and pus were leaching. The drip was doing its job of getting some more valuable but less morale- building fluid into him and the smell of something chemical smeared over the cratered scarring of a million insect bites indicated that within a day or two he might come down to a state where he just looked like he had a bad case of measles and smallpox combined, rather than something that might grace the pages of a medical textbook.

'More beer,' mumbled Mickey, sitting up a little higher. 'And what am I doing here?'

'Debrief,' answered Smithy, cracking a can from the fridge, swapping over the straw and handing it over.

'About how I found the files?' said Mickey.

'That too,' said Smithy. 'But I want you to start from the beginning. Right from the jump.'

'Uh?'

'You got shifted from your regular spot in the stick,' said Smithy. 'Why?'

Mickey tried to shrug: 'You think I got told the reason?'

'There was a Recce officer and a sergeant with you,' said Smithy.

'What's this to do with?' asked Mickey.

'Steiner marked you down as KIA,' said Smithy, with a grimace. 'We just got to do the enquiry.'

303

'And you organised a special plane for me and took me out of the hospital and brought me down to my own special ward to be looked after by *ma bru*, Andy Bridgeman just for this?' said Mickey, out of the corner of his mouth. 'You going to offer me a blow job from the President of the Republic next, hey? Because I am sure that you are not from the committee that gives out medals for bravery, hey?'

'*Ja*, well, it's to do with the files too,' answered Smithy, lying. 'You not dumb, OK, but we need to know what you were doing at Capinga right from the start. It's so we get the whole timeline about the files. Just so we can rule them out as a hoax or a plant. Then we can give you a medal or whatever you *fokken* want.'

Mickey grunted and a bubbling sound came from further down the bed.

'Is that…' asked Smithy. 'You need a bedpan?'

'Just a fart, man,' said Mickey, shifting in the cot. 'I feel like I've got a zeppelin stuck up me. Drinking lager through a straw doesn't help much either.'

'You want whisky?'

'*Lion* is just fine,' answered Mickey.

'So tell me about the jump,' said Smithy, trying to ignore the smell.

'Are you going to nail Steiner for leaving me behind?' asked Mickey, shifting painfully again.

'We just investigating at the moment,' answered Smithy, and then when the smell could no longer be reasonably ignored. 'Are you a vegetarian, or something?'

'It was just a fuck up,' said Mickey, ripping another one off. 'You want someone to blame, you should look at the pilots who overshot the DZ and dropped me on the wrong side of that river. That wasn't Steiner's fault. And no; I like meat.'

'*Ja*, we heard about that,' said Smithy, archly. 'What were you doing with the Recces?'

There was a terrible grumble from below the sheets once more.

'I just went along with them,' said Mickey, pained with a cramp. 'I was just supposed to be protection for them.'

'*Protection*,' said Smithy, trying not to sit up like a bloodhound in butchers. *Protection? Why would those animals need protection?* 'Go on.'

'They were going deep into the camp,' said Mickey. 'They'd been tasked to get to something before it was whisked away or ran away in the general confusion. It was like, secure or capture. Me and another guy were supposed to go with them just to watch their backs while they secured whatever it was they were after.'

'You didn't know what the thing was that they were after then?' said Smithy. 'Bit strange, hey? How would you know what it was when you found it if you didn't know what you were looking for?'

Mickey's stomach grumbled again.

'Did you take any specialist gear with you?'

'Like what?' asked Mickey.

'Well, like explosives or demolition gear or something like that,' said Smithy.

'Not that I know of,' conceded Mickey. 'But the Recces might have.'

'Did they have bigger packs or special jump containers?'

'Just the usual, as far as I could see,' said Mickey. 'Could you fix this pillow up for me?'

Smithy got up, helped Mickey to lean forward and flipped the pillow over. It was wet with yellow fluid, spotted with blood and stank of liniment, bush and the sickly sweet smell of fart and sepsis.

'And they didn't give any indication of what they were hoping to capture,' said Smithy, helping him to lie back. 'Just have a think, hey?'

Mickey shook his head slowly, as though mystified.

'Come on, man,' urged Smithy. 'They weren't going to demolish anything – not that there would be much left to demolish if that air strike was anything like it was meant to be – and they didn't have transport to move anything heavy, like a safe or something. Did they tell you where in the camp they were heading for?'

'Some small huts by the cookhouse,' said Mickey. 'They pointed them out on a sketch map as the objective, but that was it.'

'So, not the offices or administration building?' said Mickey. 'They weren't after some special radar or Russian missile or special weapon?'

Mickey shook his head again. 'No idea.'

'Who was the other guy that went with you?'

'Jonny Jacobs,' said Mickey. 'How is he?'

This time Smith shook his head: 'He didn't make it. KIA. Sorry, hey.'

Mickey took a moment to absorb this news and then, struggling to sit up, let off another grumbling gurgle. This time the smell was horrendous.

'You need to get the medics to give you something for that,' said Smithy. 'It smells like something crawled up there and died.'

'It probably did,' agreed Mickey. 'And is now enjoying a fine funeral in the company of all its *fokken* friends and relations.'

Smithy sat back and put his hands behind his head.

'So, there was nothing that struck you as strange about the whole business,' asked Smith, more as a question to the air than to Mickey. 'Nothing at all?'

'Only that we had our own extract,' said Mickey. 'The Recces said we had an Alouette dedicated to us for uplift once the mission was achieved. Oh, and that we shouldn't be tempted to bring back any souvenirs as there wouldn't be any spare room.'

'That's odd,' said Smithy. 'There were just four of you in that stick, right?'

'Yup,' confirmed Mickey.

'There are five seats after the pilot in an Alouette,' said Smithy. 'Looks like you were going to be bringing someone back with you.'

*

Given the state in which the files were recovered Mostert was quite pleased with the fact that they weren't completely ruined. Having been upside down and rolled through Mickey Epstein's washing machine and then pulled out by the recovery Tiffies' greased up cutting gear, oily hemp ropes and general bad temper, she was surprised that they were in any fit state at all. Fortunately the sturdy construction of the boxes and the fact that they had been lashed together in the back of the truck meant that they had tended to concertina, absorb the shock and just rattle rather than shatter. A few of the frames had bent, many of the side panels were dented and several of the drawers looked like they had been hit by a battering ram but apart from the ones that Mickey Epstein had jemmied open in search of a bottle of brandy, they were, by and large, uncompromised. Those files that had been spilled had been gathered up by oily hands and shoved willy-nilly into plastic bags like rubbish but were still capable of being sorted into some sort of order without too much of an outlay of effort.

There were no keys of course, but keys were not really necessary when Corporal Bridgeman deployed his impressive array of drills, screwdrivers and crow bars and a jemmy that she had only ever seen once before when it was in the hands of a car thief trying to lift her old Opal from outside a bar in Hout Bay. If anything, the greatest obstacle to accessing the files was not the broken locks or twisted tracking but rather the skill of SWAPO's filing clerks. Few of these people had been chosen for their administrative skill and not many of them had ever made it past primary school, but whatever the failings in their academic education they were the sort of people who knew by instinct what the real qualifications for a job were; they had degrees in spotting the person who held the power over the allocation of jobs and Ph.ds in how to tap them. The result of this practical corruption was that when a piece of paper came into the SWAPO office it certainly went over several desks, received several rubber stamps and more than a couple of signatures but not necessarily did it fly into the right file cover. Mostert had in front of her eighteen filing cabinets which in order and regularity resembled nothing more than a badly contained blizzard. To add complexity to chaos, the files were also composed in a mixture of bad Portuguese, bad English, some Spanish and dotted with some unintelligible Afrikaans. It was as though a huge multi-national primary school had been asked to translate the complete works of William Shakespeare into isiZulu over a short wave radio. If SWAPO had ever actually contemplated activating a plan to disrupt South African intelligence, then they could not have done better than dumping this mass of contradictory, confusing gibberish on the BOSS.

'There's a month's work here just sorting through what is and what isn't in need of decent translation,' said Mostert, despairingly. 'And I've got two days'.

'Would you like more coffee ma'am?' asked Corporal Bridgeman, sympathetically. 'And I can read Afrikaans and I know a little Portuguese.'

'*Lekker,*' said Mostert, pointing to the black sack full of unfiled files. 'If you can get that into some sort of order I'll be forever grateful to you.'

'Will this help Mickey?' asked Bridgeman, hopefully.

'The reason why Mickey was left behind at Capinga is probably in these files,' said Mostert, hands on hips. 'But beyond that I don't really know what I'm looking for; so as well as looking through that sack your job is to pump me and Sergeant Smith full of so much coffee that we'll still be awake next Tuesday.'

Bridgeman looked at her directly and seriously, his question made more intense by the unvarying stare of the glass eye.

'Ma'am', he said, quietly. 'I know people in the infirmary. If you want, I can get something stronger.'

'Corporal Bridgeman,' said Mostert, brightly. 'If you offer me any of that crap again I'll have you posted to a place that a *moffie* like you will not appreciate.'

'Coffee it is then, ma'am,' said Bridgeman, head down and retreating.

'Coffee,' said Mostert. 'And then that big sack of paper.'

While Bridgeman rattled pots in the kitchen, Mostert inspected the filing cabinets paraded before her and mused on where she ought to start. Contrary to what Major van der Merwe had stated, this did not represent the totality of SWAPOs intelligence collection but it was still a valuable haul and contained plenty that seemed to emanate from sources high up in Luanda in amongst matters of purely local and administrative importance. The preliminary recce had not been of much practical use but it had at least revealed the size and scale of the problem and now the real task was to transform it from a mass of almost formless information into useable intelligence. *Collect; Collate; Present* was the standard method but within each of those little words was concealed a whole cornucopia of selection, judgement and valuation, a thousand small decisions about the validity, reliability and worth of each document that added together would result hopefully in some worthwhile knowledge. Which bits to collect? Which bits to discount? Which bits to lay aside for further consideration? Which documents could be believed? Which ones were bureaucratic fictions designed to conceal a scam? She knew that many FAPLA, SWAPO and

310

ANC units contained 'ghost' soldiers who only existed on paper, but who still drew pay and rations that were gratefully received by commanding officers; what other scams were concealed in these reports? There was also the added complication of weight of evidence versus the quality of evidence; do ten documents of marginal worth outweigh one document of pristine splendour, even if they contradicted? And over all this hung the possibility that this whole truck full of paper was an elaborate hoax, a deception designed to confuse and mislead the BOSS for years to come.

Her speciality was battlefield intelligence rather than this, the secret variety. Her training had concentrated on spotting different weapon systems, distinguishing between varying types of units, knowing about the different tactics employed by different armies. She knew, for example, that the movement of a Russian SA-8 Gecko meant a big operation was being planned against the South African army because this mobile anti-aircraft missile system was a top secret piece of kit that the Americans were willing to pay large sums of hard currency for just a glimpse at the manual. If the Russians were willing to risk one of those being captured then the reward must be commensurate. It was for that reason that she was always on the lookout for them coming up to the border. She knew how to write up reports of interrogations from SWAPO deserters or captures and knew what conclusions could be drawn from the state of their kit or rations or general health; if they were ragged, hungry and poxed they were no danger; fit, tooled up and eager meant something entirely different. She knew how to build up a tactical picture from movement reports, knew how to identify infiltration routes, supply routes, unit change-overs. In some cases, she had known the names of the enemy commanders and those of their wives and families to boot, but these filing cabinets contained something that was way beyond her experience.

311

She leaned on one of the cabinets and thought harder about the problem. Was she coming at this from the wrong angle?

Actually, she decided, she was, for her brief was not to build up a complete picture of SWAPO intelligence; that could safely be left to others with more time and more manpower. Her job was to find out why Anna-Marie van Zyl was in a mass grave at Capinga so this was more of a needle-in-the-haystack search than a full intelligence work-up. She was looking for – what had Pieters called it? – a *killer fact*. That thought sent a chill through her because the several unexpected appearances of Colonel Steiner in this case was leading her to think that the *killer* in that phrase was acquiring a whole new ambiguity.

*Method*, she said to herself. *There has to be an effective way to search through these documents without going through them cabinet by cabinet, drawer by drawer, file by file, document by document and then line by line.* The obvious place to start would be to look for a file with Anna-Marie's name on it but even as she opened the cabinet marked 'WXYZ' she knew that she was being way too hopeful. *How are the files organised? Are they sorted alphabetically or by some sort of theme or subject?* Looking through the several files in the same drawer, still miraculously preserved in their original order, she could discern no obvious pattern. One file appeared to be concerned with the quality of the water supply at Capinga, another with a new type of ant-tank mine and a third with a retired newspaper editor in Swakopmund. She closed the drawer and drummed her fingers on the top.

*If these intelligence files were valuable enough to be moved*, she thought, *then they must contain valuable information.* That was obvious but from that question followed several more; what was the nature of that valuable

312

information and was some information thought to be more valuable than other pieces? Perhaps the files were organised in that way? She looked at the labelling of the cabinets and was gratified to find that although there were cabinets marked alphabetically, there were also others marked with more helpful directions; by geography, *Swakopmund, Rundu, Oshadangwa*; by unit, *Police, Koevoet, 23 Leopard, Air Force*; by subject, *Agitation and Propaganda, Student Organisations, Mobilisation of the People.*

*What I really need*, she thought to herself as Bridgeman appeared with coffee and rusks, *is the file marked: Top Secret List of Lunatic Female BOSS Agents Employed Under Cover Spying On Us By Colonel Steiner.* She also realised that she was unlikely to find it.

'Any luck?' asked Bridgeman, laying down the tray on a smart little occasional table that had recently been employed in the Officer's Mess.

Mostert took a rusk and nibbled at it. 'I just don't know where to start,' she confessed. 'I'm tempted to flip a coin.'

'When I get a load of paperwork dumped on me,' said Bridgeman. 'I start by sorting it by order of importance.'

'I thought of that,' said Mostert. 'But there doesn't seem to be anything to distinguish Top Secret from General Knowledge.'

'No, that's not what I mean,' said Bridgeman. 'A clerk doesn't care what's in the files, just who wrote them. I mean, if a General writes a memo then I make sure it gets filed in double-quick time while if some middle-ranking desk jockey sends me a load of routine *kak*, that goes right to the bottom of the in-tray. You got to prioritise if you want to reduce the amount of *kak* coming your way down the hill and the higher up the hill, the bigger the

313

load of *kak* will descend if you don't file the General's memo in triplicate, stamp it and send it on to wherever it must go as first priority.'

'You say I should look for things written by SWAPO Commissars?'

'It's a start,' said Bridgeman.

'He's got a point,' said Smithy appearing unexpectedly at the door. 'But I've got a better one. A *refinement*.' Three real eyes and a glass one turned on him. 'Look for a posh, convent educated copperplate handwriting. Mickey Epstein and the Recces were sent in to uplift Anna-Marie van Zyl out of Capinga, I reckon. Which means she was blown. Which means there will be a confession in her handwriting or at least one signed by her.'

'Anna-Marie van Zyl?' said Bridgeman, startled. 'The one with the crazy old Nazi for a father?'

*

'I guess that you have just got to accept it that in a small country like ours everyone knows everyone else,' said Smithy, leafing through a set of files. 'If ten percent of us are *moffies* – well, not *us*, or *me*, I mean, obviously – and we don't count kiddies or *krimpies*, and most of them go off to live in big towns where what they are doing will not be noticed like it will definitely be in a small dorp, then that means – Jeez!'

'You are doing the mathematics now, are you, Smithy?' sniggered Mostert, as she dropped a file back into a drawer and took out a handful of others.

'Eighty thousand *moffies* divided between Cape Town, Durban and Jo'burg!'

'Like I said: they're *everywhere.*'

'But that's like, nearly thirty thousand *moffies* in Cape Town alone!'

'They *behind* you, Smithy,' said Mostert, in a pantomime voice, eyes wide open.

'I mean, this can't be true,' said Smithy, amazed. 'I would have noticed.'

'Would you?' said Mostert, with sarcasm. 'I suppose you are a detective, hey?'

'It's a bit disturbing that they so secretive though,' said Smithy. 'Although, I suppose it is illegal.'

'What do you expect?' said Mostert, holding up a piece of paper to the light. They had been going at the stash now for nearly four hours and her eyes were tiring. 'You part of a group, you know other people in the group and they know others and soon everyone knows everyone else. It's just like a little dorp in the end – or maybe the *Bruderbond* or the *Ossewabrandwag*. A Moffie Mafia, if you like, with secret handshakes, nods, winks and the like, helping each other out, all under the noses of the Official Heterosexual and Thoroughly Calvinstic South African Republic. Except maybe there is a bit less of the politics and backscratching and more of the histrionics and turquoise hair involved.' She squinted at the paper. 'Can you imagine the bitching?'

'*Backscratching*?' said Smithy, eyebrows arching.

'You have a dirty mind, Joshua Smith, and I'm going to tell your mother.'

'Do you believe Bridgeman?' said Smithy. 'I mean, Anna-Marie was older than him and wasn't batting on the same team as him neither.'

'Like I say,' said Mostert. 'They get around a lot. And some of them bat for *both* sides.'

'You lie!' said Smithy, jaw dropping. 'I mean…how can they? You either one thing or the other, surely?'

'Liesl Aristedes obviously did.' Mostert grinned. 'She had a son, remember? Anyway, why limit your choice to just fifty percent of the population?' she teased. 'I mean, it must be worth a try, hey? Just to get the feel of things?'

'Just to get the *feel of things*?' Smithy was appalled. 'No way! Not in a million years.'

'Don't knock it 'till you have tried it, Joshua,' she said. 'And I have always believed that you should try anything at least once.'

'*Ja,*' said Smithy. 'Like sticking a red hot poker up your…like sticking your finger in a naked flame?'

'Just for the experience,' said Mostert, picking up another file and dropping her eyes coyly. 'Just to see if you like it. You want me to fix you up with Mickey?'

'That is my idea of a perfect weekend,' said Smithy. '*Ag, sies, man.* I don't think.'

Mostert scoffed and then held an imperative finger up. 'Looks like we found our first copperplate,' she said, waving a grey, cardboard file and beckoning him over to the desk.

The file consisted of several sheets of purple carbon copy, rather smudged but still legible, with a neat copperplate signature at the bottom of each one. The top sheet was what appeared to be a list of telephone numbers, complete with area codes, all of which were situated in South Africa. Mostert gave this to Bridgeman with instructions to find out whom they belonged to, a task which he considered to be well beneath his sleuthing abilities but which he undertook with his customary efficiency anyway.

'They belong to serving members of the armed forces in the main,' he said. 'Plus there are two take-aways in Vredenburg, a bar in Jo'burg and a steakhouse in Cape Town.'

'Her contacts?' suggested Smithy, once Bridgeman had retreated.

'Seems odd that there are two Vredenburg numbers,' remarked Mostert. 'Maybe all these people are Recces or places that they frequent. I'm guessing that's who they are. She gave them up. I wonder how long she held out.'

'Not long,' said Smithy, who had some experience of torture. 'Nobody really lasts more than forty-eight hours before they cough. Getting the intelligence out of people is a lot quicker than checking it isn't a load of made up *kak*.'

The second and subsequent sheets looked and smelled like a confession to Smithy. It was written – or typed up – in the stilted style of the stenographer.

> In July 1971 was recruited into BOSS by Colonel Steiner and after operational training, I was sent to London to infiltrate SWAPO networks....In 1974, I was instructed to gain employment with SWAPO at their Headquarters in Luanda where I remained until 1975. I was withdrawn from Luanda at the time of Operation Savannah when Colonel Steiner wished to conduct an in-depth

317

*debrief. This was carried out at Langebaan base which is the base of the Reconnaissance Regiment aka, the Recces and I was then re-inserted into SWAPO in 1977 with the cover story that I had been travelling in Asia to account for my absence. I was set to work at the Karl Marx Reception Centre at Lubango assessing the authenticity of foreign and South African volunteers for SWAPO. These assessments were also passed to Colonel Steiner.*

'Looks like my theory was right on the money,' said Smithy. 'She was Steiner's agent but he failed to uplift her before SWAPO rumbled her.'

'There's no phone number for Steiner,' said Mostert. 'Why not? Why could she remember all these other numbers but not his?'

'Sometimes people under interrogation hold things back,' said Smithy. 'It's why everything is checked over and over again.'

'Well, this doesn't look like it's been checked,' retorted Mostert. 'There's not much here at all when you look at it. No detail. Nothing about her training, what she did, how she did it or how she communicated. And there's no mention of why she joined BOSS either. Doesn't that strike you as strange? I mean, you would have to be pretty focussed to spend all those years of your life under cover and from what we know about Anna-Maria van Zyl, she didn't have the attention span of a soccer fan.'

'Maybe, it's just the top cover, a precis,' suggested Smithy. 'They put all the detail elsewhere?'

'Then we need to find it,' said Mostert, looking back towards the cabinets. 'Because I'm not buying this. Anna-Maria van Zyl as Matahari? Never in a thousand years.'

'That's been said before,' said Smithy. 'Ian Smith, late Prime Minister of the now defunct Rhodesia on the possibility of black majority rule, I believe.'

'No, come on, Smithy,' she replied, slightly irritated by his flippancy. 'Agents are recruited on the MICE principle – say one word about cheese and I will have you on a charge, Sergeant. That stands for Money, Ideology, Compromise and Ego, OK? So let's say that Steiner sets out to recruit Anna-Marie; he offers her lots of money?'

'Her old man is already loaded,' agreed Smithy.

'And do you think a half-English possibly Lesbian, dope smoking runaway who hangs out with the ANC at the Britannia Hotel is a likely candidate for Afrikaaner Nationalism's poster girl of the year? No, you agree with me there too. So we can rule Ideology out.'

'What's 'Compromise'?' asked Smithy.

'It means being a businessman caught with your trousers down,' replied Mostert. 'And I really can't see a bit of a scandal on those lines bothering Anna-Marie. Which leaves us with Ego.'

'She had plenty of that by the looks of things,' said Smithy.

'No, she didn't,' said Mostert. 'Formless undirected rage and just generally being pissed off at everyone you meet and every rule and every law is not the same as Ego, Smithy. Arrogant, conceited and self-centred, she probably was but that is not the same as Ego. Ego, in the intelligence business, means that a person feels so undervalued, slighted, passed over and treated so shabbily that they go over to the enemy out of sheer, blind revenge.'

'She was mad enough,' said Smithy.

'Except that according to your theory, she didn't go over to the enemy did she? She joined BOSS. If it was Ego, then she would have joined SWAPO or the ANC wouldn't she?'

'Maybe she did,' said Smithy. 'Maybe she's a double agent?'

'Then she would have to be Matahari on speed to pull the act off,' said Mostert. 'I can believe the speed bit, but not the Matahari part.'

'Back to the cabinets?' said Smithy.

'Back to the cabinets,' confirmed Mostert.

\*

'Here's something,' said Smithy. *'van Zyl is to be accommodated separately and kept isolated.* Orders to the camp commissar by the looks of things. Looks like my theory might have legs after all, Trudi. SWAPO had rumbled her and were preparing to interrogate her.'

'Why take her all the way out to Capinga then?' replied Mostert. 'Don't they have a prison camp outside Luanda? The Karl Marx Hilton or something like that?'

'The Nun saw her on the base at Langebaan,' said Smithy, reminding her. 'She's Steiner's creature.'

'But that confession…It was just all wrong.'

'Maybe the interrogator was *kak*?' answered Smithy. 'It's been known.'

\*

'Now this is a bit juicy,' said Smithy, holding up a single sheet of paper on which was printed the template of a message form. 'And after this discovery, I think I deserve a reward. Bridgeman! Break out the Klippies!'

'Hold the Klippies, Bridgeman,' said Mostert.

'*The intelligence files are to be loaded and moved back to Luanda immediately. Information received indicates the possibility of an attack on Capinga camp in the near future,*' said Smithy, reading from the screed. 'Looks like they knew Steiner's Parabats were coming.'

'If so, why didn't they prepare?' asked Mostert. 'They were taken by surprise that morning.'

Smithy looked at the file and then held up a handful of similar message forms. 'Luanda had cried wolf too often before, I'd say.'

'So just the intelligence people at the camp took note?'

'Seems so,' said Smithy.

'Why this time?'

'They knew the information was solid, I'd guess,' said Smithy. 'Which means they got it from a source more reliable than the ones they had been relying on before. Bit of a coincidence that it came just at the moment when Anna-Marie goes to Capinga? Maybe she coughed up under questioning and told them? It supports my theory that she was Steiner's spy.'

'Or maybe they were just doing what Bridgeman says clerks do,' replied Mostert. 'Following the orders without commenting on them one way or another?'

She looked up at the clock. It was late.

'Klippies,' she said. 'And then bed. *Own* beds, before you say it.'

*

'Hello, hello,' said Smithy, putting down his brandy and slipping a note out of a grubby, greasy, much handled file. It was written in spidery English, quick, hurried, like that of a Doctor writing a prescription. It was the hand of a busy man, someone who had time only for terse notes and no need or desire to explain them. It was the hand of someone in authority, someone educated, someone worldly, someone who had seen it all and could no longer be surprised by anything.

> *The white girl van Zyl is to be provided with a passport, handed over to Mason and sent to London. Comrades will understand the revolutionary logic of this decision when victory is finally achieved.*

'Now what on earth does that mean?' said Smithy.

'It means you owe me twenty bucks,' said Mostert. 'If she was a spy, then she wasn't working for Steiner when that note was written.'

'Not at all,' responded Smithy. 'It seems to me that *Comrades will understand* blah blah means that she was Steiner's spy who had been rumbled and was now being sent back on some prisoner exchange or other.'

'Come off it, Smithy,' said Mostert, necking the last of her Klippie. 'Prisoner exchanges take years to negotiate. She was at Camp Capinga for less than a week before she was killed in the air strike. They probably just got sick of her and sent her back to England. Who knows what shenanigans she was getting up to?'

'She knew too much for that,' said Smithy, wrinkling his nose. 'I'm telling you, she was the spy who got caught.'

'So why was she being sent to London? It's as good as being set free. She could be back in Steiner's arms immediately, just by changing planes. And who is *Mason*?'

'*Kak*,' said Smithy, as the penny was not flipped, but instead, dropped. 'She was a spy alright but she wasn't working for Steiner or SWAPO, was she? She was working for the *bladdy* British.'

*

12

Monday

It was only the slightest of sounds. A sound so small that considering the prevalence of strike jets, helicopters, cannons, guns, mortars and machine guns in this part of the world, it should really have gone un-noticed. It was no more than a *pop*, less noise than would be made than the drawing of a cork from a bottle of red, followed by the merest crackle, like a crisp packet being carefully screwed up in the back of the bioscope; but Corporal Andrew Bridgeman heard it.

Ever since he had heard of Mickey Epstein's miraculous re-appearance he had been so excited that he could barely contain himself. By turns he was elated, absolutely thrumming with excitement and then overwhelmed by surges of relief that welled through his body and brought a lump to his throat and tears to his one remaining eye. He could hardly keep his fingers from drumming on any available surface and small things, like the spiral caused by the twirl of a spoon in a tea cup or the smell of toast, made him inexpressibly happy. So happy, in fact that he was in danger of losing the self-control that a gay man in 1970s South Africa had learned to exercise from the very first time he had gone into the communal showers and realised that something was, quite literally, up. He was up on tip-toes all day and when he lay down in the purloined camp bed that he had set up in the store-room by the kitchen, now his self-allocated sleeping accommodation, he stretched out those same toes luxuriously, put his hands behind his head and revelled in the sharpness of his muscles and the disappearing strain in his neck.

It was frustrating, more than frustrating that he had not been able to sit in with Mickey; Pieters' orders were clear that no-one but he, Sergeant Smith or Captain Mostert were allowed into that locked room at any time, under any circumstances or for any reason. Sergeant Smith had had the glory of a long talk with him, had stolen the privilege of taking in his meals, changing the bag on his intravenous drip and Bridgeman resented all of this; well, except maybe the changing of the chamber pot, a task which Sergeant Smith had come more than close to delegating to him until Captain Mostert intervened. He desperately wanted to see him, talk to him, just be with him and he would gladly have given a testicle for the chance to nurse him back to the fullness of his health. And he was more than confident that, given half a chance, the Moffie Mafia on Grootfontein airbase could swing them both a weekend pass on the Flossie down to Cape Town just as soon as he was well enough to walk.

It was this possibility that kept him awake. He had broached the subject with one of the transport clerks (gay) and had been given the nod on condition that he found an appropriate officer or senior NCO (gay or straight) to sign off on the paperwork. Unfortunately, the (gay) NCO that he had in mind was at that moment up on the border directing air strikes onto SWAPO camps and so he was mulling over the possibility that Captain Mostert (not sure, it was difficult to tell with girls) might be persuaded to put her name to the movement order and if not, whether she was the sort of officer that a reasonably savvy clerk could get to sign a blank form or an imperfectly scrutinised piece of paper. He was pretty certain he could get Sergeant Smith (straight, boring) to do such a thing but also reasonably certain that a coppers thumb print would probably not carry the necessary weight with the Lords of Air Tasking, Logistics and Movements (stuck up, arrogant bastards, gay or straight).

It was probably because the place was so utterly and completely quiet that he heard the faint *pop* and distant *crackle*. The wind had dropped and so there was no movement in the bluegums outside, Sergeant Smith was out cold after having consumed a lot more Klippie than coke – Bridgeman had taken pity on him and had slipped him a bottle; he looked rough and Bridgeman reckoned that he had a dose of the post-combat jitters coming on – and Captain Mostert, though a light sleeper, had put her light out only moments after slipping the padlock on her door. At first he thought that the sound might just be a cockroach dropping down from the ceiling; for insects that were supposed to be super-efficient, almost indestructible examples of superb Darwinian evolution, they never seemed to have mastered the trick of not falling out of cupboards, off ceiling fans or through floorboards; but he discounted this because the stupid things usually fell off in twos and threes. Besides, they didn't crackle; the tiny feet of mice sometimes did but then the sound was longer and more sustained and in the silence of the night, somehow louder and impossible to ignore.

He got up, rolling off the cot and switching on the kitchen light. If there were cockroaches or mice, now was the time that they usually displayed their evolutionary prowess by legging it for the nooks and crannies like out-of-town Kaffirs in a passbook raid, but there was no startled movement or terrified scurrying. Opening the kitchen door, he looked out into the corridor, heard the squeal of springs as Sergeant Smith rolled over and then walked all the way down it, out of habit mainly, to check that the front door was locked. On his way back, he paused by Mickey's door, touched the lock wondering if he might just use the key he happened to have duplicated but then, deciding against it, just gave the slightest tap.

'You OK, Mickey?' he whispered, in the smallest voice he could command. 'Everything *lekker*?'

There was no answer; just the merest hint of a snore. And then, the squeak of a metal window hinge being swung open, very carefully.

'Mickey?' he said louder. 'Do you need anything?'

There was a grunt, the protest of bed springs and the clang of a light going on.

'What the *fok?*' called out Smithy, alarmed and irritated by turns, appearing in the corridor. 'Bridgeman? Are you tuning Epstein? *Jeez*! Can't you bum bandits leave off the uphill gardening for even one night?'

'I thought I heard something,' said Bridgeman, folding his arms. 'I was just checking.'

'*Ja* and I'm the Queen of Sheba,' replied Smithy, shoving his key into the lock.

'If you say so,' muttered Bridgeman.

'Just wait outside, hey?'

Smithy pushed open the door and switched on the light. The room was as bare as the last time he had gone in there; a light, a bed shoved up against the wall by the window, a drip, a chair and a heavily bandaged Parabat.

Mickey sat up and then caught himself with a groan.

'You OK?' grunted Smithy.

'I was, until someone woke me up,' replied Mickey, squinting at the light. 'Are we under attack now or are you coming to give me a blow job?'

'No and No,' said Smithy, blanching.

'*Ag, man,*' Mickey replied, pulling his blanket closer. 'Is it cold in here or is it me?'

'You OK, Andy?' said Mickey, raising a hand in greeting and then let out a sneer. 'Looks like you did alright for yourself finding this little job, hey? I always said you'd make a proper *koffie-moffie*.'

'Temper, temper, Mickey Epstein,' said Bridgeman, wagging a finger. 'Who rattled your chain?'

'Stay outside,' repeated Smithy. 'There'll be no big *fokken* John Travolta and Olivia Newton-John love scenes while I'm around. I couldn't stand it.'

'Who you calling a *moffie*?' snarled Mickey. 'Are you calling me a *moffie*?'

'Mickey, shut up,' said Smithy. 'It's three in the morning and I really do not want you chaffing me at this hour before coffee.'

'There! I knew I wasn't dreaming,' said Bridgeman, interrupting.

'I really do not want to know what goes on in your dreams, Bridgeman,' answered Smithy.

Bridgeman pointed to the window.

'The window is broken,' said Bridgeman. 'The window has been smashed.'

'What's going on?' said Mostert, arriving bleary-eyed, trouser-less, her modesty covered by the long tails of her shirt.

'Bridgeman here thinks there's a drama,' said Smithy, jerking a thumb. 'I think he *is* the drama. Or one of them, at any rate.'

'I thought I heard a window being broken,' insisted Bridgeman, ignoring Smithy and speaking directly to Mostert. 'So I came to the door to check and I was right. There is a window broken.'

'Did you use your key?' asked Mostert.

'I don't have one,' sniffed Bridgeman.

'Like the best handyman, fixer and networker in the whole of the Republic wouldn't have had an extra key cut?' said Mostert, wearily. 'Let's see this window then.'

The pane was missing.

'Did you break this?' Smithy asked Mickey.

'Yes, Sarge,' replied Mickey. 'It was too hot in here, so I woke myself up, hopped out of bed, disconnected the drip, smashed the window, reconnected the drip and got back into bed.'

'There's no glass on the inside,' said Smithy. 'That's why I am asking.'

'Bridgeman, go put the outside lights on,' said Mostert. 'Smithy, get your pistol while I put my longs on. We must just take a look outside.'

'Is that really necessary?' said Smithy.

'Get your gun.'

'I meant about the longs.'

The screen door banged loudly sending some small creature scurrying away into the bush as the three of them skirted around the bungalow. Around them, the yellow light warmed the sand from a concrete grey to a beachside tan and lit the strands of paperbark leaves from the bluegums so they looked like long leaches rolling in their death throes. Above them, the light could only blur a fraction of the blue of the night and the great cast of diamonds rolling away across the wide sky seemed to mock their search for a few shards of glass, reminding them of their insignificance and smirking at their efforts.

'Here,' said Mostert, reaching below the broken window and picking something up.

'Watch out for snakes, hey?' said Bridgeman.

'What have you found?' asked Smithy, shaking out a thorn from his flip-flop.

329

Mostert held up a loose lattice of broken glass held together by paper tape.

'What do you make of this?' she said.

Smithy's eyes narrowed: 'That's a burglar's trick,' he said. 'You tape up the window before you smash it so it makes less noise. Then you lift it out, stick your hand in and turn the lock. Nobody move. There should be tracks – that's if you haven't already trampled over them Ma'am. Have you got a torch, Bridgeman?'

'You said nobody was to move.'

'Bridgeman, don't be such a puff, will you? Now go and get a *fokken* lamp.'

Bridgeman went off in a huff and returned minutes later with a hurricane lamp. In the meantime, Smithy crouched down to examine the ground.

'Hold the lamp up, here,' ordered Smithy, searching. 'Over here,' he said, shuffling forward. 'Over here,' he said once more, casting around like a dog.

'That's odd,' he said, straightening up. 'Give me the lamp, Bridgeman.'

Smithy took the lamp and went this way and that, right up to the fence and then around the corner of the bungalow. He picked up a stick and prodded some of the brush, examined the boles of a couple of trees and then, coming back, waving the lamp like a lightship in a storm, declared: 'That is a proper burglar. No spoor left at all. Not a footprint, boot mark, scuff or scrape. Let's have a look inside.'

'He can't be all that good if he left the glass behind,' said Bridgeman, snarkily.

Back in Mickey Epstein's room, Smithy went first to the window, looked around it carefully and then stood back, hand on hips, to think.

'What was he trying to nick?' he said, running his eyes around the room.

'Is there anything to eat around here?' said Mickey. He was shivering a little and there were beads of sweat on his forehead. 'I mean, *fok*, Andy! Isn't this what you do all day? We do the fighting and you stay home and bake rusks?'

'Mickey, shut up,' said Smithy. 'I'm thinking.'

'*Ja*, I can just hear those gears grinding, Sergeant *fokken snuffelhonde*,' answered Mickey. 'Who do you think you are? Liewe *fokken* Heksie?'

'Mickey,' said Smithy, opening the window then peering up and around it. 'Shut up.'

'What are you looking for, Smithy?' said Mostert.

'I don't know, but something isn't right,' answered Smithy. 'Why did he go to the trouble of smashing the window pane and then not bother to open it?'

'Bridgeman,' said Mostert, nodding in his direction. 'He woke Bridgeman up and decided to make himself scarce.'

Smithy looked around again and then bent down to peer under the bed: 'There is nothing here worth nicking.'

'Drugs,' suggested Mostert, looking meaningfully at Bridgeman.

'What are you on, Mickey? Anything interesting?'

331

'*Ja fok,*' he replied. 'Heroin, morphine, LSD, *dagga*, the *fokken* works, *poes.*'

'Is he always this pleasant?' asked Mostert.

'You think this is bad, Missy *loskind*? Just wait until I'm out of this *kak* ward.'

'*Loskind*, is it?' said Mostert, angrily. 'You think I'm a slutty girl, is it? You should not try to get better very quickly, Private Epstein, because this ward is far more comfortable than the place you are going to when I've put you on a charge.'

'Mickey,' said Smithy, pulling him roughly forward to look behind his pillows. 'Shut up.'

'Where is this *fokken* hospital anyway?' said Mickey, gasping as Smithy slammed him back. 'What the *fokken fok* am I doing here?'

Smithy stopped: 'What did you say?'

'I said where, where...*fok*... '

'How many fingers am I holding up,' he said, anxiously.

'Four, *fokken poes.*'

'Jesus!' cried Smithy. 'He's going into shock! He's diabetic! Get some sugar into him. Bridgeman – juice, sugary water, raisins, chocolate, anything but make it quick.'

'He's not a diabetic,' answered Bridgeman.

'He *fokken* well is now!' said Smithy, pulling the drip out of Mickey's arm. He squeezed the bag of saline on its stand. A thin jet of water sprayed straight out from the top of the bag. 'Someone's stuck his bag with insulin. A hypodermic full, I'd say.'

*

'Well done, Sergeant,' said the medic, fastening his bag and preparing to leave. He was a big man, broad shouldered, narrow-hipped, blonde, tanned, sharp-eyed and Bridgeman was drooling. 'Another couple of hours and he would have slipped into a coma and then shuffled off this mortal coil. How did you know it was insulin poisoning?'

'Just something I picked up in Youth Preparedness class at school,' replied Smithy, tapping the new bag on the drip. 'In amongst how to kill a terrorist and how not to be a communist, we were taught about the symptoms in case our *krimpies* had diabetes. Sweating, cold, irritability, confusion; it was the bad temper that did it.'

'Well, it looks like we have something to thank the Education department for, after all,' said the medic, tipping a vague salute and emitting a dazzling smile from perfect white teeth. '*How beauteous mankind is! Oh brave new world that has such people in it.*'

'Huh?' said Smithy.

'It's Shakespeare,' said Mostert, dipping her eyes and taking the daintiest drag on a Lucky Strike.

'Good Lord, an educated woman!' said the medic, winking at her. 'Do you know how rare it is to find such a thing? Especially in Grootfontein? *Get thee to a nunnery.*'

333

'Been there. Done that already this week,' replied Mostert, with a coy smile and a flick of her recently combed hair. Smithy could smell perfume and it wasn't citrus. 'It couldn't have been an accident then?'

'Murder most foul, without a doubt,' replied the medic over his shoulder, as he headed down the corridor. At the door, he halted, looked back, struck a pose, chin up, arm out and declaimed: '*Good night, good night! Parting is such sweet sorrow that I shall say good night until it be morrow.*'

'*I would I were thy bird,*' said Mostert, as the door slammed behind him.

'You can say that again,' murmured Bridgeman.

'*Jeez,*' said Smithy. '*Bakvissies*, the pair of you.'

Mostert went up on her tip-toes, shook her hair and regained her composure: 'So, who and why did someone want to kill Mickey Epstein then?'

'Steiner is top of my list,' replied Smithy, on the instant. 'He left no spoor under the window and that's a Special Forces skill...'

'Apart from the broken glass,' said Bridgeman.

'Bridgeman,' said Smithy. 'You did well tonight, OK? Well done. I'll see you get a medal. Now shove off and make some breakfast, hey? You a clerk, not a detective.'

Bridgeman did as he was told but the level of his hostility to such a brusque dismissal was immediately evident by the volume of clanging that very quickly began to emanate from the kitchen.

'Was that really necessary?' asked Mostert. 'He'll be in a mood all day, now.'

'He's alright,' said Smithy, irritably. 'He just gives me the creeps sometimes; the way he looks at men is revolting. Anyway, Steiner is top of my list. He cleared his spoor – apart from the glass – and he's the only connection I can think of to Mickey Epstein and this whole business.'

'What would he gain from killing Mickey?' asked Mostert. 'I mean, it's a bit obvious isn't it? Steiner knows that he is being investigated and so goes back to the Cape to clear up the trail that connects him to Anna-Marie. Then, all of sudden, the second thing that connects him to her arrives out of the bush unexpectedly after being assumed reasonably to be KIA and then gets bumped off in mysterious circumstances. That is a coincidence that would be very difficult to sell.'

'True,' conceded Smithy. 'But it would be worth the risk if Mickey knew something that he hasn't already told us.'

'But Steiner wouldn't know what he had told us,' said Mostert. 'We're the only ones who know what he said.'

'What's better, a live witness or a dead body and an unsigned bit of paper with nothing but my notes on it?'

'*Ja*,' said Mostert, nodding and blowing out the last of her cigarette. 'OK. Shower, breakfast; then we interview Mickey again. After that, we go talk to Steiner.'

'We only have the files for one more day,' warned Smithy.

'We'll need a lot of coffee then,' said Mostert. 'Because today I am going to find out what happened to Anna-Marie van Zyl or bust.

335

'Go fuck yourself,' said Mickey, arms jammed in armpits, chin down, forehead out. 'I told you everything.'

Mostert stood by the door, leaning on the jamb and smoking a Lucky Strike, eyebrows raised, arms folded and from time to time shooting a warning glance at Smithy which stated *no torture*. Smithy, in turn, sat by the bed trying to ignore both her, Mickey's intransigence and the reflux that he was getting from the breakfast that Bridgeman had produced; the reflux he suspected was deliberate revenge for him being dismissive of him. As to torture, he had already discounted the possibility that some sort of mild roughing up might produce results on the basis that any sort of mild roughing up that he could provide would probably produce an opposite and more than equal reaction from the man in the bed. As well as that, Grootfontein was home to several hundred other Parabats and they were known to be a bit on the clannish side. Smithy didn't fancy it and had decided to try a sort of guileless pained patience.

'No Mickey, you didn't,' he said, with a sigh. 'You told us a lot but you didn't tell us everything. Like what your mission was.'

'I told you,' said Mickey. 'I went in as protection for the Recces. They didn't tell me what they were after.'

'But they told you they were headed towards the cookhouse and they told you that you would be bringing something that would require a seat in your own dedicated extract Alouette,' said Smithy.

'That's it,' confirmed Mickey.

'So at no time did anyone say: Your Mission is to go into the camp and bring *Something* or *Someone* out?'

'No,' said Mickey.

'You see this is the bit that I'm struggling with,' said Smithy, adopting a tone of wondering puzzlement. 'Because I understood that one of the things that all you Troupies do when you set off to *upfok* someone is to go through that little ritual of saying: *Mission! To go and* upfok *Someone!* And then, just to make sure the numpties in the squad have understood it, you say it again, just like before: *Mission! To go and* upfok *Someone!* Always, you repeat it.'

'It doesn't happen always,' said Mickey. 'If you are in a rush.'

'*Ja*, Mickey, it does,' said Smithy. 'So you are going to tell me what your mission was or things are going to get serious.'

Mostert shot a warning glass across the room. Mickey sniggered.

'Mickey,' said Smithy. 'You're a Parabat, right?'

'*Ex alto vincibus*,' replied Mickey. 'And proudly South African.'

'And do all your comrades share your *liberal* ideas?'

'You think I'm soft on communists and Kaffirs?' answered Mickey, the incredulity plain in his voice. 'You think wrong, man.'

'*Ja* Mickey, I'm not really talking about that kind of *liberal*.'

'Is there any other kind?' shot back Mickey. There was a warning note in his voice now.

'*Ja* Mickey, there is,' said Smithy, leaning in. 'There are those *moffie*-type liberals, Mickey. You know, *queers, puffs, chocolate speedway boys, fudge-packers*, Mickey. *That* type of liberal.'

Mickey's head came up and he looked first to Mostert by the door and then straight back at Smithy: 'Has *ma bru* Andy Bridgeman been telling tales out of school?'

'Mickey,' said Mostert, quietly. 'We know about you and Bridgeman and Sergeant – what was it? – Bilko? We don't care about your private business. We're not trying to blackmail you but...'

'Yes, we are,' said Smithy, straight at Mickey. 'She's just nicer about it than me. If it was up to me, I'd paste the news up on the camp notice board – and I mean, the *camp* noticeboard – but she's from the Cape and so a bit more *liberal* about this whole business than me.'

'We *not* trying to blackmail you,' repeated Mostert, her eyebrows up again in warning. 'We just want to know what your orders were.'

Mickey snorted: 'Is this 'your good cop bad cop' routine? You think it's good enough to get me to betray my Colonel?'

'Who's talking about betrayal?' said Mostert. 'What betrayal?'

'You trying to get Colonel Steiner stitched up because I got left behind at Capinga,' said Mickey. 'You think I'm stupid?'

'*Strength of a carthorse, speed of a racehorse,*' said Smithy under his breath. '*Brains of a* fokken *rocking horse.*'

'Mickey,' said Mostert. 'We investigating Colonel Steiner because we think he tried to kill you last night by stabbing your drip with a hypodermic

338

full of insulin. And we think he tried to do that because of something to do with your mission at Capinga.'

'*Ja*? Good luck with your next novel,' said Mickey.

'No novel, Mickey,' said Mostert. 'You think Sergeant Smith here can write?'

'You going straight into my memoirs,' said Smithy, drily. 'The bit where I try to forget about all the *mompies* I've come across in the course of an illustrious career.'

'*Fok jou*,' said Mickey, and then turning his head to Mostert. 'With all due respect to an officer, of course, Ma'am.'

Smithy pushed back and swung on two legs of his chair.

'Just tell us what the mission was,' he said, coaxing. 'And I promise we won't tell your buddies in the Parabat locker room that you're a *moffie*, OK?'

'You think they will believe you?' said Mickey. 'You think they will even care? Because no-one cares about any of that *kak* in a firefight. They just want to know you got their back covered and you know how to slot Kaffirs.'

'You probably right on that,' agreed Smithy, affably. 'Question is, when you get back to camp after slotting all those Kaffirs, will they want to drink with you? Share the latrines with you? Play rugby with you? And there is always the problem of actually being allowed to be a Parabat. How would you feel about a dishonourable discharge? And how would you feel about your father and mother and all your family knowing that you are a *moffie*?'

339

'And how would you feel knowing that I know that you name is Sergeant Smith and that you will never walk out of a bar or past an alleyway or down a quiet road at night without wondering if I'm going to pop out and hand you a beating, *hey*? Or maybe it will be several of my *special* friends, *hey*?' said Mickey, evenly. 'And maybe when they have finished with you, you will not know where your trousers are and you will be walking very gingerly for a week? Because two can play at that game, *ma bru.*'

'Can I torture him, now?' said Smithy, looking towards Mostert. 'Just a little bit, hey?'

'No,' said Mostert, stubbing out the cigarette. 'Mickey, something went really wrong in that camp and I think you were sent in to sort it out. I think you were sent in to –.' There was a sharp rap at the door.

'Bugger off,' shouted Smithy, who just knew it would be Bridgeman and Bridgeman probably still in a huff of one sort or another.

'Captain Mostert, please, open the door.'

'It's Bridgeman,' said Mostert, unlocking. 'What do you want?'

'Ma'am, I've just been on the phone and I think there is something you should know,' said Bridgeman, his head coming round the door.

'Do tell,' called Smithy.

'It's probably better you know in private, Ma'am,' said Bridgeman, ignoring Smithy but nodding at Mickey.

'Fine, just fine,' said Mostert. 'Smithy, I'm just going out the door *hey*?'

'Fine,' answered Smithy, knowing what she was referring too. She always suspected that he had tortured David Merriman when he had sent her out of

340

the room on a pretext. She was right about this too, but Smithy had never let on. 'Just time for me to wire Mickey here up to a socket.'

'Funny,' said Mostert and Mickey, simultaneously.

'I can wedge the door open if you prefer, Ma'am,' said Bridgeman.

'Really, there is no need,' said Smithy, with resignation.

Bridgeman withdrew taking Mostert with him and for a moment Smithy and Mickey eyed each other across the bed. Mickey had the closed look of the guilty, thought Smithy. The pig-headed frown of the perpetually suspicious sat on his brow like a big, stupid black crow. He had seen it often enough on the faces of suspects in the interrogation rooms and the cells and recognised the invincible self-justification, the invincible confidence in their own brilliance and the truly bovine belief that none of it was their fault anyway. None of them ever seemed to consider the possibility that they were not unique, nor did they ever pause to consider that a whole department of police backed up by a whole department of justice and another one of prisons might just outweigh them in the IQ stakes, if only by sheer weight of numbers.

'True knowledge isn't what you know,' said Smithy. 'Did you know that Mickey? True knowledge isn't what you know – .'

'*Ja*, it's knowing how to find out what you don't know,' said Mickey, finishing off the proverb. 'Did you learn that in policeman's school?'

'No, it isn't,' said Smithy, firmly. 'Anyone can find out what they don't know, Mickey. You just ask someone or go to the library or wire the suspect up to plug socket, something like that. But *true* knowledge is knowing the extent of your own ignorance. Knowing that what you know is only the tip of a very big iceberg, if you like.'

'Right,' said Mickey, lying back. 'Amazing, professor. Truly amazing.'

'See, the thing is, Mickey,' said Smithy, rocking backwards and forwards on the chair again. 'What you brought out of the jungle for us in the form of those filing cabinets is a big chunk of the iceberg but really, to my mind, the bit of the iceberg that I really need to know about before I can make sense of it all is the tip, the top, the pinnacle, like the top of a triangle, if you like. If I can get that angle at the top, then I can work out a lot about the size and shape of what is going on below.'

'There is nothing I can do for you,' reiterated Mickey. 'I'm loyal to my regiment.'

'And so you should be,' replied Smith. 'But is Steiner loyal to you, in turn?'

'You have proof that he tried to kill me? I don't think so,' said Mickey. 'Look, things go wrong all the time in the bush. So I got left behind? Not good. This is true. But shit happens, man. If everyone was pursued like this for making a mistake all you would have is a lot of flat-footed coppers and a lot of fat lawyers but no army because that army would all be sacked, in jail or awaiting disgraceful discharge. Drop it man. Colonel Steiner is a good soldier. I'm not playing, *ja*?'

The door opened.

Mostert and Bridgeman came into the room both of them had faces shut tight. Both knew what the news would mean to a soldier like Mickey Epstein.

342

'Tell him,' said Mostert.

'What would you like me to say?' answered Bridgeman.

'Just say it as you said it to me,' said Mostert. 'Go on.'

Bridgeman looked like he wanted help, saw none was forthcoming and so began.

'Mickey, you're not going to like this but you can't say I didn't warn you about Steiner,' he said.

'What are you talking about man?' said Mickey, warily.

'I told you that he only cared about himself when I lost my eye,' said Bridgeman. 'And you didn't believe me then but now maybe you will believe me now.'

'Spit it out, Corporal Bridgeman,' said Mostert. 'We don't need any *I told you so.*'

Bridgeman looked for help again and got none this time either.

'Colonel Steiner has gone AWOL,' said Bridgeman. 'He took a vehicle out at last light yesterday and told the gate he was driving up to Oshadangwa. He isn't there.'

'So?' said Mickey.

'He had no orders to go there.'

'So he was on some bit of secret business,' said Mickey. 'You know he's in with the Recces.'

'There's no sign of the vehicle either.'

'Maybe he got ambushed?'

'No reports of any contact – and the Engineers swept that road both ways last night. I checked.'

'So he went somewhere else,' protested Mickey. 'What is this?'

'Headlights were seen being switched off a hundred metres east of this bungalow just before three o'clock this morning,' said Bridgeman. 'And he drew medical supplies from the infirmary yesterday. The dispensing orderly had to go into the main storeroom to get what he wanted. When he came back, he was missing some insulin. He's sure of it and sure it was Steiner because the insulin was -,' he shot a compromised glance at Mostert and then one at Smithy. '- was *off the record* insulin and he kept it the same drawer as some *off the record* morphine and the morphine was left.'

'How do you know all this?' said Mickey, paling.

'Contacts, of course,' said Bridgeman. 'The same ones that you have.'

'Jesus,' said Mickey, lying back. 'And you swear that this is all true? You will swear that this is all true? On the Bible?'

'Not on the Bible,' said Bridgeman. 'You might be Born Again but I'm not going in for any of that sin, hellfire and destruction stuff.'

'You a Christian?' gasped Smithy. 'How can you be a Christian and a *moffie*? It isn't allowed!'

'Shut up, Smithy,' said Mostert, smartly. 'Not now.'

Mickey went quiet, his head back on the pillow as he digested all this. Steiner; a Parabat. Steiner; a Colonel. Steiner; a decorated soldier of

344

unquestionable bravery. Steiner; his officer. Steiner; who he had given his unquestioning loyalty to.

'What was the mission, Mickey?' said Mostert.

'Kill or capture,' he said, after a while, as though in a daze. 'Kill or capture a white girl. Some kind of spymaster. She was Swedish or Norwegian and working for SWAPO. One of those *kaffirboetie* foreigners who get off on black dick. Steiner said she was a big cheese. If we took her out, it would cause massive damage to SWAPO.'

'Was this her?' said Mostert, handing him the photograph that old man van Zyl had given her.

'This was taken a while ago,' said Mickey, examining it carefully. 'But yes. That's her.'

'Did you succeed?' asked Smithy.

'How the fuck would I know, you *domkop*?' replied Mickey. 'The drop went wrong. I was on the wrong side of the river, remember?'

\*

'Well, at least we know what we are looking for now,' said Smithy. 'Even though we cannot hope to find it. The only people who know what happened to Anna-Marie van Zyl are two nameless Recces who will no doubt wish to remain nameless.'

'And Steiner will be well over some border by now,' said Mostert, pushing away a plate of rusks. 'So we must just do our best with the time we have left.'

'That sounds like a funeral oration,' said Smithy, taking a third rusk and dunking it in his coffee. 'But we can read the files now from a different angle at least and so give Pieters a report that is not wholly fiction.'

'*Ja*, Smithy, that was a good hunch you had about Anna-Marie working for the British,' said Mostert. 'So we must just look for more evidence of this. If you do this thing, I'll write the draft.'

*

At five that evening, as the last of the cabinets were wheeled out of the bungalow and loaded onto a truck for Pretoria, Pieters lit a cigarette to go with the two already burning in an old fish can that served as an ashtray. He had Mostert's report in his hand and he opened it as he sat down, concentrating, already absorbed in its content, reading closely and intelligently. From time to time, he took a drag at the cigarette, but mostly his blue rheumy eyes simply winced when the smoke spiralled up into them while the rest of the time he used it almost as though it was a pencil or a pointer writing notes on an invisible pad suspended in the air. The remnants of the fish oil hissed when the stub went into it giving off an unwholesome smell that made Bridgeman click his tongue as far away as the kitchen, but was not enough to mask the overwhelming stale cumin sweat of his BO, to which Pieters, his nylon shirt stuck to his back, was clearly oblivious.

It was clear that he wanted no disturbance. Indeed it hardly seemed that he was aware of his own presence, let alone those of Mostert and Smithy and if a lock of his brylcreemed hair sometimes detached itself from the solid shiny slate of his cut, it took some small moment, a break in a sentence or paragraph before he moved a finger to replace it. The report itself was not long and Mostert had laid out the bare bones only on the upper sheets, reserving the detail for a number of appendices, but Pieters read through everything; he was not interested in a precis and he was interested in the detail, in the supporting documents, in the examples that she had provided and went back and forward between them, reading voraciously, making judgements, testing hypotheses and looking for the gaps. He was reptilian in his intensity.

*Report on the Capinga Situation.*

1. *The white female identified in the mass grave at Capinga is Anna-Marie van Zyl b.1950. (See photo recon photos attached).*

2. *Anna-Marie van Zyl appears to have had a difficult childhood, by turns neglected and indulged and lacking in stability. This resulted in deviant behaviour (see notes on the statement given by Sister Margaret of St Xavier's School, Saldana Bay) and permanent estrangement from her father.*

3. *Between 1965-68, she lived at multiple addresses, attended the University of Cape Town without successfully graduating and maintained a bohemian lifestyle.*

4. *Between 1968-70, she worked at the Britannia Hotel in Simonstown where she dabbled with ANC activities (see the notes attached on Charles Markham).*

5. *In 1971, she was arrested in Montagu and handed over to the custody of her father. Note that Cornelius van Zyl denied having any further contact with her after 1965. This is a point for a further line of investigation.*

6. *Shortly after this, she was forced to undergo psychiatric procedures with the aim of curing her deviant behaviour. The*

347

*treatment was thought to be unsuccessful and she was moved to a military hospital in Pretoria for further treatment. Colonel Steiner removed the medical records from the psychiatrist treating her in Cape Town.*

7. *It is our conclusion that Colonel Steiner came into contact with her at the time of her treatment and recruited her into BOSS but we have no available detail about what her training consisted of. We assume it was for an undercover infiltration role. Also, there is evidence that she underwent some training with the Recces at Langebaan in 1976. We have no view on her motivation for joining BOSS; her actions and behaviour are contradictory throughout.*

8. *It is possible that she worked for SWAPO at various locations in Luanda and then at the Karl Marx Reception centre in Lubango where she passed reports to Colonel Steiner on SWAPO personnel and foreign volunteers. (See the confession attached; we cannot vouch for the authenticity of this document).*

9. *At some stage, we believe that she was recruited by British intelligence, either in London or in Angola, by someone called 'Mason'. This is an area for further investigation and must be verified. (See information extracted from files various, attached; also communication tagged 'Revolutionary Logic'.).*

10. *Sometime before the attack on Capinga, Anna-Marie began to request extraction from Colonel Steiner. This was refused. We have two theories regarding this:*

        *i.  Colonel Steiner suspected that Anna-Marie had been turned and was now working for SWAPO.*

*We have no firm evidence to back this conjecture up.*

    *ii. Colonel Steiner believed that she was safe but miscalculated the risk. We have no firm evidence to back this up.*

11. *Shortly before the attack on Capinga, Anna-Marie was moved to Capinga camp in ambiguous circumstances. It is probable that she had been uncovered by SWAPO but before she underwent serious interrogation, orders were received that she was to be allowed to leave for England. (See attached communication tagged 'Revolutionary Logic').*

12. *When Colonel Steiner became aware that she was being moved to Capinga, he ordered her to comply with the direction, for reasons which are unclear to us. See point 10.i and ii above.*

13. *When the Capinga operation was about to be mounted, Colonel Steiner attached two Recces and two of his own most trusted men to the operation. Their mission was to kill or capture Anna-Marie van Zyl. We have two theories on this. They are not mutually exclusive.*

    *i. Colonel Steiner had discovered that Anna-Marie was working for SWAPO and wished to apprehend her.*

    *ii. Colonel Steiner had discovered that he had been duped by Anna-Marie and wished to cover up his mistake.*

14. *We do not know how Anna-Marie van Zyl was killed. It could have been the air strike or assassination at the hands of the Recces. It could also have been the result of some misadventure in the camp.*

*15. We believe that an attempt was made on the life of Private Michael Epstein, previously presumed KIA at Capinga, by Colonel Steiner whose motive is given at point 13.ii.*

*16. Colonel Steiner has been listed as AWOL, whereabouts unknown.*

Pieters grunted, coughed, lit up another cigarette and then, still hunched over the desk, lifted his head and looked at Smithy and Mostert sitting before him on hard chairs, as though they were being interviewed for a job.

'May I congratulate you on your report, Captain Mostert?' he said, adding a quick, small smile. 'It is quite a masterpiece.'

'Sergeant Smith did most of the work,' answered Mostert. 'I just wrote it up.'

'*Ja,*' said Pieters. 'A report that is full of information but which says nothing at all. I could not have done better myself.'

'With respect, Sir,' said Mostert. 'We did our best with what we had and in the short time available.'

'*Deviant behaviour,*' he said, smirking. 'A nice term for it. And you can give no assessment as to her motives for becoming a spy either for BOSS, SWAPO or this mysterious British agent called Mason? Would the issue of Apartheid not provide a motive possibly? I hear it is quite controversial and much discussed among young people today. And you cannot tell how she was killed, even though she is in a mass grave after an airstrike. My, my, and you an educated person too, I shouldn't wonder.'

'Again, with respect, Sir,' said Mostert, biting her lip and laying an accent on *respect*. 'I don't think this investigation was about Anna-Marie van Zyl at all.'

Smithy's eyebrows shot up at this and he had the distinct feeling that Mostert was going to say something that would drop him in deep water. As far as he understood it, their plan had been to just hand over the report, beg for a weekend pass in Cape Town as a reward and then wave goodbye to the whole baffling nonsense. Now it appeared that the object of his desire had decided to go off in a direction that was all her own and he was not comfortable with this at all; not comfortable at all. This was BOSS she was talking to and he knew just what BOSS was capable of doing to people who talked to them and did not do it in a satisfactory way. There was something in her tone that he had once used in front of a Headmaster at school and had been caned within an inch of his short life for it as a direct and immediate result. He shifted uneasily in his seat at the memory.

'No? Do, please, enlighten me,' said Pieters, taking up a cigarette from a three strong line burning in the fish can ash tray, and straightening his back.

'I think this was just a cover to get at Colonel Steiner, Sir. I think this is a private investigation on your part. Elsewise, why would you not do this officially? Why would you not use real BOSS agents?'

'And why would I want to get at Colonel Steiner?' said Pieters, closing one eye as a smoke genie spiralled up into it. 'He's a good soldier by all accounts.'

'With respect, again, Sir,' said Mostert. 'I must disagree. He was not efficient at all, either as a soldier or a spy.'

Smithy squirmed on his chair. She had not prepared him for any of this. Pieters waved a cigarette in the air, coughing up a chunk into a handkerchief as a signal for her to proceed.

'Well, firstly, Sir, he was in on the planning for the Capinga raid and endorsed the timing of the para drop. He should have known to allow more time between the air strike and the drop so that the Dak pilots wouldn't be so distracted by the spectacle. His control of the extraction wasn't of the highest order either – that's why Private Epstein was left behind.'

'It's a small point,' coughed Pieters. 'You know he has medals?'

'It's quite a big point actually, Sir,' said Mostert. 'He's got a record for making mistakes like this. People assume that because he is some kind of German Nazi that he is super-efficient. *Ja*, well, who was it that actually won the war, hey? Corporal Bridgeman - through the kitchen there – he's probably got a cup to the wall - lost his eye because Steiner made a mess of an artillery fire plan. I bet it would make interesting reading to go back through his operational reports, one by one, and then compare them with the actual reality. You know at Capinga the troops marched in the wrong *bladdy* direction before the attack? That's why the resistance was tough. The enemy got time to re-organise because the Parabats were attacking 180° in the wrong direction.'

'Jeez, Mostert,' muttered Smithy. 'You getting your knickers in a twist.'

'Fog of war,' said Pieters, shrugging. 'Cock-ups happen all the time in battles. But do carry on, hey?'

'Secondly, this spy business,' said Mostert, becoming animated. 'Who on earth recruits their spies from a lunatic asylum? And who on earth would

352

recruit someone so unpredictable, unreliable and wilfully stupid as Anna-Marie van Zyl?'

'You might be surprised,' said Pieters, as a racking cough extinguished the beginnings of a twinkle of mirth.

'And then the cover up?' she continued, as he continued to hack. 'Instead of reporting to his superiors in BOSS that his agent has been turned or captured and that this is a problem not unknown, he decides to cover up his mistakes and hopes they will not find out! And how does he do this? He starts by demanding psychiatric records from a Cape Town practice and expecting not to have this thing remarked upon? It's crazy.'

Pieters waved a hand for her to stop while he regained his breath. Smithy looked at him and wondered if he was actually laughing at the rope that Mostert was paying out ready for her own hanging. The sinking feeling that had been growing on him in these last few minutes now went ocean deep.

'And then, when Private Epstein re-appears, he panics and tries to kill him,' said Mostert, ignoring his imprecations. 'And bungles it! He leaves the taped up glass behind! And if that isn't a stupid thing to do, he then takes a vehicle and makes a run for it! Where does he think he is going?'

'He has plenty of survival skill,' said Pieters, recovering. 'He will not easily be caught.'

'He will need them,' said Mostert, a tone of exasperation taking over her voice. 'This man is a *doos*. No wonder the Rhodesians were happy to see him foisted on us.'

'You finished now?' said Pieters, laying down his cigarette and appraising her with just one eye while he rubbed a finger in the other.

'With respect, Sir,' said Mostert, calming down. 'You used us because someone in BOSS was protecting Steiner and you used us to get enough dirt on Steiner so that you could remove him from his position.'

Pieters lit up another cigarette. Smithy noted that there were now five burning; something of a record. He tapped it in the ashtray while his eyes wandered in thought and the fingers on his other hand drummed on the table.

'You are as smart as I have heard, Captain Mostert,' said Pieters, nodding as he came to a decision. 'You got the story pretty well. There are a few details missing, but on the whole, you nailed it. Well done. Steiner is finished. Thank you.'

Smithy sat up. 'I helped too,' he blurted out.

'*Ja,*' said Pieters, flicking his tongue in and out. There was a blob of white phlegm on the end of it. 'I bet you did.'

'You didn't like Steiner,' said Mostert. It was a statement not a question. 'Was it personal?'

'Cornelius van Zyl is my brother,' said Pieters, standing up, collecting up his cigarettes and cramming them into the pockets of his ratcatcher's jacket and drawing the interview to an abrupt close. 'Anna-Marie was my niece. Steiner and Cornelius knew each other through the OB, the *Ossewabrandwag*, and the OB got Steiner his promotions and his position with BOSS. And you are right about his competence. He had his successes, true, but he was out of his depth, promoted beyond his ability

354

because of his OB connection. This is not a new story in the way of the world, as I am sure you are aware. Now he is exposed for that incompetence. All well and good.'

He shuffled towards the door. From outside came the whine of helicopter rotors beginning to turn and he looked up into nowhere, fiddled with his pockets, checking that he had his cigarettes and then stopped, turned and said: 'Steiner violated my family when he recruited Anna-Marie. *Ja, Anna-Marie* was a traitor to the republic. But blood is thicker than water.'

*

'That's it?' said Smithy, as the chopper lifted off the pad and circled off to the south. 'Not even a pat on the back and a weekend pass in Cape Town for all our efforts? What a complete waste of time and effort. And I'm up to my arse in *moffies* and *mompies* into the bargain.'

'It makes you wonder who the real traitors are,' said Mostert, angrily.

'All of them,' said Smithy. 'That useless spoiled brat Anna-Marie working for the *bladdy* British, that cretinous Nazi Steiner working for the OB and that disgusting Pieters of the Bureau of State Security using us to undermine Steiner the Cretin of the Bureau of State Security because he's pissed off that he turned his worthless niece into a spy – and he couldn't care less that she was working for the enemy. Plus that thing about the SWAPO brass knowing about the Capinga operation in advance. Which loyal citizen of this fine republic told them about that? This place is leaking like a sieve.' From inside the bungalow, the sound of a ringing telephone could be heard. 'And that will be some minion telling us to piss off back to where we came from and keep schtum. Jeez! It's enough to make you want to defect.'

From the direction of the infirmary, an ambulance was approaching, kicking up the dust like a motorcyclist with his foot on the ground.

'Looks like Mickey's holiday in the private ward is over too,' said Mostert. 'I wonder if Bridgeman will keep his little hideout here?'

A window opened and Bridgeman's head poked out. 'That was HQ,' he called out. 'You're to leave all notes and issued ID with me and prepare to return to your units. Transport is being arranged.'

'Today?' asked Smithy.

'This evening,' confirmed Bridgeman.

'Well, at least we can have lunch and a few beers together,' said Smithy. 'Before we part.'

'Sure,' said Mostert. 'Let's get out of these uniforms and into civvies for a couple of hours. We'll make a braai and pretend we civilised, hey?'

She folded her arms, looked down and then up into his eyes. 'It's been good to see you Joshua and…I know what you want me to say but I can't say it. So let's get that straight from the beginning.'

'Do you?' said Smithy. 'Why don't you just give it a go and see how it turns out?'

'Because, Joshua,' she said, looking away. 'Just *because*.'

*

The helicopter came early for Trudi and with it the news that he would not be moving until the following morning. Bridgeman had stacked everything up in the bungalow ready for it to be moved in the morning and had gone off to the hospital with Mickey Epstein and so Smithy was left alone in the emptiness, partly drunk and full of the good steak that Bridgeman had blagged for them as a parting gesture. Police Post 158 beckoned and so tonight he intended to finish off every scrap of booze in the property, curse his bad luck and feel thoroughly, thoroughly sorry for himself in the matter of Trudi Mostert, who he just knew would know it was right if she just let herself go and gave him a chance.

He turned on the radio and tuned it to Radio Lesotho in the hope of hearing some uncensored music but the signal was too weak this far away and Angolan radio was just terrible so he had to settle for SABC. It was better than nothing, he supposed as he wandered aimlessly through the building. He couldn't resist going into her room in the hope of catching some faint hint of her, but Bridgeman had already had the sheets away and into the laundry, cleaned the room and swept the carpet, so the spoor was lost. He had hoped there would perhaps be a note but there was nothing. She was gone. Probably for good. *Parting is such sweet sorrow.* He made a resolution to read some Shakespeare but he knew that this was a resolution doomed to last no longer than the time it took to make it.

He went through to the office where Bridgeman had emptied the ash trays, squared the chairs and tied up the Capinga Report materials into a neat pile secured with string. On top of it was the Filofax that Bridgeman had gave him and which he had forgotten all about and now, picking it up and flipping through the pages, the hope came to him that she had written something for him in here; something funny, something witty, something poignant, just…*something.* But there was nothing.

And then the smell of citrus, of oranges, limes, lemons, tangerines suddenly rose up and filled the room. It was so strong as to be overpowering and Smithy found himself squinting and swaying with its intensity and on an impulse that he could neither explain nor understand, he took the file, removed the string and took out the report.

1.  *The white female identified in the mass grave at Capinga is Anna-Marie van Zyl b.1950. (See photo recon photos attached).*

He scrabbled to the back, found the large envelope that contained the photos and taking them out laid them out on the table. Ripping open the drawer, he took out one of the magnifying classes and then bending down he began to scour through the dreadful images with an intensity that made him almost nauseous, a desire for the answer to the question that had been nagging at his subconscious, the question that he had forced down and avoided with every effort that his subconscious brain could make, the only question in this whole, worthless episode that was worth answering.

*'Why does everything smell of citrus?'*

And, as he knew he would, he found the answer.

He knew the reason for the smell of citrus. It was the scent of the trees in Mrs Parr's garden. It was the scent that Mrs Maquondo made up from her secret recipe. It was the scent that Ayize wore.

And down in one corner of the photograph of that terrible, terrible mass grave at Capinga was a leg, with an ankle bracelet on it, brought from CNA with his own pocket money.

\*

Epilogue

Table Mountain Cable Car Station

Three Months Later.

'There really can be no disputing it, can there? This must be one of the finest views of the world.' The voice came from slightly behind and to his right, but Joshua did not turn around. 'Signal Hill, the Lion's Head, the docks, the castle, all laid out like a sand table model and all tiny when you think of the vastness of the ocean and the vastness of the sky. Bloubergstrand all the way across the bay, just the beginning of a beach that stretched all the way up to Morocco with hardly a break. Just think how long it would take a man to walk that distance and just think what adventures he might have along the way! The Skeleton Coast, the mighty Congo, the Atlas Mountains; it is breath taking to think of it. And then, just a short hop across the straits to Gibraltar and there is the old world to explore too. Africa to the north and beyond it Europe; nothing to the south but ocean and the pole. It's the vastness of it all that strikes one, does it not? Makes you realise that the concerns of the day are not as great as we think, in the great scheme of things.'

'Who are you?' said Smithy. Before him the tumbling rocks of the mountain were grey and green with moss, the line of the horizon discernible only as a difference in the shades of blue, while the sea itself lay calm, serene, perfect. Only the low shape of Robben Island broke it, like a swimmer pushing out to the Atlantic. 'And what do you want? I'm only here because Clive Merriman wanted me to meet you and I owe him a favour.'

'I'm a journalist colleague of Mr Merriman's,' replied the voice. It was an English voice, courteous and querulous, not harsh or quarrelsome, but the sort of voice that might belong to a mildly interested retired person. 'And I'm interested in the Capinga story.'

Smithy gave a small snort. 'Whatever you are, you are not a journalist,' he said. 'In my limited experience, journalists do not begin by talking about the scenery.'

'It's a specialist area, I admit,' said the voice.

'Poison gas?' asked Smithy.

'More in the missing persons line, actually.'

Smithy look along the long line of the wide horizon and then followed the sweep of the beach all the way round from Grootbai, through Milnertown and the snaking lines of the railway down to the docks where the Japanese and Korean freighters were unloading, past the sand pink pentangle of the castle and the empty spaces where District Six used to be, before alighting on the skyscrapers of the central business district. Somewhere down there was Adderley Street and the Edwardian Town Hall but he could not make them out from this angle and so turned to look at Seapoint nestling beyond Signal Hill and then strained his neck to catch the Twelve Apostles.

'Any particular missing persons? Like one by the name of Anna-Marie van Zyl?'

'Among others,' admitted the voice. 'I would be grateful for any information and my Editor would be willing to authorise a suitable reward.'

'She was killed in the airstrike,' said Smithy.

'Would you know what she was doing there?'

'I've got a fair idea,' said Smithy, turning to face the stranger. 'I guess you have too.'

The man was dressed in white bags, brogues, a white shirt, blazer and panama, the uniform of the elderly English ex-pat from the Cape to Cairo, whether planter, banker, diplomat or spy. His face was florid and clean shaven, unremarkable except for that fact that it was remarkably untanned and instantly forgettable, except for the rather inane smile that it carried, half on, half off.

'Would the name *Topollo* mean anything to you?' he asked. 'She had adopted *Freedom* as her *nom de guerre*.'

Smithy shook his head. 'Never heard of her.'

'Pity,' said the stranger.

'Do you know a lot of the names of people who were in that camp?' asked Smithy, cautiously.

'Some,' admitted the voice, optimistically. 'Some, yes, certainly.'

'How about Ayize Maquondo?'

The stranger continued to smile a smile that gave nothing away but seemed to be expectant, as though expecting more words, more questions, more information before the question could be answered.

'What is it you want?' said Smithy, turning back to look at the awesome panorama before him.

'To be quite straightforward,' replied the stranger. 'My Editor is very interested in the whole issue of missing persons and would be willing to make adequate remuneration for help in accessing the appropriate records from time to time. Nothing very sensitive, of course; nothing that might compromise your position as a policeman, of course; we like to think of ourselves as working alongside the police in these matters, rather than against them.'

'What's the name of the newspaper you work for?' asked Smithy, a little irritated now as the picture was beginning to come into focus.

'Well, to be honest, we are more in the way of a wire agency than an actual newspaper,' said the stranger, disarmingly.

'And why do you think I would be willing to work for you?'

'Clive Merriman recommended you to us,' answered the stranger. 'He understands that your background and beliefs might indicate a natural sympathy to our work.'

'In *missing persons*?'

'Indeed.'

'You'll need to make yourself a little plainer than that, whoever you are,' said Smithy. 'And you still haven't given a name. How do I know you are not the KGB?'

'Oh, I'm sorry,' said the stranger. 'My name is Mason.'

'Mason?'

'Mason,' confirmed the stranger. 'And please do not think we would insult your integrity by offering monetary payments.'

'Please, go ahead,' said Smithy, sarcastically. 'Insult me all you like.'

'How very droll,' said Mason. 'But my Editor was thinking more along the lines of helping you towards citizenship of the Irish Republic, perhaps. Would that be something that might interest you? I understand the

Emerald Isle is very popular with South Africans. The landscape there is such a contrast with here. More colourful, I hear.'

'Ayize Maquondo,' said Smithy. 'Tell me about her.'

'She was killed. We believe she was killed in the airstrike,' said Mason, sympathetically. 'She joined the ANC shortly after her brother was killed during a robbery and had been a loyal comrade ever since.'

Smithy looked out across the bay for a while as he digested this and tried hard to dismiss the thought that he was the root of all this madness. He could not have known that the boy he shot was Ayize's brother; he could not have known that Mrs Maquondo would leave so quickly for Johannesburg; he could not have known that Ayize would join the ANC and be sent to Angola; he could not have known that she would succumb to that terrible, terrible rain of tearing metal sent down by Templeton and Steiner. And yet, in retrospect, he could imagine Mrs Maquondo's utter despair, Ayize's utter desolation and it did not take a genius to work out the possibilities that would flow from the iniquities of their position in the apartheid state. He could not have known the particulars, but he had long been aware of the generalities.

'And how do you know all this?'

'The files that were lost at Capinga did not include the bulk of the personnel records,' said Mason.

'How did Anna-Marie van Zyl come to be working for you?'

'Revenge,' replied Mason, simply, as though it was the simplest thing in the world to change sides, to become a traitor to your country. 'When she was a student here, she walked in to a police station in London and offered

363

her services. She kept us remarkably well informed about both BOSS and SWAPO.'

Smithy gave a wry smile.

'Revenge?' he asked.

'Mainly against her father, who she despised as an Afrikaaner and a Nazi,' said Mason. 'What better way to get her revenge than to work for the British? Despite the international media's blanket insistence that apartheid is a tool of white dominance over black, most of those who know a little more about South Africa are aware of the certain nuance that an Afrikaaner would, in the normal run of things, usually prefer a black man's company to that of an Englishman.'

'There is certainly something to that,' agreed Smithy. 'But why should she report on SWAPO?'

'Oh that was just bloody mindedness on her part,' said Mason. 'She had picked up some crackpot theories about being above normal morality and frankly, she enjoyed the subterfuge. I doubt she had any loyalty to anyone but herself. Such are the tools one must work with from time to time.'

Smithy turned back to look out from the mountain.

'Did you know Cape Town is one of the few ports in the world that is not situated at the mouth of a river?' he said.

'The thought never occurred to me, old boy,' replied Mason.

'And did you know that there are no major navigable rivers in Africa?' he continued. 'The Nile is blocked by cataracts, the Congo by rapids, the

Zambezi goes over Vic Falls and the Niger doesn't go anywhere worth going.'

'Fascinating,' said Mason, amiably.

'So even if the rivers in Africa do reach the sea – and not all of them do, I can tell you,' he said. 'They are still no real use.'

'Amazing,' said Mason, in the same amiable tone.

'So what it means is that we South Africans are stuck here in Africa,' said Smithy, nodding out towards the landmass ahead of him, to the north. 'We can't just follow a river to the sea and escape. We are here. We have to make it work, *here*.'

'Oh, absolutely, old boy,' said Mason. 'Take your point fully.'

'I'm South African,' said Smithy. 'I can't be anything else. So an Irish passport is no use to me at all.'

'Well said. Very honourable indeed,' said Mason. 'But let's not dismiss the thought out of hand. Keep an open mind? Mull it over?'

Smithy put his hand out and touched the rock of Table Mountain, felt its solidity under his hand, felt how cool it was even as the sun warmed it, and then something came to him, floating down from some English Lit class years and years ago.

'*What profit a man that he gain the whole world yet lose his own soul?*' It was old Conway, he remembered, banging on about some play or other about Henry VIII; he had slept through most of it but this line had stuck and now he adapted it to his own situation and finished the quote. '*But Smithy, for an Irish passport?*'

He turned away, making for the cable car exit.

'Goodbye Mason,' he said. *'Get thee behind me, Satan.'*

Glossary

FAPLA: The armed forces of Angola.

SWAPO: The Namibian Liberation movement.

ANC: African National Congress. The South African liberation movement.

Toyi-toyi: a kind of dance popular for political protest.

Fok, Fokken; the usual swear word.

Poes: Pussy; female anatomy.

Brakeshoes; army biscuits.

Terrs; Terrorists.

Lekker; good. *Lekker koue een;* a nice cold one (beer). Afrikaans.

Tiffie; technician of various sorts. From 'artificer'.

Snuffelhondes; bloodhounds.

Maak'n plan: Make a plan. Afrikaans proverb.

Kak: crap, shit.

Esbit: solid fuel individual cooker issued to soldiers.

Jollers; young lads on a jolly.

Dagga; cannabis.

Klippie; Klipdrift Brandy

Piccaninis; small African children. Sometimes considered an offensive term.

Troupies; soldiers.

Fundies; technicians. From the isiZulu for 'educated'.

Boet; pal, mate.

Choti ghoti: good looking girls. Durban-Indian slang.

Bru; brother, good friend.

Babelaas; hangover. 'Baboon' in Afrikaans.

Blerrie leuenaar; bloody liar. (Afrikaans).

Bevok, Bosbefok; mad, 'Bush-fucked', combat-stressed. (Afrikaans).

Skyf; cigarette, also chips.

Chateau Libertas; cheap red wine.

Bakvissies: teenage girls. (Afrikaans). Literally, 'fish that are too young to be caught and must be thrown back'.

Dikbek domkop; bad-tempered and stupid. (Afrikaans).

Lekke anties; good tits. (Afrikaans).

367

Stoep; veranda. The place to sit and gossip. (Afrikaans).

ProNutro; popular breakfast cereal.

Sangoma; witch-doctor, fortune teller, traditional healer.

Voorkammer; Front room (Afrikaans). Traditionally the main room in the house.

Mampoer; home made brandy.

Veldtschoen; light, leather shoes. (Afrikaans).

Soet; sweet. (Afrikaans).

Laatie, Jonge; lad, young man. (Afrikaans).

Bergie; tramp. (Afrikaans).

Broekie lace; ornamental iron work. (Afrikaans).

Goffel; ugly girl. (Afrikaans).

Vlei; shallow marsh or pond. (Afrikaans).

Co-ax; co-axial mounted machine gun. It is fixed to the movement of the main gun.

Loskop; airhead. (Afrikaans).

HEAT, HE; anti-tank shells, high explosive shells.

Bakkie; pick-up truck.

Ous, Oke; chaps, boys, lads. (Afrikaans).

Ratpack; army rations.

Tronk; jail. (Afrikaans).

Kloof; narrow valley.

Mompies; idiots.

Broederbond; Brotherhood. A secret society of Afrikaaner Nationalists.

Moffies; male homosexuals.

Gatvol; 'Had a gut full', fed up. (Afrikaans).

Krimpies; old people. (Afrikaans).

Ag, sies, man; 'Oh, please stop.' (Afrikaans).

Liewe Heksie; a clever witch in a children's tv programme.

Kaffirboetie; Nigger lover (Afrikaans, impolite).

Doos; idiot.

CPSIA information can be obtained
at www.ICGtesting.com
Printed in the USA
LVHW05s0106260718
584896LV00015B/1003/P

9 781976 266164